The Wolves of Langabhat

D.A. Watson

A Wild Wolf Publication

Published by Wild Wolf Publishing in 2015

Copyright © 2015 D.A. Watson

All rights reserved. No part of this book may be reproduced, stored in a retrieval system or transmitted in any form or by any means without the prior written permission of the publishers, except by a reviewer who may quote brief passages in a review to be printed by a newspaper, magazine or journal.

First print

All Characters appearing in this work are fictitious. Any resemblance to real persons, living or dead, is purely coincidental.

ISBN: 978-1-907954-45-0

Also available as an e-book

www.wildwolfpublishing.com

For Max

Much Obliged

Good vibrations to the following fine folks who've been a big part of getting me to this point. If I've missed anyone, just assume I meant to mention you.

My agent, Judith Murray for her priceless advice on editing and untangling. The guys at Wild Wolf for taking me on. Jake Powning for weaponry info. Calum and Murdo for local knowledge on the Isle of Lewis. Tommy Barnes for help with police procedures (and nights of drunken punk rock and Johnny Cash tunes) and the nice police officer I spoke to who works in the weaponry room at the Stornoway Police Station. Carrie Francis, Emanuele Sangregorio and Claire McMaster for making my words look good with your amazing artwork and design ideas. My mates, who were among the very first to read and review my scribbles; Davie, Kev, Marco, Nicky, Jodey, Laura, Brian, Fiona, Robb, Lorraine and Tinny. My big brother Alan for scaring the shit out of me as a kid with horror movies and ghost stories, and my big brother Iain for spreading the word. Sorry I made a crap chef, bro. Cheers very much to Lorraine at the Greenock Telegraph and the boys at Inverclyde Radio for giving me my first media exposure. Thanks to all the guys at Follow Follow, Writing Forums and The Morningstar Saga websites for encouragement, advice, reviews and good wishes and to Dominique De Leeuw for the fancy beers and awesome photos. Extra special gratitude to Louise Welsh, Liam Bell and Meaghan Delahunt, who taught me all the things I didn't know about writing (which was, and still is, a lot), and who made me believe I could do any of this, and thanks to my fellow MLitt students at Stirling Uni for all the workshop critiques and good thoughts. It's been a pleasure! Endless gratitude to my amazing wife who's supported me all the way, and above all, thanks to Mags, William and Catherine Watson, for raising me right and giving me my love of storytelling.

Dominique De Leeuw for the fancy beers and awesome photos

PROLOGUE

1013 AD

He sees the knife for just a moment before it is buried to the hilt in the left side of his neck. Such is the length of the weapon that two inches of blade emerge just below his right ear, punching out from his neck in a spraying gout of blood. He is able to hear the sound of it as it happens. A hideous internal scrape as steel kisses bone. The point where his brain stem fuses with his spinal cord is torn asunder, and but for a tiny fraction of time when all he feels is a devastating explosion of agony, the fisherman's death is instantaneous.

The body slides off the massive gore streaked dagger with a liquidly metallic sniiiiick, and collapses in a boneless heap on the white sand, blood jetting from the wound onto the beach and staining it black in the moonlight. The thing standing over the corpse looks down at the body at its feet for a second, then it kneels, and fastens long, sharpened teeth over the wound.

It feeds.

Its thirst slaked, the giant marauder then rises again to its full terrifying height, and howls.

Above the beach, the islander's round huts are already ablaze. The smoke filled sea air is full of the screams and choking wet grunts of the dying, the hard clash of steel on steel, and the low meaty thuds of riven flesh and limbs cleaved. Frantic hand to hand combat rages across the beach as the giant's brothers fall upon the fishermen. It is no contest. The villagers are not warriors, and cannot hope to so much as dent a shield before being hacked to bloody chunks and devoured. The crackling roar of the flames as the tiny settlement is immolated is a hot, physical thing, the very voice of Fenrir, the screams of the slaughtered humans and their livestock praises in His name.

Another villager attempts to attack the fanged giant, this one only a beardless boy, clumsily swinging a boat hook at its head. The raider batters the whelp contemptuously aside with its great round shield, thrusting out with a spear before the boy can regain his balance. The head punches into the youth's side, and he begins to scream in ever rising shrill crescendos as the giant slowly lifts the spear and plants it firmly into the sand, the skewered boy still writhing and shrieking upon it. To the left, one of the invader's brothers charges by, launching through the air at another villager that runs to the impaled boy's aid. Deep into the shift, the brother requires no weapons of steel, and the human falls to tooth and claw, torn to quivering red pieces.

Some few of the fishermen have gained elevated ground atop the beach, and rain down an unorganised hail of arrows. Those infrequent shafts that find their mark are simply plucked out, snapped in fists and jaws, and left on the sand, no more harmful than stinging insects. Two of the raiders flank the small group of archers, and come bounding from the shadows to land roaring amongst them. One fells two of the defenders with a single swipe of a longsword. The second clamps its huge jaws on the head on another villager, crushing the human's skull between its teeth while simultaneously disembowelling a fourth with a swipe of a huge clawed hand.

The howling horde tear through the last few remaining men, women and children like a fanged storm, gorging themselves on the human's flesh, terror and souls. They feed well, and leave their victims as chewed, ragged things on the ground before burning everything in sight that cannot be killed or eaten.

When it is over, the night sky above is stained a bruised, sickly red by the leaping flames and greasy smoke rising from the village. The sea wind blowing off the pale sandy bay carries the astringent scent of blood and salt and burning flesh, and the cold howling of wolves echoes across the water.

PART ONE

1

"Are you sure he's coming?"

"He said he'd be here."

"Not the same thing though, is it?"

"Not for him anyway."

The two men stood silently for a few seconds, thinking about their friend Ian.

"How long did you say he'd been back?" asked Cal.

Clyde shrugged. "He wasn't very specific. Just said he'd been back a while."

"It's been over a year. You think he's alright now?"

"Who knows, man?" Clyde replied with a shake of his head. "A thing like that happening? That's going to fuck you up. He sounded okay on the phone last time I spoke to him. A lot better than the first time he called anyway." Ian had been on the phone for twenty minutes that first time, Clyde had told Cal. Crying mostly. Occasionally babbling some seriously weird shit. Sometimes screaming.

The salty wind blew off the ocean at their backs, a stiff sea breeze that cooled the warm air. Despite it being the middle of July, Ulapool had been battered with seventy mile per hour winds only a week ago, spelling the demise of more than one of the boats that made up the town's fishing fleet. Living in the coastal north west of Scotland and making one's living harvesting the unpredictable moods and waves of the fierce North Atlantic was not without its risks. Cal had been in a near panic, fearing that his stag weekend was set to be scuppered, but the weather had improved, and while the fifty-three mile stretch of dark water that separated the mainland from the Isle of Lewis was choppy, it was sailable. The huge Caledonian MacBrayne ferry was docked in the harbour, wallowing like an obese white leviathan devouring cars and passengers in preparation for the near three hour crossing to the port at Stornoway, the island's main town.

Scarlett and Matt walked over and joined them, Matt handing out the boarding cards he'd just picked up from the ticket office. Cal's best man was a lanky individual, long limbed, bespectacled and built like a rake, his wide intelligent forehead topped with tight brown curls.

"Any sign of him yet?" Scarlett asked. She was a tall, willowy woman with a sweet, classically featured heartbreaker's face. Standing a slim and respectable five eleven in her jeans and black denim jacket, her long burnt honey coloured hair blew wildly around her head in the wind.

"Negative," Cal informed her. "How long till the ferry goes?"

"Still got ten minutes," Matt said, glancing at this watch. "He's cutting it fine though." Cal smiled at his friend's obvious discomfort. Tardiness wound Matt up something terrible, but when you were mates with Ian, you just had to get used to it. As Cal's best man, Matt was in charge of the weekend, and had meticulously planned out the travel and accommodation arrangements to the minute. He was that kind of guy. Organised. Methodical. Efficient. It had served him well. They were good qualities for a software developer to have, evidenced by the lucrative contract he'd just won with the new and well funded electronics company in Berlin to write, test and launch their website.

"Ah! Speak of the fucker," Clyde exclaimed, pointing down the road.

Cal looked over and saw a black Ford Mustang pulling into the harbour's car park. Ian's car.

Their friend, who none of them had seen in almost three years, got out, grabbed a rucksack from the back seat and walked towards them. He still had the same familiar rolling gait to his stride, but in the time since Cal had last seen him, Ian's physical appearance had changed. Not dramatically, but more than a little.

He'd never been what you'd call a chubster, but he'd always been just slightly overweight. Now he was only a kick in the arse away from being downright gaunt. His black jeans, shirt and leather jacket hung loosely on his slender frame, his face pale and drawn. He looked like he hadn't slept the night before, and maybe not the night before that. Three days worth of dark stubble covered his cheeks and neck, and the shoulder length hair which hung lankly across his face had an unwashed look to it. Cal knew that the life of a touring musician took a toll on one's body. Except Ian hadn't been on tour in over a year. Cal knew there were other, darker reasons for his friend's rough appearance. He'd struggled with depression himself, and knew that when the black moods came at you, personal upkeep was often the last thing on your mind.

A gust of wind blew Ian's hair back from his face for a second, revealing his features. There were bags under his eyes, but the eyes themselves were focussed and alert, Cal noticed. That was good.

Cal stepped forward, smiling broadly, and embraced his friend in a manly bear hug, thumping him a few customary punches on the back.

"Fuckin' good to see you, mate," he said, meaning every word. Ian was definitely thin beneath his clothes.

Ian returned the hug then stepped back, a strange, sad smile on his face.

"Thanks, man," he said. "Good to be here."

The others crowded round and there were more welcomes, manly bear hugs and thumping of backs, especially from Scarlett, whose extra manly hug had Ian struggling to breathe for a second.

"Welcome back, you handsome devil," she growled into his ear as she squeezed his ribs to the point of breaking, planting a big wet smacker on his cheek. "Agh. You might have shaved, Ian."

"Got to keep up the rock star look, missy," Ian replied, wiping his cheek dry with his sleeve and tipping her a lascivious wink.

"Don't try your sleazy tricks with me, Mr Walker," Scarlett objected. "Well you know I'm a married woman."

"And mankind wept," Ian said, shaking his head wistfully. "How's the wee man doing?"

"Aye, he's in good form. Gorgeous as ever. Think he's going to be walking pretty soon." Scarlett took out her phone and showed Ian a picture of Reece, her eleven month old son. The baby, dressed in a black Led Zeppelin bodysuit, grinned happily at the camera through a chinful of drool, the smiling red mouth populated by a single tiny tooth in the lower gums. His mop of unruly blonde hair stood out in all directions as the baby reached for the lens, one chubby hand caught in the act of trying to grab the camera phone from Scarlett's hand.

Ian laughed at the image. "He's a wee cracker, Scarlett. I see you and Stuart are getting him into the good tunes."

"That's my doing. Stu doesn't care much for Zep."

Ian again shook his head in dismay. "And you married this man?"

Scarlett shrugged. "What can I say? He's got some size of walloper."

Ian burst out laughing. "That's just fuckin' nasty, Scarlett."

Scarlett was by far the crudest member of the group, funnily enough, the most stereotypically male, and could match any of the men pint for pint in a drinking session. She was also terrifyingly ferocious when angered, as they'd witnessed on the occasions when her good looks had attracted too much unwanted attention from some would be Romeo in the pub. That daft cunt who'd foolishly grabbed her tits in the nightclub that time... Jesus. He wouldn't be doing that again.

"Well this is all very informative folks," Matt said, "but we'd better get our arses on this here ferry before it sails without us."

They presented their boarding cards to the ticket inspector and made their way onto the vessel, laughing and talking. Although they kept in touch among themselves through Facebook and emails, and got together whenever possible back in their day to day lives, it was the first time in almost four years all five of them had been in the same place at the same time, and it was good. It was just like old times, Cal thought.

He'd wanted his stag weekend to be this way, with just the five of them. He knew many other people that he was friendly with, but aside from his fiancée Lynne, he only regarded Matt, Clyde, Ian and Scarlett as actual friends. The wedding was going to be the same. Although Lynne had a large family - just *how* large Cal had realised when he looked at the estimate for the catering bill - his four friends would be the sum of his side of the guest list. He shook off the depressing thought, grinning in anticipation of the weekend to come. The music festival in Stornoway that night, a day canoeing and back to town for the festival's final night on Saturday, then home on Sunday. Matt had it all planned out and timetabled with his usual efficient style. All the accommodation, tickets and excursion bookings had been arranged and paid for in advance. As best man, he was thus far doing a bang up job. Even as Cal had the thought, Matt was ordering drinks from the bar in the ferry's spacious lounge while Ian, Clyde and Scarlett were getting settled into a large semi circular booth in front of the long window that ran the breadth of the room, affording them a panoramic view across the choppy water. Cal joined them, taking off his jacket and slumping down into a seat next to Ian.

"How you keeping, dude?" he asked. They'd agreed not to bring up the accident unless Ian spoke about it first.

"I'm doing okay, mate. Better, you know?"

Cal nodded. "That's good. You know we're here for you."

Ian smiled his thanks. "Yeah, man. I know."

"Anything you need, okay?" Cal repeated. Ian nodded again, not looking at him.

Matt arrived with a tray full of drinks.

"Four lagers, and a vodka, soda and lime for the lady" he said, passing out the beverages.

"Shut yer ass, Connell," Clyde retorted as Matt passed him a slender highball glass. "The thinking man's drink, this is."

"Aye," Scarlett said, lifting her pint from the tray. "Thinking about what shade of lipstick goes with your blouse."

Clyde flicked an ice cube at her, which she dodged, laughing.

Matt raised his glass. "Okay people," he said. "Let's make it a good weekend. The last stand of Cal Dempster. Get it doon ye!"

"Get it doon ye!" the others chorused, as was tradition, and then drank.

2

"Get it doon ye."

The words, the first the old man had uttered in months, came unbidden from his dry throat in a hoarse, papery whisper.

He sat bolt upright, the muscles under his tattered colourless coat contracting as if he'd been sitting in an electric chair rather than on a rough hewn wooden stool. All at once his senses heightened to an intense focus. Every sight, smell and sound of the ramshackle bothy was instantly magnified a hundredfold. The sharp, earthy aroma of the peat fire filled his nostrils. He could tell to the hour when he had cut the turf from the small hillock out the back. His gaze took in the stout logs and hardened mud that made up the north facing back wall of the hut, and he could make out every tiny scratch and nick in the wood. He could hear the miniscule sounds of a mouse that had made its home in the walls as it scurried to and fro in search of food.

He rose to his feet and stood in the centre of the bothy, letting the avalanche of perception sweep through his senses. He closed his eyes and stood stock still, his hulking figure, standing close to seven feet tall, dominated the one room hut. He was intensely aware of the breath in his lungs, which worked like massive bellows in his great chest. He could hear and feel the blood coursing in red rapids through his veins, and the strong, steady beat of his heart. His enormous hands, gnarled and hardened through uncounted years of harsh living, but nimble and precise as a surgeon's when required, opened and closed as if of their own volition. They were coated red and tacky from the blood of the rabbit he'd been dressing at the table when those strange words had issued from his long unused lips. Drops of blood dripped from his fingertips to the oiled earthen floor.

His eyes snapped open. They were a fierce, icy blue that blazed from his craggy face, itself surrounded by a thick mane of long iron grey hair shot through with streaks of blonde. His beard rolled and flowed down his chest in a thick tangle of wiry pale curls.

He crossed the room in two big strides and threw open the bothy's door. The hut was nestled among a patch of rocks and bracken on a small level area of ground midway up a rugged hillside, and held an open view out across the northern end of the loch below and the surrounding hills. The harsh, windswept landscape was devoid of trees, and bare rolling moors cloaked in nothing more than tough wiry grass, rocks, heather and spiny gorse bushes stretched away to the horizon on all sides. Below him, the loch itself. Over seven miles long in total, nestled at the bottom of the steep sided valley and running northeast to southwest for around four miles before doglegging away to the southeast. From his vantage point, he could look down upon the upper portion of the loch, and the barren island which lay just off the northern shore. The island was only four or five acres in area, flat and featureless from this distance. The old man concentrated his gaze in the middle of the bleak little piece of rocky land. His eyes narrowed as he focussed his heightened vision. Nothing moved.

His senses still vibrated like tuning forks however, and for over an hour he stood completely motionless, intently surveying the little island and unheeding of the bitter wind that swept up the hillside off the loch. Eventually he turned and went back inside. The rush of sensory input was starting to fade, but an echo of sensitivity remained, like a phantom electrical current that crackled softly through his nerves.

Something was coming.

The old man went to the back wall of the hut and stood staring at the collection of objects held there in sturdy iron brackets. The double headed axe. The longsword. The bow and quiver of arrows. The pair of spears. Closing his eyes, he reached out and laid his massive bloodstained hand flat on the axe's head.

As his skin made contact with the cold steel, a single word whispered in his mind.

Ulfhednar.

His eyes snapped open again, and Sealgair, who had long awaited this moment, quickly took the axe and the other weapons down from their places on the wall.

3

Ulfhednar.

They were just over an hour into the ferry crossing, in high spirits, talking and laughing with each other when the word slithered in a sibilant whisper through Ian's head. As if he'd been given a strong electric shock, every muscle in his body contracted reflexively and the pint glass in Ian's hand cracked and then shattered as his fist clenched. A jagged frothy mixture of broken glass, lager and blood soaked his lap and the floor around his feet, and Ian shot up from his seat, knocking over his chair.

"Woah!" Cal exclaimed in amazement. "Dude, did your beer just explode?"

"Fuck man, your hand..." Matt said with concern, looking up at Ian. A large gash cut across the palm of his right hand. Blood seeped steadily from the wound and dripped on the floor amidst the spilled beer and shattered pint tumbler.

"Here," Scarlett said, quickly getting up from her seat and tossing Ian her silk scarf. "Wrap this around it and keep the pressure on." She turned to the barman, who'd looked over at the group at the sound of the breaking glass. "We need some help here," she informed him with a dangerous glint in her eye. "One of your shitty pint glasses just broke in my friend's hand and he's bleeding." The barman nodded fearfully and scampered off, presumably to find the first aid officer.

"It's okay, Scarlett, it's not bad," Ian said shakily, looking down at the wound with a strange look on his face,

"Away you go, ya silly bastard," she retorted, coming round the table and taking his bloody hand in hers. Ian pulled away from her defensively.

"Don't worry about it. Really. I'm fine."

"Mate, that's gonnae need stitches," Cal said, joining Scarlett at Ian's side and wincing at the laceration, from which bright red blood continued to flow. Other passengers in the lounge had taken notice of the scene now, and glanced over. There was nothing like a little drama and the sight of blood to liven up a lengthy sea crossing.

"Look at the man's hand, mum!" a blonde boy of about ten years exclaimed excitedly from the table next to theirs. "All the blood! Gross!" The child's mother hit him a swat on the backside, scolding him for his insensitivity. The kid started crying.

Ian backed away from the table, still staring down at his bloody hand with something like amazement on his face. "I'm just going to the bathroom..." he mumbled. "Need to clean it..."

Scarlett made to stop him. "Just wait here for the first aid guy," she insisted, reaching out and trying to pull him back by his coat sleeve. Ian shrugged her hand off angrily, still backing away.

"*Just leave it, Scarlett, for fuck's sake,*" he hissed. "It's just a wee cut. I'll be back in a minute."

Scarlett stared at him open mouthed as he backed away, hurt by his harsh words.

"Dude," Cal began. "She's just trying to…"

Ian turned and walked away quickly, drawing a few startled gasps from the other passengers as he strode from the room, still dripping claret on the carpet.

In the corridor leading from the lounge area, he pushed through the door into the men's toilets, almost knocking over a man who was just coming out. The man flinched at the sight of Ian's pale, haunted face and his bloody hand.

"Jesus, mate. Are you all right?" he asked. Ian ignored him, shouldering open the door to a cubicle and slamming the door behind him. He closed the lid of the toilet and sat down, staring at the wound and breathing rapidly. There was no pain, not yet, just a slight prickling sensation. Ian shook his head in futile denial.

"Please no, please no…" he whispered. "Not now…"

The flow of blood from the cut had stopped. The tingling prickle in his palm grew in intensity and began to burn. Ian winced as the pain came.

"No, no, no…" he pleaded. To whom, he didn't know.

The burning sensation turned up a few notches. Ian threw back his head, eyes clenched shut and grinding his teeth, trying not to cry out. He grunted in the back of his throat as the pain in his hand spiralled up in an agonising crescendo. He bit down hard on the sleeve of his leather jacket to keep himself from screaming, while behind his clenched eyes, flashes of red exploded across his retinas. Just as he thought he was about to pass out, the pain abruptly lessened till there was only a light, pulsing throb. He released his jacket sleeve from the death grip of his jaws. Ian remained there like that for a minute, facing the ceiling and trying to catch his breath. When he had himself under control, as much control as was possible anyway, he left the stall and went to one of the sinks against the wall. He turned on the cold tap and thrust his reddened bloody hand under the freezing water, rubbing at his injured palm with his other hand. The coagulated blood came off in rusty lumps and flakes and swirled down the drain, staining the water and porcelain pink.

The wound was already closing up.

4

"What the fuck was that all about?" Scarlett asked as Ian fled from the lounge, shocked at the way he'd spoken to her.

"It's all right," Cal said, putting a hand on her shoulder. "Don't take it personally. He's had a rough time. Probably the sight of the blood, you know? After what happened to the band?"

Scarlett nodded, but still a worried crease lined her forehead. "I'll go and check on him," she said, and started in the direction Ian had gone. Clyde stood up, shaking his head.

"It's cool, Scarlett. I'll go and talk to him." Before she could argue, Clyde was already making his way towards the toilets. "Can't have some chick hanging about in the men's bogs anyway, can we?" he said to her as he passed. "Even if it *is* her usual type of place to hang out." Scarlett gave him the finger.

The toilets were on the right hand side of a corridor which led out from the lounge area. Clyde knocked at the door to the men's room and opened it a few inches. "Ian, you in here, mate?" he called.

No answer.

Clyde entered the brightly lit restroom. A stringent scent of pine cleaning fluid stung his nostrils, and the low burbling splash of the automatic flushers on the urinals reverberated on the tiled walls.

The bathroom was empty.

On the floor, several small red droplets patterned the white tiles. Following the trail of bloody splashes, Cal paused at the door to the cubicle where they led.

"Ian?" he said softly. "You okay?" He pushed lightly on the cubicle door and it swung open. It too was empty, though there were several more blood spots and a few reddish smears on the floor around the toilet bowl.

Frowning, Clyde turned from the cubicle and left the bathroom. As Ian hadn't come back out into the lounge, he could only have gone the other way up the corridor which led to an ascending staircase. Clyde followed the passageway and made his way up the stairs. As he pushed through the door at the top, he was suddenly buffeted by a chill wind as he found himself outdoors on the port side of the ship. He walked out onto the open upper deck, shivering in the cold and looking around, trying to locate his friend. The only other people in the topside area were an elderly couple in bright blue windbreakers who stood at the rail on this side of the ferry, passing a pair of binoculars back and forth and pointing back at the mainland, by now a thin line on the hazy eastern horizon.

Clyde made his way to the starboard side and found a narrow gangway running up that side of the ship towards the bow. Ian was standing at the rail midway along the passage, hands in the pockets of his leather jacket and his long greasy hair blowing around in the wind, looking down intently at the foamy wake which churned out from the ship's hull as it cut through the water. Clyde walked over and stood beside his best friend.

"All right, mate," Ian said without looking up.

"Bit nippy out here, eh?" Clyde said casually, rubbing at his bare forearms. The thin t-shirt he was wearing provided little protection against the bitter sea wind, and his jaw jittered and chattered in the cold. Ian only nodded slightly, still staring down at the water.

"The hand okay?" Clyde tried.

Ian turned his head and looked at him for a second, saying nothing, before withdrawing his right hand from his jacket pocket. He studied it himself for a moment, then held it out for Clyde to see. A thin red line ran diagonally across his palm from the base of his first finger to the side of his hand beneath the pinkie. The three inch long mark looked like it had been no deeper than a paper cut.

"Just a scratch," Ian said softly, staring at the shallow red mark. He held it there for a moment longer, clenching and unclenching his fist a few times before shrugging and returning the hand to his pocket. He turned from Clyde again and went back to studying the dark water some thirty feet below.

Clyde was perturbed at the sight of the superficial wound. The blood had been fairly pishing from Ian's hand just a few minutes ago. He'd thought for sure that it would require stitches as Cal had feared, and he said as much now.

"You developed some sort of weird bleeding disorder or something? Some mad groupie pass you a dose of reverse haemophilia?"

"I guess," Ian said without turning his head.

"Ach well," Clyde continued, sensing Ian really didn't want to discuss the matter of his hand any further. "Saves us a trip to the casualty ward. I don't even know if they *have* a casualty ward in Stornoway. Shit, do they even have a hospital? Not exactly a bustling metropolis is it? Plenty of pubs right enough from what Matt said. Guess that's all we need. The festival tonight should be a good laugh, eh? Not usually into all that mad teuchter ceilidh music myself, but should be a gas anyway. Maybe get myself a dance of the Gay Gordon's with some wee farmer's daughter. You think birds from Lewis are dirty? I'll bet they are. Fuck all to do out here apart from pumping. I'd imagine they're all into some freaky shit as well. Dressing up as sheep for a shagging. Ha!"

This was Clyde's way of drawing people out of conversational reticence. If someone didn't want to talk, then he'd simply bombard them with his own words and semi coherent train of thought. Some people thought he had some form of attention deficit disorder or a mild case of Tourette's and couldn't help himself. His friends though, knew that there was method in his verbal madness. His infectious rambling patter almost never failed to raise a smile in someone who needed one, and Clyde sensed that Ian was in dire need of some levity. That intense way he was looking down at the water. It was... unsettling. But sure enough, although he could only see Ian in profile, Clyde could see a smile start to form on his friend's gloomy unshaven face.

"And we're going canoeing tomorrow," he continued. "Still not sure about that. Mind what happened to those poor cunts in *Deliverance*? Can just imagine us getting ambushed by a bunch of hairy arsed, shotgun toting island hillbillies. I've got a tenner on Matt being the one out of all of us that gets raped, even before Scarlett. The hillbillies'll be destroying his ring piece and giving it 'bleat like a sheep, boy!' All that curly hair of his, he looks a bit like sheep, don't you think? A black sheep."

Ian was looking at him now, something approaching a real smile on his face. It was good to see. Clyde paused in his meandering monologue and grinned back at him.

"C'mon, man," he said, "Let's get back inside. I'm freezing my nuts off out here. Just try not to crush any more pint glasses in your fists of fury, alright? It's a tragic waste of good beer."

Ian looked at him for a moment, then startled Clyde by turning and suddenly embracing him, clutching on with a tight desperation. Taken aback, Clyde returned the gesture after a moment. In his arms, Ian's bony frame felt rigid, like a taught steel cable. He was shaking. Not weeping, but trembling violently, as if in shock.

"Hey, man, it's alright," Clyde said.

"I'm sorry, mate," Ian whispered, his breath hot on Clyde's neck. "I'm sorry I've not been in touch. Things have been... a bit fucked up."

"It's cool, mate, don't worry about it. After what you've been though. Fuck, man."

They stayed like that for a few more seconds. Then Ian disengaged himself. He gave Clyde a brisk nod, a slap on the back, and they went back inside. When they returned to the lounge, Ian went straight over to Scarlett and apologised.

"Sorry, babes," he said sincerely. "Shouldn't have snapped at you like that. Forgive me?"

Scarlett hugged him. "Of course I do, ya daft prick," she said.

When they asked about his hand, Ian showed them all the shallow red cut running across his palm, assuring them that it was nothing, that he'd probably just nicked a blood vessel or something which made it look worse than it was. He went to the bar to get another round of drinks in.

Upon seeing it again, Clyde thought the wound looked even less serious than it had when he'd seen it up on the open deck, but he was distracted from the thought as Ian returned from the bar, handed him his vodka soda and lime, and Scarlett asked what brand of tampon he favoured.

5

The weapons laid out on the rough table before him were a thousand years old. After a millennia, normal edged weapons would lose their cutting keenness regardless of how well cared for they were. After ten centuries, even a blade sharpened daily would dull. Wooden shafts and leather bound grips would rot.

The axe, spears, bow, arrows and longsword on the table however, were not normal weapons, and the passage of ages did nothing to diminish their killing potential. Each edge was sharp enough to shave a man's forearm, the leather grips of the sword and axe were as strong and supple as the day they had been bound, and the wooden shafts of the axe, arrows and two spears remained stout and unblemished.

"Get it doon ye," Sealgair said quietly as he gazed at the ancient arsenal.

When he'd spoken the words the first time, in his mind, he'd heard them in the voice of another, and the inflection and accent of this other's voice had not been that of an islander. The words had been spoken by an outsider, but one that like Sealgair himself, walked on both sides of the veil. Their kind were rare, he knew, and the meeting of two such souls rarer still. The fact that he'd involuntarily linked minds with this nameless outsider could only be the portent for which he'd waited all his long days.

The Harbinger had come at last.

Settling himself on the stool at the table and closing his eyes, Sealgair *pushed* with his mind. Searching. Seeking another connection.

At first, there was only the heightened awareness of his immediate environment, which had stayed with him since he'd first heard and spoken the strange words. Reaching further, his net of perception widened, and he experienced the cold brackish taste of the water in the loch, the prickling sting of the gorse bushes which dotted the land in spiny clumps, and the frigid cutting wind that blew across the hills. Further he cast about, his mind and senses pushing outward, outward, until he could feel the hard tar of man made roads, hear the sound of a passing car. Further still he stretched his perception, and then there were the voices of other people in farmhouses and other isolated dwellings. He felt the warmth of their fires, smelled and tasted their food, heard the sounds of their lives, but still nothing of the Harbinger.

His closed eyes squeezed into wrinkled slits as he pushed harder, almost to the limits of his abilities, and his mental net cast wider still. Across land, air and water, a thousand sounds, flavours, textures and scents cascaded through his mind, seeking, seeking, seeking...

There.

In a cerebral lurch, Sealgair found him, and the presence of the Harbinger lit up in his mind like a fiery beacon.

There was the smell of freshly spilled blood. A feeling of creeping dread. An echo of pain in his right hand. The scent of salt water. A stiff iodine breeze. The sound of waves, and a rolling, bobbing sensation.

The Harbinger was at sea, and drawing nearer.

He rose from the table, the top of his head almost brushing the ceiling of the bothy, and shrugged into the long woollen coat which wrapped thick and warm around his massive frame. From a peg on the wall, he took down a sturdy leather belt upon which was fastened a long rawhide sheath. In the sheath was a very large, very sharp hunting knife.

Pushing out through the door, Sealgair stepped into the biting wind and looked down on the little island just off the shore of the loch below. Nothing moved. He crossed the small patch of rugged land outside his dwelling to a large object covered with a canvas tarpaulin and hauled it off, revealing the ancient rust spotted truck beneath. Existing as he did on what food and water he could harvest from the loch and surrounding hills, the gnarly vehicle was used only on the infrequent occasions that Sealgair was in need of some supply that nature itself could not provide, and he was reluctantly forced to travel into town, over twenty miles away. He squeezed into the cab, the aged suspension groaning and squeaking in protest under his huge bulk. He fired the ignition and the engine roared immediately to life.

Spraying loose stones from the half hidden trail that led away from the bothy, Sealgair sped off, the truck crashing through the undergrowth that had encroached on the rugged trail since the vehicle's last passage.

The heavy weight of the hunting knife was snug against his hip, and his purpose was intently focussed in his mind.

The Harbinger from the sea could not be allowed anywhere near the island on the loch.

6

The music festival had attracted an impressive crowd this year, and the Stornoway seafront was busy with other passengers disembarking from the ferry and others who had already arrived to enjoy the sunny weekend.

The sound of a three piece folk band in a small marquee nearby belting out a fast Celtic reel with no small measure of panache lent a lively soundtrack to the bustling atmosphere; the thumping bodhran drum beating out a frenetic pace behind the reedy strains of an accordion and a vigorously strummed acoustic guitar. A small market and fair had been set up in the harbour, and the area was buzzing with a cheery mass of humanity. Locals fished from the piers, families and couples, young and elderly, strolled around enjoying the rare warm weather. A group of baggy clothed kids on skateboards weaved their way precariously through the crowds with languidly effortless ease, and the air was full of enticing aromas emanating from the fast food stalls. Locals had stalls set up from which they hawked cheeses, meats and other local produce from the surrounding farms of the island, a smiling middle aged woman painted the faces of a line of giggling children, and an ageing hippy type sat behind a psychedelically pattered kiosk offering legal highs, skins, bongs, poppers, pipes and other class B paraphernalia. There were stalls selling clothing, CD's and vinyl records, souvenirs, artwork and books. A few fairground rides had been erected, and the piped jingling of a calliope competed with the folk group's music. There was a small Ferris wheel in operation, and kids and adults alike happily busied themselves at various game stalls, whacking moles, hooking ducks and throwing balls at weighted pyramids of tin cans in the hope of winning cheap novelties which cost about a tenth of the games' fees.

"So where's the digs?" Cal asked, lighting a cigarette.

"The Clune Brae Hotel's just over yonder," Matt said, pointing up James Street. He folded up the town map, put it in his back pocket and hefted his backpack onto his shoulders. "There's an apparently decent wee restaurant in the hotel, so we can grab a bit of scran after we've dropped the bags off, then it's drinkity, drink, drink. The main festival stage is over in the grounds of Lews Castle across the harbour, and that kicks off at seven tonight, so we can get a few pints in before we head over."

"Bravo, sir," Cal said, slapping him on the back. "Let's mingle."

They set off through the crowd in the direction of the hotel, enjoying the carnival atmosphere. Unlike the big name rock and pop festivals back on the mainland like T in the Park and Download, the Hebridean Celtic Festival, HebCelt for short, was a more modest affair, attracting only about a tenth of the larger festival's attendances and featuring mostly folk groups from the Scottish islands with a few larger acts from further afield. Van Morrison, Runrig and the like. Rather than being held in one place, the three day event was staged in several local bars and pubs, which acted as satellite venues where bands would be playing throughout the day before the night time event out at the castle grounds where the main stage was set up.

The relatively low key festival had been just the ticket for Cal's stag. He'd said to Matt when naming him as his best man and putting him in charge of organising the weekend that he wanted to do something different to the standard paintball / pub crawl / strip bar agenda that seemed to be the meat of most last hurrahs for soon to be married men. Cal had been delighted with Matt's idea when it transpired the HebCelt festival was taking place in a time frame that suited them all, and was equally stoked about his plan to go canoeing the following day.

At the hotel, after signing in at reception they split up and made their way to their rooms to drop their bags off. They reassembled in the hotel's small bar and restaurant, which was as busy as the rest of the town due to the visitors attracted by the weekend's festivities, and ensconced themselves in a corner booth that Matt had of course reserved in advance. Food and drink were soon brought to the table by a smiling waitress and as they ate, they discussed the plans for the evening.

Matt took out a notebook and his map of the town and began showing them his pre planned route of bars which would lead them to the main stage, pointing out the locations of the various hostelries on the map.

"Right, the hotel's here, we've got The Argyll pub first up, which is just a few doors along here, then there's Lafferty's; an Irish themed bar further along here. We take a left onto Lewis Street to get to the Regal bar here, then a right up Matheson Road which'll take us to The Norseman. From there, it's a five minute walk over to the castle grounds and the main stage." He glanced at his watch. "It's just after five pm now, so if we spend about half an hour in each place, we should get there about seven, in time for the first band."

"Fuck's sake, Matty," Clyde said, between mouthfuls of his steak pie. "How does Sarah put with you?"

Matt frowned. "What you on about?" he asked.

"You, ya madman," Clyde exclaimed, indicating Matt's notebook and map with his fork, where half a gravy slathered sausage wobbled precariously. "I'd go mental living with somebody that organises the weekly sock wash three months in advance and in order of colour."

"Without organisation," Matt replied, "we're nothing but savages, and the world would descend into chaos. And I'll have you know that sock washes are done according to type of use in my house. Casuals on Wednesday, work socks on Friday and sports on Sunday."

"You know, Matt," Scarlett said, grinning over the rim of her pint of Guinness, "It's scary that I can't tell if you're serious or not."

Matt produced yet another piece of paper from somewhere, this one a brightly coloured flyer for the festival, listing the performers and other attractions.

"Oh, fuck a duck," Clyde said, head in hands. "It never ends..."

"Ah, shut yer arse," Matt said with a happy grin. He was in his element. "They've got a karaoke tent, you know."

Clyde perked up. "Really?" he said. "Now that *is* worth knowing."

Cal laughed from across the table. "Am I going to have to drag you offstage again? Mind what happened the last time?"

"Pfft," Clyde dismissed him, returning to his steak pie. "Those protestant heathens wouldn't know a good song if it bit them in the balls."

"Dude, you sang *You'll Never Walk Alone* in a Rangers bar full of pissed up bears. We were lucky to get out of that pub alive."

Matt hadn't been there that night, but Cal had phoned him the next day telling him how he and Clyde had narrowly escaped a serious bleaching after Clyde, who was a Celtic fan, had decided it would be funny to sing the Gerry and the Pacemakers hit which had long been adopted as an anthem by his team's support, during a karaoke night held in a Rangers supporters club in Greenock. Several of the blue nosed regulars hadn't seen the funny side, and Cal, sensing the imminent carnage, had practically tackled Clyde off the stage before he'd got halfway through the song's opening lines, bundling him out the pub door, glass bottles and pint glasses smashing on the floor and walls around them.

Good times.

Ian had been sitting quietly nursing a pint of lager as the others laughed and joked around him. He hadn't ordered any food, and had spoken little since the earlier incident on the ferry.

"How 'bout you, Ian?" Matt asked him, wanting to draw his friend into the conversation. "Be nice to hear someone on the karaoke who can actually sing."

Ian smiled and shook his head. "I'm a drummer remember. As they say, I only hang around with musicians."

The modest reply was typical, Matt thought. Despite his natural talent for music, Ian had always been overly self deprecatory about his ability. In truth, Ian was possessed of a haunting, smoothly melodious singing voice, and could easily have been a lead vocalist. Gifted with perfect pitch, he played the guitar, bass, piano, harmonica and violin with more than considerable skill, but had chosen the drums as his main instrument of choice. Safely half hidden behind a wall of cymbals and toms, he would keep his bandmates in perfect metronomic time while simultaneously adding note perfect vocal harmonies to the singer's melodies and adding intricate flurries of percussion that perfectly embellished the songs in all the right places. Furthermore, he was a tremendously gifted composer, and had penned the string of hits that had briefly made his band, Ragged Mojo a worldwide success before their tragic end.

All this, and he'd never had a music lesson in his life, being completely self taught.

"I'm sure, Scarlett'll be up for it, though," Ian said now, smiling across the table at her.

"Dear Jesus, please no," Clyde said in exaggerated horror. "Every sheepdog on Lewis'll throw itself into the sea when they hear her. The farming economy'll go into freefall."

Scarlett picked up a chip from her plate and threw it at him. She loved karaoke, and would gleefully spend an entire evening belting out ABBA tunes with happy abandon if allowed. It was actually through Scarlett's questionable vocal ability that she'd met her husband, Stuart. Being a fan of drunken singalongs herself, Scarlett's sister Fiona had hired a karaoke DJ for her wedding reception, and a cataclysmically drunk Scarlett had spent a good part of the evening enthusiastically mangling Swedish pop hit after Swedish pop hit. Between numbers, standing at the bar and downing a pint of heavy, she'd overheard a nearby male guest critiquing her talent with the verdict that she had a voice 'like a rat pishing in a rusty tin can' and she'd taken umbrage with the would be Simon Cowell, lambasting him with a string of profane abuse and several lusty swings of her clutch bag. Stuart had taken it well, Matt recalled, and by the end of the night, they'd been slow dancing together. A year later, and Scarlett was savaging the ears of the guests at her own wedding reception while her new husband looked on proudly. Love it seemed, was deaf as well as blind.

The group finished their food and drink, then left the hotel and made their way up James Street in the direction of the first pub on Matt's meticulously planned agenda.

None of the group noticed the hulking blue eyed bearded man in the long overcoat that followed them through the throng.

7

The faint buzzing in Sealgair's blood that indicated the presence of the Harbinger from the sea grew steadily stronger as he drove his battered truck across the moors in the direction of Stornoway.

As the miles rolled past, he could feel a building sense of anticipation in his bones, drawing him onward to the island's main population centre. He was as close to surprised as a man such as he could get when the truck entered the town proper, and he became aware of the fact that there were far more people in the streets that usual. Living in seclusion out in the hills, he had neither use nor care for the comings and goings of the rest of the island's inhabitants, and knew nothing of the music festival which had temporarily swelled the population. The crowds didn't detract him from his purpose, however. The Harbinger was near at hand, and as the truck entered the harbour area, the sense of anticipation in his blood rose. Looking out to sea as he drove along the waterfront, he saw the large ferry approaching the island and knew that his quarry was on board.

He parked the rusting hulk and made his way along the seafront towards the ferry terminal. A bustling market and fair had been set up in the grounds of the harbour, and Sealgair paused, considering the best way to continue. Instinct urged him to identify the Harbinger, stride boldly through the crowd, and gut him the second he was within reach of the hunting knife.

Reason however, calmed this urge. He had waited for this encounter for too long, and there was no margin for error. The stranger from the mainland was an unknown element, and a careless approach could end in disaster. Only a fool rushed into battle knowing nothing of his enemy, so Sealgair decided to watch from a distance and identify his target before deciding on the most prudent way to proceed.

He selected a point along the sea wall on the outskirts of the fair from where he could see the ferry passengers disembarking the large vessel. He had a talent for going unnoticed when he needed to, and despite his great size and ragged appearance, no one in the crowd paid him any particular attention. His senses were still in their heightened state, and he was almost overwhelmed by the chaotic bright colours, myriad of scents and sonic assault generated by the busy market and fair that had taken over the harbour. It was all a confusing blur of many hued lights, tastes, music, laughter, sweet and salty air and jangling conversation. Sealgair was vexed by the overload of sensory input, and he began to grow concerned that he would have difficulty homing in on the Harbinger amid the jumbled torrent of perception.

"So where's the digs?"

The words stood out as if illuminated, and his glacial blue eyes were drawn to a particular group of passengers that had exited the ferry's covered gangway and now stood on the harbourside. All distractions faded from his mind, reduced to no more than faint background static.

Three men, a woman, and the Harbinger.

Although he was over two hundred meters away from where they stood, Sealgair was able to observe them as if he'd been standing next to them, and he studied the group intently.

The woman was tall, with dark blonde hair, fine features and a slim figure. She carried herself with a relaxed, graceful confidence. Sealgair sensed fire in her.

One of the men was of above average height, slightly built with a high, intelligent forehead and a thatch of brown curls atop his head. He was studying a street map. A thinker, Sealgair surmised, not a warrior.

A second tall male with close cropped hair stood by the gangly map reader, smoking a cigarette which Sealgair could smell and taste as if he'd been partaking of the tobacco himself. This one was more solidly built, broad across the shoulders and chest. His eyes held whispers of a past tainted by great sadness, but there was strength there, a deep well of courage and resolve. He was the one who had spoken.

Next to him, a third man stood. Straight brown hair, average height with a build that showed early signs of running to fat. This one had a faintly charged manner and lively, darting green eyes that suggested a roguish penchant for the absurd. A joker.

Then there was the Harbinger. Identified beyond doubt by the cold knife of foreboding that slid across Sealgair's heart as he set eyes upon him. He was thin and had an unkempt appearance, with dark shoulder length hair that hung in lank strands around his unshaven face. Sealgair sensed a great tide of fear and doubt in the man.

Sealgair stood watching, trembling with the insistent urge to simply stride over and take the Harbinger's head. Then the group moved off through the crowd in the direction of the town centre, but Sealgair saw the Harbinger hesitate a moment before following, glancing around nervously as if he sensed he was being watched.

8

The Norseman was the last stop on their way to the main stage. Matt had informed them as they approached the pub that he'd checked it out in advance (of course he had) and while it wasn't a tackily themed establishment, it was named for the strong Scandinavian heritage prevalent on the island. Viking raiders, Matt told them, had begun attacking the coastal settlements of Lewis in the ninth century, laying waste to the small crofts and fishing villages, following the Viking standard operational protocol with much plundering, pillaging and raping. After a few decades spent reaving the shit out of the island, the Norsemen had begun to integrate with the island's native population and many of them settled on Lewis. They had even over time abandoned their heathen religious beliefs and taken up the practice of Christianity, and the evidence of the Viking's presence was still evident in the Nordic originated names of many villages, streets and families on the island.

Entering the noisy pub, Ian and the others found it jumping and filled almost to capacity. It was laid out in the style of a traditional Viking drinking hall with several long trestle tables which ran the length of the right hand side of the open plan room, each bench filled with boisterous drinkers and festival goers. The bar and an open standing area took up the left hand side of the establishment, and it too was jammed tight with customers, the press of thirsty patrons waiting at the bar three people deep. The high ceiling was held in place with thick, exposed wooden beams, the walls decorated with a riotous collection of paintings featuring armoured Norse warriors and longships, colourfully patterned round shields a metre across, and several axes, spears and swords that looked authentic enough, but were probably dull edged replicas. A huge open fireplace blazed merrily away in the left corner at the far end of the large room, and a small raised area lay along the back wall. On the stage, yet another folk band, this one featuring a four piece of greybeards, hammered away lustily at a fiddle, a mandolin, a banjo and an acoustic guitar, belting out a furious, rousing jig. Several punters in front of the stage whirled around in boozy abandonment, taken up and transported by the exciting music. The air was filled with a cheery wall of noise; loud conversation, laughter, hooting, rhythmic clapping of hands and stomping of feet, the occasional smash of a glass and a chorus of cheers accompanying each breakage.

"Same again, fuckers?" Scarlett yelled above the jovial din. The four men answered in the affirmative, and Scarlett began threading her way through the crowd in the direction of the bar to get another round in. Ian watched her go, and despite the throng of customers already pressed up at the bar waiting to be served, he knew they wouldn't be waiting long for their drinks.

He saw Scarlett pause for a moment, thoughtfully selecting a likely insertion point. She adjusted her top slightly and then moved to an area in the press of waiting punters that was mostly made up of males. As Ian had expected, they parted before her like magic, gallantly giving up their places in the queue and allowing her through to be served before them.

"After you, hen."

"On ye go, sweetheart. Ladies first."

"Archie! Get yer fat arse oot the way and let the lassie through!"

Scarlett smiled sweetly at the suddenly courteous gentlemen, thanking them gushingly for their fine manners in the presence of a lady and complimenting them on their sweetness.

There were advantages in going out drinking with a beautiful woman, Ian thought, and Scarlett was certainly not above using her looks and natural feminine charm to get what she wanted, especially when what she wanted was a pint.

A minute later, and the group were furnished with fresh drinks.

"You're shameless, Mathie," Cal was saying to Scarlett, "and we love you for it. Here's to drinking with bow legged women!" he exclaimed, raising his pint in salute. *Jaws* was Cal's all time favourite film, and he never passed up an opportunity to drop one of its lines of dialogue into conversation, though more often than not, like now, he misquoted the script despite having seen the film about a thousand times. Scarlett hit him a cuff on the shoulder, stating that her legs were in no way bowed.

Despite the day's cheerful and lively atmosphere in the presence of his old friends, Ian had been unable to shake off the pervading sense of wrongness that had haunted him ever since the incident with the pint glass on the ferry. Try as he might, he couldn't shake the feeling that something was most definitely *up*.

Ulfhednar.

He'd never heard the word before. He'd involuntarily plucked it out of the ether like he was some sort of fucked up radio receiver, but he knew that somewhere, someone else had spoken or thought the word to themselves. He had no idea what it meant. And yet it terrified him.

He tried to tell himself that it was a fluke. Some random Gaelic word spoken by an islander on the ferry that he'd subconsciously heard and unwittingly stored in his memory. If he'd had a smart phone, Ian might have tried Googling the strange word, but he'd always been something of a technophobe, relying on the same bells-and-whistles free Nokia which had served him faithfully for seven years and two world tours with the band. And in the last year or so especially, his thoughts had been otherwise occupied. Modern gadgetry and keeping up with the technological times was way down the list of things he'd had on his mind. He wasn't about to ask one of the others to look up the weird sounding word either. He didn't even want to think about it, never mind research it. After leaving the bathroom on the ferry, his recently gashed hand tingling in the aftermath of the unnatural healing, and the alien sounding word repeating itself like a whispered mantra in his head, he'd found himself standing up top at the ship's rail, looking down at the water, and wondering what it would feel like, plunging into the churning wake of the ferry, being dragged deep under the ship's keel and mangled by the great propellers. If Clyde hadn't come up and found him at that moment...

On top of that, ever since stepping off the boat, he'd had a powerful perception of being observed by some unknown, yet thoroughly menacing presence, and had been constantly checking over his shoulder, studying the bustling, noisy crowds in the streets and pubs, trying in vain to locate the unseen watcher that he instinctively knew was there. The unfocussed feeling had been steadily building over the past hour, thick with the type of pent up energy that precedes acts of violence.

Now, with the sensation of being observed like icy crosshairs on the nape of his neck, Ian decided that after this pub, he'd quietly take Cal aside and apologise for bailing on his weekend, but bail he would. The sense of impending danger was too strong, and if his presence was somehow putting Scarlett, Matt, Clyde and Cal in jeopardy, he had to be gone. Simple as that. He'd apologise, say something about not being ready to be in an environment where there was a stage and a large crowd, go back into town, collect his bag from the hotel and catch the next ferry back to the mainland. They'd be disappointed he knew, but he thought they'd understand. They were good people. His only friends. And that was why he had to go.

The drinks were soon finished, and they left the Norseman, heading out of the busy town centre. They crossed the narrow river that emptied into Stornoway Harbour and entered the large park and woodland area encompassing the grounds of the local golf course, the college and Lews Castle. The footpath towards the main stage area in front of the castle was hemmed in by woods on either side and crowded with a happy flowing river of other festival goers that streamed around them. With his constant sense of unseen danger now reaching an almost suffocating level, Ian was just getting ready to tell them that he was leaving when Cal said that he needed a pish.

"Why didn't you go in the pub, ya dipshit?" Matt asked, swaying slightly from the beer and frowning at his watch. "We're cutting it fine here!"

"Obviously I didn't need to go in the pub, did I? Ya time obsessed rocket," Cal answered smartly and stepped off the footpath. "Just going to quickly water the shrubberies," he announced cheerily as he stumbled off into the shadows between the trees.

Ian saw a chance to slip away without making too much fuss. Rather than address all four of them, it'd be easier and quicker to just explain his decision to Cal alone and then quietly leave. He knew that if he spun the lie about not being able to face a large music venue, Cal would get where he was coming from, having dealt with a great deal of tragedy and post traumatic stress himself when he was younger.

"Hold up, dude," he called after Cal and followed him. "I'll come with you. Could do with a slash myself."

"Jesus jumping Christ," Matt groaned after them as they disappeared between the tree trunks. "Bunch of slack bladdered bufties around here. Move yer arses!"

Although the day was still light, the shadows were thick beneath the leafy canopy and between the tree trunks. They walked a short distance into the wood before Cal stopped at a large clump of Rhododendron and unzipped, sighing with deep satisfaction.

"Good for what ails you," he declared as his stream of urine spattered on the ground around the base of the foliage.

"Cal, listen, dude…" Ian began, but never finished the sentence.

A huge shadow detached itself soundlessly from the murk between two thick pine trees on his left, and lurched soundlessly towards them.

The shadow was holding a very large knife, which swung in the direction of Ian's throat.

PART TWO

The Valkyrie :   Of the Berserkers lot would I ask thee,
thou who batten'st on corpses.
How fare the fighters who rush forth to battle,
And stout-hearted stand 'gainst the foe?

The Raven :   Wolf-coats are they called. The Ulfhednar.
The warriors unfleeing,
Who bear bloody shields in battle.
The darts redden where they dash into battle,
And shoulder to shoulder stand.
'Tis men tried and true only, who can targes shatter,
Whom the wise war-lord wants in battle.

Thórbiörn Hornklofi, *The Lay of Harald*

1

Breck jerked awake as the first cries of alarm carried on the still night air up the hill to the small hut above the settlement. He cursed himself for falling asleep on watch, threw off his warm sheepskin blanket and scrambled to his feet, heart already pounding beneath his tunic. He looked down the night darkened slope in the direction of the fishing village of Eanach, his home.

Already, a few fires were blooming like flickering orange flowers in the darkness. There were more shouts, and a terrifying chorus of guttural war cries, then the ringing clang of steel on steel. More points of red firelight appeared in the darkened bay, and then a terrible howling filled the air.

Fear slammed through Breck's chest, and he bolted back into the hut to shake his sleeping companion awake. "Egor, wake up. The village." Egor came to, throwing off his own sheepskin and scrambling up from the earthen floor.

Breck ran outside again, taking a flaming branch from the small fire that had helped keep him warm during his watch, and throwing it on the much larger pyre that stood nearby, ready built and soaked in oil. The signal fire roared instantly into life.

Egor stood beside him, looking down at Eanach, his hands fisted in his hair and dismay twisting his features. More roundhouses and the village's small fishing fleet had been torched, and the whole settlement and beach were now lit up in a wavering fiery glow. From their elevated vantage point, they could see the longboat anchored in the shallows of the bay, and the shadowy figures of the enormous raiders that moved up the beach and through the settlement, burning and killing.

"Lord save us," Egor mumbled in a choked voice. "Breck, my mother. My sister..." He reached for the knife on his belt.

Breck grabbed him roughly by the shoulder and pulled him away from the edge of the hill, pushing him in the opposite direction.

"No," he said. "It's too late. We have to go. Run!"

The neighbouring settlement of Acker was just over a mile inland. The signal fire lit, it was Egor and Breck's duty now to make their way with all speed to the next village. The two boys scrambled down the small hill and raced away along the narrow trail that led west. The sky was clear and the moon and stars above cast a silvery light across the surrounding moors as they pelted along the path.

Breck understood his friend's desire to help. He had two brothers in Eanach himself, but he forced himself to run, trying not to think about that. It had been many years since the feared Norsemen had last raided any of the coastal settlements, and the Vikings had even begun to settle on the island, marrying into native families, raising crops and establishing their own communities which lived in peace with their neighbours. Most natives believed that the days of living in fear of the longboats were over, but Garron, Breck's father and Eanach's chieftain, had lived through previous raids in times past, and had ordered that the lookout post on the hill behind the settlement continue to be manned night and day. Now it seemed, Garron had been tragically right to insist on what many considered an unnecessary precaution.

The path to Acker ran through the bottom of a shallow valley with rocky moorland sloping up on either side, and Breck could hear Egor's laboured panting behind him as they raced along the valley floor. His own terror quickened breath burning in his throat as they ran, Breck soon caught sight of the torches of Acker, flickering in the darkness ahead.

"We're here, Egor," he gasped as they passed between the torches and ran into the crofting village. Acker was a little larger than Eanach, with a population of around sixty, its buildings consisting of roundhouses, several animal pens and a few large barns. The village was deathly still at this late hour, and deep shadows pooled between the small dwellings where the settlement's inhabitants slept in blissful ignorance of the carnage in their neighbouring village. Breck had hoped that the population would already have been roused by their own watchmen, who should have been alerted by the signal beacon he had lit. Apparently though, the people of Acker had not thought the threat of sea raiders was as serious as Breck's father had, and had not bothered to keep watch for their neighbour's warning pyre. Their indifference, Breck supposed, was understandable considering there hadn't been a raid in almost a decade.

Egor shattered the village's peace as he began yelling shrilly. "Help us! Please! Marauders have come! Eanach is under attack!"

Breck was familiar with Acker, and knew in which hut Drostan, the village chieftain dwelt. He ran across central clearing of the settlement, heading for one of the larger roundhouses as Egor continued to raise the alarm, running from hut to hut and pounding on the walls, shouting to wake the villagers who slept inside.

Breck reached Drostan's hut and pulled aside the heavy sheet of leather that served as a door. He could smell the earthy smoke of the peat fire in the centre of the roundhouse, and in the low orange glow, could make out a figure struggling up from beneath a pile of furs on the floor.

"Who is that?" the figure demanded with irritation. "Who wakes an old man from his rest at this hour?"

"Drostan, it's me, Breck of Eanach. You must rouse your people. Raiders have come. Eanach burns."

"Breck?" Drostan said in alarm as he threw off his sleeping skins and pushed himself quickly to his feet. His wife Ceana sleepily mumbled some admonishment at the disturbance and pulled the coverings over herself again. Drostan nudged her ungently with his foot. "Wake yourself, woman," he grated, then came to Breck in the doorway. "What has happened, boy?" he demanded.

"Please, Drostan, you must call out your men. The northmen have returned," Breck pleaded in desperation, close to tears.

Drostan looked at him sceptically. "Vikings? There's not been a raid in many years, Breck..."

Breck grabbed the old man by his jerkin and hauled him outside, pointing eastward. There was an orange tinge to the night sky in the direction of the coast, and the smell of burning blowing in from the sea. "See for yourself!" Breck cried. "Where are your watchmen? It was agreed at the last gathering that you'd keep a vigil, as we do."

Drostan freed himself from Breck's grip and stood in shock, gazing at the hazy orange glow in the east. "We never thought... it has been years..." he was saying, shaking his head in disbelief.

By now, others awoken by Egor's frantic shouting had emerged from their huts and stood around in the settlement's central clearing, rubbing at sleep tired eyes and looking at one another in confusion. Egor was still running among the roundhouses, banging on the walls and yelling. "Marauders! Marauders have come!" he cried as he went. "Wake yourselves! To arms! To arms!"

The wakened villagers looked at another in alarm, their weary eyes coming fully awake at the threat of sea raiders, a deadly menace they all thought long past. An anxious buzz of worried conversation filled the air, and there were a few small screams from frightened women and the squalling of small children.

"Please, Drostan…" Breck was saying, pulling at the old man's sleeve again. The chieftain looked down at him as if really seeing the boy for the first time, then shook off his confusion.

"TO ARMS!" he roared. *"MEN OF ACKER! TO ARMS!"*

Torches around the central clearing were lit, and Breck could now see the men of the village who had come out from their huts immediately duck back inside to re-emerge moments later carrying an odd assortment of weapons, which he saw were mostly made up of farming and metal working tools; pitchforks, hammers and the like. A few of them, mostly the older ones who had lived through the years when Viking raids had been frequent, were equipped with real weapons and held swords, shields, spears and bows. There were a few old scraps of armour on show, a rusting helm here, a dented breastplate there. It was obvious that there had been little preparation amongst the men for such an event, and they stood around the central clearing in unorganised, frightened groups, looking at one another, unsure what to do next and awaiting instructions. There were around thirty of them, ranging from beardless boys of no more than twelve summers to bent greybeards.

Drostan went running over to the nervous armed men and began trying to rally and organise them. Breck saw Egor accompanied by a tall blonde haired man of muscular stature hurrying over to join the makeshift band of defenders. The big man was better equipped than the others, carrying a long handled axe and a spear, as well as a large rounded shield. A metal helm sat atop the man's head, his long pale hair flowing free from underneath, and he wore a heavy mail vest. Breck had seen the man on previous visits to Acker, and knew he was a Norseman going by the name of Vandrad, who had settled in the village. Knowing that Vandrad was not the only Norseman who'd made a peaceful home on the island, Breck looked around and saw the other one, Ulfar, a hulking dark haired man, similarly adorned with mail vest, helm and shield. Ulfar was armed with a great longsword that he wore in a scabbard across his back, and had two throwing axes tucked in a wide leather belt across his waist.

As Breck made his way towards the band of men to join them, a fearful scream rang out from the darkness somewhere towards the rear of the settlement. The buzz and bustle of the villagers abruptly ceased at the sound, and several people turned in the direction it had come from. The desperate wail of terror and agony went on for a few seconds, rising in pitch before being cut off suddenly. Drostan pointed and barked a few curt orders, and a group of four men began to hurry off to investigate. They stopped in their tracks however, as a deep, rumbling snarl sounded out from the shadows.

Breck froze, the blood in his veins turning to slush at the otherworldly growl that seemed to reverberate in his bones and through the very ground. He saw the villagers glance fearfully at one another. Women held their children close. The men tightened their grips on their weapons. He noticed Vandrad and Ulfar share a look, and heard Vandrad mutter a strange word to his companion.

Hamrammr.

Ulfar nodded slightly, still looking towards the darkened rear of the settlement. Breck saw the giant Norseman's hand flex on the handle of one of his throwing axes, as if he were readying himself for imminent battle.

The four man search party broke their paralysis and made towards the shadows again, but Ulfar stepped in front of them holding up a hand, shaking his head and speaking a few quiet words. Breck walked over to stand amid the armed men, feeling small and scared.

"You no go," Ulfar was saying, his words thickly accented. "No good."

Vandrad and Drostan joined them. "Drostan, we must bring everyone here into the centre of the village," the Norseman was saying. "Everyone. Bring the women and children from their huts. We must have torches and as much oil as possible…"

A second scream from somewhere in the darkness shattered the tense atmosphere. Closer this time. A man, wailing in stark panic. Between the desperate shrieks, Breck could hear something snarling. Something that sounded very big, and very hungry.

"FORM A CIRCLE!" Vandrad roared, hefting his axe in a two handed grip and looking around at the men standing in frightened confusion. "Get the women and little ones in the centre and protect them! The beast is upon us!"

2

The tension and fear that had been slowly building in Acker since the men had been called to arms erupted into full scale panic.

That second scream and the terrible sounds that followed - hoarse grunting growls and an unnerving wet snapping sound like a large predatory animal at a kill - had at first frozen the settlement's inhabitants immobile. Vandrad's bellowed command to form up broke the spell, and suddenly the central clearing was a chaotic confusion of people running to and fro. The men who had gathered with their meagre arms and armour broke and rushed off to find their loved ones, women clutching small children aimlessly dashed around, frantically seeking some safe refuge. Drostan was shouting over the confused racket, holding his hands aloft and appealing in vain for order, but only Vandrad and Ulfar, Breck saw, were keeping their heads. The two Norsemen remained in the central clearing, standing back to back with their weapons drawn, seizing and bawling at the men dashing around them to form a defensive ring and calling for torches and oil to be brought. Seeing his friend pass by, Breck grabbed Egor by the shoulder and hauled him over to stand by the two warriors. Two women joined them then. The short, dark haired homely woman stood by Ulfar, and spoke to him in his native tongue, a look of deep anxiety on her face. Again, Breck heard that strange word, *hamrammr*. Ulfar's wife mumbled something incoherent and made a quick gesture with her hand, and although Breck did not know the language of the Norse people, the gesture and tone of the words had the quality of a prayer, and he knew Ulfar's wife had offered up a request for divine protection.

The second woman, Vandrad's wife, was a native islander named Sileas. Breck and Egor both knew her, as she was originally from Eanach and only a few years older than them. She spoke to Egor now, concern lining her face. "What has happened, Egor?"

"They burned it, Sileas," Egor replied, shaking his head, tears shimmering in his eyes. "Everything. The boats, the houses, the church... everything."

"Did many others escape?" she asked. Sileas' father and sister still lived in Eanach. *Had* lived there, Breck supposed bleakly. What little he had seen of the attack from atop the hillside had been brutal, and he held little hope of any survivors. Again, thoughts of his own family rose in his mind, and he fought to hold back tears. His mother has died from the wasting sickness two years ago, but Garron, his father and Maon, his elder sibling, would have been involved in the fighting. Airill, his younger brother, was only five summers old...

More villagers began to take refuge within the ragged defensive circle now starting to form under the urgent commands and gestures of Drostan, Ulfar and Vandrad. Several of the men returned to the clearing with their families and joined the outward facing circle, their weapons drawn. More villagers came running from the shadows between the roundhouses to join the swelling huddle, and Breck saw that many of them carried flaming torches and clay pots of oil as Vandrad had commanded.

"We must arm the men with the torches and oil, Drostan," Vandrad was saying to the village chieftain. "Weapons of steel will do little good. We must burn it."

"What is it?" Drostan asked, his eyes flicking among the patches of darkness pooled between the roundhouses surrounding them. "Those sounds…"

"I will explain it to you if live through this night," Vandrad replied in a grim tone. "If you value the lives of your people, you must do as I urge and place an urn of oil in the hands of every second man, and a torch in the hands of the one beside him. Every third man should hold whatever weapon he possesses"

Drostan nodded and began organising the defenders, distributing the flaming torches and oil pots as instructed. The tide of villagers arriving in the settlement's centre dwindled until the entire population of Acker pressed tightly against one another; the women and children in the centre, and a ring of men holding weapons, torches and oil pots surrounding them.

"When it comes," Vandrad called out, "those men with pots and urns must soak it in oil for those with torches to light. The beast will come swiftly, so be true and do not let fear steal away your nerve. Stand firm now, and be ready."

The frightened whimpering and muttering of the villagers died away eventually, and a strained hush fell over the circled crowd.

They waited.

Nothing moved in the darkness beyond the light cast by the men holding torches, and a palpable tension filled the air. Breck was breathing rapidly, his palm sweaty upon the hilt of the small belt knife he clutched in his fist. Egor stood by his shoulder, a torch in his hand. The night seemed to hold its breath in anticipation, the men watching the shadows nervously, glancing this way and that, jumping at the slightest sound.

When it came, though, it came in silence.

From the corner of his eye, Breck saw the shadows between two huts on his left writhe for a split second before some huge animal sailed soundlessly from the darkness. He had a momentary impression of a soaring mass of tawny hair, pointed ears, claws and yellow eyes. The thing *flew* from the darkness, bounding clean over the heads of the outer ring of armed men, and before anyone could so much as shout a warning or scream in terror, it was right there amid them.

The tense silence shattered in a mass of panicked shrieks, and the night fell apart into bloody chaos.

It happened with such shocking suddenness that Breck was still facing outwards when a splash of warm wetness slapped the nape of his neck. He tried to turn, but was knocked roughly to the ground as the press of villagers in the centre of the clearing scattered outwards in a panicked stampede, pushing, barging, stumbling and trampling each other in their frantic efforts to flee from the monstrosity that had suddenly appeared in their midst. The ring of armed defenders disintegrated as those behind ran into them, and the night was suddenly alive with a hellish cacophony of screams, confused shouts and blood freezing animal roars. Somewhere Breck could hear Vandrad desperately trying to rally the men. *"STAND FIRM! HOLD YOUR GROUND! THE OIL! THROW THE OIL!"* But it was useless. Any semblance of order had vanished in the terror that swept through the villagers' hearts, stealing their courage and prompting mass hysteria.

Lying stunned in the mud, Breck saw the thing through a shifting confusion of running villagers, and the sight of the gigantic beast unmanned him. He could only lie there, staring in terrified disbelief. It was easily seven feet tall, a huge creature coated in tawny fur, standing on two powerfully muscled, dog jointed legs. A massive upper torso it had, with long sinewy arms and human-like hands, long fingers tipped with talons. It had the head of a wolf, but such an animal had surely never existed on God's good Earth. The eyes blazed an unholy yellow fire, and the elongated snout bristled with a mouthful of daggers.

It leapt with terrifying speed around the clearing, striking down the panicked men, women and children around it in an indiscriminate orgy of slaughter. As he lay there, shocked into immobility by the sight of the roaring demon, Breck witnessed the thing pounce upon a fleeing woman and tear open the back of her neck, gnawing on her briefly before springing up again with impossible speed and laying open another villager's torso with a swipe of its claws. The man, an old greybeard carrying a spear, screamed horribly and spun away to the side, his intestines trailing through the air after him in a dripping wet tangle of bloody ropes.

Already, torn bodies lay all around Breck, and the dusty ground of the clearing was slicked with blood. He could only gape in numb, stupefied disbelief at the horrific carnage the beast had wrought in the space of mere seconds.

Over the constant screams of the fleeing villagers, Breck heard again the ringing battlefield voice of Vandrad cutting through the chaos. *"BURN IT!"* he was bellowing from somewhere behind him. *"THE OIL! THROW THE OIL!"*

Breck turned his head and saw a group of armed men, Drostan, Vandrad and Ulfar in their centre. They threw, and several clay urns and pots trailed glistening arcs of whale oil as they sailed through the air towards the monster.

Turning back, Breck saw the creature bound towards the men in a sudden burst of speed. The thrown jars and pots flew harmlessly over it and it ran, coming straight at Breck, who screamed in fright as the wolf-like creature's eyes met his. He tried to scramble away, his heels digging at the ground, but already the monster was airborne, the hatred and hunger in its eyes burning into Breck as it descended on him, dripping jaws agape.

Breck's view of his impending death was suddenly blocked as a huge figure stepped over his prone body, bellowing a fearful battle cry. There was a tremendous clatter and Breck instinctively rolled away to the side, coming quickly to his feet to see Ulfar standing there, crouched behind his great round shield and brandishing the massive longsword. The wolf, denied its kill, roared in fury as it stalked toward the Viking, then a spear point erupted from the centre of its broad chest, punching out through the golden fur in a gout of blood as Vandrad, standing behind the monster, held tight to the shaft. The beast threw back its massive shaggy head and screamed, then twisted at the waist, clawing at the air behind it. Vandrad saw the blow coming and ducked beneath the flailing arm, circling further to the right behind the beast and keeping hold of the spear. The wolf shrieked in rage, then brought both its huge mutant hands to its chest and grasped the head of the spear which impaled it. With a great heave and an ear splitting howl, it pulled the shaft straight through its own body in a wet red torrent and snapped the spear in two like a twig, tossing the broken pieces aside contemptuously. Ulfar ran at the monster then, bellowing his war cry and swinging the longsword at its head. The wolf dodged nimbly beneath the attack and countered with a swipe of its left hand which Ulfar only just managed to block with his shield. Splinters flying, the force of the blow sent the big man crashing to the ground, and the wolf closed in, snarling in victory. Then Vandrad was there, standing between the advancing nightmare and Ulfar, swinging his long axe in a furious series of cuts. Ulfar scrambled to his feet again and took up a position to the side of Vandrad. The two Norsemen spread out slightly, circling, keeping the creature between them. The monster roared and swiped, snarled and lunged at them, but the two warriors kept their distance, one darting in and striking whenever the towering horror turned its back to slash at the other.

Another oil jar flew through the air, this one cracking open on the beast's back. The creature turned, its eyes flaring in fury, and bounded across the clearing toward the young dark haired lad who had hurled the missile. The boy turned and ran, but was swiftly borne to the ground, crushed beneath the huge body as the monster fastened its jaws around his neck. With a hideous crunch, the screaming boy's head was torn away, spraying a wide fan of blood across the ground. As it rose up again, Vandrad and Ulfar charged, Ulfar hurling his two throwing axes on the run, each of which zipped through the air to thud meatily into the thing's chest. The creature merely flinched, then bounded back across the clearing toward the advancing Norseman, Ulfar's axes still deeply embedded in its body.

Breck knew the two men couldn't keep the fight going much longer. The wounds they'd inflicted upon the hellish creature seemed to have no effect, and he could see they were tiring. Something urged him at that moment to look down, and he saw there was a torch lying discarded on the ground by his hand, a weak flame still fluttering at its end.

The great wolf and the two Vikings came together with a brutal crash as the Norsemen simultaneously raised their shields in a two man wall and braced themselves. The wolf crashed against the barrier of hard wood, driving into the shields with a thick shoulder and knocking the two men to the ground. The warriors rolled away and got halfway to their feet, but the wolf lunged forward again in a bristling blur of movement, catching Vandrad across the chest with a swipe of a clawed hand and sending him flying a full ten strides across the clearing to land in a senseless heap. Ulfar roared and thrust out with the longsword, going for the wolf's groin area, but in a lightning fast left-right combination of slashes with its claws, both sword and shield were torn from the big Norsemen's grasp, and the snarling fiend barrelled into him, bundling him to the ground again. It was upon Ulfar in an instant, pinning him down by the shoulders and leering into his face, savouring its triumph. It reared back its head, the cavernous maw agape for the killing bite.

Then it burst into flames as Breck thrust the burning torch into the oil soaked fur of its back.

Like a dried out gorse bush ignited by lightning, the creature seemed to erupt, instantly engulfed in flames. Breck jumped clear and scrambled to a safe distance as it leapt off Ulfar and whirled away, screaming in a horrible high pitched mixture of animal and human tones that made Breck hold his hands over his ears. It flailed and leapt, rolled and thrashed, and the air was thick with the stink of its burning hair and flesh.

Breck saw Vandrad stagger back to his feet, then he and Ulfar rushed towards the howling pyre with their weapons aloft. Vandrad was shouting something about blood and waving his long axe forward as he ran, bidding the other villagers to rally to him. They responded to his call and several more men charged towards the burning monster that staggered aimlessly around the clearing, baying in agony.

It went down, and the men crowded around the flaming body, reigning down vengeful retribution, hacking, stabbing and pummelling at the screaming creature. Breck lost sight of the burning beast as more men joined the angry shouting mob, and all he could see were the backs of the violent huddle as their weapons rose and fell, rose and fell, until the unearthly animal shrieking finally ceased.

When it was over, Breck pushed his way through the throng of bodies who stood motionlessly staring down at the dead beast. The wolf-creature had been reduced to a smoking, mangled carcass, riven and cleaved and scorched raw. It had been dismembered in the frenzied attack, and severed limbs, chunks of fur and viscera littered the blackened ground around it. The stench of burned meat and hair was sickening, and the sight of the butchered monster burned itself into Breck's mind.

Then Ulfar stepped out from the crowd of men towards the smouldering collection of body parts. He grasped hold of the severed head, the charred broken shape of the lupine skull partly exposed where the fire had scorched away hair and meat. He planted a foot on the thing's head, and with a grunt and a twist of his massive arms, Ulfar tore off the huge fanged jawbones and lifted them aloft to the night, bellowing a fierce roar of victory. The villagers raised their weapons and joined in the cry, the savage chorus rolling through the village of Acker and out across the surrounding hills.

Eventually the triumphant yelling died down, and the men's blood cooled as they looked around the clearing. All around in twisted heaps lay the bloody remains of the slain. Bodies of villagers littered the hard packed earth, small red unrecognisable pieces of people, scattered haphazardly around, and everywhere were congealing pools, streaks and splashes of blood. Those who had fled the clearing now returned to look upon the devastated scene, which had the look of a battlefield after some vicious melee, and then the night was full of weeping and wailing as loved ones were discovered amongst the human wreckage by their kith and kin.

A strong hand came down on Breck's shoulder, startling him from his shocked state of detachment. He flinched and looked up into Vandrad's blood splattered face.

"You have iron in you, boy," the Norseman said. "In all the legends, there are less than a score of men that have vanquished one of the Ulfhednar."

"Ulfhednar," Breck repeated faintly. "Is that what it was?"

Vandrad nodded slowly, his flinty eyes coldly looking down upon the maimed corpse at their feet. Breck expected more of an explanation as to what exactly the thing had been, but Vandrad just squeezed his shoulder, nodded again and walked away.

3

"The Devil has come to our island," Drostan said, looking gravely at the men around him.

He'd called an immediate council even as the men had been standing staring at the demon's smoking carcass, and the large roundhouse in which he dwelt was crowded with people, the thick smoky air inside the chieftain's home rife with fearful tension and the smell of sweat and burned animal hair, which clung sickeningly to the clothing of those in attendance.

Vandrad stood. "The Devil would be a blessing, Drostan," the tall Norseman said. He turned to address the others. "The evil that has landed here is not of your Christian religion, but of the Norse. Our gods…"

"Blasphemy!" one man shouted over Vandrad. "There is only *one* God! Your pagan ways have brought Satan among us, *raider*," he spat. A few voices muttered in agreement with the pious villager, a heavy set man with a red beard and angry, close set eyes.

"Peace, Sionn," Drostan said. "Vandrad has lived among us for many a year as well you know. I do not believe he, nor Ulfar, are the cause of this wickedness."

"Their heresy has been tolerated here for too long," Sionn continued, ignoring his chieftain and looking around at those who nodded along with him. "We must purge our land of their sacrilegious ways. Exile them!" His gang of supporters loudly proclaimed their accord with this judgement, and calls of "Cast them out!", "Begone, marauders!" and "Banish the Vikings!" rang out. Vandrad and Ulfar shared a look, and both fingered the hilts of their weapons.

"*Still your tongues!*" Drostan thundered, sensing the gathering was on the verge of boiling over into violence. "Have you all so short a memory? If it were not for Vandrad and Ulfar, all of you, everyone in this village, would be dead. Where were *you*, Sionn, when the beast was slaughtering our people?"

Sionn sat down again, his face taut and sullen. His followers muttered, but none spoke out again for fear of incurring the wrath of their leader.

"Each of us here owes our life to these men," Drostan said, pointing at the two Norsemen, "and I will hear no more talk of banishment. Press me on this and I will let you take it up personally with those you accuse. What say you, Sionn? Uallace? Conn? If you wish exile upon Vandrad and Ulfar, I give you my leave to challenge them in combat."

Vandrad and Ulfar grinned hopefully at Sionn and his friends, who each suddenly discovered something of great interest lying on the ground between their feet.

When it was clear no challenge or further demand for the deportment of the Norsemen was forthcoming, Drostan continued. "This beardless stripling here," he said, indicating Breck who sat hunched silently in the corner, "is perhaps the one with the most courage in this room. Stand and be recognised, Breck of Eanach." There were raucous shouts and much stamping of feet as Breck got shyly to his feet.

"From this day on," Drostan proclaimed, "Breck and Egor are of *our* people, and I bid them welcome under my roof." There were nods and sounds of approval at his announcement. Embarrassed, Breck sat down again next to Egor, who was gazing into space, still in shock from the night's bloody mayhem.

The chieftain turned again to Vandrad. "It is clear to me from your actions that you and Ulfar have some knowledge of the beast. Is it not so?"

"It is so," Vandrad replied softly.

Ulfar nodded. "So," he grunted.

"Then share what you know with us," Drostan said.

The chieftain sat down and Vandrad stood again, looking over the men in the room, who returned his gaze with a mixture of expectation, mistrust and hope. He glanced at Ulfar, who simply shrugged.

"They were once known as the Ulfhednar," Vandrad said. "In our tongue, the name means 'wolf coated'. Long ago, they were shock troops in the army of Harald Fairhair, first King of Norway. Berserkers, who wore the skins of wolves in battle. The stories say they were invincible fighters when in their battle frenzy, unfeeling of pain, and each one the match of any ten men. The Ulfhednar took no prisoners, slaughtering all who stood in their path, be they enemy or ally. It is said the other warriors in Harald's army would make sure they stayed far from the berserkers when in battle, lest they fall under their spears themselves. It was whispered that the Ulfhednar fought not for their King, but for the wolf god Fenrir, son of Loki, whom they worshipped, and they spat upon the name of Odin. Because of this they were shunned, feared and despised by the other soldiers of Harald's army."

No one spoke, and when Vandrad paused, Drostan indicated that he should continue.

"Despite this," Vandrad went on, "the Ulfhednar brought many victories for Harald, accomplishing many heroic deeds, and it was said they won him his crown at the battle of Hafrsfjord, after which he was recognised as the ruler of all Norway. To reward them, Harald made the Ulfhednar his personal king's guard, a position of great honour, but they refused and spurned him. The Sons of Fenrir, as they called themselves, were warriors, not nursemaids to some mortal with a crown, they said. Enraged by their arrogance, the proud Harald commanded that the Ulfhednar be put to death for treason, but the berserkers slew those guards who came against them at the King's order and fled, killing many more of Harald's men before vanishing without a trace."

"What lies are theses?" interrupted Sionn. "The pagan Harald won the battle of Hafrsfjord almost two hundred years past, and that was no man in a wolfskin last night."

Vandrad ignored him. "Not long after," he continued, "stories began to spread in the northern lands of raiders who came from the sea at night, attacking coastal settlements. They took nothing of value, but burned and slaughtered at will, leaving few survivors. Then the stories began to change. They were not mere men, these raiders, but demigods who walked as men, and as wolves. They were *hamrammr*, shapeshifters. The stories said that those the Ulfhednar wounded but left alive *changed*, became *vargulfen*. These poor souls were transformed into great ravenous wolves, never again to take human form, forever hungering for living flesh, and let loose upon the land.

"Over time, the legend of the Sons of Fenrir passed into myth, and they became feared throughout the lands as evil spirits who came in the night, appearing from the sea only to burn and slaughter in the name of Fenrir, infecting the land with their *vargulfen* offspring, before disappearing again."

For a moment, there was a perfect silence in Drostan's smoky roundhouse as the men of Acker took in Vandrad's tale. The Norseman sat down again by Ulfar, who clapped him companionably on the shoulder, muttering something in their native tongue and chuckling.

It was Sionn who broke the uneasy quiet. "Blasphemy," the bearded man whispered contemptuously, shaking his head. "You speak of heresy, *raider*, with your many gods. I say the beast is a minion of Satan, sent to punish us for allowing these pagans to live among us with their ungodly..."

"*ENOUGH!*" roared Drostan, suddenly striding across the room and hauling Sionn to his feet with a fluidity and strength that belied his age. "The raider's ship lies still on the sands of Eanach," the chieftain hissed in Sionn's face. "Be they of Satan or of the Norse gods, they are *still here*, you fool." He had sent out scouts immediately after the attack on Acker, and they had returned from the coast soon after, pale faced and trembling at what they had seen. A massacre, they'd said, with the invaders' longboat still there, beached on the sands. Drostan kept hold of Sionn's tunic, staring the fat man down with a burning intensity in his eyes. Sionn's mouth opened and closed soundlessly like that of a gasping fish on land, and he visibly quailed before his chieftain's anger. Drostan released him and turned to the others who sat gaping in shocked silence at the outburst. "We must find and kill these beasts," he said, "and I will hear no more of religion in this matter. The next man to utter accusations of heresy or blasphemy will be used as bait in a trap, and we will see how the Sons of Fenrir like the taste of pious Christian flesh."

There were a few gasps of disbelief at Drostan's threat, which itself bordered on sacrilege, but so evident was his conviction that none doubted his resolve. The chieftain turned again to Vandrad and Ulfar. "I would ask that you advise us in these dark times," he said. "Lead us in the hunt for these creatures, and tell us how they may be destroyed."

"Fire," Vandrad said simply. "It is the surest way, but I have heard tell that weapons stained with the blood of *hamrammr* are thereafter deadly to their kind. Such was my thinking when I bid you all strike down the beast as it burned."

Breck, who had been sitting listening with growing horror to Vandrad's tale, remembered the warrior urging the villagers forward as the wolf had spun blazing and screaming about the clearing in its fiery death throes. He'd been shouting something about blood.

"If this holds true," Vandrad said, "then many of you now possess weapons with the power to combat this evil."

Several men in attendance nodded approval, fingering the shafts and hilts of their weaponry and looking at the old spears, rusty swords and worn pitchforks with something like religious awe.

"But first," Vandrad said getting to his feet, "we must burn their ship."

4

The bay of Eanach usually boasted clear blue waters and fine white sands that rose in pale gentle dunes, normally a tranquil, picturesque place of natural charm.

Now, in the pale dawn light, it had a battered and raped look to it.

When they arrived at the coastal settlement, Breck, Egor and the thirty or so men who accompanied them, including Drostan, Vandrad and Ulfar, were met by the sight of a seared, bloodstained wasteland. The rising sun in the east cast crimson rays over the devastated village, and the chilly morning was eerily quiet, the only sound the soft sigh of gentle waves lapping languidly at the white shores.

Nothing moved among the shells of the burnt out roundhouses, every one of which had been reduced to a few boulders and charcoaled pieces of wood. The small church had likewise been incinerated and lay in a sorry pile of singed stone, scorched timber and ashes. There was nothing of human remains but a few blackened bones.

On the beach there were many bodies, those who had attempted to defend the village. As in the central clearing at Acker, but on a much larger scale, corpses lay spread about in twisted red repose. All around the grisly cadavers, the soft white sand was churned and stained rust red, a few weapons lay scattered about and a few arrows protruded from the beach.

Among the dead, Breck found his father and his elder brother. Both had died very badly. Of little Airill, there was not a trace, but Breck, crippled with shock and grief, refused to give thought to foolish hopes that his younger sibling had somehow escaped. He knew in his heart that Airill was gone. Nothing more than dead cinders spread amid the burned out huts. Of Egor's mother and sister there was also no sign, and the two boys, the sole remnants of the people of Eanach, held each other and wept bitterly, grieving with each other over the loss of their families and home.

The small flotilla of vessels that had made up the village's fishing fleet was gone. All that remained were charred pieces of kindling that washed up sadly where the still bloody waves of the ocean met the land. The only ship still intact in the bay was the invaders' sleek longship, which had been beached on the sand, its presence terrifying evidence that the inhuman raiders had not left after the attack, but were still somewhere on the island.

The longship sat like a brooding dark sentinel, gloating over the bloodstained sands and the flensed corpses of the fallen. The men had come from Acker equipped with clay pots of oil and torches, intending to set the invaders' ship afire, but now they looked upon the vessel with cold dread in their hearts, such was its fearsome appearance and the thoughts it inspired of the inhuman crew it had carried to their shores. It was the length of perhaps ten men, wide and shallow drafted, designed for speed and balance in the rough waters of the northern seas. At both prow and stern, the hull of the vessel narrowed and rose tall, giving the ship a symmetrical shape. Atop each high reaching end, there snarled an intricately carved figurehead, a great wolf's head, wide jaws agape and fangs bared. The skill of the craftsman who had carved the figureheads was evident in the naked hatred and hunger etched upon the beasts' faces. So fearful to look upon were they that many of the men shrank back before the sight of them and averted their gaze, feeling as though the lupine faces marked them somehow with their dead wooden eyes. The very wood of the longship seemed to emanate a deathly chill, and the men of Acker hesitated to approach it, many of them nervously crossing themselves as they stood there on the sands, whispering prayers for protection.

Conn, one of the men who had earlier agreed with Sionn's proposal to banish Ulfar and Vandrad, meekly approached Drostan, who himself stood looking upon the longship with a mixture of fear and loathing in his expression.

"Is this wise, Drostan?" he asked his chieftain. "Would it not be better to leave this ungodly vessel untouched? The raiders will return eventually and be gone from our shores, but if we burn it…"

"You would have the slaughter we witnessed last night visited upon others, Conn?" Drostan enquired, his face set.

"We cannot fight this menace," Conn muttered, looking away from the older man's eyes. "You saw yourself what but one of their kind did to us. This ship must hold forty or more."

"Yes, Conn. I saw what befell our village," Drostan said, looking back to the longship, "and I see what has become of Eanach. I would not have such a thing happen again,"

"Please, my chieftain," Conn begged. "I implore you. We are crofters and fishermen, not warriors. Let the devils leave this place."

Drostan turned his gaze back to Conn. The man was badly frightened, but his fear was understandable. He himself had debated the wisdom of destroying the marauders' vessel, and had seriously considered leaving the ship alone. It was as Conn said after all. They were farmers, not fighters, and he could not begin to imagine how they could possibly defeat forty or more of the demons, considering what just *one* had done to his people.

He knew himself, though. If he failed to act, he would be haunted by guilt and shame for the rest of his days. He could not knowingly let the Ulfhednar continue on their bloody way, bringing chaos and death to untold others. Thirteen of his own people had been torn apart the previous night. How many more would fall to the teeth and claws of these monsters if he gave in to fear? He would not have it so.

"I'm sorry, Conn," he said, then turned to Vandrad, who stood waiting at his other shoulder. "Burn it."

The Norseman nodded once and began shouting orders. Several men stepped forward and hurled their clay pots of whale oil into the hull of the longship. Others uncorked the urns and stoppered animal skins they held, and soaked the outside of the ship in the viscous liquid. When the oil was spent, Vandrad barked another command. Torches were lit and thrown. The oil caught immediately, and flames leapt up over the low sides of the longboat's hull. Within minutes, the ship was fully ablaze. Flames crawled up the mast, and the large square sail billowed in the fearsome heat, seeming to writhe and dance amid the fire that engulfed it. The wolfish figureheads snarled through the blaze, and many men would later swear that as they watched those terrible faces burn, they could hear enraged bestial snarls in their minds.

The men of Acker stood and watched the longship of the Ulfhednar burn, yet there was no sense of victory in this act. Many of them had the feeling that they were witnessing their very lives being reduced to ashes.

PART THREE

1

Cal had just zipped up his fly when the huge shadow seemed to separate from the surrounding gloom between the trees and lunged silently toward them.

Ian has been about to say something, and Cal only caught the shadow's movement as he'd turned towards his friend. Something metallic glinted for a split second in a stray beam of dusklight that penetrated the foliage overhead, and the word *blade* leapt into Cal's mind.

He threw himself forward instinctively, leading with his shoulder and aiming for the dark looming shape. As he barged into the half-seen figure, there was a low grunt, a dull thud, a yelp of pain from Ian, and then Cal was desperately grappling with the massive shape, his arms around the assailant's midsection, trying to heave them off their feet. He felt freakishly strong hands seize him, then he was lifted from his feet and found himself flying through the air. He collided with something, a tree, spun, and hit the ground, tumbling away through the underbrush. There was no initial pain in the surge of adrenaline, and he was back on his feet immediately, charging back through the bushes and shouting for help. Pushing his way through a clump of undergrowth, he saw a bearded giant in a long black coat crouching over Ian, a huge curved knife in his hand. Cal burst forward and kicked out, catching the attacker's wrist with his boot and sending the oversized blade spinning away into the shadows. The giant was instantly up again, and Cal only just managed to duck under a monstrous haymaker of a punch that swept towards his head. He lashed out another kick, going for the giant's groin, but his blow was turned onto a thick meaty thigh as the giant nimbly swivelled his hips, then a huge hand closed around Cal's throat like an iron clamp, and he was lifted into the air, his oxygen abruptly cut off. Gagging and spluttering, kicking in the air and clawing at the enormous hand constricting his windpipe, he felt the crushing vice-like grip squeeze...

*

Scarlett hadn't thought to wait for Clyde and Matt when she heard Cal's shouts for help coming from the woods at the side of the footpath.

She immediately took off in the direction of his voice, and was sprinting through the trees and bushes half a second later, vaguely aware that Clyde and Matt were following somewhere behind, urgently calling out for her to wait. She wasn't about to do that though, and she blundered on, heedless of the low pine branches and brambles that snagged and whipped at her as she passed.

Somewhere up ahead she could hear the sounds of a struggle, low grunts, muted cries of pain, and a then a horrible strangled croaking, as if someone were being violently throttled. A second later she burst into a small clearing, and saw Cal dangling a clear three feet off the ground, legs kicking, his throat seized by a huge long haired figure. Ian lay senseless on the ground nearby. The huge stranger had his back to her, and with an enraged snarl in her throat, Scarlett ran forward, and putting everything she had into the kick, punted the huge man between the legs from behind. She felt the impact all the way up to her hip, and briefly remembered her dear departed dad instructing her in the finer points of self defence as a child.

Doesn't matter how big they are, sweetheart, he'd told her. *You plant a good boot in a man's plumbs, and he'll go down like a tart's knickers.*

The giant didn't go down, but he immediately dropped Cal and staggered to the side, half doubled over and groaning. Scarlett felt a fearsome rush of pleasure, which immediately evaporated as the huge fucker turned toward her and stepped forward, a terrible black fury twisting his craggy bearded face as he reached for her. She backed away, and stepped on something hard on the ground. A knife. A really big knife. She swept it up and stepped to the side, circling round till she was standing protectively over Cal and Ian lying on the ground, and began slashing at the air with the massive knife as the giant came at her.

*

The band of steel around his windpipe suddenly loosened, and Call fell once more to the ground, landing hard on his back and sucking in great lungfuls of precious air.

Opening his eyes, he saw Scarlett standing over him, brandishing the enormous knife, screaming threats and very unladylike obscenities at the top of her voice. The bearded giant advanced on her, then Matt and Clyde were there, running from the shadows between the trees and crashing as one into the man from behind. All three went down in a tumbling tangle of flailing limbs and thrashing bodies. Cal regained his feet, and with Scarlett at his side, rushed to join the struggle. Matt and

Clyde each clung desperately to one of the huge stranger's enormous arms, trying with little success to restrain the enraged behemoth while Cal and Scarlett laid into his head and body, kicking and stomping with furious abandon. Then there were sudden bright lights, shouts, and a peripheral glimpse of several yellow jacketed figures rushing towards them. Someone grabbed Cal around the waist from behind, trying to haul him away. Swept up in the old black fury, the kind which he hadn't lost himself in for many years, Cal blindly lashed out behind him with an elbow, felt a hard, crunching impact and heard a cry of pain.

Then something crashed into the back of his skull, and the fight instantly went out of him as he crumpled senselessly to the ground.

2

"There's always one, isn't there?" Constable Lorna McDaid said to her superior, sighing and watching as five of her colleagues manhandled the huge semi-conscious bearded man into the back of the police van. "You say this big nutter's a local, Sarge? Never seen him before."

Sergeant Murdo Harrison nodded, keeping a close eye as the van's rear doors slammed shut. It had taken a considerable effort to subdue the suspect. He'd fought ferociously, throwing his officers left and right in a frantic effort to get to the long haired guy who'd been lying bleeding and unconscious on the ground. They'd managed to eventually calm him down only with sheer weight of numbers, the aid of quite a few baton digs to the skull, and liberal doses of incapacitant spray. Even thus weakened, battered and burning eyed, the big man had continued to struggle, but he'd been groggy enough, just, for the five constables to get the restraints on him and bundle him into the back of the van.

"Aye," Harrison said to McDaid. "I've seen him in town once or twice. Hard to forget the big bastard once you've clapped eyes on him. No idea what his name is though. Think he lives out in the hills somewhere."

"And he's never caused any trouble before this?" Lorna asked.

"Nope."

"Well, he's making up for it now," the young constable said.

Harrison nodded in agreement. He'd already been briefed on the incident by Niall Wallace, one of the first officers who'd arrived at the scene, accompanied by a few of the festival security staff who'd come running at the sound of shouting and screaming. Niall was currently sitting in the bay of the nearby ambulance, in surprisingly good humour considering his broken nose, which was being attended to by a paramedic. The guy who'd inflicted the injury, one of the mainlanders going by the name of Cal Dempster, was cuffed up and safely ensconced in the back of one of the three patrol cars present at the scene. Three of his companions were each talking separately to officers, giving their version of events. The fourth, the guy who'd been knifed, had already been taken to the local hospital. He'd live, Harrison had been informed, but it'd been close. If the guy who'd broken Niall's nose hadn't tackled the assailant, that huge knife would have been buried in the guy's neck instead of just nicking it.

The annual music festival always saw a slight temporary rise in the local crime rate, Harrison knew. A minor scuffle in a bar, or some drunken concert goer having a pish in a public doorway. Nothing serious, and all to be expected when the population was swelled by an extra five thousand or so people. The rest of the year, the small police presence on the island had it pretty easy compared to those working in cities and towns on the mainland. The population of the whole island was under nineteen thousand, the great majority of which inhabited Stornoway and the surrounding villages, and lawlessness was limited to the odd drunken bar fight, underage drinking, vandalism and petty drug abuse. The most serious thing to have happened in recent years was the seizure of a negligible stash of cocaine and cannabis resin found in a small time dealer's house. Even with these infractions, the Isle of Lewis enjoyed one of the lowest crime rates in the whole of the UK, and as such was one of the safest places to live in the British Isles.

In the thirty years Sergeant Murdo Harrison had lived and worked here, there'd never before been an attempted murder.

He walked over to the patrol car which held Cal Dempster, opened the door and helped the guy out of the vehicle. He positioned the man with his back against the car door and stood for a second, studying him. He was about six foot two, wide across the shoulders and chest, short cropped hair, solidly built and with the look of someone who knew how to handle himself. Harrison sensed no threat from the younger man, though, despite what he'd recently found out about him when doing a procedural background check.

"How's your head, son?" he asked, not unkindly.

"I've had worse," Cal replied, a contrite look on his face. "Look, I'm sorry I hit your guy. I didn't know he was a polis. With everything that was going on... I just felt someone grabbing me and swung an elbow without thinking. Is he alright?"

"Ach, just a broken nose," Harrison said. "Niall's a member of the local boxing club. That nose of his must have been broken fifty times. You may well have improved it. He's a good lad, though, not the sort to hold a grudge. He knows you didn't do it on purpose."

"Really?" Cal asked, eyebrows raised in surprise.

"We're not all arseholes you know, Cal," Harrison said. "I understand you've had a few problems with the law before?" He'd run Dempster's name through the computer, and found the man had previous. The record made for very interesting reading in fact. Harrison noticed the way Dempster turned his eyes downward at the mention of his chequered past.

"You could say that," Cal said, looking at his shoes.

"It's alright. What happened before's got nothing to do with what's gone on tonight. You did what you did and you served your time." With that, he turned Cal around and undid the restrains around his wrists. "Keep your head down for the rest of the weekend though, okay? You'll need to come back to the station and give a formal statement, and you'll probably be summoned as a witness when this goes to trial."

Cal nodded, rubbing his wrists. "Much appreciated," he said. "You mind if I head over the hospital before coming into the station? I want to see how Ian's doing."

"On you go, son," Harrison replied, nodding. "Come by the station tomorrow first thing though, right?"

"First thing."

"Okay then," Harrison said. He paused for a second, and then said, "You know, it took balls to do what you did. You saved your mate's life."

Cal shrugged. "He'd have done the same for me."

Harrison chuckled. "Maybe. I doubt he'd have been able to do much though. Your pal's built like a jockey's whip. Do I know him from somewhere by the way? His face looked familiar."

"He was in a band," Cal said. "They were pretty big for a while. Ragged Mojo?"

"Jesus, my son's got their album! Are they playing at the festival?"

Cal shook his head. "Nah. They... broke up."

"Ach, too bad. My boy would've loved to see them. Maybe your mate'll sign an autograph for him?"

"I'll ask him," Cal promised. "Thanks again, Sergeant. Really. I'll see you in the morning. First thing."

"See you then, Mr Dempster," Harrison replied. "A real life rock star in our sleepy wee town, eh?" he said, laughing as he walked away.

3

It was happening again.

Eighty thousand pairs of hands clapped impatiently, the steady rhythmic *crack* of one hundred and sixty thousand palms crashing together underscored by the constant wave of whistles, shouts and cheers from the multitude. They began chanting, the huge crowd's combined voices adding to the clapping to make a vast wall of noise.

Mo-jo
Mo-jo
Mo-jo
Mo-jo

The sense of anticipation in the air crackled. The crowd, soaked and filthy, had waited two days for this moment, enduring ceaseless downpours of torrential rain that had turned the ground underfoot into a muddy swamp that sucked hungrily at their feet. They pressed together, a haze of steam rising from their close packed sweaty bodies and floating above the heaving, shifting throng. Flags and banners waved in the clammy night air, hot and jungle moist. The chanting increased steadily in volume, until it was a colossal, syncopated pulsing roar like the voice of God.

Mo-jo
Mo-jo
Mo-jo
Mo-jo

The raised area beyond the chest high barriers that kept the seething swarm of humanity back was darkened but for a few small orbs of white light that bobbed around randomly, flitting this way and that. They faded and disappeared, and a sudden huge crackling noise followed by an ear splitting, wavering shriek rent the night apart. The ululating, whining howl leapt over the crowd like the shrieking cry of some lupine deity. The fanatical horde screamed as one.

The large darkened area before the frenzied mass abruptly erupted in a blaze of rainbowed light, and the howl of amplified feedback gave way to a towering three piece wall of sound that swept down and drowned out the noise of the crowd in a vast sonic avalanche. The band that had recently been described by a *Rolling Stone* journalist as the best and most important group of the last twenty years took the stage, and they rocked.

Drums boomed, crashed and banged in a complex flurry of precise metronomic pops and snaps. Great slabs of distorted guitar chords roared from the massive stacks of Marshall cabinets, clanging relentlessly through the air like concordant slaps from a giant's hand. The thick fuzzed-out bass notes grumbled and pulsed like the heartbeat of a behemoth, flawlessly complimenting the rattling drums as the low frequencies weaved and twisted around and under the frenetic backbeat, shaking the bones of the multitude that pushed forward, crushing those at the front helplessly and joyously against the barriers.

Several bodies began to roll over the heads of the bouncing throng, surfing the crowd, smiling and laughing in delirium, waving their hands in the air and occasionally dropping out of sight when a gap opened up in the press of humanity. Those that made it all the way to the front were seized by large men in yellow jackets and firmly escorted to the side, whereupon they found gaps in the press of bodies and rejoined the ecstatic crowd. A pit formed, and several figures began to leap and rush at each other, barging, pushing and colliding in a hysterical outpouring of violent joy. Some went sprawling through the mud, blood flowing from split lips and broken noses, but were immediately helped back to their feet by others to immediately rejoin the other whirling, dancing combatants.

Above them all, on a huge stage flanked by massive video screens, Ragged Mojo let loose in an enormous melodic blast of auditory adrenaline.

At the rear centre of the stage, elevated on the drum riser, Ian Walker sat behind his Tama five piece fusion kit, sweat already coating his wiry bare torso as the stage lights baked him in their fluorescent multi-coloured glare. He battered away with tightly controlled ferocity at the straining skins of his snare and toms, nailing the intricate beat together. Like an octopus on amphetamines, his flailing limbs a-blur as they pounded out the elaborate heartbeat of the band in a complex series of flams, triplets, rolls and paradiddles, Ian's head was turned to the left, facing a microphone as he simultaneously sang a flawless falsetto harmony over the main vocal of Ryan Kessler, frontman and guitarist, who stood in front of Ian, slightly to the right of centre stage. Ryan opened his throat with perfect gravelled pitch, shredding out a deliciously evil riff on his Gibson Les Paul, and the adoring crowd in the palm of his hand. To Ryan's left, Mad Tambo McGrath stood, legs wide apart, his head a blurred mass of thrashing, swinging hair, his fingers frenetic upon the thick strings and wide frets of his Fender Jazz bass.

The trio poured out their souls in a thousand watts of sound that measured close to one hundred and sixty decibels, louder than a jet engine.

The crowd were going berserk, loving every note and singing along like the world's biggest backing choir as they bounced and heaved in a joyous rolling sea.

Ian rattled out a long, rapid fire snare fill in the build up to Ryan's solo break, his head tilted back on his shoulders, looking up towards the massive lighting rig above, just as it lurched and wrenched with a tortured squeal of failing metal...

...There is iron in you, boy, the tall man with the long blonde hair said.

The main stage of the Reading Festival was suddenly gone, and Ian was standing in what looked like some sort of medieval village. Lots of little rounded huts made of stone, thatch and hardened mud. It was night time, and there were dead bodies lying everywhere. Torches. People crying. A large, unidentifiable charred figure lay on the ground nearby. A huge black haired man was standing over it, roaring and holding what looked like a pair of giant jawbones in the air. Jawbones ridged with ridiculously large pointed teeth.

Ulfhednar...

*

Ian bolted upright in bed, a scream lodged in his throat and rank nervous sweat coating his brow. His hair hung in greasy strands, plastered to his face, and his hands shook in the aftermath of the dream. Ian let out a long shuddering breath.

Across the hotel room, Clyde muttered some random nonsense sentence in his sleep, something that sounded like "protect the bag of hamsters." God only knew what *he* was dreaming about.

Ian lay back in the bed, the memory of the nightmare already dissipating, his heart gradually slowing. He scratched absently at the wide bandage that covered his shoulder from neck to upper left arm. He'd been extremely lucky, the doctor at the casualty ward had told him. Just a little deeper and the wound could have been fatal. As it was, the long but shallow cut running from the left side of his neck down across his shoulder was largely superficial, without the need of stitches, and after the application of a sterile bandage and a few precautionary shots to ward off any infection, he'd been allowed to leave. Accompanied by Scarlett, Clyde, Matt and Cal, who'd all arrived at the hospital together after they'd given statements to the police, he'd gone back to the hotel. Freaked out and mentally exhausted over the violent episode, they'd all agreed that they should call it a night, get some much needed kip, and discuss what happened in the morning.

Now, Ian closed his eyes again, despite the knowledge that any attempt to fall back asleep would be an exercise of the utmost futility.

Just a little deeper and the wound could have been fatal.

When the doctor had said that, Ian had laughed in a strange, fractured way, causing the physician to frown at him in confusion. He wondered what the young doctor would say if he were to tell him that he'd *felt* the huge dagger pierce deeply into his flesh, and had been all too aware of the horrible scrape as the blade had brushed his cervical vertebrae.

He wondered, not for the first time, exactly what it took to kill him.

Ian had discovered his new deathless state two weeks after the on-stage accident that had killed Ryan and Tambo. Weeks later, back home in his three million pound mansion on the outskirts of Glasgow, Ian's head had been in a very dark place, lost in a black chasm of depression and survivor's guilt by day, and every night tormented by vivid nightmares of falling lighting rigs, whipcracking steel support cables, eighty thousand screaming fans and the crushed bodies of his bandmates.

He hadn't written a note. He'd just lit some candles in his luxury bathroom, drew a nice hot bath, downed most of a bottle of Glenfiddich, and slid into the steaming water. No bubbles. Just the straight razor. Then a lot of blood.

Gratefully giving himself to the merciful death chill that stole through him, supplanting the unwanted warmth of the Scotch infused blood which spilled eagerly from his opened forearms and turned the steaming water into a thick crimson soup, Ian had been on the very verge of fading out, feeling the life leaching from him in pulsing red waves.

And then the pain had exploded in his rent wrists, and he'd experienced the healing for the first time, watching in disbelieving horror as the long vertical slits in his forearms knit themselves back together before his eyes.

Already a badly damaged man, Ian's mind had very nearly been broken beyond repair when he'd discovered that the only thing he wanted, the only thing that every man eventually *got*, had been taken from him. The revelation that Death had deserted him had almost driven Ian to unrecoverable madness, and driven him to further acts of deranged and experimental self harm. The blender incident for example. Jesus, he'd been in a bad way that night.

But it all proved futile, as his bleeding, broken, abraded, electrified and poisoned body proved, as it stubbornly reset itself, time after time after time. Large quantities of sleeping pills were not a viable method of suicide. They'd just made him a bit sleepy and had caused extremely painful stomach cramps. Likewise, hanging had proved a most inefficient means of taking his own life, leaving him not with the broken neck he grimly craved, but merely with a serious rope burn across his throat, a cunt of a crick in his neck, and the loss of his voice for a couple of days. Shit, he'd even been able to breathe as he'd dangled from the big chandelier in his living room, feeling like the world's biggest fanny, his toes three feet clear of the cheesy guitar shaped rug beneath him. Getting himself down again had been a nightmare.

The wound beneath the wide bandage was itching like mad now, as if a swarm of carnivorous ants were happily munching away at the tissue.

The last thing he remembered was standing with Cal in the undergrowth by the footpath leading to the festival grounds, that huge shadow coming at him from nowhere, a brief glimpses of a ridiculously oversized knife, then that terrible penetrative impact, which he'd felt punching into his neck, brushing the upper regions of his spinal cord with a cold grinding kiss, then withdrawing quickly to slide down his neck and across his shoulder. Then there'd just been blackness.

He'd come to his senses again lying in the back of the ambulance, a paramedic attending to him and his friends anxiously looking on. When they'd joined him at the hospital a bit later, Cal had told him what had happened, filling in the blanks in Ian's memory.

As shaken as he was following the attempt on his life, Ian was aware that the menacing sense of being watched, which had been with him ever since they'd set foot on the island, was now gone. The man who'd tried to kill him had evidently been the source of that creepy feeling of impending danger, which had now had ceased with his attacker now locked away at the police station.

It left Ian with a few questions though. He knew that the man hadn't attacked him at random. He'd *known* there was something different about Ian, and had purposefully targeted him. Why this might be, Ian had no clue, but in all probability his would-be murderer was the one who'd spoken that weird, foreign sounding word that had involuntarily sprung into his mind on the ferry. The same word he'd heard whispered in his nightmare as he'd stood in that strange little village, broken bloody bodies all around.

Ulfhednar.

On the other bed across the darkened hotel room, Clyde grunted and snorted in his sleep, turned over onto his back and babbled something about not attending the Bar Mitzvah. Then he let out a girlish high pitched giggle, said "space hopper," and started to snore lustily.

As if getting to sleep wasn't hard enough already, Ian thought ruefully.

4

Sealgair paced the concrete and steel confines of his cell.

His eyes still burned from the stinging liquid that the police had sprayed him with, and his bones and muscles ached all over from the administrations with their clubs. He paid no attention to his injuries, however.

When his senses and strength had returned, not long after he'd been confined in the cell, he'd immediately thrown himself in a fury at the steel door, desperately hammering at it with fists and bare feet. He'd kept up the frenzied assault for a full hour, attacking the metal door, kicking with all his fearsome might. At one point, he'd heard someone in the corridor beyond the door, ordering him to calm the fuck down. He ignored the command. Blind with rage, he'd continued to bludgeon at the cell door. His enraged screams and the great hollow booms of his fists and feet striking the metal bounced and reverberated around the cellblock in a deafening racket.

The policeman on the other side had soon been joined by a colleague who'd apparently come to investigate the disturbance.

"We'll need to go in there," Sealgair heard the first one say. "The big bastard's going to do himself an injury if he keeps this up."

"Fuck *that*," the newcomer stated. "If you want to go in there, Luke, be my guest. You know it took five of us just to get him into the van earlier? The guy's a fucking bear."

The first officer apparently saw the sense in this, and Sealgair heard no more from the corridor outside. He'd kept battering away at the door, but it was to no avail. He'd put several dents in the steel, but it was solidly constructed and held firm. Finally coming halfway to his senses, he conceded that he couldn't force his way out, and that continuing the assault was a futile enterprise and a waste of energy. He'd reluctantly abandoned his escape attempt, and began pacing, his mind fevered with frustration.

The Harbinger was still alive, saved by his friend at the very moment he should have perished.

He cursed himself for this failure. Incarcerated, he could do nothing as the Harbinger ran free. Just the very thought of the interloper at liberty was enough to drive Sealgair half mad, and he muttered and cursed loudly as he paced back and forth in the cell, seething and desperately trying to form a plan of action. It was difficult, however, to think rationally while the loch and the island lay unguarded. If the Harbinger were to go there while Sealgair remained caged... He could not think of that. Thoughts of failure and what would follow would only cloud his mind further, and he needed it to be clear. Although he was powerless to do anything about the situation, he still had to know the location of the thin long haired man whose very presence on the island was a dire herald of unimaginable suffering.

Forcing himself to calm, Sealgair crossed the cell to the narrow bunk against the wall. He sat down and closed his eyes, taking a long series of deep breaths. His frantic thoughts began to settle and cool, the rapid thumping of his heart slowing and steadying. When he was finally at peace and his mind and spirit were relaxed and open, he *pushed*. Feeling. Searching. Reaching out into the night beyond the walls of his cell, seeking out the signature of the Harbinger's mind.

His mind cast out its widening net, flying free in search of the now familiar presence. He didn't have to search far. With that same lurching sensation in his head, Sealgair found his quarry close by, sleeping in a hotel room less than a mile from the police station.

As frustrating as it was to have his target so close yet unreachable, Sealgair was relieved that the Harbinger was still in the local vicinity. He fought against the urge to attack the cell door again, and lay down on the thin bed bolted to the wall, calming his troubled thoughts and maintaining the mental link between himself and the sleeping man.

All he could do was watch and wait. The police would come to his cell sooner or later.

He must be ready when they did.

5

Matt Connell's head was being viciously crushed.

The terrible squeezing sensation in his skull was such that he thought that his brain matter would surely burst from his ears in chunky grey ribbons. His whole body ached and quivered, and a sickening roiling nausea greasily swirled and sloshed in his gut. He couldn't move. To move would be the death of him.

In the darkness, he heard someone else groaning in anguished misery, and recognised that this other unseen unfortunate shared his torture. They weren't going to make it, he thought in despair. He prayed for this horrific ordeal to be over. He wished for the mercy of a quick death.

"Kill me," he whimpered pitifully. "Please, God, just kill me."

"Aaaahhhhuuuugh," the other voice slurred. Matt heard the total bleak desolation in the drawn out expression of abject wretchedness.

The door to the dark room suddenly crashed open, banging loudly against the wall. The sound caused a piercing new spike of pain in Matt's already brutalised head, and he had to make a conscious effort not to scream. He heard the other one in the room hiss through their teeth, then blurt, "Sweet Jesus! Please, I'm begging you, don't do that! Just leave us alone!"

"Get the fuck up, ya lazy shower of lightweights," a woman's voice said cheerily.

"Fuck off, Scarlett," Cal groaned from his bed across the gloomy hotel room. "We're dying here."

"Awwww. Poor wee lambs," Scarlett said in mock sympathy. "Can't handle your drink, boys? You know what they say, if you can't do the crime, stick to cranberry juice, ya buftie."

"It's not the drink!" Matt protested, poking his disintegrating head out from underneath his blanket. "It's the drink *and* the concussion."

Scarlett said "Pffft," in a most uncaring way, then crossed the room to the window and mercilessly opened the blinds. Hideous bright sunlight lit up the dim, stale smelling hotel room, and Matt and Cal both yelled in dissent at the same time, letting loose foul mouthed torrents of ungentlemanly abuse in Scarlett's direction. Scarlett stood by the window, backlit by the terrible sunlight which cast a glowing halo around her freshly washed and brushed hair, fresh as a daisy and grinning down at them, heedless of their coarse insults.

Matt hated her, and her freakishly unnatural resistance to hangovers.

"Rise and shine, my lovelies," she sang merrily as she grabbed the bottom of Matt's duvet and dragged it off the bed. He tried to catch hold of the retreating blanket, mewling in protest like a distressed kitten, but Scarlett tore it from his grasp and dumped it on the floor. The room was brutally cold without the coverings, and Matt squirmed on the mattress, his head pounding and feeling like he was on the verge of violently vomiting. He wanted to cry.

"Breakfast's downstairs," Scarlett said as she ripped Cal's duvet from his weakened grasp and dumped it unceremoniously on the floor beside Matt's. "See you girls in the dining room."

She left the room then, cackling and maliciously slamming the door behind her in what Matt thought was a particularly cruel and intentional parting shot. He heard her laughing as she strode away down the corridor.

*

Feeling only very slightly better after a quick shower, Matt looked around at his companions gathered at the table in the busy dining room. His resistance to hangovers had always been feeble at best, and though he was famished, he couldn't eat the large fried breakfast that the waitress had placed in front of him, such was the precarious control he had on his troubled stomach. He'd broken his fast instead with large quantities of water, coffee and paracetamol. He ached all over, having taken several hard blows to the head, body and limbs while trying to hold down the giant lunatic who'd tried to kill Ian the previous night. Clyde, boasting a painful looking swollen black eye which he'd sustained in the struggle, was at least able to eat, and was absorbed in intently devouring a massive plate of scrambled eggs on toast. Next to him, Cal was likewise looking pretty dishevelled, wincing when he sat down after limping into the dining room. Ian, despite what had happened to him, actually looked okay all things considered, and though he was somewhat distracted and moved stiffly, he for sure didn't look like someone who'd come within millimetres of death only a matter of hours previously. Scarlett, damn her to Hell, was just fine and dandy. Infuriatingly radiant.

"So," Matt said, leaning forward in his seat and wincing as the slight movement caused a wave of hurt to roll through his aching body. "What's the plan, folks? Game's a bogey or keep calm and carry on?"

Cal was the first to speak.

"Personally, I don't mind heading back after what's happened. We can pick this up another time and do the weekend again." He looked around at his friends' faces to gauge their reactions.

"I think your right," Scarlett said, glancing quickly at Ian, who caught her look.

"Look, if you guys are worried about me," Ian said, "then don't be. I'm fine, really."

"Dude, you got *slashed* last night," Cal said.

"It's just a scratch," Ian said dismissively. "I'd be dead if it hadn't been for you. What kind of mate would I be if I thanked you by fucking up your stag do?"

Cal laughed, shaking his head. "Fuck's sake, mate, don't worry about *that*," he said. "Wouldn't hold it against you. Ian, between gashing your hand on the ferry and being chibbed last night, you must have lost about a gallon of blood."

"Aye, Ian," Clyde agreed. "It's really not a good idea."

"Look," Ian said, putting down his coffee mug. "I'm honestly okay. Please, don't worry about me. The shoulder's a bit stiff and itchy, but you heard the doctor yourselves. It's not serious. We're here, and we've got this canoeing thing booked for today, plus we've all paid in advance for the hotel, the festival and the return tickets for the ferry tomorrow. Aside from all that though, really, when's the next time we're all going to be able to do this?"

He had the right of it, Matt conceded. It had been a minor miracle to find a time slot for the weekend that had been suitable for all five of them. He personally travelled quite a bit with his work, and was frequently out of the country overseeing web development projects abroad. He spent less time than he'd have liked with his family already, and Scarlett was also married with a baby. Cal would soon be in the same boat, and knowing Ian, he'd more than likely be away again sooner rather than later, probably on one of his extended travels abroad which he often went on by himself. It'd been a lot easier to arrange time together when they'd been in their teens and twenties, and didn't have the ties that came hand in hand with careers and families. Clyde was the only one that didn't have many demands on his time, being single (most of the time) and working for himself at his little recording studio, which meant he could pick and choose his hours.

"If you're sure," Clyde said to Ian, "then I'm good for staying."

Scarlett and Matt agreed, and the four of them looked to Cal. It was, after all, *his* stag, and it was only right that he should have the final say about whether to go home or stay on the island and try and enjoy the rest of the weekend. He shrugged and held out his hands in a *what am I to do?* type gesture.

"I'm outvoted then," he said, and grinned. "Fuckin' love you guys."

6

Gordon McLeod, manager of the Calanais Visitor Centre, was in his office going through a pile of invoices and receipts when Jack Powning, his adopted son, came in and told him about the dead birds.

"Found them out by the main circle when I was doing the rounds," the young man said. "Five of them. Sandpipers. Just lying together there on the ground."

Gordon looked up and regarded Jack from under his bushy white eyebrows.

"Together?"

"Aye. Lying there in a wee pile. Was weird."

Gordon frowned. The standing stones, the main attraction of the Calanais Visitor Centre, sometimes attracted the attention of certain locals, and it wasn't the first time strange objects had been found in the vicinity of the ancient monoliths. There was a small group of Celtic Reconstructionists on the island who practiced a form of Paganism, and the CRs, as they called themselves, often left small tributes - trinkets, amulets and food offerings near or on the stones as part of their ceremonies. Never before though had they left anything that had been killed. Animal sacrifice had no place in their gentle religion, centred as it was on the worship of life and nature.

Weird indeed, Gordon thought, but a mystery for another day. With the music festival in Stornoway that weekend, a welcome influx of visitors had invaded the island, and as one of the main tourist attractions on Lewis, he expected the Calanais Visitor Centre to be busy for the next two days. The mystery of the dead birds was intriguing to the old historian nevertheless, and he resolved to ponder it and investigate further when he had more time.

"Well, nothing we can do about it right now," he said to Jack, checking his watch and rising from the desk. It was eight forty five am. "We all ready?"

Jack nodded. He'd already been round the entire site, picking up the odd bit of litter, checking everything was presentable and ready for the coming day, and had fired up the forge. The working blacksmith's shop was a popular feature at the centre, where visitors could watch Jack at work as he skilfully formed, heated, sharpened and finished raw metal, forming tools, armour and weapons using the same ancient techniques that would have been used in centuries past. As he carried out these demonstrations, moving confidently and efficiently around the workshop like he'd been born and raised there and could have done it blindfolded, he'd give light hearted, entertaining talks to the watching tourists about the methods and practices of antiquated metalworking techniques, and would allow them to handle and wear the various swords, daggers, chain mail and breastplates he made. He had a friendly, easy going manner and was able to speak about the potentially dull subject in a way that made it enjoyable to listen to. The fun factor of his metallurgy lectures was also greatly enhanced by the astonishing display of skill and dexterity involved in the knife throwing demonstrations which were the climax of his talks. The kids loved him. The dads wanted to be him.

The two men now left Gordon's office and made their way out through the main building of the centre, greeting the other employees who were turning up for work.

"Morning, Isa," Gordon greeted a cheerfully heavy set woman with graying hair as she came through the revolving doors into the reception area, resplendent in a brightly coloured floral print blouse. "Looking fabulous as usual," he complimented her.

"Och, behave yourself, Gordon," Isa Shaw said with a demure smile and a girlish blush as she passed by them on her way to the cafeteria where she was in charge of the kitchen and waiting staff. Gordon and Isa were both widows and in their sixties, and it was the centre's worst kept secret that they were an occasional item. What the younger ones called 'fuck buddies' these days, Gordon thought with amusement, enjoying the memory of Isa's energetic performance the previous night. The woman may have had a few summers behind her, he considered, but she was a bona fide tigress in the sack. He gave her rump a playful swat as she passed, and she squealed in delighted outrage.

"Oh! You *beast!*"

"You love it," Gordon replied, tipping her a sleazy wink. He turned to Jack, who was rolling his eyes at the pensioners' inappropriate behaviour as they exited the building and made their way in the direction of the blacksmith's workshop. "What did you do with them?" Gordon asked.

"The birds? They're at the forge. I had a feeling you might want to take a look at them."

"Good lad," Gordon said, clapping Jack on the shoulder. The younger man had come to know his mind well in the long years they'd been acquainted with each other. He'd first seen Jack at the centre when the boy was eight years old, in the company of a tired looking but smiling mother, who wearily followed her excitable child around the glass cased exhibits, the child goggling in amazement at the displays of ancient coins, knives, swords, arrowheads and other archaeological finds which had been discovered in the local vicinity. The kid and his mother became regular visitors to the centre, recently moved to the area and living in Callanish, the nearby village where Gordon also lived. Over time, he'd got to know the woman and her young son well on their almost daily visits to the centre. They were from the mainland originally, near Edinburgh, but had been forced to leave on account of some trouble her ex husband had been in. She didn't know where 'the prick' as Sylvia Powning would often simply call her ex, was. Neither did she care. *Dead in a ditch*, she'd said with vehement hope more than once.

When Sylvia Powning died four years later, finally succumbing after a lengthy battle with cervical cancer, Gordon had taken in the bereft twelve year old Jack, a boy with no other known family, and whom he'd already come to look upon as a favoured nephew, already employed as an unofficial helper around the visitor centre. Gordon and Mary, his late wife, had never been blessed with children of their own.

They came to the forge, the large open fronted wood and stone blacksmith's shop where Jack worked. To the left of the squat building, there was a rectangular area of empty grass about the size of a cricket pitch, at the far end of which, in front of stacks of hay bales, stood five wooden mannequins secured into the ground by thick stakes. Each dummy featured slender throwing knives embedded in their oaken foreheads and throats. Jack liked to get a little practice in each morning before work, and now walked over to the target dummies and began pulling out the blades stuck in their wooden flesh.

"I'll come by and take a look at the birds this afternoon," Gordon said as he walked on, leaving Jack with his knives and wooden men. Behind him, the *thok-thok-thok* sound of steel biting into wood echoed pleasantly across the calm morning air. Although Jack had already made the morning rounds, checking the grounds were ready for visitors, Gordon liked to visit the stones at the start of each day, wandering among the various arrangements of monoliths, endlessly fascinated by their ancientness, their inherent and enduring air of mystery. In almost forty years of working at the centre, he'd never grown tired of them.

To Gordon's right, the outer ring of the Calanais Stones reached skywards. The arrangement of Neolithic obelisks was made up of around fifty stones in total, some of which protruded almost five metres from the ground, and was laid out in a rough cross shape centred on an inner circle, within which lay a chambered tomb. The site had been excavated back in the eighties, and was estimated to be between four and a half to five thousand years old. As with other similar sites like Stonehenge, debate surrounded not only their means of construction, but the purpose of the stones. The best guess was that they had some form of astronomical significance. What was unusual about the Calanais site however, was that while working on the dig, archaeologists had discovered that around a thousand years after it had been constructed, the area had been levelled and abandoned, the reasons for which were still the matter of scholarly debate.

As Gordon walked by the massive upright chunks of roughly hewn stone, he noticed something out of place, and paused. There was something dark in the grass at the foot of the stone closest to him. Frowning, he walked over, and stood staring down in consternation at what he saw.

In a heaped feathery black pile, five large crows lay broken and dead on the ground.

7

Cal was the last to leave the police station that morning. He met the others, who'd already been formally interviewed, in a café across the road from the police station. He'd met with Sergeant Harrison and had given his version of last night's events, and when what he'd said more or less matched up to the statements Ian, Scarlett, Matt and Clyde had given, Harrison had thanked him and said he was free to go.

"What about the big guy that jumped us?" Cal had asked as he was leaving the interview room.

"He's still down in the cells," Harrison replied. Cal noticed a troubled look pass briefly across the Sergeant's features as he said this.

"Did something happen?" Cal asked.

"Made a hell of a racket last night when he came to, that's all."

Cal had a feeling that Harrison was holding something back. The big copper had for some reason looked almost scared there for a second, but deciding not to press him further, he thanked the Sergeant again and left.

In the café, Clyde, Scarlett, Ian and Matt were sat at a table with large colourful mugs of strong coffee before them. Matt was looking a bit fresher, Cal noted. He'd been in some state earlier. Never could handle hangovers well. He took a seat, nodding in thanks to Ian who pushed another of the big brightly coloured mugs towards him.

"I'll save your life too one day, dude," Ian said to him. "But for now, I can only repay you with a double cappuccino."

Cal grinned and toasted Ian with the big garish mug. "De nada," he said.

Matt, back on form it seemed, had his trusty map of Stornoway on the table in front of him and was scrutinising it closely.

"Right people," he addressed the group. "Car rental place is on Shell street down by the waterfront. 'Bout a five minute walk from here."

"Ugh," Clyde said with feeling. "Walking no good. Clyde need bed." He was obviously struggling with his hangover and concussion as well. His black eye was an absolute cracker.

"C'mon, liven yourself up, Farley," Scarlett jeered from the seat next to Clyde, poking him in the ribs mercilessly. "A few hours canoeing will sort you out."

"Uuuuuugh," Clyde replied with yet more gravitas, and lay his head on the table next to his huge coffee cup.

Cal smiled at the irony at play here. It had been Clyde's idea in the first place to hire canoes at some point of the weekend as a wee nod to the past, in tribute to how the five friends had come together originally. A high school trip to the highland outdoor centre of Ardentinny in their early teens, where their high school geography class had spent a week paddling on a few of the great many inland and sea lochs in the western highlands of Scotland. Cal had loved the idea. Clyde, on the other hand, was now in all likelihood thinking it was the worst idea he'd ever had.

The five of them finished their coffees, shrugged on their jackets and backpacks, left money for the bill, and exited the café, heading toward the seafront.

It was another fine day outside, and already the streets were busy with locals and those visitors there for the festival. As they got closer to the waterfront, Cal could smell the salt in the air and breathed deeply, filling his lungs with the briny freshness of it. The sea air was pleasantly bracing, and his head continued to clear as they made their way along the waterfront road to the car rental office. He was still a bit tender from the previous night's incident, but the cold shower, hearty breakfast, hot coffee, water and Anadin were taking the edge off his discomfort. Like he'd said to Sergeant Harrison, he'd had worse. Much worse, evidenced by the old knife wounds and the extensive patch of burn scarring that mottled most of his back.

He'd been fortunate, the police and fire brigade had told him at the time, that he'd made it out of the burning building alive. His parents and younger sister hadn't been so lucky. The other scars that patterned the flesh beneath his clothes had come as a result of all that had happened in the aftermath of the blaze that had orphaned him. The deliberate blaze.

As he'd learned to do, Cal forced the bad memories aside, refusing to dwell on them as the group walked up to the car rental place.

When they arrived, Matt was inside for only a minute before he came out of the office again accompanied by a young slick haired man in a suit who held a set of keys and a handful of documents, both of which he gave to Matt as they walked towards the minivan he'd hired.

"So where you folks off to then?" the rental guy asked with a friendly smile, trying not to stare too much at Scarlett's chest. His name badge said his name was Chris.

"Off down to Ardvourlie," Matt told him as he opened up the boot of the vehicle. "Doing a bit of canoeing." They all threw in their backpacks and jackets. The day was getting downright hot, and it was a long drive, Matt had told them, to the outdoors centre where they would hire the kayaks for the day.

"You should check out Loch Langabhat when you're down that way," Chris was saying. "It's close to the outdoor centre. Absolutely beautiful spot."

As Matt signed the rental agreement fastened to Chris'clipboard, nodding distractedly at the rental man's travel tip, the others climbed aboard the spacious vehicle, making themselves comfortable for the twenty-four mile journey. Matt climbed into the driver's seat, and gave the waving Chris a thumbs up through his window as they pulled out onto the main road that ran back along the seafront of Stornoway. They reached the outskirts of the town, and Cal could see from his place in the passenger seat the narrow road before them that wound south west down across the moors, through the forests and skirting the scores of inland lochs of the Isle of Lewis. There was practically nothing in the way of civilisation between Stornoway and the outdoor centre at Ardvourlie, just miles and miles of empty uncaring wilderness.

*

Chris McBride watched the mini van and its five passengers drive away from Stornoway Auto Hire with a slightly confused look on his face.

As busy as the car rental business had been over the past few days thanks to the number of tourists in town for the music festival, he'd given out several tips and suggestions to his customers about interesting places to visit on the island, which roads to take, local beauty spots and such. There were many such attractions on Lewis. Lews Castle, the Norse mill, the standing stones at Callanish and several stunning white sand beaches. Having been a resident of Lewis all his life, he'd been to them all over the course of his thirty-two years.

Loch Langabhat was the largest of the island's many inland waters, and he supposed that made it worth seeing to a tourist. Maybe. Strange thing was, he had no idea if it was an 'absolutely beautiful spot' as he'd assured the group that'd hired the mini van.

Maybe it had been because of the woman that'd been part of the group, he thought. A stone cold fox. With ample chestage too. He'd always been nervous around women, and whenever he'd tried to chat them up, no mater how cool he tried to be, he'd invariably find himself babbling nonsense. He reckoned that mentioning Loch Langabhat was just yet another example of his idiot mouth flapping before his brain was engaged, a clumsy attempt to make conversation with an attractive member of the opposite sex.

He'd never been to the loch after all, but for some reason he'd suddenly felt very compelled to throw in the suggestion to visit it, and the words had sort of fallen from his mouth involuntarily, before he was even aware of what he was saying.

8

The Harbinger was on the move.

All night, Sealgair's body had remained perfectly still, not so much as a muscle twitching, while his disconnected mind was an unseen presence watching over the sleeping man in the hotel room a few streets away. That morning, he'd observed the Harbinger rising from his bed, dressing and meeting with his companions in the hotel dining room before making his way to the police station. Sealgair had almost lost control at that point. Having the Harbinger in the same building was almost more than he could bear, and it had taken all his self restraint to remain focussed on watching him instead of immediately attacking the cell door again. Fighting the burgeoning sense of impending dread that he felt clamouring for attention in his mind, he'd managed to keep himself under control as the Harbinger had again left the station and rejoined the other mainlanders in a building across the street. Sealgair's calm, watchful focus had remained shakily intact as the group had then set off through town, heading along the waterfront. He prayed that their intention there was to board a ferry back to the mainland, but the group passed by the harbour area and instead entered a car rental lot. He held on to his focus even as the group began loading a large vehicle with their backpacks, but Sealgair's control finally broke when the slick haired rental man mentioned Loch Langabhat.

Sealgair's panicked mind broke the connection, and he flew at the cell door with renewed ferocity, screaming wordlessly and hammering at the thick steel.

It wasn't long before he heard voices outside ordering him to quiet down, but he didn't. Couldn't. His frantic rage reached terrible new levels, blocking out everything else. There was just the black, doom laden foreboding that filled him, flooding through his mind, body and very soul, fuelling his muscles with furious desperation, hardening his flesh and bones as he beat his fists bloody on the cell door again and again and again in savage panic.

More voices outside the door. A heated discussion. The sounds of hurried movement. A small plate sliding open in the door. Something dropping inside. A flash of light and a deafening bang. Smoke filling the cell. The door violently pushed open. Several armoured men carrying tall shields. The crackle of electricity. Clubs.

*

Sergeant Murdo Harrison stood in the corridor in the detainment block listening to the incredible bedlam coming from cell seven. It sounded like there was an enraged rabid gorilla imprisoned in there rather than just a man. Constant incoherent roars of fury and relentless pounding echoed chillingly through the tiled corridor as the suspect hammered frenziedly at the door. The incredible racket was unnerving, and he had to make every effort not to let his unease show on his face. Constables Luke Simpson and Peter McAuley stood alongside him, gaping in bewilderment at the cell door that was all that was separating them from the enraged giant inside. Their repeated orders for the prisoner to settle down had gone unheeded. If anything, he was getting worse.

"What the fuck do we do, Sarge?" McAuley asked nervously.

Harrison tried to think. McAuley and Simpson had reported to him that morning, informing him of the prisoner's violent episode the previous night when he'd first tried to batter the cell door down. He'd glossed over the episode when Cal Dempster had asked about the suspect earlier that morning after giving his official statement, saying only that he'd had made a bit of a racket when he'd regained consciousness. He hadn't mentioned the frightened expressions that had been evident in McAuley and Simpson's faces when they'd told him about it.

"Luke, go and get Inspector Scally," he said now. Luke Simpson nodded once and hurried away down the corridor, glad to be away from the deafening clamour. He returned a few minutes later with an irritated looking Inspector Martin Scally, the ranking officer on duty at the station that morning. The pinched-faced CO angrily strode towards them, holding his hands out as if to ask what all the fuss was about and why they were wasting his valuable time. Scally'd been at the station for around four years. Transferred from the mainland. Harrison had heard rumours about him dicking a collegue's wife back in Aberdeen.

"Jesus Christ, Harrison," the Inspector spat, forced to raise his voice above the furious din from the cell, which continued unabated. "What the fuck is gong on down here?"

"Disorderly prisoner, sir," Harrison replied tightly. *What the fuck do you think is going on, you silly bastard?*

"Well, take a couple of the boys and go in there and calm him down," Scally said, as if explaining a simple maths problem to a particularly stupid child.

"With all due respect, sir," Harrison began, "I'd rather not send my constables in there…"

"I don't give a dog's dick what you'd *rather*, Sergeant," Scally interrupted loudly, glaring at his subordinate. "I gave you a direct order. Subdue the suspect."

"Sir, it took five of my men to arrest this man last night. Three of them had to receive medical attention afterwards."

As Scally opened his mouth to reply, the ferocious assault on the cell door next to them abruptly reached a new level of violence, the frenzied hammering becoming more rapid, taking on a quick paced rhythmic regularity until it seemed like there was some sort of automated battering ram in there. Harrison saw Inspector Scally frown and take a few steps towards the cell door, reaching for the viewing slot. A tremendous rending crash exploded from within, even more powerful than before, and the commanding officer reeled back across the corridor.

"*Christ on a bike!*" Scally gasped as he fell on his arse. He looked up at Harrison from the floor, a more understanding expression now on his face. "How long's he been going like this?"

Harrison checked his watch. "About twenty minutes now, sir. He was at it for an hour last night, but not as bad as this."

And still it went on; an insane fusillade of rending booms, bangs and never ending roars and screams. Surely no man could keep up that level of fury for this long?

Then the cell door started to move.

As Harrison watched in utter disbelief, the steel door actually shuddered under the continuous brutal impacts from within. The wall plaster close to the upper right hinge had cracked, and with each new assault, a puff of dust escaped the growing hairline fracture.

"No," he said, shaking his head. "That's just not fucking possible..."

On his feet again, Inspector Scally now saw what was happening, and his already pale face blanched completely.

He turned to McAuley and Simpson. "You two, get as many other constables as you can find in the building. Suit up in the riot gear and bring some flash bangs. NOW!"

*

Sealgair barely felt the electricity that flashed through his flesh as the prongs of the first Taser bit into him. Nor was he fully aware of the stinging in his eyes, the ringing in his ears or the impact of the policemen's batons. A terrible black wrath, borne of sheer desperation had taken an inescapable grasp of him, and there was no pain. He was above and beyond physical sensation. Free from thought. Absent of mercy or conscience. There was only the fight. Only the task that was his sole reason for existence. The men who crowded into the cell with him, the armoured police with their tall shields who zapped and battered him meant to stop him fulfilling that task. That could not be allowed to happen.

They were in his way.

As they closed in, crowding and trying to overwhelm him with their superior numbers and the force of their combined attack, Sealgair zeroed in on a small gap in the wall of shields in front of him and pumped out a straight right hand, obliterating the protective visor of one man's helmet, sending him reeling across the cell, blood splattered across the inside of the smashed facial shield.

One down.

He grabbed a second assailant to his left, picked him up, spun on his heel and flung the man through the air, scattering his colleagues. The man's body struck the wall with brutal force. He slid to the floor and didn't move.

Two down.

There were still another four men facing him. Two of them rushed him from the front, crouched low behind their riot shields which they held close together, reforming the barrier of hardened plastic. Sealgair lurched forward to meet them, bellowing in rage. He aimed his shoulder for the point where the two shields overlapped and crashed into it with colossal power. The impact spun the men in opposing directions, splitting their combined guard. Sealgair spun round, and before the armoured men could regain their balance, he had the one to his right by the back of the neck, his monstrous hand finding a gap above the collar of the man's riot vest He swivelled his great shoulders, propelling the armoured figure across his body right to left, and flung him with brutal strength into the second guard as he was getting to his feet. The two men clattered together with sickening, bone breaking force, and dropped in limp heaps.

Four down.

Another stinging prickle in his back. Sealgair pivoted, spinning and lashing out backhanded with his left fist in an almost balletic movement that would have seemed graceful, if not for the intent of extreme violence. He didn't even see the officer on the receiving end of the vicious blow fall. He was already engaged with the sixth man, who was circling him, keeping a cautious distance with his shield raised and baton ready. More wary this one. More experienced. Sealgair moved for him, but the man nimbly dodged to the side, bringing the extendable baton down across his scalp and landing a ringing blow. A good hit. Not enough though. Not by a long way. Encouraged, the last armoured man closed in, raising the baton again. But Sealgair's clamp like hand was suddenly wrapped around the shaft of the metal club. The policeman tried to wrench his weapon free, but Sealgair's grip was as iron. He pumped a massive tree trunk leg forward, planting his bare right foot square in the armoured man's midriff, sending him flying backwards straight out the cell door to crash against the facing wall in the corridor. He came to rest lying face down on the tiles.

Sealgair, still clutching the last man's baton, stepped calmly over the motionless men strewn around the cell floor. Pausing only to pick up another of the extendable metal clubs, he left the cell block, and violently embraced his freedom.

He moved through the police station, pitiless as a hurricane, contemptuously swatting and throwing aside all who tried to block his path. There were more clubs and Tasers, more bursts of incapacitant spray, but they were feebly ineffective in the face of his wrath, and uniformed men and women flew left and right, lying in battered and bruised heaps in the giant's wake.

He eventually found a rear fire exit that opened up on to a car park filled with police vehicles. During the course of his escape, he'd had the presence of mind to take several sets of keys from unconscious officers, and he was soon behind the wheel of one of the patrol cars, his huge bloody fists tightly wringing the steering wheel as he roared away through the town, once more in pursuit of the Harbinger.

PART FOUR

A hungry wolf is bound to wage a hard battle.
The Laxdaela Saga

1

"We cannot stay here," Vandrad said.

Drostan, who had been staring silently into the peat fire of his roundhouse as if searching for answers to their situation in the flames, looked up at the Norseman's words. The chieftain had summoned Vandrad, Ulfar and Ailde the blacksmith to his hut immediately upon returning from the ruin of Eanach. The two Norsemen and the blacksmith were the only three men in Acker who had any real fighting experience, and as such, were the only war council Drostan could assemble to discuss their course of action.

"The Ulfhednar will return to their ship sooner or later," Vandrad went on, "and when they do, and find it in ashes, they will track us back here. In truth, they probably know we are here already. Their scout will no go unmissed. Acker is not safe."

"We have no time to organise defences," Drostan stated.

"No, we do not," Vandrad agreed. "That is why we must leave. All of us. Now."

"And go where?" asked Ailde. The big blacksmith had been sitting silently, looking at the ground between his feet, his dark shoulder length hair hanging in his face as he absently fingered the long handle of his smith's hammer. Ailde had been the first to join Vandrad and Ulfar as they bludgeoned and slashed at the monstrous creature as it had capered, screaming in flames around the clearing in its death throes the night before, and the heavy iron head of his hammer had been well annointed in its blood. In the aftermath, he had found the body of his fourteen year old son among the dead. Laid open from belly to shoulder. An ex soldier who had fought in the fyrd of the English king Harold at Hastings, Ailde was no stranger to battle, carnage and the death of comrades, but Laise had been his only child. His wife, Nula, had died the previous winter, and now, with Laise gone to join her, the loss of Ailde's family was a bitter, rotten thing that ate at him, more hate than sorrow.

"The nearest village from here is Neig," Vandrad answered the blacksmith. "It is large enough, they have walls, close to a hundred men, and the settlement lies atop a hill in a defensible position with a clear view of the surrounding land on all sides."

Ailde merely grunted and nodded in response.

"When we reach Neig, we must recruit more men to our cause," Vandrad continued, looking at the others. "If their ship was filled, there may be as many as forty of the Ulfhednar. We do not have enough men here to fight them." The Norseman paused then, a troubled look on his face. "There is something else to consider though," he went on. "We do not know where the beasts are now. They attacked Eanach, and one of their number then came here to Acker. Neig is the next closest village. It is possible they may already have gone there."

Drostan's jaw tightened at the thought. "I fear we have little choice," he said after a moment. "Neig itself is a three hour walk from here for a man travelling alone. To move our entire village there will take longer, and the next closest settlement is too far inland to reach before sundown. We will be fortunate to reach Neig before nightfall as it is."

Vandrad saw the truth in this. "Then we should delay no further," he said, rising. "With your leave, I will begin organising the people."

"See to it," Drostan said, also getting to his feet. The four men left the roundhouse, Ulfar accompanying Vandrad, and Ailde stalking off back towards his forge, alone. Drostan watched as the big blacksmith walked away, and felt the man's grief keenly. The chieftain and his wife had lost their own son to the sea when a storm had taken his fishing boat some years before, and he knew all too well the heart rending grief of losing a child. The blacksmith's son Laise had been a good boy.

The chieftain of Acker walked to the bronze village bell that hung on a wooden post in the charred central clearing. The dull clanging sounded out low and flat in the sombre atmosphere that hung over the settlement. A jarring, morose sound that spoke of death. Soon, a crowd of grim faced villagers had gathered, and looked at him expectantly, waiting for him to tell them what happened next. Several had lost loved ones in the night's bloody chaos, and they now looked to him to make sense of the madness and set things right. Drostan gazed sadly out among the frightened faces of his people, and prayed he was doing the right thing in asking them to further upset their simple lives and abandon their homes. He felt the burden of leadership weighing heavily upon his ageing shoulders like never before.

"We have agreed that we must take shelter from this evil elsewhere," he addressed the crowd. "The council are of a mind that the beast last night was but one of many, and that more will come here. Maybe this very night. We are too few, and cannot resist them as we stand. Acker is no longer safe. We must leave."

There were a few muted cries of confusion and protest, a low babble of worried conversation among those gathered, and several questions were thrown at him at once. Drostan raised his hands in appeal for their attention. "We make for Neig," he said, pitching his voice with a calm authority that he in no way felt. "I bid you now, my neighbours, to gather yourselves and your families, take only those possessions that are essential, and do so with all speed. We must reach the gate of Neig before nightfall."

2

Breck and Egor sat on the ground outside Drostan's roundhouse, watching as the people of Acker rushed around the settlement, urgently gathering their possessions and herding their livestock in preparation for the exile. Ceana, Drostan's wife, was inside the large hut also making ready for the journey to Neig. After she had seen the boys fed and clothed with fresh tunics and leggings, discarding their old garments which held the grim reek of burned flesh and death, the two boys had been put straight to work, assisting Ceana load up a cart with the bulk of essentials that she intended to take with them, and the wooden wagon now sat piled high with furs, grain, tools, cooking utensils and other items. Breck had been thankful for the work, which he recognised as an effort on Ceana's part to distract them as much as possible from their grief, and had thrown himself into it. Focussing on lifting and carrying, the pull and flex of his muscles, trying not to think about churned and blooded sand, torn body parts and blackened fanged skeletons. He had tried to talk with Egor and Ceana while he worked, chatting mindlessly of trivialities in a strained, desperate way, and Ceana had obliged him, but Egor had remained brooding and silent since they'd returned from the devastation of Eanach, and Breck's friend now sat staring intently at the blackened patch of ground in the village's central clearing where the monster had burned and died. Someone had disposed of the creature's remains, and all that was left was a seared area of hard packed earth. The bodies of those the beast had slain had also been removed, but there were still several large dark stains on the ground around the clearing, and the villagers who bustled around in preparation for leaving Acker averted their eyes from these bleak blemishes.

Breck had continued to try and bring Egor out of his dark mood, but had so far met with little success, receiving only monosyllabic replies and distracted grunts from his companion. He was about to try and get his friend to talk again by asking if Egor had even been to Neig before, even though they both already knew that he hadn't, but Egor suddenly began to speak of his own accord.

"You were very brave last night, Breck," he said, not taking his eyes from the scorched clearing. "Very brave."

There was something wrong with Egor's voice, Breck thought. His friend had until yesterday been a light hearted soul, always ready with some foolish joke, and would spit words with a jovial rapidity that he accompanied with much waving and gesturing with his hands. Those hands now lay limply in his lap like two pale dead fish, and the tone of his voice was jagged, brittle and somehow... empty. Lifeless. Breck opened his mouth to say that he had never been so scared in his life, but again Egor spoke before him.

"Do you think it's true what Vandrad said? That the monster was really a man in a wolfskin?"

"I don't know, Egor," Breck replied quietly. Thinking about it scared him. Stories of shape shifting beasts were before last night only that. Stories.

"I think it was," Egor said, still in that fractured, ghostly tone that was an empty imitation of his usual lively voice. "A man turned into a wolf," he added absently, nodding as if speaking to himself. He turned abruptly to Breck, who flinched back at the fevered, desperate look in his friend's eyes. "Did you see what it did? Did you, Breck? The way it killed everyone? Such a thing... There was so much blood. So *much*."

"Yes, Egor," Breck began, "I saw it..."

As if he hadn't heard, Egor continued, his voice growing louder. "Did you see it bite that one boy's head off? The one who threw the oil on it? Did you hear how he *screamed?*"

Breck noticed Vandrad, who had paused at the sound of Egor's voice as he made his way across the clearing. The Norseman was looking at them with a strange expression on his face.

"Calm yourself, Egor," Breck said, placing a hand on his friend's trembling shoulder. "It was a terrible, unholy thing. But it's over now."

"No! Don't you see, Breck?" Egor shouted, shaking off his friend's hand. "It's not over. It's *not*. They're going to come back. Lots of them, Breck. A score of them. A *thousand*. They'll kill us all and eat us, or they'll leave us alive and then *we'll* become wolves like Vandrad said, wolves that kill everything *but eat nothing*." Egor's jagged voice raised in pitch and volume as he went on, his eyes growing wilder by the second. Other villagers had taken notice and looked over at him, unnerved by his desperate babbling.

Suddenly Vandrad was there above them, roughly hauling Egor up by the back of the neck and pushing him inside Drostan and Ceana's roundhouse. Breck scrambled up from the ground and quickly followed them inside. Ceana looked up in surprise as the tall blonde warrior marched inside her home, clutching Egor by the neck. He was still raving, squirming in the big man's grasp, a frightening vacancy in his eyes. "We'll run and howl and kill eating men and women and babies..."

"Apologies for the intrusion, Ceana," Vandrad said to the chieftain's wife, then turned Egor around and backhanded him hard across the mouth. The boy spun around with the force of the blow and fell on the hard packed earthen floor, his frantic cries suddenly cut off. As he tried to rise, Vandrad stooped and seized him by the shoulders, pushing Egor back to the ground again and holding him there with their faces mere inches apart. Egor's eyes had cleared, the haze of terror gone to be replaced by a shining awareness, and the only thing coming now from his mouth was a thin stream of blood trickling from his split lip.

"Quiet yourself, and listen well to me, boy," the Norseman grated as he crouched over Egor, icy blue eyes blazing down at him. "You have seen much that you should not have. You have witnessed horrors unfit for a child's eyes, and you have lost kin. You are right when you say it is not over. It is certain that more, many more, will die before this is over, and you will see much of blood and death. This is the way of war. Make no mistake, Egor of Eanach, we *are* now at war, and your childhood has ended before its time." Egor drew a breath, his face twisting in anguish. He let go a bitter sob of purest grief. Vandrad slapped him again. "It is not the teeth and claws of the Ulfhednar that inflict the most grievous wounds," he said, "but the *fear* that they breed and spread. When we are unable to master that fear, it reduces us to babbling frightened fools, such as I now see before me. The fear infects others and spreads like a plague among our friends and allies, and the enemy has won even before a sword has been drawn. Do you understand?"

Egor stared up at him with his mouth agape, blood glistening on his chin, shocked into silence.

"*DO YOU UNDERSTAND?*" Vandrad roared into his face.

Egor flinched and nodded rapidly. "I understand," he gasped, cringing away from the intense fury on the big man's face. Vandrad hauled him to his feet once more and pushed him against the wall of the roundhouse. Holding Egor in place with his left hand, Vandrad reached down to the boy's waist and snatched the small, crudely made belt knife from its worn leather sheath. He brought it up to Egor's face and held it before his eyes.

"This blade is shit," he said. "We are not skinning rabbits here, boy." He contemptuously cast the small knife away, then drew a much larger dagger from his own belt, and pressed it into Egor's hand. "This weapon has tasted the blood of the Ulfhednar. Master your fear, Egor of Eanach. Drown it in wolf's blood, and see those you have lost avenged. Turn terror to wrath. Slay the monsters that would have you as fodder. Kill them, rend their flesh and take their heads - and do not stop until *every last one of them* is sent to the underworld."

He held Egor's eyes a moment longer, then released him, undid the belt holding the dagger's sheath from around his own waist, shoved it into Egor's arms and abruptly marched out of the roundhouse, leaving Egor, Breck and Ceana staring after him.

Breck walked over to where Egor stood by the wall, looking in wonder at the huge knife Vandrad had just presented him with. It was a simple thing, a weapon designed for hard use, not show. The length of Egor's forearm from pommel to tip, it was almost sword like in appearance when held in the boy's slender hand. The only decoration was a single runic character etched into the steel at the base of the broad blade. Double edged with a smooth, well worn antler wrought handle below the iron hilt, the blade parted the flesh on the pad of Egor's thumb when he lightly ran it along the edge. Blood immediately welled up from the small wound, and Egor gazed upon it in fascination, his eyes switching back and forth from the cut to the blade and back again, from the cut to the blade and back again.

"Terror to wrath," Breck heard him whisper, and saw a new, dangerous light begin to smoulder in his friend's eyes. The vacant, lost look that had dulled Egor's gaze since they had seen the burned bloody ruin that had been their home that morning was gone.

In its place was naked hatred.

3

Vandrad stood to the side of the trail watching as the small caravan of villagers, carts and livestock slowly passed through the west facing gate of Acker. He would have had them move faster. The settlement of Neig lay some seven miles to the west, and Vandrad estimated it would take at least three hours for them to make the journey along the floor of the narrow valley. As the sixty or so residents of the settlement filed past and set off along the trail that ran between the two villages, led by Drostan and Ceana at the front with the armed and watchful Ulfar bringing up the rear, the sun had already reached its zenith in the clear blue sky and would soon begin its descent to the western horizon. Darkness would be upon them in perhaps three and a half hours. It was going to be close.

From among the slow moving column, he saw Breck break away from the villagers and head towards him. The courage the boy had displayed the previous night had impressed him. The lad acted when most all others had frozen, and in setting the shapeshifter to flame, Breck had saved Ulfar's life and probably that of many others, including Vandrad.

"Can I walk with you, Vandrad?" Breck asked as he approached. "I need to speak with you." Vandrad appraised the boy for a second before answering.

"I intend to scout ahead of the column," he replied. "I must be in Neig ahead of the rest of us to let them know of our coming. I will be moving swiftly, and it may be dangerous."

"I can keep up," the boy answered. Vandrad considered a moment longer. Breck was carrying only a small pack upon his back and was lightly armed with a simple fishing spear given to him by Drostan. Vandrad himself was similarly unencumbered by excessive weight, and had adorned himself for stealth and speed. Dressed in a tunic, woollen leggings and cloak, he carried only a small belt pouch containing food, a compact water skin, his spear, and a bow with a quiver of arrows slung across his back. His helmet, chain mail and shield were too heavy and made too much noise for scouting, and he had left them with Sileas.

"Keep your eyes open," he said to Breck, "go quietly but with speed, and move under cover when you can. If you see anything, raise your hand to the height of your shoulder in a fist. I will be watching you. Questions?"

Breck shook his head.

"Let us be to it then," Vandrad said, and turned to the west, setting off at a fast run. He smiled to himself when the boy appeared at his side a moment later, matching his pace stride for stride.

They quickly overtook the column and were soon well out ahead of the villagers, moving swiftly along the path. At Vandrad's instruction, they separated and quickly established an overlapping pattern where one would move slightly ahead of the other, pause briefly under cover of rocks and scrub to check the way ahead, then signal for the other to move ahead of them. They continued along the valley floor in this fashion, constantly scanning around them for any sign of danger as they went. The worn trail was hemmed in on both sides by steep hills cloaked in heather, gorse, wiry grass and rocks which provided ample cover, the path running alongside a thin meandering river which occasionally broadened into small inland lochs. It was by one of these lochs that Vandrad and Breck paused to rest and take on food and water.

As they ate silently, their backs against a large boulder, Vandrad felt the boy's eyes upon him. "Where are you from, Vandrad?" Breck asked.

"My home is a settlement called Birka," Vandrad replied between mouthfuls of dried meat. "A trading centre on the island of Björkö on the Mälar sea."

"Your homeland has many strange names," Breck said. "I do not know these places."

"I do not expect that you would," he said. "Ah, such a wondrous place it is, Breck. The trade route upon which it lies brings ships from many far off lands, lands at the end of the world. The ships carry traders, exotic men such as you have never seen. Men of yellow and brown skin, who speak in a thousand tongues and dress as women in long robes. They bring with them many fantastic stories and the treasures and marvels of their land. Spices, silks, strange metals, jewels and gold. All the gold in the world flows through Birka." He sighed, remembering the bustling merchant port fondly.

"Why did you leave there?" Breck asked, his eyes wide as he imagined these strange, far off places.

"I desired to grow old and fat," the Norseman said. "My people do not usually live long, Breck. In my land, a man who reaches forty summers is considered to have lived a very long life. The Norse lands to this day are squabbled over by this king and that would be ruler. The earls of each province fight one another for land, and war is everywhere. Fair Birka, rich because it is a trading centre, is fiercely fought over, often attacked by raiders who come for its plunder."

"You were a soldier there?" Breck asked.

Vandrad nodded. "A captain of the guard. The settlement resembles a fortress more than a town, and there is an entire garrison of men employed to defend it, mostly ex soldiers, mercenaries, all experienced fighters."

"The way you and Ulfar fought last night, I have never seen the like. You have been in many battles, I think."

"I have seen my share of war," the Norseman said, looking away.

Breck seemed to pick up Vandrad's discomfort at the turn in conversation. "The men in Acker, Sionn and his followers," the boy said carefully, "they call *you* a raider. Is it true?"

Vandrad faced him again. "Few great things in this world are ever made without spears and the shedding of blood, Breck," he said. "No king has ever sat upon a throne without stepping over the bodies of those he has slain to get there. The port of Birka has changed hands many times."

"Will you teach me? To fight?" Breck asked after a moment. Vandrad regarded him seriously, gauging the boy.

"How old are you, Breck?" he asked.

"Sixteen years this autumn."

"Old enough, but it is no small thing you ask," Vandrad said. "Do not think there is glory or heroism in the ways of war. It is a dark path, Breck."

"I do not want glory," Breck stated simply, "only the skill to be able to defend myself and my people."

"Defending your people is a noble cause, but it ever requires the death of another's," Vandrad said. "Even a man who is evil in your eyes may have a loving family who see him as righteous, and who would mourn him. In the face of war, the difference between good and evil is sometimes unclear, and often does not exist at all. As it is with all legends of heroes and monsters. Often it is not easy to tell one from the other."

"But those beasts, those devils that destroyed Eanach. They have no families. No one would mourn them."

"No. They would not."

"Then teach me, if you will."

There was a grim resolution in the boy's eyes, Vandrad saw, and he knew then that Breck would fight whether he was taught the ways of the sword or not. There would be dark times ahead, and the boy's chances of surviving them would be increased, even if only very slightly, if he had some training. As was true of all the natives. It was something Vandrad intended to see to, but they first had to reach the safety of Neig's walls.

"As you wish," he said, relenting and offering his hand. Breck took it and smiled. "But first, let us continue," the tall warrior said, getting to his feet. "The day grows short and we have lingered here too long."

They set off along the trail again, naturally falling into their overlapping scouting pattern. There was perhaps an hour and a half until nightfall Vandrad reckoned, and he prayed to Odin that the people of Acker, his wife among them, were not too far behind.

4

Egor was near the head of the marching column that evening, walking alongside Sileas when they rounded a bend in the trail and the settlement of Neig hove into view, perhaps half a mile away up on their left. The walled village was perched on a plateau above a small pebbled bay on the southern side of Loch Shiphoirt, with a wide path running from the gate, down through the thick covering of heather of the slope to the stony beach below, where sat a handful of fishing skiffs and a few small thatched huts.

"Neig draws close," Drostan called out from the head of the column, turning to the villagers behind him and pointing up the hill.

There was a noticeable lightening in the mood of the column at the sight of their destination, Egor noticed, and even a few ragged cheers. The journey from Acker had been slow and difficult. Carts and wagons heavy with villagers' possessions and those too old or young to walk the path, had several times become mired in muddy patches along the trail, causing frequent delays as the travellers were forced to dig and bodily heave the wheels of the carts free from the ground beneath before they could continue. Their progress was also hindered as the livestock the villagers brought with them had been skittish, repeatedly bolting from the herd.

And all the while, the sun dropped closer to the horizon.

Throughout the journey, the caravan had carried a subdued and uneasy air about it, the people constantly casting worried glances at the shadowy scrub covered hills that loomed above on either side. They had known that the passage along the valley floor to Neig would be hazardous, the lay of the land making them especially vulnerable to attack, and Drostan, under advisement from Vandrad, had organised a mobile defence of the column. Those men carrying weapons that had been used against the wolf-demon the night before formed the outer lines of the moving caravan. Ailde the blacksmith and Ulfar, bedecked in full armour and armed with his great longsword and throwing axes, yet moving as easily and quickly as if dressed in only a light tunic, constantly patrolled up and down either side of the line, keeping the other armed men equally spaced, bolstering their courage with encouraging nods and slaps on the shoulder, ensuring they remained vigilant while all the time keeping a close and wary eye on the hills themselves. Before they had departed Acker, Egor had watched in fascination as Ulfar had taken the charred upper half of the wolf's huge skull, and nailed it to a tall stake planted in the centre of the soon to be abandoned village. An act of defiance.

As they rounded the curve in the path and Neig at last lay in sight, the sun's lower edge was only a finger's breadth from touching the western horizon. Darkness would very soon be upon them, in all likelihood before they reached the settlement gate.

"I fear we'll not make the gate before daylight fades," Egor said now to Sileas at his side, turning to face the tall woman. Sileas returned his anxious look with a calm smile. She and Egor had spoken at length during the journey. She had sought him out among the crowd as they left Acker, and they'd walked the road to Neig together, taking comfort in each other by reminiscing of happier times spent in Eanach, telling light hearted stories of those who'd been lost.

"I am not worried," she said to Egor. "Only a fool would come against us while you are so armed." She pointed to the large sheathed dagger that hung at his hip.

"Your husband is a kind man," he said, feeling the comforting weight of the big knife on his belt. "It is a gift much appreciated." The consuming terror that had been clouded his mind had lessened slightly after Vandrad had slapped it out of him and stiffened his spine with the steel of the big knife. Although he was still badly scared, Egor's mind was now clear, and he knew what he had to do, as troubling as it was.

The column of people, animals and wagons reached the bottom of the hill and started up the trail that climbed to the gates of Neig. Looking to the western sky on his right, Egor saw that the sun was now dipping below the horizon.

A shiver that had nothing to do with the cooling evening air rippled across his flesh. Looking around, he could see that the shadows cast by the caravan and the land itself had already deepened and grown long. Feeling the weight of the pack he carried more keenly as the land steepened on the uphill path, Egor made an effort to quell the nervous trembling in his bones. They would make it, he told himself, and be safe within the sturdy walls of Neig before long. It was a secure place, he thought, glancing once again at the sinking sun, now half obscured beneath the surrounding hills. The sky above blood red in the west, deepening to the purplish shade of twilight in the east. They would be safe in Neig., he told himself again. Salvation was at the top of the hill, now a mere quarter of a mile away.

The dusk was torn apart by a ragged shrieking howl that rang out across the valley, immediately followed by another, then more, the cries rising and combining to create a nerve freezing chorus of animal screams that seemed to come from everywhere at once.

Instant wails of terror rang out from those in the column, which had frozen stupidly still on the hill path at the unearthly sound. Egor, his heart hammering in his chest, skin prickling with fear, saw the armed men on the edges of the column turn outwards, frantically looking this way and that among the deepening pools of darkness that gathered in the ridges and dips of the hilly terrain.

"*Keep moving!*" Drostan roared from the head of the line. "*Do not stop! Make for the gate!*"

His command broke the paralysis that had gripped the caravan, and they rushed up the hill in panic, the armed men on the outskirts struggling to keep themselves in position as the column ascended. Ulfar remained at the rear, facing down the hill with his sword drawn as he jogged backwards, scanning left and right as he went. The terrible baying continued all around them, the sound echoing off the loch below and the surrounding hills. It was getting louder, closer. Amid the howls of the unseen demons, Egor could now discern a garbled mix of grotesque half human tones that shouted in a strange language.

There was a crash from downhill, and Egor saw that in the stampede, one of the pony drawn wagons had careened off the trail and overturned in the scrub, scattering its cargo of grain sacks, furs and equipment. The frightened animals pulling the wagon screamed in terror, thrashing in the undergrowth and fighting to free themselves of the entangling harnesses. The beasts and the wagon were left behind as the frightened villagers rushed past, streaming up the hill in a terrified rabble as the chilling screams of the monsters grew nearer.

Expecting at any moment to see some fanged nightmare spring from the growing shadows surrounding them, Egor looked uphill and saw that the gates of Neig had been thrown open for the people of Acker who rushed inside the settlement. Egor ran to join them. But then there was a shrill scream of pain from somewhere on the trail behind him, a man crying out in agony, accompanied by a deep, guttural snarling. Egor could not help but look back, and in the last of the rapidly failing daylight, he saw several large hunched shadows moving swiftly through the undergrowth below, rushing through the gorse and thick heather and converging on the trail from both sides. On the wide trail itself, through the press of running villagers that pushed past him, he glimpsed struggling figures at the rear of the column and heard the ringing clash of steel on steel.

He was suddenly grabbed from behind, and yelped in alarm, spinning round to see Drostan's fierce eyes boring into him. "Draw your weapon, Egor," the chieftain grated, before releasing him and charging down the hill, lowering his spear.

Egor could not move. He stood there on the trail, the last of the villagers surging around him as they fled for the safety of the settlement above. His very soul ached to join them, to turn his back on the fight below and run. The skirmish was intensifying. He could hear more men's voices bellowing in fear, rage and pain, the clatter and scrape of edged metal clashing together, and above it all, the terrible roars of the gathering wolves.

He closed his eyes.

Turn terror to wrath.

His hand slipped inside his tunic, and he lightly fingered the shallow wound on his chest. It was not serious, just a scratch, but it had burned steadily since he had sustained it the previous night during the attack on Acker, when the monstrous wolf had leapt among the gathered villagers in the clearing, laying about it with its terrible claws. The creature had torn the entrails from the body of the man who'd been standing next to Egor, and its gore coated claws had then raked along his chest in passing, sending him spinning to the ground. He thought he'd been killed for certain, but when he looked down, he'd found only the thinnest of tears in his tunic, barely even noticeable. The scratch beneath had begun to itch and burn soon after, and he'd intended to have the wound tended to, but then he'd heard Vandrad's tale, and learned the fate of those unfortunates whom the Ulfhednar wounded but did not kill.

He'd almost told Breck that morning. Had been trying to, but then Vandrad had taken him in hand, slapped him to his senses and given him the knife. Egor had known then that he would not say anything about his wound, and he'd resolved to see Breck and the others to safety at Neig. He would then go in search of the monsters himself, to take what little vengeance he could before he died, if he did not turn first.

Now, he opened his eyes again, and he tasted the hard iron tack of blood in his mouth as his gums bled and opened around his growing teeth.

Egor drew the great dagger from its sheath and sprinted downhill into the fray, letting loose an ear splitting scream from the very pit of his stomach, baring his long, pointed fangs to the dusk.

5

Fourteen years ago, just a foolish young man who had sailed from his island home in search of adventure, and somehow finding himself fighting for King Harold's army at Hastings, Ailde had been struck with disbelief at the sight of the advancing Norman force. By that time he'd already seen combat at Gate Fulford and Stamford Bridge, fighting against the Norse invaders, but the sight of the approaching Norman army had overwhelmed him. Thousands upon thousands of men had poured across the land like a great flood, bristling with banners, swords, axes, pikes and halberds. The hooves of the heavy cavalry's armour-clad horses had been as thunder, and then the sky above had darkened with a terrible storm of arrows which rained down among Harold's ranks, spitting and skewering men by the hundreds before the brutal hand to hand combat had commenced in a clashing, roaring, screaming wave of sound that had rolled across Senlac Hill. With Harold's army eventually defeated, Ailde, amazed to find himself alive amid the horrific carnage, had fled, vowing to himself that he would return north to his island home, and never again complain about the dull life of a blacksmith's son.

Now, fourteen years later, he found himself in battle once more, but this time facing a foe even more terrifying than the immense legions of William of Normandy.

They converged on the hill path in a shrieking wave of steel and fangs. It was hard to see in the failing light, but with a sick lurch in his gut, Ailde counted at least eight of them. A hellish mix of tall armour clad warriors still in human form, and walking nightmares. Monsters bedecked in helms and chain mail, brandishing axes, swords and spears, their faces and limbs twisted into grotesque animal forms. Ailde could scarcely believe what he was seeing as the unspeakable pack came on, leaping from the underbrush on each side of the trail and falling on the men of Acker as they tried to retreat up the hill in a half-formed defensive line.

He saw Donnan, a young man who'd been a friend of his son Laise, jabbing fearfully at one of the towering wolves with a pitchfork. The beast, black furred and barrel chested, grabbed hold of the improvised weapon with one huge clawed hand and tore it from Donnan's grasp, then lashed out with its other forepaw, opening up Donnan's neck in a wide red slash before pouncing upon him, fastening its immense jaws on the wound and bearing him to the ground. Ailde saw Mungan, his own cousin and a skilled whaler of some local renown, desperately fending off another of the bestial attackers with a harpoon. He was barely managing to keep the thing at bay, thrusting and slashing the heavy weapon at the advancing creature as he retreated up the path. His head suddenly leapt from his shoulders in a spray of blood as a statuesque yellow eyed warrior still half in human form attacked from his blind side, beheading Mungan with a swipe of a longsword. His twitching body, still grasping the shaft of the harpoon, was leapt upon by two more of the enormous wolfish warriors, and torn to pieces.

There were many others. Friends and neighbours he saw being bitten, stabbed, clawed and slashed by blade and fang as the Ackerians retreated backwards up the path, their blood staining the ground as they went, and their numbers rapidly dwindling.

Ulfar, Ailde saw, was faring better. His longsword was a constantly moving blur in the fading light, and baptised in the blood of the beast from the previous night, its blade was death to the encroaching enemy, who seemed to sense he wielded a weapon that could do them harm. The big Norseman jabbed and slashed and hacked, keeping the huge creatures pursuing them at bay, battling ferociously, leaping about the trail with a speed and deadly grace rare for a man his size. Even as Ailde looked, Ulfar's sword found a gap in the armour of one partially transformed beast, and the blade split the snarling creature's neck open. It shrieked in a hideous half-human gurgle and fell to the path, blood fountaining from the yawning wound.

Ailde's smith's hammer was heavy in his hands as he frantically looked left and right, trying to make sense of the brutal melee raging around him. He locked eyes with one of the attackers, a tall, blond haired axe wielding brute wearing scraps of armour. As he advanced on Ailde, the man's face bulged and stretched beneath his helm, the mouth and nose twisting and elongating into a fang filled snout. The wild eyes within the helm burned a sick ochre, and the hands that gripped the haft of its long axe broadened, curved talons pushing out from the fingertips in rivulets of blood. The thing roared and came at him, swinging the long handled axe in a low sweep aimed at Ailde's knees. The smith quickly lowered his hammer, managing to block the attack, the axe and hammer heads meeting with a grinding clash. Instinctively, muscle memory taking over, Ailde stepped back and brought his hammer upwards in a massive uppercut, his great shoulders, powerful from a life spent at the anvil, bulging under his tunic. The hammer head crunched into the underside of the monster's jutting muzzle, sending a spray of broken fangs into the air. The creature screamed and staggered to the side, and Ailde, bellowing in mindless fury, brought the hammer down and around in a second mighty swing. The unforgiving weight of the hammer crashed into the side of the thing's helm, and the monster spun and dropped. Even before he could set his feet again, Ailde was immediately battered to the ground, smashed aside by a broad shield. The enemy, this one a black haired rangy man still mostly in human form, advanced on him, raising a spear over his shoulder, eyes glowing with hunger and grinning a mouthful of sharp teeth. The warrior drew back the spear for the killing blow... and was bundled out of sight as some screaming thing armed with a dagger leapt upon him, stabbing and hacking.

*

Drostan woke up lying on the trail, his head pulsing with agony. He remembered a shield, with a snarling wolf's head sigil painted on it, smashing into his face. Then nothing.

Now, as his senses slowly returned, he could hear all around the screams of the dying, the clash of weapons and the constant roars and howls of the beasts that decimated his people, who continued to fall like straw before the scythe.

Pushing himself up on his elbows, he looked dazedly around him. Pious Sionn was a short distance downhill on Drostan's right. He went down beneath a pouncing wolf-demon, dragged screaming into the darkness at the side of the path. Drostan saw Conn, who had questioned the wisdom of burning the longboat in Eanach, pitched backwards, an axe planted deep in his chest. Close by on the path below him, he saw with confusion a huge spear wielding wolf embroiled in a vicious fight with what seemed to be one of its own brood, though the thing that snarled, bit and stabbed at the creature was smaller, no bigger than a boy, and dressed in a simple tunic. It was only when the smaller of the two figures raised its head that Drostan recognised the boy, Egor. The lad's face was barely human, twisted and gaunt. His sunken eyes glowed like hot coals, and long sharpened fangs protruded from his distended jaws. The boy rose from the ground, his deformed face a dripping red mask of his enemy's blood, and their eyes met for a moment. Then Egor, a lad who Drostan had only that morning taken into his care, turned away, leaping at another of the creatures, frenziedly stabbing with the great knife which he clutched in one clawed hand.

Pushing himself to his feet, Drostan tried to rally his few remaining men. *"To me! Make for the gate!"* he yelled desperately. Their defensive retreat had stalled in the ferocious intensity of the skirmish, and the men of Acker were now scattered along the trail, falling on all sides under the relentless attack of the roaring creatures. A score of armed men had left Acker that afternoon, and in the last few minutes, most of them had been annihilated. The few that remained responded to Drostan's command, and began converging on the chieftain, harried all the way by the pursuing demons.

Drostan then heard from behind him a strong, clear voice barking a command, and the scuffling of many running feet. The chieftain turned and there above him was Vandrad. The Norseman was accompanied by a rank of bowmen, who stood along the top of the wall to either side of Neig's gate.

"*Loose!*" Vandrad cried.

At the Norseman's order, a hail of flaming arrows streaked guttering through the dark night.

"*The gate!*" Drostan bellowed as fire filled the air. "*Make for the gate!*"

The sudden appearance of the flaming arrows had caused a precious moment of distraction among the attacking horde, and at Drostan's order, the surviving men of Acker turned and fled up the trail, bolts of fire flashing over their heads, and ran inside the walled settlement, barring the gate behind them.

Not a single one of the fiery projectiles planted itself in the body of a foe, but each one found its mark, landing amid the oil drenched heather and gorse on either side of the narrow path. With a great roaring *whoosh*, the underbrush that coated the hill suddenly erupted in flame, engulfing several of the bestial marauders and causing instant panic among the rest.

"*Again! Bring them down!*" Vandrad roared, and a second hail of arrows zipped downhill, this time aimed at the wolves who staggered around screaming, their bristling hides ablaze. Above the thunderous rolling wave of hot crackling sound as the air and land were in moments consumed by the flames, the hideous half-human shrieks of the dying Ulfhednar could be heard with a terrible clarity.

Drostan and the handful of other survivors stood upon the high wall alongside Vandrad and the archers of Neig, safe from the reach of the flames, and watching dispassionately as the monsters were engulfed in the firestorm below.

6

When the screams of the dying wolves finally ceased, the fire continued, and burned through the night. By the time the sun rose once more, limpid and wan through the haze of smoke, the wild vegetation that had covered the hill had been completely consumed in the flames, and only a heavy rain that came with the dawn stopped the fire from spreading further afield. Neig itself had been saved from the flames due to the wide mud filled trench that Vandrad had had dug around the walls as a fire break.

The blaze extinguished, a party of men emerged from the gates of Neig in the iron grey morning light, and began picking through the smoking wet ashes, removing burnt corpses and salvaging what weapons and anything else useful they could recover from the charred, body littered hill. It was grim and sickening work. The salvage party uncovered the remains of ten of the shapeshifters that morning. There was no celebration or sense of victory in finding the monstrous charred skeletons of their enemies though, as among them, there was almost twice as many which were all too human. Twenty three armed men had had set out from Acker, and their doomed struggle had held the wolves back just long enough for the rest of the villagers to make it safely through the gates of Neig.

Only five of the twenty three had lived. Drostan, Ulfar, Ailde, Gabhran and Uallas.

They found the Ulfhednar's weapons. Unlike the few iron and steel weapons wielded by the Ackerians, which had been distorted and warped in the heat of the fire, making them useful only as salvage metal, the swords, axes and spears of the enemy had remained undamaged by the fire. Fine pieces of steel they were, huge double edged long swords, axes and great heavy spear heads intricately inscribed and twice the size of a man's hand.

The high quality weapons could have armed another twenty men, had they not been so accursed.

Any man who so much as touched the wolves' weapons was instantly beset with terrible cramps and experienced sickening visions of slaughter that flashed in their minds. Vandrad had every last piece of the unclean weaponry tied securely in heavy burlap sacks and dropped in the deepest point of Loch Shiphoirt, never again to be held in human hands.

Soaked, filthy, reeking of smoke, burned hair and flesh, the men left the seared killing fields some time later, and gathered in Neig's large meeting house where Odhran, the chieftain of the settlement, wished to address them.

7

When Vandrad, the tall Norseman from Acker, and the young lad with the haunted eyes accompanying him appeared at his gates late the previous afternoon, Odhran, chieftain of Neig, had already been dealing with his own problems.

All morning, the settlement had been subdued, the gloomy quiet broken by the wretched wailing of a bereaved mother. The woman's son, a shepherd boy who had been watching over his flock in a nearby pasture the previous night, had failed to return to the village that morning. When the boy's father had gone out in search of him, he'd returned not long after in terrible bewildered anguish, white faced, red eyed and babbling. It had taken some time to get the story from the father, but eventually he told of how he'd found his meadow strewn with the mangled bloody remains of his flock. He'd also found the body of his son. Butchered and gnawed. The only trace of whatever had wrought the unspeakable carnage had been a set of huge paw prints.

When Vandrad had arrived at his hut, accompanied by the young lad as well as Ospak and Osvald, twin brothers also of the Norse people who had settled in Neig, the blonde haired warrior had recounted what had befallen his own village. Odhran, a swarthy man in his middle years with iron grey hair, kind eyes and broad shoulders, had listened without interrupting, but at first had been sceptical of Vandrad's outlandish tale of monstrous shapeshifting wolves.

Then the Norseman had shown him the massive jawbones of the creature he claimed had decimated Acker.

Seeing the huge fanged mandibles, which still stank of smoke and burnt hair, a deep squirming coldness had roiled in Odhran's gut. No creature that he knew of was equipped with jaws and teeth of such unnatural size, not the wolves, or even the great brown bears found on the mainland. Ospak and Osvald actually recoiled in superstitious fear upon seeing the jawbones, nervously touching the hammer shaped pendants they wore around their necks and muttering prayers to their gods. They backed up Vandrad's tale about the mythical Sons of Fenrir, recounting almost exactly as Vandrad had the same story regarding Harald Fairhair's renegade berserkers. There was no doubt, they said. These were the jaws and teeth of a shapeshifter, and it was obvious that such an abomination had also been responsible for the death of the shepherd boy.

After that, Odhran decreed that Neig be made ready to receive the refugees from Acker. He was a friend to Drostan, and relations and trade between the two settlements were good. Neig was large enough to accommodate their neighbours, and he ordered that room be made wherever possible in his own people's dwellings for the Ackerians until further huts could be constructed to house the new arrivals. Furthermore, he organised a defensive force from among the men of his settlement and placed them at Vandrad's disposal. The Norseman thanked him, then immediately ordered a wide, shallow trench excavated around the settlement walls. He then had the men soak the gorse and heather covering the hill outside in oil, and had a ready supply of fire arrows prepared.

In truth, despite Vandrad's tale and the testament of Ospak and Osvald, Odhran had still not completely believed the idea of monstrous wolf-sprits that walked on two legs and fed upon the living, but it was good for the frightened people under his leadership to see him taking decisive action, even if he had his doubts about the nature of the threat.

Those doubts had been brutally shattered when he had seen the monstrous beings with his own eyes, bursting from the shadowy undergrowth outside Neig as the sun set, falling upon and slaughtering the retreating Ackerians.

Now, in the large stone and wood barn that served as Neig's meeting hall, Odhran regarded the bedraggled men who had come in from searching through the ash field outside. He had intended to try and cheer the men with rousing words, praising the heroic deeds of those who had fallen, but seeing the vacant, dazed expressions of Drostan and the others in the room, he decided that they were as yet too close to the tragedy, and that his words would be better spoken at another time. Instead, he chose to simply welcome them and offer what small comfort he could.

"I know you are all weary and heartsick," he began gently. "Neig shares your sorrow, and bids you welcome at our hearths. Beds, food and drink have been made available for you all, and I would see you rested and given time to recover before we speak further."

Drostan, the lines of his haggard face etched deeply on his cheeks, his eyes haunted, rose slowly and regarded Odhran. The chieftain of Acker, a man Odhran had known and respected for many years, was a fearful sight to behold. Clad in a stinking coat of wet ash and dried blood, ghastly faced and moving stiffly, yet still grimly clutching his spear, Drostan had the appearance of a walking corpse. Odhran knew he had not slept after last night's battle, but had instead elected to personally inform the wives and children of the men who had fallen of their deaths. He had then sought out Odhran and thanked him for taking in his people before going to the walkway behind the wall. He had stood there watching the burning hill below, and had not moved until the sun rose and the fire died down under the morning downpour several hours later. Even then, he had not rested, and had led the salvage party in searching among the bodies and ashes.

"I thank you again, Odhran," the chieftain of Acker said quietly, his eyes downcast, "for your kindness and the help you have provided us in these dark times. Your offer of shelter is much appreciated." He paused then and looked up, meeting Odhran's eyes before he spoke again. "But I fear we have slain only a few of the demons. Their ship, which we found on the beach of Eanach and burned, was of a size capable of berthing many more of the creatures. I fear that we have much more to do, and I would speak of ending this. I would speak of hunting."

PART FIVE

1

The weather had turned suddenly during the drive down through the island from Stornoway.

With the island's main population centre diminishing in the rear window of the minivan, the morning had been bright and fine, and the rugged moors, lochs and hills of Lewis had rolled easily by as they drove south under a deep azure sky. By the time they'd reached the outdoors centre at Ardvourlie, the clear blue above had clouded over and darkened to a stormy slate grey, and the warming sun had vanished behind a vast gloomy curtain of grim looking clouds. The temperature had dropped, a strong wind had picked up, and even as Ian and the others stepped out of the minivan, they'd seen that Loch Shiphoirt, a long stretch of saltwater which doglegged inland from the sea, was a rough choppy expanse of white capped waves. The churning surface of the water would make canoeing a hazardous ordeal rather than the relaxed pleasure it was meant to be, and the group stood by the lochside, cold wind biting at them as the owner of Ardvourlie Watersports confirmed what they already suspected. Terry Scullion was a tall rangy man of around forty, with the healthy weather-bitten appearance of one who made their living in the outdoors.

"Sorry, mate, but I can't hire the gear to you when the weather's like this," Terry was saying to Matt with an apologetic shake of the head and shrug of the shoulders. "Of course, you'll get your deposit back. I'm as annoyed as you guys are, truth be told, 'cause I've got a whole bunch of bookings marked in for today. With the crowds coming in for the festival this was supposed to be the busiest day of the year for me." He shook his head and shrugged again, obviously as pissed off at the changeable Scottish weather as Matt and the others were.

"Can't you take us somewhere else instead?" Scarlett asked.

"Sorry, love. My operating permit's only for Loch Shiphoirt here, and besides, I need to be here for when the other bookings show up to give them the bad news."

"Fuck a duck," Clyde spat, kicking at the stony ground in annoyance. He'd crashed out again on the drive down and his hangover had lessened considerably. He'd woken up actually looking forward to a few hours paddling about on the water.

Ian, who'd been standing slightly behind the others and gazing thoughtfully at the choppy loch stepped forward. "Can I speak to you for a second, mate?" he said to Terry. He looked back over his shoulder and winked conspiratorially at the others as they stepped away.

When they were out of earshot, Ian turned to the other man. "Listen, I know this is as much a pisser for you as it is for us. We're here for my mate's stag and this was supposed to be a good day, know what I mean?"

"Absolutely," Terry said, "and like I said to your pals, I wish there was something I could do, but this is my business. It's an insurance thing, and if anything were to happen to you folks out there - and with this weather it probably would - this place is done. I can't risk it."

"Understood," Ian said agreeably. "If you don't mind me asking, how much money are you losing today because of this weather?"

Terry considered for a moment. "Close to two grand," he said, wincing to himself as he realised just how costly the inclement conditions were to his livelihood.

"Jesus," Ian said, nodding in sympathy. "That's pish. Maybe we can help each other out. You take credit and debit cards here?"

"Aye, of course," Terry said, "but it's not about the money. I couldn't let you take the boats out for any amount. It's just too rough out there."

"Wouldn't ask you to, mate," Ian replied with a smile. "Let's go in your office."

Five minutes later, they re-emerged from the one storey building that served as the premises of Ardvourlie Watersports. Both men smiling broadly.

Ian walked over to Cal. "Early wedding present, mate," he said, presenting him with a thin folder.

Cal frowned, and opened the light document holder. Inside was a hastily drawn up bill of sale for five canoes, complete with all necessary clothing and equipment including life jackets, spraydecks and paddles, and a three spar centre post trailer capable of holding up to eight boats. Ian had modestly blanked out the amount he'd paid Terry Scullion for the gear, which had been enough to cover the cost of the equipment and enable the owner of the centre to replace it. Cal gaped in disbelief as he realised what Ian had just given him.

"Dude, are you fuckin serious? You *bought* the canoes?"

"And the trailer," Ian said, shrugging his shoulders. "We can take them anywhere we want now and find some calmer water. Wouldn't want the weekend getting fucked up."

Cal regarded his friend in amazement for a moment. "Mate, this is too much. That must have cost you a fortune."

Ian shrugged again. "What else am I going to do with all those royalties?"

Cal looked at him for another moment, then took him in a powerful bear hug, laughing.

Terry removed the large canvas tarpaulin from the heavy kayak trailer that sat at the side of the office, and with Ian and the others' help, loaded it up with five canoes and stowed the other assorted gear, then securely attached the trailer to the back of the hired minivan.

"Pleasure doing business with you," Terry said, shaking Ian firmly by the hand. "Where you thinking of going with your new toys?"

Ian thought for a second. "Matt, what was the name of the place that car hire guy mentioned?"

Matt thought for a second. "Loch Langa... something."

"Loch Langabhat?" Terry asked.

"That's the one," Matt confirmed

"You're practically there," said Terry. "Just head straight down that way," he said, pointing across the road behind the outdoors centre. Ian could see the beginning of another, smaller road that wound away to the west through the moors towards distant hills on the horizon. The road was narrow, but looked wide enough to accommodate the van and trailer. "Loch Langabhat's just on the other side of those hills," Terry said. "The road'll take you through a wee valley that runs between them. The drive should take you about fifteen minutes or so. The road's a bit rough, but drivable."

"Thanks again, Terry," Ian said, shaking his hand again as the rest of the group eagerly clambered into the van, their good mood restored. Matt started up the engine.

"Thank *you*," Terry replied as Ian joined them. "Very much indeed."

2

The moors and lochs of Lewis flew past the speeding police car's windows in a blur as Sealgair roared down the winding country road, his massive gnarled hands wringing the steering wheel of the stolen vehicle as if he meant to violently throttle it.

His bare right foot kept the accelerator pressed to the floor, letting up only slightly on bends, which he screamed around, heedless of any oncoming traffic or the risk of losing control of the vehicle. His senses, still in a supernaturally heightened state, detected every slight deviation in the rural road's surface and any other potential hazards with unerring accuracy. He drove with a separated part of his consciousness flying high above the speeding vehicle, seeing the road and any oncoming traffic ahead. He pushed the car onwards, the engine screaming in protest as he went flying along the twisting south bound road at suicidal speed. Grit sprayed in wide stony fans behind the car as he drifted round the bends in long perfectly controlled skids, decorating the road with streaks of smoking tyre rubber in his wake.

The Harbinger could not escape again.

He could still feel the presence of the gaunt long haired man, still some distance away, but drawing ever closer as the police vehicle sped down the road. The ethereal signature of his quarry was like a splinter in Sealgair's mind, prodding and twisting in his brain. He ground his teeth together, every muscle in his body bunched and rigid. The car blazed round a tight bend onto a long straight section of road. Sealgair shifted the gears, coaxing yet more acceleration from the roaring engine as the speedometer reached sixty, seventy, eighty, ninety miles per hour and beyond.

The part of his awareness that was locked to the presence of the Harbinger told him that the other man and his companions were at that moment unmoving, in a location close to water, and he discerned a strong salty wind in the air. Near the coast then, mercifully not in the sheltered valley region of the loch. As long as they remained in place, Sealgair would soon be upon them.

But then the perceived briny tang of coastal wind lessened, and with cold dread Sealgair sensed the Harbinger on the move again. He focussed all of his concentration on the quarry, the watchful part of his mind that monitored the road ahead losing focus as he brought his entire psyche to bear on the ineffable spiritual beacon that marked the outlanders' position.

There.

Moving west.

Moving inland.

Not three miles from Langabhat.

Roaring in desperation, Sealgair pounded the wheel of the rocketing car, trying to coax every last ounce of speed from the already maxed out engine.

He could not fail. He *must* not fail.

The straight section of road was running out, a tight turn to the right rapidly approaching, looming large through the windshield. Sealgair kept his foot down, his maddened mind intensely focussed elsewhere.

He saw the Harbinger in a large van towing a trailer loaded with canoes. With every sense tuned to the horrifying vision of the man approaching the loch with the apparent intention of setting out on its waters, the image was so horribly vivid that Sealgair was blind to all else, driving practically sightless, only peripherally aware of the diminishing road ahead.

The police car was travelling at almost a hundred miles per hour, and was less than a hundred metres from rapidly approaching the bend in the road when the sheep wandered out of an adjacent field and stepped in front of it.

Sealgair was violently brought back to himself when there was a tremendous crunching impact and the windshield abruptly turned a chunky liquid red. His mind snapped back to the here and now, and he fought desperately for control, but the car was now an unstoppable two ton metal beast and the steering wheel took on a life of its own, spinning wildly through his hands. With a jarring thud, the hurtling vehicle mounted a low incline on the outside of the right hand turn and burst through a barbed wire fence to go soaring into the air as if shot from a cannon.

The world spun as the airborne car performed an almost long, almost graceful triple twist, the merciless and irresistible G-forces throwing Sealgair's great bulk around inside its shell. The vehicle's flight seemed to last for hours, then gravity overcame momentum, and with a tremendous crash, the car met the earth once more, the right hand wing of the vehicle gouging into the ground. The car executed yet more mechanical acrobatics and flipped end over end, twisting and turning in the air and bouncing along the field in a grinding, banging cartwheel of shattering glass and flying steel debris. It finally came to an inelegant, crunching halt, lying on its roof.

The battered, dented wreck lay there in the field, smoking and ticking as the alarmed cows who'd been grazing in the paddock cautiously approached the strange object, regarding it with bovine amazement. After a few seconds, there was a shriek of tortured metal, and one of the doors, warped in its frame, was forced open from within the crumpled metal shell. A bloodied screaming monster emerged from the twisted wreckage, long hair and beard matted and stained red, staggering with one arm dangling at an unnatural angle. The curious cows scattered at the appearance of this frightening, noisy creature, mooing in alarm.

Sealgair unsteadily got his feet beneath him, then fell back, leaning his battered body against the trashed vehicle and trying to regain his equilibrium. Breathing was very painful. A grinding flare of agony flashed through his ribs with each breath. His left shoulder was a similar bright ball of fiery pain, and something felt separated and disjointed in there. A sheet of blood coated his face from the deep gash across his forehead, and his broken nose jutted far left of centre. His right wrist and both ankles also throbbed intensely. It seemed his entire body was awash with waves of pain.

But the hateful beacon of the Harbinger's doom laden presence was still flaring in his head like a maddening unscratchable itch.

Gritting his teeth and putting the nuisance distraction of his injuries to one side in his mind, Sealgair pushed himself away from the destroyed police car, and began sprinting south.

3

The bumpy narrow trail that wound west through the deep valley terminated at a small sandy bay on the eastern shore of Loch Langabhat. Cal, Matt, Scarlett, Clyde and Ian emerged from the minivan and stood looking out across the gunmetal grey loch. Enclosed on all sides by the surrounding hills, the waters of the loch were sheltered from the high winds that had buffeted and churned the coastal inlet of Loch Shiphoirt, and the surface of Langabhat was glassy smooth. There was a curious stillness in the air, the harsh practically barren landscape deathly silent, with not so much as the faintest gust of wind to stir the scraggly heather and tall wiry grass that clung tenaciously to life on the rocky terrain. The dark waters of the loch stretched out left and right from where the group stood, before twisting out of sight on either side where it bent around jutting peninsulas. The size of the loch was impressive, and Matt took his trusty map of the island from an inside pocket of his weatherproof jacket, unfolding the glossy piece of paper and closely studying it.

"Looks like it's about seven miles long in total, and we're roughly in the middle just now," he said. He pointed out their position, showing the map to the others who crowded around.

"There's a bunch of wee islands there towards the northern end," Ian noted, pointing at the map. "Might be cool to head up in that direction and stop on one for lunch."

"Cool n' the gang," Cal said, nodding.

They unloaded the five canoes from the trailer, got into the waterproof clothing that Ian had bought from Terry Scullion along with the other gear, loaded the sealed storage compartments on the small boats with backpacks containing spare clothes and provisions for lunch, and were soon pushing off from the small bay onto the mirror flat water, quickly finding their centres of gravity as the shallow canoes wobbled beneath them, before beginning to glide smoothly through the water with a few propelling strokes of their paddles.

"*Yaaaaaassss!*" yelled Scarlett, obviously enjoying the silky forward motion as the canoes cut northwards along the surface of the loch, leaving gentle wakes in their languid passing.

"Fuckin' canoein', man," agreed Cal, smiling broadly. "That's what I'm talking about."

Their voices and laughter rang out across the water, hanging long in the still, fresh air. It was a fine sound, Cal thought to himself with a deep satisfaction. A strong, simple feeling of rightness filled him, and he sighed in contentment, enjoying the pleasant feeling of his arm and shoulder muscles flexing as he paddled. This was exactly what he'd wanted.

"*Eskimo roll!*" Clyde suddenly shouted from his left, before purposefully capsizing himself and thrashing with his paddle once he'd gone under in an attempt to propel himself back to the surface. When the upside down canoe wobbled slightly but refused to roll upright, the other four laughed heartily at their friend's feeble attempt at the manoeuvre. When Clyde broke the surface again after a few seconds, treading water, spluttering and grimly holding onto the underside of the canoe like it was a life raft, the others mercilessly splashed him with their paddles, raining down barbed but good natured abuse and questioning his sexuality. After several valiant but failed attempts to get back inside the canoe, during which he endured further harsh heckling from his friends, Clyde finally managed to seat himself in the shallow body. He resolved to leave Eskimo rolls to the Eskimos for the remainder of the trip, and stick to straight forward paddling. Slow paddling.

"Jesus," he gasped breathlessly. "That was a lot easier when I was fifteen."

"So was your mum," said Matt, grinning. Clyde pretended to take the insult to his sainted mother in his stride, responding only with a sarcastic chuckle and a riposte involving a lewd comment concerning Matt's sister. A few minutes later, he casually paddled over to the blindside of Matt's canoe and capsized him with a sudden push.

"Vengeance is mine!" Clyde declared proudly as Matt went under with a startled squawk.

Cal laughed at the antics of his mates, not noticing as Scarlett innocently paddled to the side of his vessel. Next thing he knew, the world tilted sideways. He had time to think *sneaky bitch*, and then he was suddenly upside down underwater, engulfed in the shocking cold of the loch. He heard Scarlett crowing and gloating on the surface above, then heard a scream and a splash as *her* canoe was overturned, probably by Ian who'd been just behind her. When he freed himself and swam to the surface again, he saw Ian and Clyde's canoes were now side by side in the water, bumping into each other as the two men grappled and attempted to sink each other while they laughed and rained down colourful insults.

What a great day, Cal thought, treading water and grinning.

4

Gordon McLeod should also have been a happy man that day.

By lunchtime, the Calanais Visitor Centre was enjoying what was undoubtedly the busiest day of the year so far, with a steady stream of paying visitors arriving at the centre ever since he'd opened up at nine am that morning. Standing now against a wall in the cafeteria as he thoughtfully slurped at a mug of tea, Gordon could see that every table in the modest restaurant was occupied with groups of patrons, and there was a further queue of waiting customers at the self service counter. There was a lively murmuring buzz of conversation in the air, the clink of cutlery on plates and the voices of the kitchen staff busily calling out food orders. The cafeteria workers were rushed off their feet, and Gordon should have been overjoyed with the day's thriving business. Such prosperity was rare at the often deserted tourist attraction, and the profits taken in for the day would mean he could have a brief respite from worrying about the place closing down due to lack of business.

All morning though, ever since finding those dead crows at the foot of the stones, he'd been bothered by a nagging unease that had grown as the morning had progressed. It had been a funny sort of day so far, and not in a knee slapping ha-ha sort of way.

Just five minutes after he'd opened the doors to the centre, Isa had come out of the cafeteria to inform him that one of her staff had been involved in an accident in the kitchen and was being taken to the hospital in Stornoway. Jill, one of the commis chefs, had been careless when prepping salad for the day it seemed, and had cut herself rather badly, almost severing a finger while chopping heads of lettuce. Gordon had winced in sympathy and asked Isa to see if she could get any of the other staff who weren't working that day to come in and cover Jill's shift. She'd nodded and gone into the office, re-emerging a few minutes later saying she'd managed to talk one of the kitchen porters into coming in. As she walked back to the cafeteria she mentioned that there'd been a lot of static on the line while she'd been on the phone, and maybe Gordon should get it looked at. The girl working at the reception, Claire, had also mentioned the bad connection to him not long after, and he'd promised to get it seen to during his lunch break.

Then there's been the whole thing with the little ones.

He'd been standing by the main group of monoliths a little later, speaking with an elderly American couple about the history of the stones when the screaming had begun. Gordon looked over at the sudden outbreak of piercing shrieks, and had seen a young family standing within the ring of stones. They had a baby with them, a little blonde haired boy of maybe a year old, and the kid was having the mother of all tantrums. The wean was in his father's arms, the anxious looking dad struggling to keep hold of the thrashing, kicking child. Scrunched up red face awash with tears and screaming at the top of his little voice, the baby sobbed raggedly and yelled, unleashing a barrage of small punches at his defenceless father's head.

"*Ow!* Stop it, Gary! Bad baby!" the father scolded uselessly, turning his face away. The kid then landed a solid right hook on his dad's nose that made Gordon wince. *Cracking shot*, he thought.

"*Jesus fuck!*" the man exclaimed more in surprise than anger, tears springing from his eyes and holding the howling, unruly tyke safely at arms length as blood ran from his left nostril. The young woman with them, presumably the hysterical kid's mother, stepped in and took the child from her injured husband. The kid never let up though, completely ignoring its mother's gentle soothing words and attempted hug, continuing to kick and wriggle violently as he screamed in a high warbling wail that set Gordon's fillings ringing. The mortified looking mother walked quickly out of the ring of stones, still holding her little angel at a safe distance. The bloodied father followed her, still wearing an expression of disbelief and holding a red stained tissue to his face.

"There's one for *Super Nanny*," Gordon joked quietly as they walked away, turning back to the American tourists who chuckled.

"Poor thing," the elderly woman said in a broad New York accent, favouring the departing family with a sympathetic look. Gordon wasn't sure if she was referring to the kid or the bloody-nosed father.

As busy as the day had become, there were several other families visiting the centre, with a fair amount of small children running about the grounds, happily chattering, yelling and laughing.

Except when in the vicinity of the Calanais Stones.

As Gordon wandered around the grounds of the centre, greeting and chatting with the tourists, giving out information and nuggets of historical lore, he'd noticed more temper tantrums erupting from some of the smaller ankle biters. A set of infant twins had simultaneously erupted into hysterical screeching when their mother pushed their double pram along the gravel path beside the main group of monoliths, when two seconds before they'd both been cooing quietly, looking about in wide-eyed wonder at the fascinating world around them. Half an hour after that, he'd seen an older child, maybe two years old, having a similar reaction when passing by the stones, for no reason suddenly thrashing about frantically in his pushchair and wailing in sudden, apparently unprovoked misery. When the concerned father quickly took the kid from the pushchair, the toddler had clung tightly to the confused dad as if terrified, looking fearfully over his shoulder at the standing stones. Gordon watched as the kid slowly raised one chubby arm, and pointed with a small trembling finger in the direction of the great stones. Among the tears and the wet, hitching sobs, Gordon thought he heard the weeping child mumble something. Something that sounded like 'monsters', and a cold finger seemed to gently stroke the nape of his neck.

Then a seagull had nearly hit him.

He'd been standing there, still feeling those icy digits on his upper vertebrae and looking at the weeping child, when there'd been a shrill screech from above, a sudden buffeting of air, and something big and white flashed screaming by his head, missing him by inches. He'd let out an involuntary yelp of alarm, and had very nearly fallen flat on his arse, but had managed to stay on his feet, just. He heard a few other people letting out little wordless exclamations of fright, and turned just in time to see the gull, a big one with a wingspan close to two metres, soar directly into one of the stones. Gordon had come terribly close to bursting out laughing at the absurd noise the gull made when it hit. Its piercing screech cut off suddenly with a horrifically comical off key *squawk/splat*, that for some reason made him think of punching a clown on the nose. He'd only just managed to get a hand over his mouth to stop himself letting loose a loud bray of amusement, which would have been wildly inappropriate at that moment.

Its spectacular kamikaze dive bomb at an abrupt end, the gull seemed to hang there on the face of the four metre tall block of unyielding granite for a second, it's wide wings spread out as if it were giving a dying embrace to the ancient monument, before sliding down and landing in a broken tangle of soft red stained feathers. A few small white feathers stuck to the bloody splatter mark, which glistened in the sun and dripped slowly down the stone, marking the passage of gull's final undignified landing at the foot of the monolith.

For a second, there was absolute silence. The milling crowd of tourists who'd witnessed the gull's demise had frozen still, shocked into wordless immobility by the suicidal seagull's exit from the land of the living. Then the moment of stupefied hush abruptly ended a moment later, as there were more screaming white streaks filling the air. There was a rapid succession of those hilariously horrible *squawk/crunch* noises as another four gulls came soaring from the heavens and ploughed beak-first into the same stone, before falling pitifully to the ground where they joined the first dead and broken bird.

The second unbelieving silence that followed the bizarre incident was rudely broken as someone behind Gordon loudly enquired, "What the purple *fuck?*"

Standing now in the cafeteria, mug of steaming tea in hand and brooding over the morning's bizarre events, he decided to make a call to Aaron Latharn. His friend was a keen ornithologist as well as local historian and folklorist, and Gordon hoped he could provide a rational explanation for the odd spate of mass avian suicide.

For some reason though, he didn't think this would be the case.

Three separate incidents. Each time five birds.

He thought of the screaming babies, and in particular, that one little terrified boy, pointing at the stones over his father's shoulder.

Monsters.

Shaking off a sudden chill, Gordon left the cafeteria, heading for his office. He paused as he passed through the glass walled reception foyer. Outside, a gusting wind had sprung up, and the bright day was rapidly becoming grey and overcast as a vast bank of dark clouds rolled eastwards, low above the Atlantic, heading in the island's direction.

He made his way to his office, sat down behind his cluttered desk, picked up the phone and dialled Aaron's number. There was indeed a fair amount of crackling on the line, making the sound of the ringing phone on the other end gritty and distorted. The next call he made, he thought, would be to BT to have an engineer fix the faulty connection.

His friend picked up after three rings. Aaron's voice was fuzzy and echoing due to the bad connection.

"Hello?"

"Aaron. Gordon here."

"Gordon, you old whoremaster. How's that prostate of yours?"

"I'm sixty-five years old, Aaron. How do you think?"

"Hmmmm. Wise words received with empathy. The onset of old age is a trying bugger, eh?"

"Och, don't talk shite, Aaron, you're not even fifty yet. Can you hear me okay by the way? We've got a bad connection here."

"You're coming through loud and clear on this end."

"Must just be a fault here then. Listen, Aaron, I wanted to get your expert opinion on something."

"Aye? What's the story?"

"It's kind of strange, but it seems that the local bird population around here's suffering from mass depression."

"Eh?"

"Jack found five dead sandpipers this morning, heaped in a wee pile at the foot of one of the stones. I found five crows myself later on, right at the same spot, and five gulls just came fleeing out the sky and flew right into the exact same stone just ten minutes ago."

"Wait a minute, Gordon. You're telling me the birds are killing themselves on the stones? The same stone?"

"That's what it looks like. You ever hear of this kind of thing before? I've seen birds fly into windows and patio doors before, but this... I thought maybe some kind of sickness or disease. Someone's smeared something on the stone that's attracting them? I don't know."

Aaron was silent for a moment. "I heard about a flock of red winged blackbirds that fell out of the sky in Arkansas last year. Thousands of them, all found with broken bones, but the experts think the most likely explanation was that they were caught in a high altitude hail storm. That kind of thing's actually quite common. You're saying there were five of them each time and they actually flew into the stone on purpose?"

"Aye, five each time, and about them doing it on purpose, the gulls certainly did. I saw it with my own eyes. Like I said, when Jack and I found the sandpipers and crows earlier, they were already dead, but because they were lying at the foot of the stone, I can only assume they did the same as the gulls. Damndest thing."

Again, Aaron hesitated before speaking. "Gordon," he said seriously, and was that a note of nervousness in his voice? It was hard to tell through the distortion and static. "Has anything else strange happened this morning? Any... accidents or... anything?"

Gordon frowned. "As it happens, aye. One of the commis chefs in the kitchen had to go to the hospital this morning. Gave herself a bad cut chopping up some lettuce. And there's been a lot of kids throwing tantrums around here today, but that's just weans for you, eh?"

"The wee ones," Aaron said, "were they near the stones when they were having these tantrums? Were they scared of the stones?"

Gordon felt a peculiar tightening of his throat at his friend's words. Again, he thought of that toddler, pointing at the Calanais monoliths.

Monsters.

Those frigid fingers returned, scuttling along the length of his spine like icy spiders.

"Aye. That's what it looked like."

"And you're having problems with the phones?"

"Aye."

Another moment of silence, then Aaron Latharn spoke again, very slowly and deliberately. "Gordon, listen to me very carefully and don't ask questions. You wanted my expert advice?"

"Aye...?"

"Close up for the day. Right now. Go outside and tell the tourists that you're very sorry, but there's been a gas leak or something. And send your staff home."

"What? Aaron, what are you on about?"

"What'd I just say about asking questions? I'm fucking serious. You need to get everyone away from those stones. Now."

Gordon had known Aaron Latharn for over thirty years. In that time, he'd never heard his friend sound the way he did now. Something was very, very wrong. The cold fingers on his neck slid round and gripped his throat.

"Aaron, I don't understand. You want me to evacuate the centre?"

The hiss and crackle of static on the line was getting worse. Aaron was speaking to him, the urgency in his voice unmistakable, but Gordon only heard snatches of what he was saying.

"…have to listen… …erous… some… ing… way…"

"Aaron? Aaron, can you hear me? I can't make you out."

The distortion on the line increased, became louder, and Gordon was forced to take the receiver away from his ear. The hissing crackling white noise was now underpinned with a series of violent *pops* and a low ululating whine like the sound of an old radio searching for a signal in empty airwaves. It increased in pitch, scaling and spiralling upwards until it sounded almost… canine.

Gordon actually shuddered as he realised that the strange electronic howling was almost a perfect imitation of a baying wolf.

"Aaron? Are you there? I can't hear you." The cold hands on his throat were now running all over Gordon's body as a very real fear gripped him. Then his friend's voice broke through the crackling, hissing, popping wall of static and ghostly wolfish howling. Aaron was shouting loudly down the phone, and he sounded badly frightened.

"I said you have to listen, Gordon. It's dangerous. Something's coming through and you have to get away."

Outside the centre, someone screamed.

5

He was coughing up blood now.

The agony in his battered body was a constant, spiteful thing. As the miles fell away under his relentlessly pounding bare feet, the pain of his injuries became more insistent, more demanding of his attention. A living, clawing presence that tore at him.

Sealgair continued to ignore it, and ran on, spitting red froth as he went.

Hurdling a barb wired fence in a single huge bound and landing smoothly on the uneven ground of the field beyond without breaking stride, Sealgair was aware that the Harbinger and his companions were now on the waters of Loch Langabhat, and were making towards the group of islands at the northern end. A desperate panic began to rise in his chest, but he forced it down. There was no time for such thoughts. The hills that surrounded Loch Langabhat were now in sight, just on the other side of the large field which he now ran across.

He scattered a startled herd of sheep who bleated in terror as he blew through them, bowling over one unfortunate ewe that was too slow to get out of his path. He leapt the fence on the far side, powerful and agile as a deer, but faltered on landing, his bare foot coming down on a large rock hidden in the tall grass. The boulder tilted sideways under his great weight, his weight came down off balance, and with a hot, crunching wrench, his already damaged ankle shattered.

Sealgair screamed and went sprawling along the wet muddy ground, his foot bent at a hideous outward angle and a sick explosion of pure white hot hurt tearing through his lower left leg. Instantly pushing himself up again, he tried to run on, but regardless of how much he tried to thrust the agony aside in his mind, it would be denied no longer. The limits of his endurance for pain finally reached, he crashed helplessly to the ground again, the broken ankle unable to support his weight. He felt the jagged ends of his broken ribs stab into his insides as he hit the ground, bringing a fresh gout of blood bursting from his lips.

Lying on his back amongst the reeds at the foot of the steep hill, Sealgair screamed and bellowed wordlessly in frustration. Even injuries such as these would heal in few hours time, but his body must be at rest. And there was no time. No rest.

Even as he lay there, broken and bloodied, he could feel the Harbinger drawing ever closer to the island. The sense of impending disaster filled Sealgair like a rising black tide, rushing and roaring in his ears. He was so close. His bothy and the weapons within were a mere two miles from where he lay, just over the crest of the large hill that rose up before him.

Sealgair tried to rise again. And fell again.

The Harbinger was less than a mile from the island. Sealgair could feel the languid forward motion as the intruder propelled his canoe towards the small patch of rocky ground that broke the surface of the dark waters.

Gritting his blood stained teeth and summoning every last ounce of his will, Sealgair began to crawl up the hill, hauling himself upward, using the pain to goad him on like a cruel spur.

6

There were several islands on the loch, and they could have stopped on any one of them.

As it was however, Matt, Cal, Scarlett, Clyde and Ian paddled right on past them as they made their way unhurriedly towards the northern end of Loch Langabhat. The going was in fact so pleasurable that it seemed a sin to stop, and so they carried on, bypassing the many little islets that rose out of the surface.

The guy at the car rental place had told them it was a beautiful place, and in a strange way, it was, Ian thought. The surrounding hills were not dramatically sweeping snow capped mountains bedecked with lush forests of many dazzling colours, and the water was not a deep aquamarine of the sort that would inspire an artist to render its likeness in oils or watercolours. Rather, the undulating featureless hills that surrounded the loch were rocky, barren and dull, with only that sparse, uniform coating of pale scraggly grass, brownish heather and dried out gorse bushes for decoration, and the water itself was a sullen dark grey. Nevertheless, there was an appealing starkness to the place, a haunting, desolate quality that made it intensely atmospheric and strangely attractive. They saw no wildlife on the slopes of the surrounding valley, nor in the water itself. No deer or rabbits moved on the hills, no birds took wing above, and not a single fish was to be seen momentarily breaking the surface to snatch a low flying insect. The absolute stillness of the loch, and the ashen sky above lent a brooding feel to the day, a strange, melancholy atmosphere of desertion that made it possible to believe they were the only people left alive on Earth.

"Weird place," Clyde remarked, looking around as he paddled alongside Ian. "Kinda nice though."

Ian nodded slightly in agreement. "It's bizarre, eh? There's just something about it..." He let his sentence trail off. Since they'd arrived at the loch, he'd been more relaxed than he'd felt in months. In truth, it was the first time he'd felt truly at peace since the accident. In some indefinable way, coming here, to this place, had inspired a beguiling feeling of coming *home* somehow. Of belonging.

An artistic soul by nature, Ian had felt emotions stirring in him that had long been absent as he'd piloted the canoe along the surface of the loch. Before they'd set out on the water, acting on a hunch, he'd gone into his rucksack and had taken out a pen and the battered notebook he always kept on him wherever he went in case inspiration for a piece of music should suddenly strike. He'd put it safely in the waterproof inside pocket of his jacket, and his intuition had proved very worthwhile, as an idea for a song had started to bloom in his mind almost as soon as they were on the water.

Paddling along, he'd found himself quietly whistling a strange melody. A good one. Full of catchy little hooks and cool lilting intervals. Near fully formed ideas for drum patterns, guitar riffs, bass lines and chord progressions had come to him, seemingly from nowhere, and he'd been amazed and overjoyed at the wealth of melodic and rhythmic concepts that just kept on coming, cropping up in his head like flowers blooming after a long hard winter. It was as if a dam had been breached in his imagination, letting loose a torrent of musical ideas that had been stifled by his depression and unbalanced mind. Now, his head alive with a delightful jostling buzz of imagined music, he stopped paddling, took out the small notebook and pen and began putting the tide of ideas down on paper, making them real and tangible. The last time he'd written anything down in that notebook had been over a year ago while on tour. Just before Reading. Ever since the incident that had ended the lives of his bandmates, song writing, the thing Ian loved above all else in life, had become an alien concept to him, the imaginative, artistic part of his mind barren and dry as a desert. Now though, the creative juices, the *mojo* after which he'd named the band, was once more flowing, and flowing well.

He quickly sketched out a series of musical staves, populating the five horizontal lines with an array of rising and falling crotchets, whole notes and semi quavers that meandered elegantly across the bars. He added more staves below to indicate harmony lines, and heard them in his head as he scrawled them onto the paper, the different melodic lines wrapping around, caressing and embellishing each other in perfect harmonious chemistry. He added a series of guitar chord progressions, hearing them as if he actually held a Strat in his hands. For the first time in a long, long while, he felt that delicious *rush*, the tickle in his gut, the prickle of his skin, the almost audible *click* in his brain and the increase in his heart rate that always came when he hit upon a really good idea for a piece of music.

He looked up from the notebook and saw that he'd fallen behind the others as he floated there, totally absorbed and hunched over the notebook as he poured the music in his mind onto the page. Adding a few last ideas for song titles, he put the notebook and pen back in the sealed pocket of his jacket and took up the plastic double bladed oar again, powering swiftly through the water and catching up to the others, feeling more alive than he had in God knew how long.

"What you smiling about?" Clyde asked as he drew alongside.

Ian looked over and grinned. "Nothing, mate. Just thinking this is a good day. A *damn* good day."

"That it is," Clyde concurred, sighing in contentment. "Starting to get a bit peckish, right enough. How 'bout you bums?" he called to the others. "Time for lunch?"

"Aye, I could eat," Scarlett replied looking over. Her long hair was plastered to her scalp and hung in wet tresses around her flushed, pretty face.

"Good call. Wood carvin' over here," Matt added. The others looked at him quizzically. "Starving," he explained.

"Dude, the acknowledged rhyming slang for starvin' is Hank Marvin," Cal said. "You can't just make shit up and expect us to know what you're on about."

"Thinking outside the box, dude," Matt said, with a self satisfied nod. "Breaking away from convention and exploring new linguistic grounds."

"Or just talking shite," Scarlett suggested, splashing him with her paddle.

"You's want to stop there?" Ian asked them, pointing ahead and slightly to the right towards a small island that lay just offshore up ahead. It was a thoroughly unremarkable, flat outcropping of boulder strewn land that rose only a foot above water level, as lifeless and dull as the rest of the surrounding hills, with a tiny shingled cove where they could beach the canoes.

"Looks good," Cal said.

The paddled over and dragged the canoes up the small beach, ditched their paddles, removed their waterproof jackets, and took the packs containing their prepared sandwiches from the canoes' watertight storage compartments. Matt surprised them by also producing a couple of six packs of lager from his canoe, and was rewarded with a hearty cheer from the others.

"You, my friend, are a prince among best men," Cal complimented him as he took an offered beer from Matt. The others agreed, and toasted their friend's forward thinking. They reclined there on the little beach, chatting and laughing as they attacked their lunch and washed it down with tinned Tennant's.

They were discussing their plans for that evening when Ian, who'd been standing looking around the flat jut of land, noticed the hawthorn.

A small, low lying sprawl of thorny green leafed branches lay in a shallow dip between a collection of large boulders near the centre of the islet. The colour of the vegetation was what drew Ian's eye initially, the bright, lustrous green leaves standing out from the dull grey of the surrounding rocks and faded yellow of the threadbare grass that grew in rough patches here and there. It was the first bright natural colour he'd seen in hours, and intrigued, he wandered over for a closer look. As he approached, he could now see that there was something on the ground beneath the hawthorn's thorny twisting limbs.

The stone cairn was roughly rectangular, thin, about seven inches long by five wide, and coloured a dark grey that set it apart from the paler surrounding rocks. It lay face up on the ground beneath the hawthorn branches, and had a deliberately fashioned look to it that gave it an appearance almost akin to a headstone, albeit a very small and clumsily rendered one. Looking at the thing, Ian felt something. An odd shifting sensation in his stomach. There was something about that little piece of stone that drew his attention, something more than the dark colour and purposefully manufactured look of it. In some remotely ineffable way, it seemed to draw him. To *call* him.

Bending closer, his heart for some reason beating a little harder, he could see now that there was some sort of near faded marking etched into the surface of the slate. Then he saw it, and for a long moment, he was struck breathless. The world seemed to spin and his vision swam.

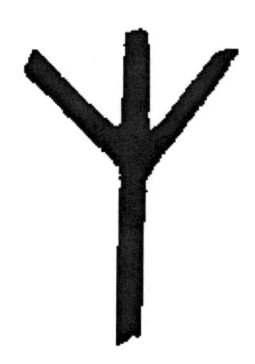

He knew that symbol, and he knew it well. He had, after all, designed it himself, and had it tattooed on his left shoulder.

Four years ago, after Ragged Mojo had finished recording their first demo and they'd been discussing designs for the CD cover, Ian had suggested a tribute to Led Zeppelin, a band that was a major influence on Ragged Mojo. His idea was that each band member design a stylised monogram incorporating their initials, kind of like the four symbols thing Zep had used on their legendary fourth album. Ryan and Tambo had loved the idea.

The etched marking on the piece of slate under the hawthorn bush was an exact replica of the monogram Ian Walker had drawn out for himself.

His heart pounding, Ian reached out slowly and touched the cairn. At the instant the pad of his middle finger came into contact with the cold surface of the slate, a current of electricity seemed to jolt through his hand. He jerked it back, gasping in surprise, and fell on his backside, sending small stones beneath him skittering and rattling across the rocky ground.

The others looked round at the noise.

"What you up to?" Clyde asked. "Did you just fall on your arse?"

Ian looked round at his friends. He found he couldn't speak.

"Ian? You okay?" Scarlett asked, concern in her voice as she got to her feet and came towards him.

Ian looked back at the little flat stone under the hawthorn shrub, his eyes goggling in disbelief.

"Dude, what's up?" Matt was saying behind him.

Ian unsteadily pushed himself to his feet. "You're not going to believe this," he said shakily, stepping towards the hawthorn bush again.

Matt, Cal, Clyde and Scarlett joined him and looked down at the bright green shrub.

"That's kinda weird," remarked Cal. "It's just a bush though, mate."

"Underneath it," Ian said, pointing.

The others crouched down and saw the flat grey marker.

"Woah. What *is* that?" Clyde said, reaching for the stone.

"Wait, don't touch it," Ian said urgently, but too late. Clyde picked up the flattened piece of rock and stood, seemingly untouched by the strange jolt that had flashed through Ian's hand.

"Cool," said Clyde, examining it. "Check out the wee symbol." He paused, frowning at the marking in puzzlement. "Dude, where do I know that from?" he asked, looking at Ian.

"My tattoo," Ian replied, a slight tremor in his voice. "The band's first demo. It's my monogram."

"Holy shit, so it is," exclaimed Cal, leaning in for a closer look at the strange piece of slate in Clyde's hand.

"Christ on a space hopper," Scarlett muttered, and the others turned towards her.

She was kneeling on the ground, looking under the hawthorn bush at the space where the weird marker had been. The exposed earth there was dark and moist looking, and a large object the yellowish white colour of old bones was partially revealed, half buried beneath the soil.

"You've got to be shitting me," murmured Cal, bending down beside Scarlett, brushing the dirt aside with his hands and lifting the object out of the hole.

It was a skull. Not a human skull, but what looked like that of some large predatory animal. The wedge shaped cranium was huge; easily a foot across and about eighteen inches long, the front end stretching to an elongated snout. And the teeth. Holy Jesus, the *teeth*. Each one was a full six inches long, tapered to a wicked point and serrated along the curving underside like a steak knife. Something had been carved across the huge skull's brow, etched into the bone, a faintly visible scrawling of strange runic symbols, similar in style to the one on the slate.

"Dude, what the *fuck?*" Ian said, gaping in amazement.

At that moment, there was a soft whirring noise in the air. It lasted only a brief second before someone said *"Ack!"*

Ian turned and saw Clyde looking at him in pie-eyed amazement. He was about to ask him what was wrong when he noticed with confusion that something seemed to be protruding from under his friend's jaw. Before he could properly discern the nature of the strange object, Clyde sank to his knees and then pitched forward, landing face first on the ground at Ian's feet, the long shaft of an arrow buried deep in the back of his neck.

PART SIX

"This is indeed one of the true tragedies of lycanthropy, that the subject of such evil pacts and nefarious deeds is ignorant of his place in the plot that besieges this humble hamlet."

<u>The Trial of John Goode</u>, Gabriel Salmon

1

The sword smashed into the side of Breck's head. The blow spun him and he fell to the muddy ground in a heap, his own blade falling from his fingers.

"You're dead," Vandrad said, looking down at the dazed youth and pressing the point of the wooden practice weapon against Breck's throat. "Never lower your shield when you thrust. Keep your guard up at all times." He stooped, offering Breck a hand. He took it and pulled himself to his feet for what felt like the thousandth time that morning.

Breck shook his head, trying to dispel the waves of dizziness that pulsed nauseously through his skull. His entire body ached from Vandrad's instruction. His arms, legs, body and head boasting an impressive covering of fresh and fading abrasions and bruises. The steel helm he wore was heavy and stifling upon his head, limiting his vision, and the weighted wooden sword and shield pulled down on his tired arms.

"Again," ordered Vandrad.

Breck wearily raised his sword and shield again, setting his feet as he'd been instructed and crouching slightly, keeping his centre of gravity low. He lunged forward, this time remembering to keep the shield strapped on his left arm raised as the wooden sword in his right hand thrust out towards Vandrad's upper torso. The Norseman easily parried the thrust, then spun on his heel, whirling away to the left in the blink of an eye. His peripheral vision hindered by the cheek guards of his helm, Breck lost sight of his instructor. How was it possible that the man could move so quickly? A ringing impact crashed across the back of Breck's helm, and he stumbled forward a few steps, almost going to ground again, but just managing to keep his feet. He turned and instinctively raised his shield again, just in time to block Vandrad's thrust.

"Better," Vandrad said, nodding slightly as he circled his student.

Breck grinned. Emboldened by this small success, he feinted to the right, thinking to catch Vandrad out with a false attack, then raising his shield high to protect his head, he brought his sword across from the left in a low backhanded swipe aimed at his teacher's knees. Vandrad casually stepped over the attack, and Breck felt the point of the tall man's sword somehow roughly poking him under his exposed left armpit.

"You're dead," Vandrad informed him. "A fair attempt, but do not raise your shield too high. A skilled opponent will direct his blow *beneath* your guard, and the heart is exposed through the side of the chest and under the arm. Again."

And so it went all that morning, as it had every morning since they had arrived at Neig more than a month previously.

Breck had thrown himself into his weapons training with grim commitment, finding that the pain of the many injuries he sustained in practice and the ache of his strained and pulled muscles helped distract him from the deeper ache that tore at him. The loss of his village, his family and finally Egor, his good friend, was a wound far more grievous than any he sustained on the training field, and one that would take years to heal. Initially, he had tried using his sorrow and anger when training with Vandrad, imagining he was swinging the practice weapon at one of the hated Ulfhednar, but the Norseman had recognised the clumsy fury with which Breck attacked, and had immediately beaten the folly out of him on the first day.

"Only a fool attacks in anger, boy," he had growled down at Breck, standing over him, staring with those grim icy eyes. Breck had looked back up at him, seething, blood sheeting down his lower face from his nose, broken on the flat of Vandrad's wooden sword. "Your mind must be clear when you fight," the Norseman said, "not clouded by anger, hate or thoughts of vengeance. Focus on the *fight*. Bend your mind to your blade and your enemy's blade, or join your family and your friend in the afterlife."

By the end of that first day's training, Breck had learned his lesson, falling painfully into his cot that evening covered head to toe in stinging welts, throbbing abrasions, dried blood and tender bruises. From then on, he pushed the sadness and hate aside during his lessons, focussing intently on Vandrad's instructions and giving his full concentration to his tutor's spoken commands and the movements of the practice swords. As long as he was thinking of his lessons, he was not thinking of what had been taken from him, and so he trained, submitting to Vandrad's teachings. When each long practice session came to an end however, and his mind was not occupied with thrusting, parrying, ducking, dodging, lunging, ripostes and keeping his guard up at all times, he found that the black thoughts and crushing sorrow came creeping back to him, and so he would continue to train alone.

As part of his instruction, Vandrad had also had a bow made for him, explaining that a warrior should be adept with as many different forms of weaponry as possible, and so each day when the lessons with the sword were over, Breck spent long hours drawing and loosing arrow after arrow at practice targets. He found that the intense concentration and stillness of mind required for archery further helped to block out the memories of Eanach afire and the screams of his people being slaughtered. He drew and released, drew and released, until the first two fingers of his right hand were rubbed raw from the flax bowstring and his shoulders, back and arms ached and trembled from the strain of drawing the bow.

There had been no further attacks by the Ulfhednar after the terrible carnage on the night the people of Acker had arrived at the hilltop settlement. The combined force of the men of Acker and Neig had spent the time in preparation for taking the fight to their enemy, and Breck was not the only new student of warfare that suffered and bled under Vandrad's instruction. Assisted by the giant Ulfar, Ailde the blacksmith and the Norse twins, Ospak and Osvald, Vandrad had spent most of his time since they arrived training the men. He had also seen to the improvements of the settlement's defences, ordering weaknesses in the walls repaired and reinforced and organising a constant watch pattern. When he was not engaged in training Breck and the other men or seeing to the defences, Vandrad spent long hours in counsel with the chieftains Drostan and Odhran, planning for the hunt. Several trackers and scouts had been sent out in well armed groups of twos and threes in search of some sign as to where the beasts might be. Not all of them returned, and the ones that did reported that they could find no trace of the shapeshifters.

Ducking under a high cut from Vandrad's sword only to find his feet somehow swept from beneath him, Breck crashed to the ground on his back again, the breath exploding out of him.

"An experienced enemy will vary his attacks," Vandrad lectured, standing over him and extending his hand again, "and he will combine and disguise them. An easily dodged attack to the head is often a ruse to distract you from a cut that would sever your legs."

Breck nodded, reached up and took his teacher's hand, hauling himself up yet again and once more taking position. Vandrad's instruction was nothing if not informative, and the Norseman had a knack for painfully illustrating his lessons with practical examples.

As Breck prepared himself for another painfully enlightening blow from his teacher's sword, perhaps to the groin this time, a thin red haired boy about his own age came running up. Vandrad turned toward him, and Breck was grateful for the chance to rest and catch his breath. Removing his helm, he recognised the other boy as Fionn, the chieftain's son.

"My father wishes to speak with you urgently, my lord," the lad shyly informed Vandrad. Since that first night when the hilltop had burned and consumed the Sons of Fenrir, the children of Neig, and not a few of the men, had come to look upon Vandrad with some degree of wonder, regarding him as a heroic slayer of monsters and a warrior of obvious legendary quality. Ulfar likewise was held in the same almost worshipful esteem, tales of his deadly prowess during the battle spreading among the hilltop populace.

"Is there news from the trackers?" Vandrad asked, turning to the boy, who nodded.

"Yes, my lord," Fionn replied nervously. "Of a sort."

2

"Abhainn is gone," Odhran said, looking up grimly as Vandrad entered the roundhouse.

"Gone?" Abhainn was a small settlement a day's walk from Neig.

Odhran was sat by the peat fire aside Searc, one of the two trackers Vandrad had sent out in the last few days. Searc looked exhausted, travel stained and badly shaken, flinching and looking up in alarm when the tall Norseman entered the room.

Three days before, a crofter had come in from the hills to the northwest seeking sanctuary, babbling about hearing strange unearthly howling in the night and of finding his flock of cattle slaughtered. Vandrad had sent Searc and his brother Neas to investigate the incident.

"Burned, my lord," said Searc, nervously meeting his eyes. "And worse." His hands were visibly trembling.

"Tell me," Vandrad said, taking a seat opposite the tracker.

Searc paused a moment to collect his thoughts, then slowly began speaking.

"Neas, my brother and I set out from here three days past, my lord. We headed into the hills, taking direction from the crofter who'd reported his herd killed..."

Vandrad and Odhran sat silently and let Searc speak without interrupting. As the tracker told his tale, it seemed a slow chill stole into the warm roundhouse.

It took most of the first day to find the pasture the crofter spoke of, Searc said, and he and his brother arrived on the scene as the sun was setting. The crofter had already disposed of the remains of his dead animals, and all that remained when Searc and Neas came upon the pasture were several large patches of discoloured grass where blood had been spilled, a few scraps of hide and small splinters of bone.

With the daylight fading, they took shelter in a nearby cave the crofter had told them of, where he often slept when keeping watch over his animals. They found the cave undisturbed, and after making sure there was no danger, they set in for the night, Searc's brother Neas taking the first watch.

"It was not my brother, but the howling that woke me some time later," Searc said, looking into the peat fire and shaking his head slightly. "Coming from the east, in the direction of Abhainn. Such a terrible sound, my lord, it stole the heart of us. We could smell smoke on the air, but I am ashamed to say we were too afraid to venture out."

The howling didn't last for long, Searc told them, but after it faded, he and his brother spent the rest of the night awake and fearful, only daring to leave the cave when the sun rose again.

"In the morning," Searc continued, "we set out in the direction of Abhainn." He paused here, eyes downcast, as if reluctant to go on. "May God spare me from ever seeing such a sight again, my lord," Searc muttered. "The settlement was destroyed. Everything burned to the ground, with not so much as a pig pen left standing. All that remained were piles of stones and ashes, and what the demons left behind."

They discovered the severed heads of every villager, every man woman and child, even the livestock, mounted on stakes in what had been the centre of Abhainn. Of the victims' bodies, there was not a trace. Save from huge clawed footprints, neither was there any trace of the monsters that had committed the atrocity.

"We decided to make back for Neig to report what we'd found," Sear went on, "and arrived at the crofter's cave again later that day. We knew we would not make Neig before nightfall, so we chose to stay there that night."

Searc took the first watch, he told them. Although he was badly frightened by what they'd found during the day and half expected to eventually hear the dreadful cries of the wolves closing in, the night was still, and his watch passed without incident. He woke his brother to relieve him after a spell, and settled down to sleep.

"When I woke this morning, my lord, Neas, my brother... he was..." Searc, still staring into the fire with wide horrified eyes, stumbled over his words, his hands now shaking more noticeably than before.

"What of your brother?" Vandrad asked quietly.

The tracker looked up sharply from the flames, meeting the Norseman's gaze with a despairing intensity in his eyes. "They left him as they had the people of Abhainn, my lord. His head mounted on a stake at the cave entrance, facing towards me. Looking at me." The tracker held Vandrad's eyes for a moment longer, then broke down in bitter tears. Vandrad and Odhran sat silently, letting the man grieve for his dead brother. After a while, Searc raised his haunted tear streaked face again. "Why, my lord? Why would they take my brother yet leave me unharmed? Why did they not kill me as well?"

"Fear," Vandrad said simply, laying a hand on Searc's shoulder. "They left you alive so that you would spread terror amongst us with your tale, my friend." A troubling thought occurred to Vandrad then. "When you woke," he said, "were you at all marked?"

"Marked, my lord?" Searc asked, looking up.

"Were you injured in any way? Scratched? Bitten?"

"No, my lord. Why?"

Vandrad saw no lie in the man's eyes, but he had to be beyond doubt. "I must ask you to remove your clothing," he said.

"My lord?"

"I am sorry, Searc, but I must check your flesh for any injury."

The tracker looked to his chieftain doubtfully.

"Do as he says," Odhran said with a nod.

The bereaved tracker hesitated, but seeing that Vandrad and his chieftain were resolute, he slowly undressed and stood naked before them, shifting uncomfortably from foot to foot as Vandrad inspected the man's body closely.

Drostan had told Vandrad of the lad Breck's transformation during the battle the night they had arrived at Neig. He had since spent a considerable amount of time thinking about infection. Searc, it seemed, had escaped such a fate, as Vandrad found no marks on the man that might indicate he'd been purposefully infected by the Ulfhednar. "Thank you, Searc," he said to the tracker when he was satisfied.

Searc dressed again. Odhran thanked him, then bid him go home to his wife to take food and rest. The gangly dark haired man nodded and trudged tiredly from the hut.

3

After leaving Odhran's hut, Searc trudged wearily home, finding his anxious wife Una pacing nervously outside their small roundhouse. Upon seeing him, Una ran to her husband and embraced him tightly, weeping grateful tears and thanking the Lord for returning him safely home. She helped her exhausted husband indoors and instructed him to rest while she prepared food.

But Searc could not find comfort in his home, nor in his caring woman. He lay down upon a pile of soft furs near the fire, but each time his eyes grew heavy from sheer physical and mental fatigue and he was on the verge of blessed sleep, ghastly images of pale wax skinned severed heads impaled on stakes flashed across the insides of his eyelids, and he would lurch awake again.

His discomfort was added to by the fact his skin felt clammy and irritated. He scratched at himself as if under attack from a hungry swarm of midges, but found no relief no matter how much he clawed at his maddeningly tingling flesh. He could not be still. The itch and a buzzing nervous restlessness caused him to rise from the furs again to begin pacing back and forth inside the gloomy, stifling hut, faithful Una looking on worriedly. Although his skin was moist and cold to the touch, he also felt an internal fever raging in his body, and was plagued by a parching thirst that would not be slaked regardless of how much water he drank from his water skin. Indeed, it seemed that the itch, thirst and restlessness grew worse the more water he took.

He could not turn his mind from what he had seen in Abhainn and in the crofter's cave, and the hideous memories his mind insisted on repeatedly calling up became more and more disturbing, more vivid with each recollection.

He paced and paced, muttering and whimpering softly under his breath. His mind a dizzying whirl of sickening images of mutilation, his skin and flesh crawling relentlessly on his bones. The heat inside the little hut was oppressive, the normally delicious aroma of the stew Una was preparing for him on the fire nauseating. He needed to be outside in the fresh air.

"Please, Searc," Una said softly, reaching for her agitated husband and gently laying a hand on his shoulder. "Lay down and take some food. You must rest."

Searc shook his head irritably, shrugging off his wife's hand. "Do not touch me. I need air," he mumbled. He pushed past Una and made for the door, throwing aside the cured cow hide that covered the entrance and stumbling outside.

The afternoon was bright, and his eyes stung painfully in the glare as he stood among the other circular huts that surrounded his own, taking deep breaths and trying to calm himself. The terrible itch that scoured his body lessened slightly, but he felt a queer trembling in his legs.

Although exhausted, he felt a manic urge to run.

A sickly squirming sensation seemed to twist his guts, and the urgent desire to take to his heels was almost unbearable. He began walking, ignoring Una's confused and worried appeals for him to return as he strode quickly away from the hut, staggering between the roundhouses of his neighbours. Other villagers passing by hailed him, offering condolences and prayers for his brother, but he barely acknowledged them, pushing past them and grunting monosyllabic responses to their good wishes. Passing by the smith's forge, he winced in sudden pain and clutched his hands to his ears, the shrill ringing of the blacksmith's hammer piercing his head like barbed arrows.

He stumbled on, his mind reeling with noise and mental images of dead staring eyes and ragged red and black neck stumps. The world tilted and swayed under him, and all the while a whispering voice in his head hissed at him, insisting that he must run, run, and keep running.

Someone else was speaking to him, but he could not see who it was. He felt a firm hand on his shoulder, realised he had stopped moving and was now standing still, hunched over and mewling pitifully. Searc tried to take a step, the desperate yearning to be in swift motion consuming him, every nerve in his body crackling with the need for release. He pushed away whichever villager it was that was speaking to him, a sound almost like a snarl escaping his throat. He blundered on, managing a few more faltering strides before the ground under him seemed to heave and buck, and he pitched forward, slumping to the ground to lie senseless in the mud.

4

Una leaned over her unconscious husband and pressed a dampened rag to his burning forehead. She could feel the fever radiating from his skin, coming off him in sickly hot waves, and the close air in the roundhouse was stifling and rank with his sweat.

He'd been like this ever since Vandrad and Drostan had brought him back to the hut and lay his limp body down on the floor that morning. All day since, her husband had slept deeply, unmoving but for an occasional twitch or violent shudder accompanied by soft mutters and whimpers, and all day she had tended to him, stripping him out of his sweat soaked clothing and covering him with fresh sheepskins that had to be regularly changed as they became sodden from his sweat.

When they'd brought him in, she'd taken his waterskin with the intention of trying to force Searc to take a drink, but had recoiled at the foul smell that assaulted her nostrils when she had removed the skin's stopper. Before he had pushed past her and rushed from the hut that morning, Searc had been drinking continually from the skin, and she worried that the spoiled water within was the cause of his raging fever. He had not vomited however, only laying there by the fire all day, deeply asleep as his flesh had continued to expel moisture and emanate that fierce diseased heat. She could almost see the weight dropping from his bones as she watched. Searc's eyes had sunk into bruised yellowish hollows, his bloodless lips seemed thinner, and his cheek bones stood out in grim detail, giving his face a ghastly skeletal appearance. When last she had changed his sweat soaked coverings, she had been frightened to see how thin and wasted his body had become since the morning, his ribs clearly visible, the hip bones jutting up beneath the skin.

Putting the damp cloth aside, she now reached out and took hold of the sheepskin under which her husband lay, and found it too was now soaked with his sweat. The fever simply would not abate. She had already changed Searc's coverings four times that day, and had been forced to borrow fresh sheepskins from a neighbour when her own supply had been used up.

Una gently drew back the damp woollen covering under which Searc lay, then recoiled in shock, a wordless exclamation of horror escaping her lips as she beheld what had become of her husband.

*

He runs.

Through meadows of tall grass and dripping evergreen forests, he runs.

Across windswept rocky mountains and vast barren plains, through snow and rain, sun and storm, he runs, his blood coursing, singing in exultation in his veins as he powers across the land, low to the ground, the endless miles falling away beneath him and the world a banquet of scents. He can smell the earth, the trees, the grass, water fresh and salted, and the very air itself, each individual scent holding within it countless further traces of everything that has previously passed through.

The world is his and his alone. He is master of it all.

Dim echoes of thoughts whisper somewhere in the back of his mind, strange, complex urges and indistinct memories half recognised as those of another.

Those of a MAN.
The name SEARC.
A place of wood, earth and stone upon a hill that overlooked water.
A dark haired woman.
A brother.
Other MEN.

But he is not a MAN. MAN is weak and stupid, clumsily blundering through the world with their pitiful senses and dull, useless teeth. Ignorant MAN, who knows nothing of the thrill of running down and hamstringing prey, who knows nothing of the exquisite flood of warm salty blood in the mouth and the crunch of bones between teeth.

He runs, razored senses experiencing the Earth and everything in it in exquisite detail, the tiny voice of the MAN diminishing, fading till it is no more than the ghost of a thought. Soon, even that is no more, and the last flickering vestiges of humanity fall away, the small irritating noise at the back of his consciousness finally still.

He runs, boundless and elemental. Thick pelt warm on his body and four powerful legs devouring the land beneath him in great, loping strides.

He is a force of nature.
He is a hunter.
He is WOLF.

*

Una knelt there by the peat fire, gaping at her sleeping husband in mute shock. The world seemed to tilt sickeningly under her.

Beneath the sheepskin, Searc's body had... changed.

Where before there had been a thin, wasted torso, all jutting ribs and hip bones, there was now the lean muscled body of a beast. Her husband's limbs, coated in thick black fur, had shortened and distorted into the legs of an animal, his hands and feet transformed into canine paws from which thick curving nails protruded. Even as she watched, beneath the wispy writhing hair sprouting on his naked torso, she could see the skin seeming to melt and reform like hot candle wax. She heard the soft pops and liquid snaps as Searc's bones and tendons rearranged themselves.

Una, shaking her head in horrified disbelief, raised her eyes to her husband's face, and finally screamed.

5

Breck sighted down the length of the notched arrow, his arm, back and shoulder muscles quivering under the heavy pull of the bowstring. He controlled his breathing as he focussed intently on the straw target down range.

In and out, in and out, slowly and evenly.

The arrow head dipped into place as he exhaled one last time, and he loosed. The arrow flew true, whirring through the air and burying itself almost dead centre in the target.

"A fine shot," Vandrad said behind him. The straw man at the end of the range was pinned with several arrows, the majority well placed in the central mass of the target's chest area. Breck turned and grinned up at the Norseman.

"I think I've found my weapon of choice," he said.

"I think perhaps you have," Vandrad agreed, "but a good warrior…"

"…is skilled with all weapons," Breck finished for him. "I know." Vandrad smiled down at him, and Breck felt a warm rush at his tutor's approval.

"Again," Vandrad said, nodding at the target.

Breck turned back to the straw man and was reaching back over his shoulder to draw another arrow from his quiver when a shriek of terror rang out from somewhere in the village. He turned towards the sound, and saw that Vandrad was already moving, rushing back towards the concentration of roundhouses where the scream had come from, roaring commands for the men to come to arms. Breck ran after him, bow in hand.

Between the roundhouses ahead, he could see the dim figures of villagers running to and fro in the dying light of the day. There were shouts of alarm and confusion, the bawling of a small child, and above it all, the high wavering scream of a woman. As they drew nearer to the huts, a villager emerged from the deepening shadows ahead and ran towards Vandrad.

"Searc's hut," the man gasped, his eyes wide, grasping the Norseman's arm and pointing in the direction of the collection of dwellings at the rear of the village. "There is something in Searc's hut, my lord." Breck felt a frosty squirming on his scalp at the man's words, but forced the fear down, determined to not show himself as a weakling in his teacher's presence.

Vandrad disentangled himself from the villager's grasp and calmly told him to join the others at the gate. He nodded once and rushed off,

142

only too happy to obey. More villagers followed in the frightened man's wake, running out from the paths that ran between the huts, many of them looking back over their shoulders as the woman's screams continued, ringing out from the shadows.

Una, Breck thought. *That was Searc's wife's name.*

She kept screaming. Then stopped.

Seeing Vandrad, several armed men came forward and rallied to him, awaiting orders. Breck saw Odhran, his son Fionn, Ulfar, Drostan and Ailde among them. Also present were Camran, the resident blacksmith of Neig, along with Ospak and Osvald, the Norse twins.

"A wolf," Drostan informed Vandrad in a tight voice. "Uallas swears he saw a great wolf emerging from Searc's hut."

"Where is Uallas now?" Vandrad asked quickly. Uallas and Gabhran, Sionn's followers from Acker who had previously called for his and Ulfar's banishment, had proven themselves stout of heart during the hillside fight with the Ulfhednar, and their animosity towards the two Norsemen had ceased.

"I sent him and Gabhran to organise and watch over the villagers at the gate," Drostan said.

The small knot of assembled men now looked to Vandrad expectantly, even the chieftains Odhran and Drostan deferring command to the younger man. He quickly divided them into three groups, first addressing Ulfar and the twins Ospak and Osvald in their native language. The brothers nodded simultaneously at some instruction spoken to them, then hastened off in the direction of the forge. They returned within moments bearing torches and a sack containing several small, rounded clay urns of a size that would fit snugly in the palm of a man's hand, and began passing the items out among the three groups. The purposefully thin walled clay vessels sloshed with the oil within.

"Odhran, take Camran and go with Ospak and Osvald," Vandrad instructed. "Make your way to the south side of the village and work inwards between the huts." He turned to another two villagers whose names Breck did not know. "Diarmad. Macrath. Go with Ulfar and take the north side. Ailde, you go with them," he said to the big blacksmith, who silently nodded his assent, fingering the haft of his smith's hammer. "I will take the centre," Vandrad continued calmly as more villagers streamed about them, fleeing the darkened living quarters. "Drostan, I would ask that you come with me. You too, Taran," he said to another man who stood by. Breck saw fear in the young villager's eyes, but Taran nodded and set his shoulders. "You all have blooded steel, yes?" Vandrad asked, using the term they had taken to use for those few weapons they possessed which were effective against the Ulfhednar. No serviceable arms had been scavenged from the ashes that first morning after the Ackerians had arrived at Neig. The weapons the men of Acker had wielded had been either consumed by the flames, or warped and blunted in the blaze's heat. Ailde and Camran had managed to rebuild and sharpen a few short swords and spearheads that were not too damaged, but Vandrad had ordered that all the rest of the recovered metals be melted down and reforged into arrowheads.

The men all answered in the affirmative, brandishing their assortment of spears, axes and swords, and Vandrad nodded. "Be ready, and stay in your groups."

The men turned towards the huts and began to trot away into the gloom, the last of the villagers fleeing the living quarters running past them to gather in a frightened huddle in front of the gates at the north end of the settlement.

"What of me?" Breck asked, not wanting to be left behind.

"You and Fionn go to the others. Stand with Uallas and Gabhran and keep watch," Vandrad answered before turning away again.

"But I want to go with you, Vandrad. I can fight," Breck insisted, starting to follow the Norseman. Vandrad rounded on him suddenly and Breck fell back in alarm at the thunderous look on his teacher's face.

"I said stay with the others," Vandrad growled in a low voice that brooked no argument. "I have no time to argue with you, boy. Do as you are commanded."

Breck held his gaze for a moment before dropping his eyes. "Yes, my lord," he said. He turned to Fionn, who was at that moment likewise petitioning his father for permission to accompany him, and receiving the same order from Odhran to fall back with the other villagers. The chieftain of Neig embraced his son quickly and bid him go and see to his mother and sister. Fionn nodded reluctantly, but joined Breck as the armed group of men split into their three parties and spread out. The two boys watched them go sliding into the shadows, then turned and reluctantly made their way back to the gate where the rest of Neig gathered.

6

The taste of the shrieking woman's flesh and blood still warm and fresh in his jaws, the great wolf pads silently through the thick shadows between the dens of the humans.

The night is an endless myriad of scents and sounds that tell him all he needs to know about the world, his very being lit up with sensory information.

The smells of the humans who live in this place, their food, their filth, the scents of their bodies, the sound of their crackling fires and the odour of the peat and oil that fuel them.

And their fear. Fresh and strong.

A large group of the hated two-legs huddle together like a herd of stupid frightened sheep very close by, and the perfume of their terror sings in his mind. He knows also the musk of the human's livestock, who in turn sense the presence of a predator in their midst and cower in their pens at the far end of the settlement. Horse, sheep, pig, fowl, each animal carries its own individual olfactory signature, clearly separate and distinct to the wolf's sensitive nose. He can hear their nervous bleating and squealing, and his great red jaws salivate at the nearness of further prey. One of the sows is pregnant, the stink of her dung covered hide unable to mask the separate odour of pregnancy that wafts from her pores. At the thought of tearing open the sow's belly and feasting on the developing young in her womb, a delicious anticipatory quivering runs the length of the wolf's spine beneath his bloodstained pelt.

As he is deciding which herd to feast upon first, the two or four legged kind, the wolf becomes aware of more men drawing near. A split pack of them, not yet upon him, but slowly closing from three directions. Four moving in from the north, four from the south and a further three to the east, directly ahead of him.

He growls low in his throat, slinks soundlessly into a deeper pocket of darkness, and waits.

7

Searc's wife had been torn to pieces.

Vandrad stood over Una's butchered remains as Drostan shepherded a badly shaken Taran out of the roundhouse. The young man had known Una well, and Vandrad had to grab him and quickly cover Taran's mouth to stop him giving voice to a scream when they had entered the blood splattered hut. Leaving him on guard outside, Drostan re-entered and shook his head sadly at the wet red mess that had been Searc's wife. Vandrad had seen more than his share of carnage in his lifetime, but that had been in battle. This small, bloody tragedy in this isolated village had a coldly personal feeling to it that was at odds to the anonymous slaughter wrought in large scale conflict.

He couldn't understand what had happened. He had checked Searc, and the man had shown no physical signs of being marked by the Ulfhednar. Yet he had turned all the same.

The thick turgid air in the cramped hut was rank, clogging his senses with the stench of blood, excrement and an overpowering musk that was the unmistakable scent of a wild animal. Scanning the roundhouse quickly, Vandrad noticed the pile of sweat soaked furs lying on the floor by the low peat fire. Crouching down and casting around the area where Searc had lain as he underwent his transformation, Vandrad's eyes stopped on a waterskin that lay nearby. Earlier that day, when the tracker had been in Odhran's hut recounting his ill fated scouting mission, Vandrad had noted how often the man had paused to drink from his waterskin, but had thought nothing of it. The man had obviously had a thirst after having run all that morning, fleeing back to Neig in terror after waking to find his brother's impaled head staring at him. Now though, a very troubling thought began to form in his mind and he picked up the waterskin, finding it almost empty. Vandrad lifted the vessel to his nose and recoiled at the foul acrid stench wafting from within. His own words, spoken in instruction to Breck, came back to him.

An experienced warrior will vary his attacks, and he will combine and disguise them.

Cursing himself for a fool, Vandrad realised that a warrior with some two hundred years experience of conflict would be familiar with *all* means of warfare, including the quieter methods of overcoming an enemy that did not involve pitched battles. He had heard tales of the plains savages in the far eastern lands of the world, how they sent catapult loads of plague ridden corpses over the walls of their enemies to spread sickness among those they wished to conquer. A fearful and

146

terrible thing it was, to use disease as a weapon, disease that hid in blood and water.

Again cursing his own stupidity, Vandrad cast the waterskin aside in disgust and rose to his feet, turning to Drostan.

"He was poisoned," he muttered. "Infected with the wolf's spit or blood in his waterskin, and left alive to infiltrate us."

Drostan, his eyes widening in horror at the implications of this, was opening his mouth to speak, when outside the roundhouse, something roared.

8

Every muscle in his body rigid with nervous tension, Taran stood clutching his spear in sweat slippery hands, constantly scanning the darkened narrow paths that wound between the huts around him.

He tried in vain to block out the memory of Una's hollowed out and dismembered body, but the image kept replaying in his mind. Even standing outside the hut, the smell of her blood reached him, and he couldn't stop his traitorous mind from gleefully suggesting what kind of beast could have wrought such unspeakable damage on a human being. He caught himself whimpering in the back of his throat and he swallowed, desperately trying to master his terror. He was a man, he told himself sternly, not some snivelling child, but his attempt to marshal his courage did little to quell the quivering of his knees and the watery looseness in his bowels.

Seventeen summers old, Taran had not been among the party of archers that had rained fire on the demons the night the people of Acker had sought refuge behind Neig's walls. He had been among the rest of the villagers, hearing the screams, the ringing clash of weapons, and the terrible animal howls and shrieks that echoed across the hill outside as the beasts had fallen upon the Ackerians. He had been regaled with stories of the battle afterwards though, had heard horrifying descriptions of the monstrous wolf creatures, and he had seen their blackened skeletons. Even the sight of their charred and misshapen bones had been enough to induce nightmares for weeks afterwards.

The training had helped somewhat. Vandrad had been quick to organise a fighting force in the days following the battle, and a hastily made spear and shield had been thrust into Taran's hands. The rigorous instruction under the tutelage of Ospak and Osvald had gone some way to stiffening his spine against the fear of the strange new threat that roamed the island, but now, standing in the shadows outside Searc and Una's hut with some unseen monster stalking the darkness, he felt his small store of bravery dwindle. He took a series of deep breaths in an effort to calm himself while trying to remember all that Ospak had taught him about the use of a spear.

Keep your feet apart, one behind the other. Bend slightly at the knees. Aim for the chest. Do not throw your weapon. Stand firm with the spear planted and let the enemy's own weight impale them.

It was as he was running through this list of instructions that something warm, wet and very sharp suddenly clamped with crushing force around the top of his head, and he was plucked off his feet, dragged up and across the roof of Searc and Una's hut, and swallowed in the shadows before he could even scream.

9

Ulfar was enjoying himself.

The weight of the throwing axes on his wide belt, the comfortable feel of the leather bound grip of the sword in his right hand, and the heavy security of the great round shield strapped to his left arm were all familiar and right. Although his huge calloused hands had until recently become more accustomed to holding a pitchfork than a sword, he would have been lying if he'd said he didn't miss the feeling of a keenly sharpened and well balanced weapon in his fist.

In truth, following Vandrad from their home in Birka to settle on this island had mainly been the desire of Kadlin, Ulfar's wife. He would have been just as happy to remain in the trading port, training the settlement's guards and fighting off the occasional raiding parties that sought to relieve Birka of its fabulous wealth. But a woman's will was a powerful thing, and though he enjoyed his life in the trading port, he loved his wife more, and he reluctantly recognised that he could not wield a sword forever, much as he would have liked to. And so eventually, he had relented and agreed to accompany Vandrad west across the northern sea to make a new life on the windswept islands on the edge of the great ocean. His father had voyaged and fought with the raiding parties that had come to the islands in years past, and upon his return, heavily bedecked with plunder, he had spoken well of the rich fertile lands.

At first, the idea of Ulfar laying down his weapons and becoming a farmer had amused him, but he had grown into the role after a time, and had come to find a measure of quiet satisfaction in the peaceful life of a crofter. A man possessed of a fearful and quick temper, Ulfar had initially struggled to deal with the mistrust and suspicion that some of the islanders still harboured toward Norse settlers, but as had always been the case, Kadlin was the cool water to his fiery nature, and he had mellowed somewhat, learning to ignore the occasional jibes and insults directed at him, whereas in times past he would have settled a personal slight with brutal and efficient violence.

But even as he settled into his quiet new existence in the village of Acker, he found that a life tending fields and animals greatly lacked the high blooded excitement of battle, and although he had been horrified and angered by the sudden appearance of the dread Ulfhednar on his island home, he had relished the need to once more take up arms.

In the recounting of the fierce Battle of Neig, as it was now being called among the villagers, it was whispered that Ulfar had bellowed laughter and fearlessly taunted his nightmarish foes as he clove a bloody swathe through their ranks. Ulfar would neither confirm nor deny such if anyone asked him if the tales were true, but he noticed the perplexed look the smith Ailde now regarded him with as they crept silently between the roundhouses of Neig, and Ulfar realised he was grinning.

In front of him, Diarmad, a sandy haired, brawny fisherman led their small group, a torch held aloft in his left hand to light their way and an oil pot held ready in his right as they wound their way quietly between the huts. Ailde walked by Ulfar's side, his long handled hammer held ready. Ulfar had witnessed Ailde strike down one of the Ulfhednar during the hillside melee, and respected the big blacksmith's courage and ability in warfare, as basic as it was. He had been impressed to learn that the blacksmith had fought in the great battle on the mainland some years ago when the foreign conqueror William had invaded and slaughtered the troops of the English king Harold. Ulfar was glad of the blacksmith's combat experience, an asset their small force had little of. Bringing up the rear of their party, also equipped with a torch and oil urn, was Macrath, a pock faced man with a scraggly beard who had proven very capable with a bow on the training field.

"Searc's hut is just ahead," Diarmad whispered over his shoulder. Ulfar nodded once and indicated the younger man to lead them on. In the time he had lived in Acker, Ulfar had learned only the basics of the islander's tongue, but out of necessity, his grasp of their language was now slowly improving day by day, though such things did not come easily to him. His natural talent lay in weapons and warfare and the shedding of blood, not foreign tongues.

As they turned a corner, at the edge of the orange glow cast by Diarmad's torch, the group was met by the sight of the lad Taran being snatched neatly and silently from the ground, his head gripped in the jaws of an immense wolf that crouched on the roof of a roundhouse. Although cloaked in shadow, with only the head and front quarters dimly visible, Ulfar saw that the beast was of enormous size, far larger than any natural wolf. For a moment, the animal locked eyes with him, yellow fire flashing balefully in its stare, before it vanished like a ghost into the murk, dragging the still kicking body of Taran after it. Without conscious thought, Ulfar released his grip on his sword and in a single fluid movement drew a throwing axe from his belt and let fly, hurling the weapon into the darkness where he judged the beast to be. He was rewarded with a cry of animal pain, and knew he had scored a hit.

"*Here!*" Ailde was bellowing. "*The beast is here!*"

Ulfar quickly crouched to take up his sword again, and was thrown to the side as something powered into him. The world spun. He heard a scream and a deep snarl, and rolled smoothly to his feet once more in time to see the gigantic wolf clamp its enormous teeth around Macrath's shoulder, snatching the archer from his feet before bounding away into the shadows, still carrying the screaming man in its jaws. Ulfar dropped his sword again, drew the second throwing axe and launched it after the creature, but this time heard no answering howl of pain. Vandrad and Drostan burst from the hut Taran had been standing outside and ran over to join him.

"*Where?*" Vandrad demanded. In response, Ulfar snatched up his longsword and sprinted after the wolf with Ailde, Diarmad, Vandrad and Drostan close behind.

*

Odhran and his search party heard the shouts of the others a split second before the wolf burst from between two huts behind them and leapt into their midst.

Before he could even turn to face the threat, there was a warning yell, someone collided with his back, and Odhran was thrown face first to the ground, his torch falling from his grasp. As he tried to push himself to his feet, something very large and heavy stood on his back, squeezing the breath from his lungs, and he was pushed back to the earth. Sharp claws pierced his tunic, sinking into the flesh of his shoulders. There was a deafening roar, so loud and close to his ear that it that blocked out the world, and he felt hot rank breath on the nape of his neck. Then there was a yelp and snarl of pain, and the tremendous weight on his back was gone. Wheezing in a great breath, Odhran rolled onto his back, and in the half light of his dropped torch saw the smith Camran lying against the wall of a hut to his left, the blacksmith's tunic torn and blooded, while the Norse brothers Ospak and Osvald rolled on the ground, locked in a desperate violent struggle with a huge black coated wolf. The twins wielded short swords, which they struggled to bring to bear in such close quarters, and the brutal fight was punctuated with the sound of snapping jaws, guttural snarling, cries of pain and bellows of rage.

"*Away!*" an accented voice from behind him thundered. At the command, Odhran saw the two brothers disengage from the fight and try to break from the huge animal, but the wolf lunged forward and clamped Ospak's left leg in its jaws as he tried to free himself. There was a sharp wet snapping sound, and the stocky Norseman was lifted into the air, roaring in agony as the monster shook him and gnawed at his thigh with bone-crushing force. Osvald leapt to his brother's aid, but was immediately knocked aside as the huge wolf suddenly spun in a tight circle, knocking him aside and sending him crashing head first into the stone wall of a hut. The beast shook and swung Ospak again. There was a crunching *rip*, and the twin spun and twisted through the air spraying arterial blood, falling to the earth by Odhran's side in a screaming bleeding heap, his left leg missing above the knee.

The huge animal, eyes blazing with amber hate, its black coat glistening bloodily in the torchlight, snarled and rushed forward like a fluid nightmare, comging straight at Odhran. He threw up his arms in futile defence and whispered a quick prayer, fully expecting to die.

Then there was a low cracking sound. Odhran caught a sudden stench of whale oil, and was aware of a brightening of the night as a torch sailed through the air, thrown from somewhere behind him. The wolf suddenly changed direction, veering away from the prone chieftain, nimbly dodging the hurled torch and vanishing once more in the shadows between the huts.

10

Breck, his bow lowered with an arrow notched and ready, stood among the line of defenders. The single rank of men stood in tense watchfulness, arranged in a protective semi circle formation that bristled with steel, fire and oil. Behind them, the frightened villagers of Neig huddled in a crowd with their backs to the main gate. It had taken some time for Uallas, Gabhran and the other men to herd the frightened populace into place and quiet them, but eventually the crowd bunched up and settled down behind their armed protectors, the noisy hubbub of their fear lulling somewhat to a low, nervous murmur.

Breck had to make a conscious effort to hold a twitching sense of dread at bay. Vandrad had long lectured him on the debilitating effect fear could have on a fighting force. Fear, he said, had to be mastered and beaten into submission, and while it was useful in controlled doses, and could help motivate and focus a man, it was an animal that easily slipped its leash, and once let loose, spread like disease, infecting soldiers with panic.

Breck closed his eyes, willing his thumping blood to slow, taking long, even breaths. He cleared his mind, visualising his heart in his breast, imagined it pumping, pumping, slower and slower, finding an easier rhythm and settling to an easy, regular pulse. And then it was so. He opened his eyes again and concentrated on his surroundings, scanning left and right ceaselessly as Vandrad had taught him, searching for the slightest movement, the first sign of danger.

To his left, on the eastern side of the settlement, was Camran's forge, a few squat barns, a weaver's cottage and several animal pens. The area was well lit with torches, and but for the occasional bleats and squeals of the frightened livestock in their enclosures, it was still and nothing moved. In front of Breck, the large open area of Neig's central green was likewise motionless. Again, several torches had been driven into the earth around the open expanse of ground, and their glow illuminated the area that served as the village's common ground, and more recently, its training field.

To Breck's right lay the darkened western side of the village, where Vandrad and the others had gone in search of the wolf. On hearing Una's screams, the villagers had hurriedly evacuated the area as the sun was setting, and in their rush to flee, had neglected to light the torches that were placed among the narrow paths winding between their dwellings. As such, as night claimed full dominion, the western side of the settlement was shrouded in a deep darkness, only the first row of huts lit by the torches bordering the central green before shadows claimed the rest of the living quarter. It was to this gloomy area that the defenders and the villagers behind them glanced with cold expectation. If a threat were to come from anywhere, Breck thought, it would come from the pools of blackness amid the roundhouses.

A tense hush descended on the scene, the armed men and those in the nervously shifting crowd behind both falling to near silence in the eerily loaded calm. The lull was such that Breck could discern the quiet guttering made by the flame of the torch held by the man beside him as it flickered and danced in the cool evening breeze that blew through the hilltop village. Breck rolled his shoulders and rotated his head, stretching out the muscles in his neck, back and shoulders, readying himself.

The quiet became absolute, heavy and pregnant with foreboding, then was shattered.

A cry rang out from somewhere in the shadows amid the huts, quickly followed by an escalating series of shouts, screams, and a low, brutish growling. The villagers behind Breck murmured and shifted nervously, some crying out in fright at the sudden uproar. The noises from the gloom became more urgent, intensifying into a sustained cacophony of angry shouts, screams of pain and the hoarse grunting snarls.

There was the low *whump* of igniting flames, and a flickering orange light suddenly bloomed amid the huts on their right. Behind Breck, the people of Neig crowded closer together, the intensifying sounds of the unseen struggle unnerving them. Several children in the crowd were weeping, and many of the men in the defensive line had begun glancing at each other uneasily, shifting restlessly where they stood, as if on the brink of running.

"Be steady there," Breck heard Gabhran's voice call out sternly. "Hold your courage and stand firm." The men settled somewhat at the command, planting their feet and closing ranks a little tighter. Breck held onto his nerve, and continued scanning his surroundings for sign of the quarry.

The creature broke cover at the far end of the darkened living quarter, a massive black shadow that erupted out from the gloom and came hurtling across the open green toward them.

"There!" Breck cried in warning, raising his bow. Several shouts rang out from the armed men as they too now spotted the rapidly advancing beast. As it bore down on them, Breck could see the thing in detail. But for the twisted half-human monstrosities that had burned his village and slaughtered his people, he'd never seen an actual wolf

before, the animal not being native to the island and found only on the mainland. He doubted however, that natural wolves grew to such a fearful size. It ran low to the ground, sleek and darting, powerful muscles rippling under its pelt. Its eyes glowed and its long fangs were bared. As it closed on the villagers, Breck could hear the beast's snarl growing louder, louder.

Arrows began raining down around the charging wolf, but it easily dodged the projectiles, weaving left and right without even breaking stride. Although they had been instructed by Vandrad only to use them at close range, several of those armed with spears, flaming brands and oil likewise launched their missiles. The air was suddenly full of the improvised artillery, a mass of the fragile vessels and burning torches arcing through the night. The wolf was too fast though, and the barely trained men's panicked aim was poor. Not one missile was on target, though a few torches landed close to broken urns, and flames leapt up in the creature's wake, as if the beast's very passage set the earth afire.

The great wolf a mere fifty paces out and swiftly drawing nearer, the fear that Vandrad had often warned him about set its teeth firmly into the men's courage. From the corner of his eye, Breck saw a male villager three places to his right throw down his pitchfork, turn and run, stupidly trying to force his way through the crowd behind him. It was just like Vandrad had said, and Breck watched in horror as he witnessed the terror spread, leaping from one man to another like wildfire. A second, then a third gap in the line appeared as the men bolted, turning back toward the crowd behind and trying to push their way through to escape the settlement via the gate. Somewhere, Gabhran and Uallas were roaring commands to hold the line and reform, but it was too late. With the onrushing wolf upon them, pouring on speed and veering to Breck's right where the line had faltered, Neig's defenders broke.

Breck ran.

He did not retreat, but instead dashed forward a few paces to keep the massive animal in his line of sight. Without thinking, with no time to think, he turned, raised his weapon, drew back the bow string, and loosed.

There was a chorus of terrified screams as the wolf launched itself over what remained of the defensive line. It seemed to hang in the air for a moment, suspended and almost graceful in flight, its red jaws agape, pointed ears flat against its broad skull, claws eagerly reaching for the human cattle beneath it.

There was a sharp yelp, and the huge animal abruptly pitched to the side, landing heavily on the grass with a weighty *thump* at the feet of a young woman. The girl gaped, staring at the huge hairy corpse that had fallen before her as if suddenly snatched from the air, a single arrow skewering the wolf's neck.

PART SEVEN

"Growing up, I was taught that a man has to defend his family. When the wolf is trying to get in, you gotta stand in the doorway."

<u>B. B. King</u>

1

Every last shred of his body and will bent to the climb, Sealgair's mind was an almost a perfect blank during of his final agonized push to reach the loch. Crawling up the hill, his awareness of the world seemed to fade in and out through a red haze of intense, unremitting pain. His broken ribs and ankle crunching and pricking inside him. Every once in a tortured while, he would get a mental flash of the Harbinger and his companions, drawing ever nearer to the island.

Clutching at rocks, tufts of wiry grass and gorse bushes, ignoring the sharp spines that pricked and stabbed at his hands, he continued to bodily haul himself up the steep side of the valley.

He finally reached the crest of the hill, coughing blood and half crazed with desperation as he clawed his way over the summit to the cliff edge on the other side, and looked down across the northern end of the loch, feeling his heart plummet as he saw five brightly coloured canoes dragged up on the tiny shingle cove of the island. The interlopers sat nearby, completely oblivious to the disaster their presence signified. A wave of despair swallowed him at the sight.

Then he'd been falling, and for a while, there was nothing.

When he returned to his senses, he was lying in a heap on the flat area of rocky land at the foot of the cliff, not far from the humble earth and wood hut where he had lived and kept watch over the island for such a long, lonely time.

He had no idea how long he'd lain unconscious at the foot of the cliff, and paying no mind to the fact that he was once more *able* to stand, his body having already begun to heal itself while he'd been lying senseless, he lurched to his feet and hobbled to an outcropping on the edge of the hill that sloped down to the loch.

The group of intruders were standing grouped around the cluster of rocks and the bright green patch of hawthorn at the centre of the island.

Sealgair turned from the sight, refusing to accept that it was over, and stumbled to his hut, returning to the outcropping carrying the ancient bow in one hand, a full quiver of arrows in the other.

His mind cold and blank as a snowfield, looking through the blood matted hair that fell in a blonde, grey and red tangle across his face, he sighted down the hill at the group of figures. Not yet fully healed from his injuries, his vision at this range, normally raptor-like, was hazy and indistinct. As such, making out individual details of the group was impossible, and he saw only vague figures. Unable to pick out the Harbinger among the blurry forms, he simply selected the closest figure.

He detached himself, purposely separating his damaged, aching body and his compromised eyesight from his mind. His muscles and reflexes took on the fluidly methodical action of a well oiled machine.

He drew back the bowstring, and loosed.

Sealgair saw the target twitch convulsively before falling limply to the ground. A clean kill.

There was a moment of utter stillness before the woman screamed.

Sealgair didn't think about compensating for wind speed and direction or the downward angle of his shots. He simply let instinct and wrath take over, and his great arms worked by themselves as he notched another arrow and loosed.

Notched and loosed.

Notched and loosed.

2

Matt was standing in wordless astonishment, looking down at the impossible sight of Clyde's body on the ground and only half hearing Scarlett's initial scream when it seemed like someone punched him, hard in the chest. Then he was stumbling backward, tripping and falling painfully among the rocks and hawthorn behind him.

Everything had happened in the space of maybe two seconds, and it took his normally quick mind a moment to catch up with the unfolding situation. Amid Scarlett's screams, he heard Cal roaring to get down, get the fuck down. There was a series of rising whirring noises as more arrows began flying around them, then someone grabbed his collar and he was being dragged across the rocks before being unceremoniously dumped behind the cover of a large boulder. More arrows zipped through the air above him, the continuous hiss of air parting in their wake regular and mechanical as the ticking of a clock, as if the arrows were being fired from some sort of automated war machine.

He looked up, and saw Ian looking back down at him. His friend's face was very pale but for a few small droplets of blood. The eyes were too big and shiny, and his mouth was wet and slack. He was shaking his head slightly, as if denying some foolish thing that Matt had said. It was only then that he became aware of the pain. Matt looked down and saw the shaft of the arrow embedded in his chest.

"*Dude...*" he said. Then could think of nothing else to follow up with as the pain really settled in, burrowing ragged broken nails into his chest. Agony flooded through him, radiating out from a point deep within his flesh, and Matt groaned in the back of his throat. His eyes were screwed shut in pain, but somewhere nearby he could hear Scarlett cursing and screaming Clyde's name, then more high pitched whistles of displaced air as the arrows continued to pour down with terrible relentlessness. There was a shout of pain from Cal. Matt tried to push himself up, but Ian forced him back again and knelt beside him.

"No, don't," his friend was saying quietly. "Just stay here. It'll be alright. We're alright. Alright..." There was a strange quality to Ian's voice. A liquid bubbling, as if he were speaking through a clod of wet mud lodged in his throat.

Matt tried to think. It was difficult. The pain was like a huge block of red concrete that weighed down on his chest, his tongue and mind. Hard to breathe. He concentrated, trying to mentally push his way through the fog of hurt and fear that clouded his thoughts, and applied all his mental focus. "Scarlett? Cal?" he asked, his eyes still tightly clenched closed in agony.

"They're by the canoes," Ian said, in that weird burbling voice. "Cal's been hit."

Hearing this, Matt opened his eyes again and looked at Ian. For a moment, he forgot all about the pain that ravaged his body.

"Ian... your...neck," he said, his voice rising jaggedly on the last word, as if he were asking a question.

Incredibly, Ian just nodded, still not looking at him. The shaft of the arrow embedded in his friend's throat bobbed up and down in obscene sympathy, waggling like a conductor's baton.

3

Beneath Cal, pinned under the weight of his body, Scarlett struggled furiously, repeating Clyde's name over and over in hoarse, anguished sobs. The sound of it broke Cal's heart, and he clung desperately to the frantically thrashing woman, trying to use his weight to prevent her from rushing out into another lethal hail of arrows.

"Stop it, Scarlett. He's gone."

"No. *No!* We've got to help Clyde," Scarlett insisted.

"We can't help him."

"Get the fuck off me, Cal."

"No."

"*CAL!* Get the *fuck* off me. Clyde's hurt…"

"Clyde's dead, Scarlett."

"*Shut up! Shut the fuck up!* He's not dead. We've got to help him. He's hurt…*Clyde!*"

Cal continued to hold tight to her, knowing that her protective nature would get her killed if she managed to escape his grip. He was also trying to deal with the sight of Clyde dropping to his knees with that arrowhead punching out of the skin of his throat, and the long fletched shaft of the arrow protruding from the nape of his neck.

The following seconds were blurry with the surge of shock and adrenaline that had flooded his veins. Scarlett had screamed and started towards Clyde's body. As Cal grabbed her, shouting at the others to get down, he'd seen Matt from the corner of his eye, pitched backwards, another arrow buried deep in his chest. He'd hesitated, momentarily frozen by the sight, and then Ian had grabbed Matt by the collar and was dragging him to cover behind an outcropping of large rocks.

That was when Cal had been hit. Scarlett had inadvertently saved his life by trying to break from his hold on her and run back to Clyde's body. The force of her desperate lunge pulling him in that direction had changed the angle at which he'd been standing, and instead of taking him directly through the throat, the arrow had ploughed a bloody furrow through the muscle above his right collarbone, before clattering off the rocky ground behind him. He'd felt nothing but a strong tug on his shoulder at the time, and remembered nothing of getting back to the canoes. He'd come back to his senses lying flat on the sandy ground of the tiny beach, taking what cover he could behind one of the shallow vessels, which he'd tilted onto its side to provide better cover, though he had no recollection of doing so, while Scarlett fought and squirmed and cursed beneath him. Eventually, Scarlett's struggles died down and she clung to him, shaking with grief. All Cal could do was hold her, his own tears running freely down his face. They lay there now, clutching tightly to one another and trying to come to terms with the bewildering, bloody onslaught.

Cal realised that the arrows had for the moment stopped flying. He cautiously raised his head above the tilted body of the canoe, saw a quick blur of movement on the hill above, and instantly ducked down again, feeling the air part an inch above his scalp as another arrow zipped overhead and ricocheted off the body of the canoe behind him.

"Jesus Christ," he gasped into Scarlett's ear. "It's him." In the brief glance he'd managed to take, Cal had glimpsed a tall, long haired figure armed with a bow, standing amid the paler rocks and shrubbery of the steep hillside that rose up from the shore of the loch. Although the archer was some distance away, his size had been evident, and Cal had instantly recognised the same long haired giant who'd attempted to kill Ian the night before. He briefly wondered how that could be so, when Sergeant Harrison had told him the crazy fucker was locked up in the cells.

The big hermit's skill with the bow was astonishing, Cal thought with an awed sense of dread. With his first three shots, fired from a range of some two hundred metres or so and aiming at a downward angle, the man had killed Clyde, probably killed Matt, and would have killed Cal too if not for Scarlett pulling him off balance at the crucial moment. All in the space of a few heartbeats. Cal, who had once been a promising medical student and had some knowledge of such things, had seen the fletched end of the arrow jutting dead centre from the base of Clyde's skull, and had known that his death had at least been instantaneous. The arrow would have severed the brain stem, splitting the spinal column between the top two vertebrae. Somehow, he knew that the huge killer had placed the shot deliberately, but hitting such a small spot at that kind of range didn't seem humanly possible.

The fog of panic and adrenaline began to lift somewhat, enabling Cal to think clearly again, and he looked toward the collection of hawthorn covered boulders at the centre of the tiny island. Lying close to the ground between two of the canoes, the vessel on his left blocked Cal's view of where he'd last seen Ian dragging Matt's skewered body.

Jesus, was Matt dead? Was Ian?

"Stay here," he said softly to Scarlett, who clutched him a little tighter.

"No, Cal. Don't go out there. Don't move."

"I'm just going to crawl forward a wee bit. I need to see if Ian and Matt are alright."

Scarlett saw the sense in this, her own concern for the others overcoming her fear. She nodded and released her hold on him.

"Stay here. Keep your head down," Cal advised her.

"Oh, really? What the fuck do you *think* I'm going to do?"

Cal simply nodded, and began inching slowly forwards, keeping his head below the level of the half upturned canoe on his right. When he reached the point where the point the hull of the canoe narrowed toward the bow, offering less cover, he dared to creep forward, so very slowly, just a few more inches, craning his neck forward and trying to see round the obstructing body of the canoe on his left, towards the rocks where he prayed Ian and Matt had found cover.

A sudden hissing-whirring noise caused Cal to quickly jerk his head back. Another huge arrow buried itself in the ground where his head had been just a split second before, peppering Cal's face with a stinging spray of grit. He quickly shuffled back behind the canoe, gasping in fright.

Gradually able to work some spit into his mouth, he called out to his unseen friends, unconcerned about the sound of his voice giving away his position. The still quivering arrow embedded in the ground, mere inches from his face, was all the proof he needed that the murderous hillbilly knew exactly where he was.

"Ian? Matt? You alright?"

"Cal?" Ian replied from somewhere ahead and to the left. His voice was half choked and had a peculiar wet rasp to it. Nevertheless, Cal breathed a shaking sigh of relief to know that Ian at least, was alive.

"Ian, thank fuck. Is Matt with you?"

"Aye. He's been hit. He's alive, but there's a lot of blood, Cal, and I think he's in shock. I don't know what to do. What do I *do*, Cal?"

"It's cool, mate. Just chill. What about you? Are you hit?"

"I'm... no. I'm alright. I'm alright," Ian replied with an odd hesitancy, then blurted, "Scarlett? What about Scarlett?"

"I'm here, Ian," Scarlett called from behind Cal. "I'm okay."

"Thank Christ," Ian's fractured voice came back. He paused for a moment, then spoke a single word that broke Cal's heart all over again.

"Clyde..." Ian's voice dissolved in a series of rasping sobs. Behind him, Cal could hear Scarlett weeping again at the mention of their friend's name. He could see Clyde's body from where he lay, just ten metres away on the cold rocky ground. Face down. Motionless. Dead. The shaft of the arrow still embedded in the nape of his neck.

4

Sealgair stood unmoving but for the regular side to side flicking of his pale eyes, constantly switching between the canoes where two of the intruders had gone to ground seeking shelter, and the burial site, the far side of which gave cover to the remaining pair. He stood now with an arrow nocked, the bow string partially drawn to half tension.

Waiting.

But for a sense of urgency that demanded he soon make a decisive move, he would have been prepared to stand still and wait for as long as it took for the slightest opportunity to bring down the remaining mainlanders. But Sealgair needed to know if the grave had been disturbed, and the only way to know for certain was to go out to the island and see for himself.

He turned and limped back to his hut, went inside, and took down the pair of spears from their iron holders on the wall. He left the dwelling again, the weight of the foot long leaf shaped iron spearheads and the grain of their well worn wooden shafts familiar and right in his hands.

Outside the hut, his heart pumping with a potent mix of cold dread and white hot wrath, he limped along a narrow zigzagging trail that descended in a series of tight switchbacks down the face of the hillside to the shoreline. All the while he kept his gaze fixed on the island, alert for the slightest movement.

At the bottom of the trail, the hillside ended in a muddy bank, thick with shoulder tall reeds and slippery boulders half submerged at the water's edge. Sealgair stepped carefully off the trail, favouring his good leg, and began making his way through the marshy bank along a series of large stepping stones that formed a path through the dense undergrowth. Pushing the reeds aside, he made his way carefully along the trail of slippery rocks, continually keeping half an eye on the island for signs of movement. The path of stones ended at a small clearing in the reeds, hidden by thick clumps of wet bracken. In the tiny patch of flat land lay a one man rowing boat, covered with an oiled tarpaulin and raised off the ground on large flat stones. Sealgair tore aside the thick protective canvas, dropped his twin spears into the battered little boat which he used for fishing, and dragged the vessel off the supporting stones, through the loch side reeds and into the water. He clambered in, took up the oars and began rowing for the island, every few seconds glancing over his shoulder at the small jut of land where the Harbinger and his companions waited and bled. His great thick muscled arms worked the oars, driving the tiny skiff across the loch's dark surface at speed, every deep stroke powering him closer.

Finally he had him. It may already be too late, but the only thing that Sealgair knew as a certainty as the weathered little boat cut through the cold water, was that no matter what, disturbed burial site or no, the Harbinger would be dead in the next few minutes.

5

Despite the insanity that had unfolded all around him, not to mention the huge arrow still sticking out of his chest, Matt was at that moment surprisingly comfortable, all things considered.

He half recognised, in a groggily exsanguinated way, that his sleepy listlessness was due to him being in shock, plus the fact that he was losing quite a bit of the old claret. He was getting cold as his lifeblood vacated his body. The act of breathing was a hassle, and he thought he'd probably suffered a punctured lung. When he shifted slightly where he sat, Matt could half discern a slight tacky feeling of stickiness under his arse, and thought there was a good chance he was sitting in a spreading pool of his own blood. Or maybe he'd just shat himself. Probably both.

The huge arrow protruding from his chest still hurt. A lot. Matt was disappointed to discover first hand the falsity of that particular movie myth, that shock numbs the grievously wounded to the feeling of pain, but to be fair to Hollywood, the hot, pulsing hurt *was* slightly more manageable than it had been just a few minutes ago. That might have had something to do with the added distraction of what had happened with Ian, right enough.

Being shot at, with arrows of all things, by some homicidal hillbilly was one thing. But seeing Ian sitting there next to him, quite the thing, with another massive arrow hanging out of his throat, well, that was a whole other flavour of crazy.

Matt's ordered and methodical mind had a hard time trying to assimilate this new set of rules about what was possible and what wasn't, and it wasn't just shock and blood loss that was the cause of his semi-catatonic state. A part of his mind just flat refused to accept what he'd witnessed, and took a figurative cigarette break at the sight, as if to simply say *fuck that*.

He'd done his level best to rationalise what he'd seen. Maybe it was one of those medical miracles like he'd seen in that show on the Discovery Channel. What was the programme called again? Body Invaders, that was it. Some crazy shit on there. That one with the lassie that had been blitzed at a party and had fallen out a window, right onto the iron fence outside her flat. Took a railing spike right through the underside of the jaw, the point of it coming out of her cheek. She'd been just fine and dandy. Well, as fine and dandy as anyone could be with a fence in their face. Point was, she survived, and even though she ended up with a peach of a scar, the girl had suffered little in the way of real physical trauma, despite the gruesome appearance of the wound. Shit, there hadn't even been that much blood.

The situation with Ian was a bit different.

For a start, unlike the drunk girl on the telly with the extreme piercing, Ian looked like someone had dipped him in a large vat of dark red ink. And his throat was torn to fleshy tatters. Matt was no doctor, but he knew where the jugular vein was, and the whole left side of Ian's neck had been laid wide by the massive arrowhead that had torn it open. And although he'd been thoughtful enough to turn his back to Matt while doing so, Ian had then proceeded to rip the barbed arrow from his own flesh, as if he'd been removing a large and particularly nasty splinter. When Ian had then slumped down next to him, twitching and slevering like someone zapped with a Taser, his eyes rolled back to display only the whites, Matt had thought that his friend was dying, that the horrific wound was killing him after all.

But then he'd seen Ian's mangled neck knit itself right back together. Right in front of his eyes.

Crazy shit indeed.

Now they were sitting side by side, he and Ian, their backs to the large boulders that sheltered them from the madman and his arrows, looking west across the beguilingly calm waters of Loch Langabhat. The bowman had for the moment paused in his raining of fletched death upon them, and Matt was drowsily enjoying the peace and quiet. No one was screaming, which was always nice, and there was just the soothing sound of the water lapping quietly at the little island's grey stony shore.

It was pleasant. Peaceful even.

He was getting really sleepy. Could barely feel any pain now. It had sneaked away, like a sneaky wee... baby fox... or something.

Matt closed his eyes.

And someone slapped him square across the chops.

"Who disturbs my slumber?" Matt blearily demanded. Where was that line from? Some Disney film. Aladdin. That was it. Cave of Wonders. Robin Williams as the genie. Funny as fuck.

The slapper slapped him again.

"Dude," the slapper said.

Matt slowly opened his eyes and saw Ian's blood spattered face before him.

"Alright, Ian. How you doing, man?" Matt slurred.

"I'm good, mate. You're not looking too grand though."

"Feelin' groovy."

"As long as you're awake."

"Dunno 'bout that, mate. This feels like a dream. Not the best one I ever had, I must say. Not like that one I had about fighting the midget terrorists at the airport. That was a good dream..."

"Aye, you told me about that one. Got to keep an eye on those midgets, eh? Shady wee bastards."

"You're not 'sposed to say midgets anymore though," Matt cautioned. "Little people. That's what's politically... correct..."

"Little people," Ian agreed.

"Not... arrows," Matt said, having had a flash of inspiration.

"What did you say, dude?"

"Not arrows. See the size of 'em? Like... javelins... for midgets... I mean little people.... The midget terrorists came back... to even the score..."

"They're pretty big. The arrows I mean. Not the midgets," Ian agreed cordially. Matt knew in the back of his diminishing mind that he was rambling a lot of pish and Ian was just trying to keep him talking. Keep him awake. That was nice of him. It was hard though. So hard to stay awake.

"Mmmm. I mean... what would you hunt... with arrows that big? Fuckin'... elephants?"

6

Aged twenty-two, and well on his way to gaining his degree in medicine, Cal Dempster hadn't been a violent man, and had never been drawn to conflict in the way that some are.

In truth, he was a friendly, though rather shy, timid sort, who would go out of his way to avoid confrontation. He'd been old enough to know that his parents had some pretty serious financial problems after his dad's plumbing business had gone under, but he hadn't known just how serious the situation had become, and certainly didn't know that his father had been so desperate that he had gone to Alza for a loan. Cal only found this out when his mum had tearfully related the news to him over the phone one night.

Alan 'Alza' McGurk was a wealthy local businessman who owned several bus and taxi companies. It was also common whispered knowledge that he was a gangster, who'd been implicated in, but never arrested for, a number of serious crimes. He also ran a line in money lending, and when Alza decided, because he could have knees broken at a word if he felt like it, to add another couple of grand to the previously agreed repayment amount, it was a couple of grand that Peter Dempster simply did not have. When Cal's dad had failed to come up with the money, McGurk had their house torched, with Cal, his parents and his younger sister asleep in their beds inside.

Lying face down in a hospital bed in the burn ward, Cal, later revealed to the authorities his father's dealings with McGurk. The sergeant taking his statement had assured him that no evidence of arson had been found, and that the case was being treated as a tragic accident. Possibly an electrical fault. Cal, despite the horrendous agony that crawled all over the scorched raw flesh of his back, noticed that the policeman had avoided meeting his eyes when telling him this, and recalled rumours he'd heard about how the well connected McGurk even had several policemen snugly in his back pocket.

Cal discovered his talent for violence when he was discharged from hospital some time later, when in a very dark frame of mind and not quite himself, he marched into The Waterline Bar, a known private hangout spot for McGurk and his crew, and just started laying waste with a baseball bat.

He couldn't recall many details of the carnage that had ensued, but at the end, he'd found himself standing over a cowering Alza McGurk, the bat in his hands already slick with blood. And he just kept on swinging.

For the second time that year, he'd woken up in a hospital bed some indeterminate time later. This time, he found himself handcuffed to the bed's railings. Apparently, he'd been repeatedly stabbed during his one man assault on The Waterline, and while unconscious through massive blood loss, he'd been arrested on several charges of aggravated assault with a deadly weapon and attempted murder.

His lawyer, paid for by legal aid, had managed to get the attempted murder charge dropped on the grounds of diminished responsibility and the fact that Cal had pled guilty at the initial court hearing. The other charges stood however, and Cal spent the next six years as a guest in HM Prison Barlinnie, during which time he had ample opportunity to further develop and hone his new found aptitude for violence and survival.

McGurk knew people on the inside. Quite a few of them, including the screws. But Cal, a very different person to the softly spoken young medical student he'd been not so long ago, came out on top more often than not in the repeated assaults, and after several failed attempts on his life, he was eventually left well enough alone.

Now, lying prone on his belly between the two canoes and trying to think of what to do next, Cal heard the faint sound of splashing from the water, and sneaked a glance over the side of the canoe on his right.

The little rowing boat and the giant that powered it were about twenty metres offshore, and closing.

Although dread swelled like vomit in his throat, at least it resolved the problem about what he should do next.

When the big crazy bastard dropped the oars, grabbed what seemed to be two very long spears, clambered over the side of the boat and started wading through the waist deep water towards him, all Cal's hard won survival instincts kicked in. He'd learned in the 'Linnie that attack most often really was the best form of defence, and that when challenged, it was advisable to get the first dig in, and to follow it up by being as vicious and relentless as possible until the fight was over.

Pushing himself to his feet, he snatched up a double bladed paddle from one of the canoes. In front of him, he saw Scarlett do the same.

"Get out the way, Scarlett," he said softly, keeping his eyes on the advancing killer.

"Go fuck yourself, Cal," Scarlett replied evenly, true to character and glaring defiantly back over her shoulder at him, those bewitching eyes flashing, her face flushed, radiant with righteous anger. She was beautiful.

"Fair enough," he said, and then suddenly ran forward, sprinting into the loch ahead of her, cold water flying around his legs as he ploughed into the shallows to meet the huge psycho. He took a moment's satisfaction from the momentary flicker of surprise he saw in the man's eyes, and then swung the paddle.

He caught him a thoroughly decent dig, right in the mouth, and even glimpsed a few teeth go sailing through the air as the hard plastic paddle blade smashed edgewise into the nutter's craggy, bearded face.

Then there was a blur of movement. It felt like a train hit him, and he was suddenly spinning through the air.

The loch caught him in its cold arms, enfolding Cal and dragging him beneath the surface.

7

Sealgair, spitting blood and pink fragments of broken teeth, didn't even look as the first mainlander went under the water. The woman had quickly followed him, screaming in his wake, and was already upon him. He saw her swing her paddle, and easily blocked the attack with the shafts of the spears clutched in his right hand. A backhanded blow with the long shafts caught the woman across the jaw, and she too spun away, knocked senseless even before she hit the ground.

Sealgair had barely broken stride since getting out of the boat.

He stepped over the woman's still form, his eyes locked on the pile of hawthorn coated stones at the island's centre, and broke into a limping run, stumbling up the little beach and over the uneven ground beyond.

As he drew closer to the grave and began to realise what had happened, a very deep and very cold stillness seemed to settle on him. He staggered to a halt, unable to breathe, and a terrible wave of despair and failure blew through him.

The cairn had been disturbed.

The rune marked skull beneath had been removed from the earth, and lay to the side of the little pit. Grinning up at him. Staring with its empty dead sockets. It's dagger teeth bared to the world.

For a moment, Sealgair could only stand there, dripping water on the ground, goggling idiotically at the disturbed grave in front of him.

He had failed.

After everything. After so long.

Failed.

The concept seemed too much to comprehend. How could it be so?

Sealgair whipped his head round to the left as he heard something move, and there he was.

The Harbinger. His throat a gaping bloody mess. Clutching one of Sealgair's arrows in his fist.

Sealgair turned toward the interloper, dropped one of his own spears and pointed the other at the man. There was no real cause anymore to kill him. With the grave disturbed, the damage had already been done, and nothing could change that. It was too late. The Harbinger's death would be meaningless.

Sealgair didn't care. He gave himself over to the blind rage that flooded through him, blocking out everything else.

If nothing else, he would extract some vengeance in advance for the many who would now perish because of the Harbinger's intrusion.

8

Half concealed behind the rock formation, Ian watched helplessly as the huge maniac casually swatted Cal and then Scarlett aside, and came loping up the beach in his direction.

The guy was beat to shit, his face heavily bruised, swollen and patchy with dried blood from the multitude of cuts and scrapes that scrawled over his grim bearded face. His tangled mass of greying blonde hair was matted and hung in ropes, thick with congealed blood, and he was limping heavily. The expression on his face was like nothing Ian had seen before. An inhuman, ageless look of displacement burned in his bloodshot eyes. So much rage. So much fear. An absolute lack of pity. Ian quailed before the giant's advance, and slumped down behind the rocks again. "He's coming, man," he said, turning to Matt, but Matt didn't answer. "Matt?"

Something chill and jagged sank into Ian's belly, then rushed back up his throat in a ragged wet sob as he beheld the sightless, glassy glaze in his friend's eyes. The slumped stillness of his body.

His *body*. His remains. His corpse.

Ian's mind tilted, threatening to loosen his already precarious grip on it. The word DEAD, writ large and insistent, flickered in his mind in strobing neon. Ian buried his face in his hands, and could only squat there behind the rocks beside another dead friend, shuddering in shock and tearing grief as the crunching footsteps of the enormous bearded maniac drew closer.

He forced his eyes open, and saw that his right fist now clutched the oversized arrow he'd torn from his throat.

Javelins for midgets.

He reached out and cupped Matt's waxy cheek with his free hand. "Sweet dreams, brother" he said, his voice little more than a broken whisper. "I'll see you on the other side. Probably in a couple of minutes."

He took a deep breath, let it out, and giving Matt a final goodbye ruffle of his curls as he passed, Ian stepped out from behind the rocks and faced the man who'd hunted him relentlessly ever since he'd set foot on the island. The fact of his impending death was rendered with a further sense of the ludicrous as he beheld the size of the killer's twin spears compared to the suddenly puny arrow he clutched in his sweaty, shaking grasp.

They locked eyes for a moment. The giant dropped one of the spears on the ground and pointed the other at Ian, then before Ian could so much as blink, the killer stepped forward and rammed the spearhead deep into his belly.

There was no pain at first, just an awareness of an awesome collision, maybe like being sucker-punched in the gut by God. Then Ian felt the earth fall away beneath his feet and realised he was bring raised off the ground, impaled on the grinning - yes, he was actually grinning - maniac's spear. The pain arrived then, with all its agonising red bells and bloody whistles. Ian tried to scream, but all that came out was an odd, drawn out gargling noise. He felt his insides fill with blood as the massive spearhead chewed through him, the weight of his own body driving it deep. Then he was swung through the air, and Ian saw the rocky earth beneath rush up to violently catch him as he was slammed to the ground. A new level of ripping, tearing agony exploded in his flesh, but his stubborn body refused to grant him the mercy of passing out. He was face up, looking up at the roiling grey thunderheads that rolled across the sky above. The spear was yanked brutally from his stomach, and he found yet another new plateau of sheeting white agony. He felt the warmth sucked from his flesh as blood vacated his body in a thick coppery gush. Surely to Christ he must die now. *Surely.*

Someone kicked him in the side. Hard. More pain. Plenty. He was rolled over by the force of the blow and found himself facedown now. Then something cold, hard and extremely pointy pressed against the base of his skull, right at the top of his spine. Ian, in some way he didn't understand, knew that whatever the extremely point thing was, it was going to kill him.

He smiled into the dirt and welcomed death.

Then there was a curious *whizz-thok* sound, and a lumpy wet mass of something warm splattered the back of Ian's head and the ground around him. The sharp pressure at the back of his neck, that jaggy object that had been about to finally push him the fuck off the mortal coil, was suddenly gone.

A split second later he heard the short, sharp report of a gunshot echo across the dark water of the loch. Something huge and heavy then fell on top of him, a massive crushing weight, and Ian at last blacked out.

9

The police marksman, lying on the crest of the hill behind the little hut overlooking the tiny island, watched through the high powered sight of the Heckler and Koch PSG1 rifle as the man he had just shot fell to his knees, then onto his stomach, before slumping heavily on top of his unfortunate victim.

"Suspect down," he reported calmly into his radio. Paul McShane, the Armed Response Officer assisting in the search for the man who'd escaped the Stornoway police station that morning, had never killed a man before. Had never even had cause to draw his weapon or take aim at a suspect. He was surprised, and not a little disconcerted, at the calm he felt. He knew the full import of what he'd just done would come later though. They'd taught him that in training. Shakes, nausea, vomiting and/or fainting. Part of the job was dealing with the joys of post traumatic stress.

Paul had watched through the scope as the huge spear wielding bugger impaled the thin, long haired man and lifted him into the air like a grisly human flag before slamming him to the ground. The suspect had been moving too much for Paul to get a clear shot, but when he paused with the apparent intention of driving the spear through the back of the prone figure's neck, the crosshairs of Paul's scope had come to rest on the back of the giant's head, and he'd fired. The single 7.62 x 51 mm NATO round had been slightly off centre, tearing away a large portion from the top of the huge man's skull in a big fan of bone, blood and brains. Not the cleanest of kills, Paul thought, downright messy in fact, but a kill nonetheless. And it was his first.

Then he threw up.

10

Murdo Harrison, despite the double dose of Cocodamol he'd swallowed, was still in some amount of pain.

He thought maybe he had a cracked rib, and knew for certain that he had a bad case of whiplash. His neck was rigid and tender, and he couldn't turn his head even slightly without a bright flare of hot pain shooting up the thick tendons at the back of his neck. If it hadn't been for the riot helmet he'd been wearing, he thought there was a very good chance the back of his skull would've been stoved in when the big crazy bastard had kicked him out of the cell and sent him crashing against the wall in the corridor of the cell block. Even with his skull protected by the helmet, he'd been knocked unconscious, only coming to a few minutes later, hearing screams and shouts, crashing and banging from elsewhere in the station.

They'd requested air support from the mainland, but tracking the escaped fugitive by helicopter had been made impossible due to the sudden onset of bad weather. A thick fog bank had rolled in from the east, giving zero visibility, and the wind had picked up to almost gale force. When the dog squad had arrived at the scene of the wrecked police car in the field to aid in the search for the escaped criminal that afternoon, Harrison had watched as the well trained animals picked up the fugitive's scent right away, but had then howled and run in maddened circles, squirting urine and their tails tucked between their legs, stubbornly refusing to follow the trail despite the commands of their handlers.

Normally, when conducting a manhunt, a law enforcement officer would have at least basic details of the quarry with which to work. A name, an address, details of family and friends. This suspect however, had been a blank page. A ghost.

Following the man's rampage and escape that morning, a plea had gone out on the local radio station asking for the public's assistance in tracking him down. A description was released, and anyone who had seen or had any information on the fugitive - who was not to be approached under any circumstances and considered extremely dangerous - was urged to immediately contact the police. Aside from complaints from the public about a bearded behemoth tearing through the town centre in a police car that morning, the appeal for information on the fugitive yielded precisely fuck all in the way of useful intel.

With nothing else to go on, and considering the only thing known about the man was that he had tried to knife someone the previous night, Harrison could only work on the assumption that the suspect intended another attempt on Ian Walker's life. He called the Clune Brae Hotel where the rock star and his friends were staying for the weekend, and was informed by the receptionist that no, Mr Walker and his friends weren't in the hotel, but yes, as a matter of fact she did know where they were.

Within a minute, Harrison was having a phone conversation with Terry Scullion, owner and operator of Ardvourlie Watersports. A minute after that, Harrison, accompanied by the broken-nosed Niall Wallace, had left the search party in the field by the wrecked cruiser and headed south, eventually finding the hired minivan and empty boat trailer on the shores of Loch Langabhat. With no sign of Walker and his friends, and with helicopter support still grounded due to the worsening weather conditions, Harrison had radioed his position and requested a marine unit to search the loch. Without waiting for the boat crew to arrive, he and Niall had then turned back and driven north again in the hope of finding another route down to the lochside. They'd been some six miles along the main road that led back to Stornoway when Niall spotted the tiny, almost invisible unpaved track that branched off from the left side of the road. Harrison radioed the other search party, informing them of their position and intended heading, and Sergeant John MacAllan responded, advising that the dogs had eventually taken the scent and were leading them up the east facing side of a steep hill, on the other side of which lay Loch Langabhat. The two groups were only a mile or so apart, and they arrived at the loch practically at the same time, Harrison via the overgrown dirt trail which ended at the fugitive's bothy, and MacAllan's group at the top of the hill above him.

Harrison had exited his vehicle in a hurry, seen the bright coloured canoes beached on the little island just offshore beneath him, and looking through a pair of binoculars, had seen his quarry, the huge maniac who'd so violently busted out of jail that morning, rag dolling several police staff en route.

Down on the rocky islet below, he was now brandishing what appeared to be a spear, and advancing on the already blood soaked Ian Walker, who stood facing him, holding a single arrow in his hands. What appeared to be three bodies lay on the ground nearby, with a fourth figure, which Harrison recognised as Cal Dempster, staggering through the water toward the island.

He'd immediately radioed the order for their ARO Paul McShane to take the suspect down the second he had a clear shot. It seemed like that moment came too late however, and Harrison watched helplessly as Walker was stuck through the torso by his attacker, lifted into the air as if he were the catch on the end of a fisherman's spear, then smashed onto the rocky ground before receiving a brutal kick in the ribs for good measure. Paul McShane had then dropped the suspect before he could thrust the spear through the back of Walker's neck.

Accompanied by two ambulance medics, Harrison and officers Lorna McDaid and Peter McAuley hurried down the narrow trail to the lochside and crossed the short stretch of water to the island in an inflatable raft, part of all ambulances' equipment on Lewis due to the loch dotted nature of the island. Cal Dempster was crawling groggily out of the water, half drowned, coughing and wheezing. One of the medics rushed to help him onto dry land while the second ran to where the suspect and Ian Walker lay in an gory blood-and-brain splattered tangle of limbs. Lorna went to check on the woman, Scarlett Mathie, who was lying motionless at the water's edge by the canoes. Harrison himself quickly scanned around for the other member of the group, Matt Connell, and spotted a familiar crop of dark curly hair, half visible behind an outcrop of large boulders. He'd sent Peter McAuley to check on him.

Harrison walked over and crouched down by the still form of Clyde Farley. He didn't even bother to check for a pulse, grimacing as he saw up close the huge arrow skewering the base of the man's skull. There was hardly any blood, a sign that at least his death had been quick. Instantaneous in fact, Harrison thought. Poor bastard would probably have been dead in his shoes even before the arrow's shaft had stopped quivering.

With a sigh, he rose to his feet and walked over to where the second medic, a burly, middle-aged bald headed man by the name of Frank Gillen, was struggling to roll the suspect's massive corpse off what Harrison assumed would be Ian Walker's dead body. As he approached, he tried not to look too closely at the gore splattered ground, or the red scrambled mess that Paul McShane's bullet had made of the suspect's head.

It helped that his attention was instead drawn toward Frank Gillen, who for some reason had begun to hyperventilate and murmur in a squeaky whisper. As he drew closer, Murdo Harrison saw that the ambulance man was visibly shaking. Then he made out what Frank was whispering in that tight, almost panicky undertone, and knew there was some new level of awfulness here, because Frank Gillen, a man who Harrison knew from experience to be reliably stoic and professional in his sometimes gory work, was praying.

"...hail Mary full of grace the Lord is with thee blessed art thou amongst women and blessed is the fruit of thy womb Jesus..."

Harrison looked over Frank's shoulder,

The medic had already cut away Walker's clothing to examine the wound beneath, revealing a gaping red fissure in his lower torso, all blood, torn skin and ripped bulging innards. It looked like a small bomb had gone off in the man's guts. Then Murdo Harrison saw something that couldn't possibly be real, and the world seemed to take a peculiar side step.

The wound was healing itself.

Walker's intestines slowly slithered back into his open stomach cavity like a squirming mass of fat purple worms seeking shelter from the sun, and the ragged edges of the hideous injury drew together as if manipulated by invisible hands, the tattered bloody flesh and torn skin seemingly self generating new tissue as the hole in Walker's torso drew shut like a puckering mouth. The musician was seemingly unconscious, but his limbs and head twitched and convulsed violently as if he were in the midst of an epileptic fit as the terrifying, miraculous regeneration of his body took place.

Thought it seemed much longer, it took less than a minute for the horrific rent in Walker's belly to completely seal itself. The two men then watched the skin of his abdomen literally crawling, as out of nothing, mottled scar tissue appeared where just moments before there'd been a huge – and undeniably fatal - open wound.

After a few failed attempts to speak, Harrison found his voice. It was less than steady.

"I guess that spear didn't actually go into this guy, eh Frank?" he muttered, still unable to tear his eyes away from the blood-soaked impossibility lying on the ground in front of him.

"Fuck me," the medic replied in a cracked whisper.

"Spearhead must've just got snagged in his clothes."

"Fuck... *me*."

"I mean, if he'd actually taken a spear in the guts and then swung about like that, he'd be lying here all torn up to shit, right?"

"Holy Jesus. Holy *fucking shit...*"

"But he's not, is he, Frank?"

"I don't... I mean... I've never..."

"I think when I write this up, I'll say that the spearhead deflected off this guy's belt buckle, slid off and got caught in his shirt without actually touching him. That sound about right to you?"

"Didn't touch him. Aye. That sounds... *fuck me*."

"Aye. Might be an idea to make sure we both say the same thing, know what I mean? Think you can write something along those lines when you do your report?"

"My report. Aye. I think that's just what I'll say. Deflected off his belt buckle. Lucky bastard. A miracle..."

"Aye. A miracle."

Walker's spasmodic twitching and trembling had lessened and eventually ceased while Harrison and Frank Gillen got their stories straight. The musician then opened his eyes, gave one final massive lurch as if from a strong electrical shock, and turned his head toward the two men, a look on his face that was part dismay, part guilt and part alarm. He clutched at his miraculously restored belly, finding it whole. When he opened his mouth to speak, Harrison cut him off before he could say anything.

"You're alright, son. I was just saying to Frank here how lucky you are that that spear came off your belt buckle. Isn't that right, Frank?"

"Aye," confirmed the trembling, white faced medic at his side. "You're... lucky."

Harrison saw Walker understood what they were, and weren't, saying.

"Sergeant, I..." he began.

"No. Don't say a fucking word, pal," Harrison interrupted. "We sure as shit aren't going to. Deal?"

A look of abject misery had creased Walker's face then. He covered his face with both hands, and gave a single nod. Harrison thought he was weeping behind his blood caked fingers.

Later, Murdo Harrison watched from outside the doorway of the tiny earth and wood bothy where the nameless giant had evidently lived, as the nylon suited forensic team carefully removed his weapons and deposited them in plastic evidence bags. The longsword and the massive double headed axe. The longbow and half full quiver of oversized arrows.

He felt a chill of disquiet at the sight of the arsenal. Just by looking at the antiquated weaponry, he could tell they were old. Very old. He felt certain though, that were he to run his finger along the edge of any one of them, he would part flesh and draw blood.

Turning way from the shack, Harrison looked down the hill and watched with a heavy heart as the bodies of Clyde Farley and Matt Connell were ferried across the short stretch of water separating the island from the loch's shore. He'd already taken a statement, the second in as many days, from the heavily concussed Cal Dempster, who'd spoken in a hollow monotone, staring intently at the ground and pressing a thick gauze pad to the arrow wound on his shoulder as he related what had happened to his group on the little island. Dempster and Scarlett Mathie, who'd also suffered a concussion as well as a suspected cracked cheekbone, were now sat in the back of Peter and Lorna's car. Their injuries, though no doubt painful, weren't life threatening.

Harrison watched as Farley and Connell's bodies were loaded into the ambulance. The corpse of their murderer would make the trip into town in the back of the police van. He turned away and walked towards his own car, deeply troubled by the day's horrific and impossible events. He climbed wearily into the front passenger seat, nodding a silent acknowledgement to Niall Wallace who sat behind the wheel, and shooting a nervous glance at Ian Walker, who sat in the back. Neither man spoke. Harrison didn't know whether to feel sorry for the musician in the back seat, or be terrified of him.

He just then noticed how dark it was getting, though it was the height of summer and barely four in the afternoon.

Then he remembered.

The eclipse.

It'd been all over the news the past couple of days, but with all that had happened, watching the majestic waltz of the heavens had not been at the forefront of his mind. The moon passing in front of the sun. Whoop-de-fucking doo. Compared to certain other things he'd witnessed that day, a solar eclipse was really not that impressive.

Nevertheless, with nothing better to do right then than think very dark and disturbing thoughts, he ducked his head out the car window and looked up. The sky overhead was veiled with a thin vaporous overcastting of cloud which shaded the sun's glare, making it possible to see that a fair portion of the moon had already passed in front, and was at the second contact phase of the eclipse. Harrison had read up a little on eclipses in the past few weeks, and had actually been looking forward to the event.

As they waited for the vehicles behind to clear the single lane trail so they could set off, the car's radio crackled to life. The comms controller back at the station was informing all officers of a reported serious disturbance at the Calanais Visitor Centre.

What a fucking day, Harrison thought tiredly, pinching the bridge of his nose.

11

Jack Powning was looking downrange at the wooden man twenty metres away, the blade of a throwing knife held lightly between the fingers of his right hand, cocked back over his shoulder. The small group of eager spectators standing behind him were holding their collective breaths in an expectant hush.

Then someone screamed from somewhere in the direction of the stones. Frowning, Jack lowered his throwing arm and turned towards the sound.

"Excuse me a minute, folks," he said to the watching group, all of whom were also looking curiously in the direction the cry had come from. Jack stepped back behind the work bench of the forge where he's just finished his second metalworking demonstration of the day and deposited the throwing knife on the rack of finished steel, then hurried off in the direction of the stone circle, a nervous tightening in his stomach. With the earlier incident involving the birds, it had been a strange day so far to say the least, and now this, whatever it was.

Arriving at the ancient monoliths, Jack saw an agitated group of people, their backs to him, crowded around something on the ground. Someone was urgently calling for a doctor. He walked over to the huddle of visitors just as Gordon came hurrying along the gravel path to his right, a look of concern, and something else, on his face. Jack noticed how pale his boss and mentor looked.

"What's going on?" Gordon asked, a noticeable quaver in his voice.

"No idea," Jack said as they drew closer.

It was a young woman that lay on the ground, her eyes closed, apparently unconscious.

"Move back please," Gordon was saying as he gently pushed through the press of bodies surrounding her. Dressed in a pair of jeans and a plain white top, she was breathing rapidly, and beads of sweat covered her brow. Occasionally, her half flexed fingers would twitch.

"Please, people, move back," Gordon urged the crowd as he crouched by her side. No one paid much attention to him, reluctant to miss being so close to the little drama. An anxious looking young man knelt next to the unconscious woman, gently patting her cheek. Her boyfriend, Jack assumed.

"Sharon?" the guy was quietly asking her, his voice tight with concern. "Sharon, you okay, babe?" The unconscious woman didn't respond.

"What happened?" Gordon asked, feeling the woman's sweaty brow with his hand.

"I don't know," the guy replied shakily. "We were looking at the stones here when she just screamed and then keeled over."

"You were looking at the stones?" Gordon asked, as if aghast at the idea. Sharon's boyfriend gave him a quizzical look.

"Well... yeah. That's why we came here, you know? To see the st..."

He never finished the sentence. From behind the little crowd of onlookers, there came another high pitched shriek of fright. Jack looked round to see a teenage boy of about fifteen wearing a Metallica t-shirt, staring with a look of absolute terror at the stone obelisks. Jack followed the lad's stricken eyes, searching among the tall stones for whatever had freaked the boy out, but could see nothing. Turning back to the kid, Jack saw him backing away, his hands raised before him as if warding off some unseen threat.

"*Whatthefuckwhatthefuckwhatthefuck...*" the teenager was gasping in a continuous breathless stream, his eyes unnaturally wide and a string of saliva spilling from his slack lips. Then he fell to the ground in a dead faint, straight down, as if his legs had suddenly turned to tissue paper. The group of tourists began to shift nervously and glance at each other in fear as they realised something very wrong was happening.

That was when Jack felt it. A weird, sick pressure in the air and inside his head, like you might feel when diving to uncomfortable depths in a polluted swimming pool. A roiling greasy nausea in his stomach.

He started to become afraid then, and looking around wildly, saw several of the other visitors wincing and shaking their heads, putting their hands over their ears as if to block out some unpleasant sound. He heard someone retching. Someone else screamed.

Then things really went to shit.

As if gripped by an abrupt mass hysteria, the crowd scattered, shouting and crying in sudden panic, pushing and shoving each other out of the way in a terrorized stampede to be away from... whatever was going on. Jack heard Gordon somewhere, trying to keep his raised voice calm, but not making a very good job of it, instructing the crowd to start making their way to the exit gate. Another sound came from somewhere to Jack's left. More of a high pitched, grunting bleat of pain than an actual scream. The sound of it brought to Jack's mind an image of an animal being clumsily slaughtered. Someone barged into him, knocking him to the grass. From his ground level point of view, Jack saw a shrieking woman lifted kicking into the air as if suspended on invisible wires. His eyes closed and he clutched the sides of his head as a terrible cacophony then erupted inside his skull. A hideous, garbled mixture of deep gurgling laughter, and a chorus of discordant howling.

Jack was half aware that he was rolling on the ground, futilely trying to get away from the horrible noise in his head, whimpering in the back of his throat and fighting for breath. Still the riot in his mind intensified. The awful gravelly sniggering. That unearthly wolfish shrieking. Becoming louder, louder, louder...

The vile uproar in his mind ceased as if it had never been, and Jack was left with a strident ringing in his ears. He sat up, gasping for breath and looked around.

The area around him and between the standing stones was littered with bodies.

For a moment, Jack's mind reeled at the sight of some forty odd lifeless corpses strewn around the grass, and he felt the air punched from his lungs. Then the corpses began to move, and he realised they weren't dead bodies after all, just people who had fallen to the ground as he had. The visitors gradually sat up, looking around in confusion as if they'd fallen asleep and then woken up in a strange place with no memory of how they'd got there. Jack saw Gordon a few metres away, sitting with his head between his knees. He pushed himself to his feet and went over to crouch by the older man, laying a hand on his trembling shoulder.

"Gordon, you okay?" he asked.

Gordon jerked his head up at the mention of his name, fixing Jack with a strange expression. For a moment, it seemed he was trying to speak but had been struck dumb.

"Did you hear it, Jack? That *noise?*" he said after a moment.

Jack held Gordon's traumatised stare for a second. He considered saying he hadn't heard anything, a means of trying to convince himself that that hideous chortling and the baying of wolves in his head had been a figment of his imagination, but he couldn't do it. It had been real. He was at a loss to explain it, and frightened to even think about it, but it had been real. Very much so. That glimpse he'd had of that woman, seemingly levitating as she screamed and kicked...

He just nodded, averting Gordon's eyes, and in doing so, saw that the visitors were now hastening away towards the car park, their thirst for historic culture apparently sated for the day.

Jack realised Gordon was saying something, whispering under his breath, and he turned back to his employer and adopted father, still sat on the ground with his head bent between his knees like someone fighting the urge to vomit.

"What did you say, Gordon?"

Gordon McLeod raised his eyes, and Jack felt a fresh wave of fear at the stricken look he saw there.

"Something's come through, Jack."

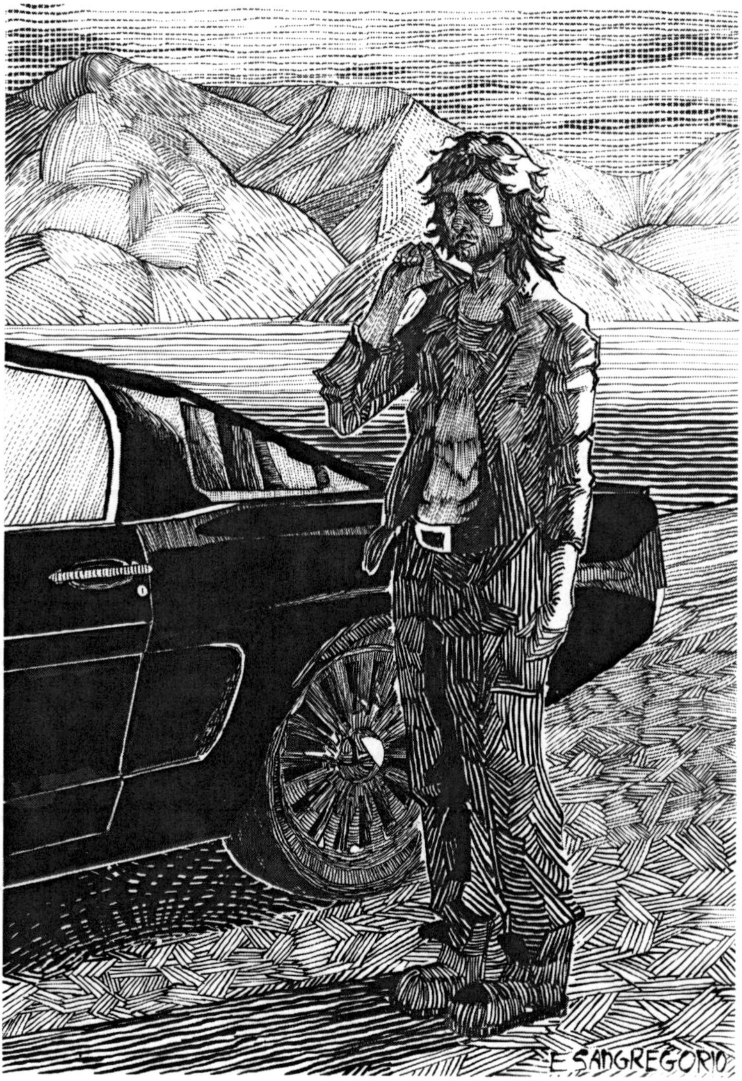
E. SANGREGORIO

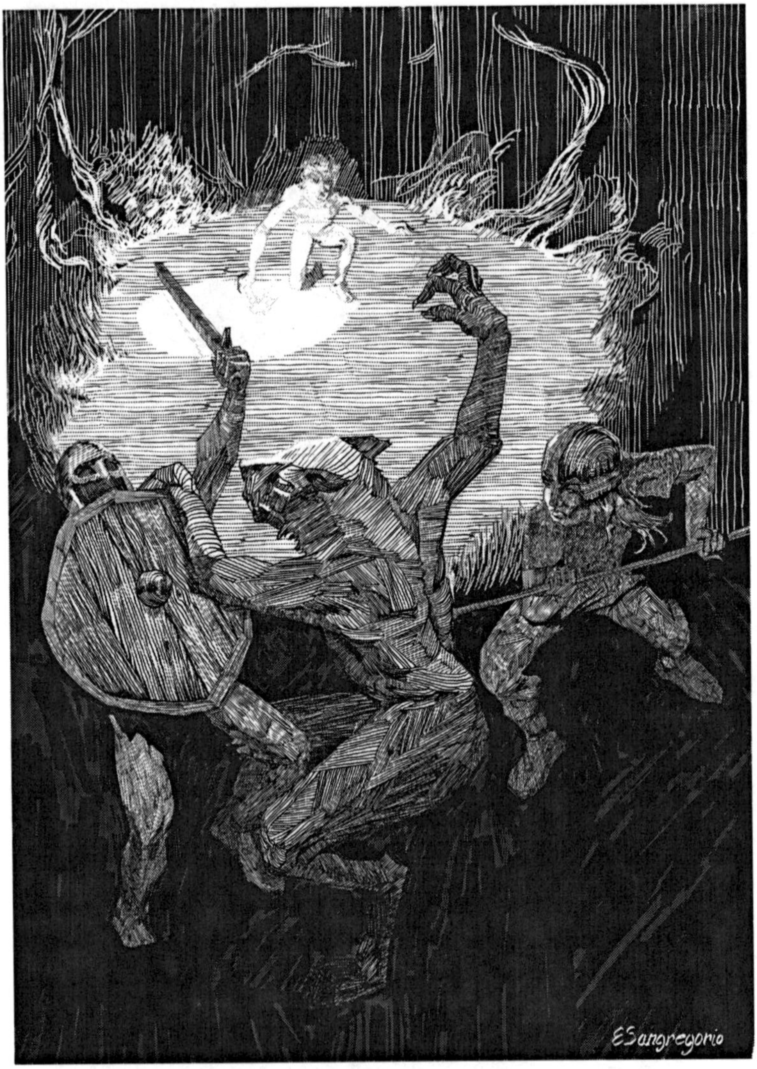
ESangregorio

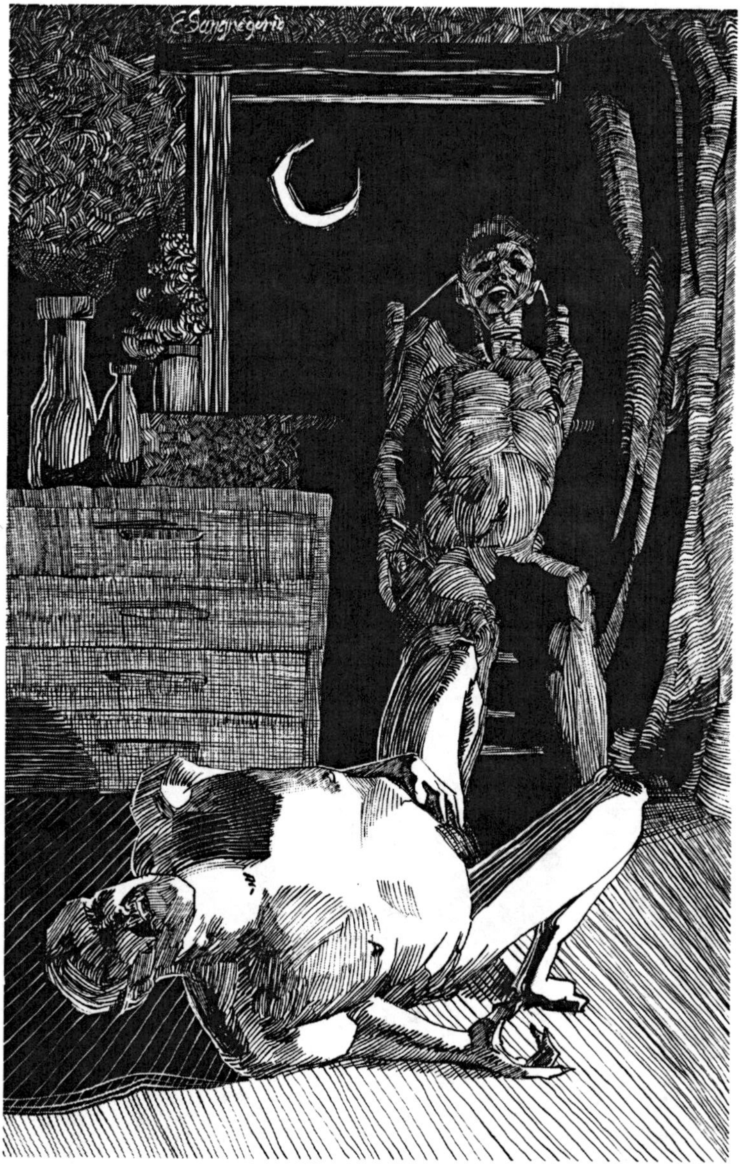

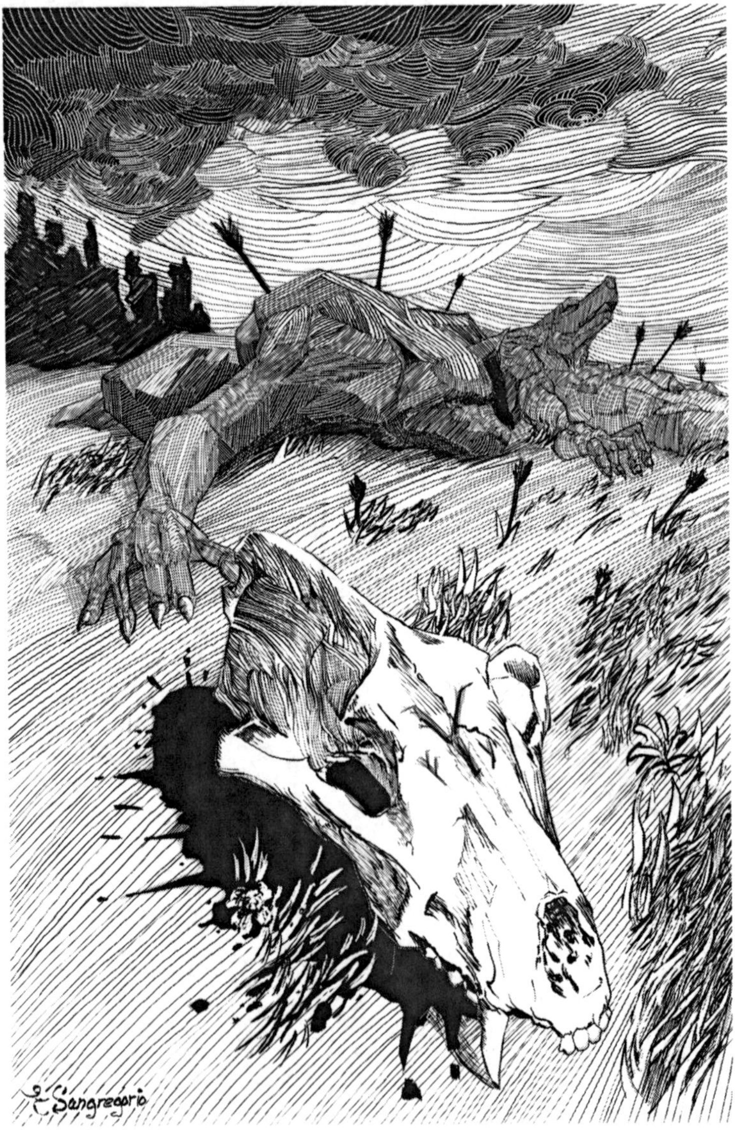
Sangregorio

PART EIGHT

Gestumblindi:
What is that lamp which lights up men,
But flame engulfs it,
And vargs grasp after it always?

King Heidrek:
Good riddle. It is the sun.
She lights up every land and shines over all man,
And Skol and Hati are called vargs.
Those are wolves, one going before the sun, the other after.

<u>The Saga of Hervor and King Heidrek the Wise</u>

1

They found young Taran's body in the shadows behind what had been Searc and Una's hut. His chewed and half crushed head, they found nearby.

The corpse of Macrath, the tall archer who'd been part of Ulfar and Ailde's group, was discovered soon after. He'd been bitten almost in two through the chest.

Ospak, one of the Nordic twins who'd taken on the great wolf with their swords, lingered for two days before finally succumbing to a fierce infection that spread outward from the suppurating stump of his severed leg, ravaging his body with fever despite the application of the white hot brand they'd used to seal the stump and hopefully purge the wound. Ospak's heartbroken twin Osvald had stayed with him the entire time, taking neither food nor sleep as he sat by his dying brother's cot, keeping vigil, keeping watch in case his brother turned, as Searc had. The grim faced Norseman kept his sword close, drawn and ready through those two black days as his sibling thrashed and raved, maddened by the foul infection that ran amok through his flesh. He did not turn however, and when he finally moved on, Osvald spent a whole day reverently washing and preparing his brother's wasted body before placing it, fully clothed and armoured, sword in hand, atop a pyre of oil soaked wood and bracken which he then set to flame.

Camran, the blacksmith of Neig followed Ospak into the afterlife the next day. His belly had been torn open by the cruel talons of the wolf.

Odhran too was stricken with the burning infection. As was the case with Ospak, the searing use of heated irons did little to clean the weeping puncture marks on his back where the claws of the vargulf had pierced him. It was expected that he too would perish.

But Odhran clung grimly to life, refusing to be beaten by the infection, and survived the blight of his blood. Out of respect for the stricken chieftain, any discussion about how the survivors would proceed with their struggle against the shapeshifters had been postponed until Odhran either recovered, or died.

Seven days later, Odhran rose unsteadily from his bed, and immediately called a council. Vandrad, Breck, Drostan, Ulfar, Ailde, Gabhran, Uallas and Osvald soon arrived in his hut, and after they greeted the recovered chieftain, embracing him and complimenting him on his strong constitution, Odhran bid Vandrad begin, and after a moment's thought, the warrior spoke.

"I have until now underestimated our enemy. The *hamrammr* are no mindless killers. They are skilled warriors with centuries of battle experience. They are cunning, able to strategise. The Ulfhednar are aware that we possess some knowledge of their kind, which is why they have not directly attacked Neig again. It is the reason they let Searc go and sent him back among us, poisoned, not bitten. They knew we would check him for wounds." He paused, making sure everyone understood what he was saying. "And their plan worked," Vandrad went on. "The vargulf that consumed Searc left five of us dead. And yet just a single arrow of plain wood and iron brought it down. And what a mighty arrow it was," he said, turning to the Breck. "Never have I seen such a shot."

Breck nodded in silent modestly while the others harrumphed in agreement with Vandrad, yet again praising Breck's deadly bow skills and slapping him on the back.

Vandrad continued, raising his voice slightly. "Either we stay here and wait for them to try and infiltrate us again, cowering behind these walls and everyday fearful of what may be lurking beneath our neighbours' skins, or we march out and finish this."

The others in the room nodded eagerly. "*FIGHT!*" Ulfar loudly opined, thumping a great ham sized fist on the table. That much of the islander's language he understood.

"I am not one for cowering," Vandrad said, leaning forward, "And as cunning as our enemy is, no foe is as sly as a house burning down around them. I suggest we increase our number as much as we are able. We swell our ranks with men, and women, from every village, farm, homestead and settlement we can reach, and we arm and train them with fire and bow. Then we find these mongrels' lair, and we burn it, and those within, to ashes."

2

The following days saw the people of Neig throw themselves into their training and preparation with a new level of grim urgency, and the hilltop fort became a bustling hive of activity. The villagers had been sorely wounded by the deaths of those lost to the jaws of the vargulf that had run amok behind their walls, and it had not taken long for their grief and shock to turn to thoughts of retribution.

Knowing the darkening mood of his people and their desire for action, Odhran had called an urgent village gathering after the council had broken up, in which he laid out the plans they had decided on.

The populace were to a man in ready agreement with their intended course of action, to marshal their full strength, then march out with the intention of finding and incinerating the lair of the demons, adding to their number with anyone willing to join them as they went. The chieftain called for anyone who could fire a bow to come forward, women included. There was no shortage of volunteers, and Vandrad found his little army suddenly swollen by some thirty odd vengeful mothers, daughters and sisters, bringing the total number of fighters under his command to almost a hundred.

The women of Neig quickly took to their new vocation with a steely determination. Many were already well familiar and skilled with the bow, hunting game being part of their daily routine, and Vandrad was pleased with the swift progress they made. He altered the training regime, spending less time on hand to hand combat practice while doubling the amount of archery training, and every villager not part of the fighting force was set to work as either a fletcher or bow maker, providing arms and ammunition for the archers.

Then the survivors from other settlements began to appear.

Alone or in small, tattered groups of twos and threes they came, stumbling in from the wilds exhausted and terrified. They came from villages and settlements that lay to the west of Neig, built along the inland fringes of the large coastal forest which provided plentiful game, building materials and fuel for those who lived within its reach.

What they spoke of was horrific, and all too familiar to Breck, who listened with dismay to their fearful accounts.

They had come from the woods in the night, the survivors said, and fallen upon their homes while they slept. Great wolf like creatures that walked on two legs, some of them armed with swords, axes, and spears, others laying waste with claw and fang. Burning, maiming and killing at will. Most of the settlements along the eastern edge of the forest were gone now, they said, burned to the ground and the populace within slaughtered or fled in terror from the demonic raiders.

Also, there had been whispers of great wolves the size of ponies roaming the inner depths of the forest. The ones the monstrous raiders infected but left alive. The cursed unfortunates devoured from the inside out, twisted and transformed into *vargulfen*.

Several torn corpses, both animal and human, and empty blood splattered cabins had been found in the woods, while other forest dwellings had been discovered reduced to ashes, their inhabitants vanished without trace. No one dared venture into the western woods anymore, and even the outlying villages that had not been attacked had been abandoned for fear of the evil that had taken up residence in the dark regions beneath the treetops.

By the time a month had passed, over a score of refugees from the west had arrived at Neig's gates. After that, they heard no more of survivors.

When they had first begun to show up, there had been some heated debate about whether to admit the frightened and desperate people to the fortified village. They could well be infected with the same accursed sickness as Searc had been, some said, and they were reluctant to open Neig's gates to strangers. As a solution, Vandrad ordered holding pens of thick stout logs hastily constructed, and made sure that every survivor, man woman or child, who sought sanctuary behind their walls was kept under constant armed guard for three full days. They were given food and water while secured, and were carefully checked for bites, scratches, fever or any other sign of infection. Only after three full days had passed in isolation were they allowed out of the pens to move freely about the settlement.

Another full moon passed, and once again in Odhran's roundhouse, the council gathered around a table, scrutinising a large map of cured cow hide that described the island. "Every one of those who have found their way here have come from the west," Gabhran was saying as he pointed out markings on the map showing the destroyed settlement's locations. "Feisidh, Dìobaig, Bhatain and Galltair. Abhainn also lies to the west of here, and now there have been attacks within the forest itself. They *must* be there."

"It seems likely," Vandrad agreed, nodding slowly. "There have been no reports of raids from the north, east or south."

Breck looked on as the elder members of the council discussed the possible whereabouts of their enemy. It made sense that the Ulfhednar had seemingly moved further inland and attacked the west. The north, south, and much of the central area of the island was for the main part composed of treeless uninhabited scrub, a harsh expanse of rocky infertile moors, high mountain ranges, marshes and peat bogs where little grew and the rare inhabitants lived in remote crofter's cottages and tiny fishing settlements along the lochs and inlets of the eastern coast. The western half of the island was for the main part far more populated and richer in resources.

"If you march south, down through the mountain pass," Odhran said, leaning forward and tracing a line down the map with a finger, "you may be able to recruit more men and women from the settlements along the coast. Halastra, here, is especially well populated."

It had been decided by the council that when they set out, Odhran would not be with them, weakened as he remained from his slowly healing wounds. He had at first been angered when Drostan told him, but eventually saw the sense in the decision, and had reluctantly admitted to himself that there was no way he could keep up with a marching force, and would only slow the company down. Just walking from one end of Neig to the other caused his legs to soften and his head spin with dizziness. He had grudgingly submitted to the council's will, agreeing to remain behind and watch over Neig and its inhabitants. "You could strike north up the coastline from Halastra," he continued, his thick index finger still tracing a route along the leather map, "and approach the forest from that direction." The other men gathered round the table nodded in assent, pointing out other villages and habitations they knew of along the way that could be scouted for further recruits and resources.

"If we are all in agreement then, it is settled," Vandrad concluded, rising to his feet. "We move at first light."

3

As dawn crept over the eastern horizon the next morning, Vandrad stood before the assembled army of Neig on the open green in the village centre.

In the slowly burgeoning light of the new day, a cold brisk wind slid through the hilltop settlement, mournfully whistling through gaps in the high timber walls, moaning along the gloomy paths between the roundhouses and causing the flames of the tall torches planted in the ground to flicker and waver. The shifting guttering glow of the torches and the first rays of the rising sun cast an eerie, shadow flecked half-light over the silent ranks of men and women who stood before Vandrad, equipped and ready for their journey. About the armed company stood those villagers who were staying behind, a collection of some forty folk, mainly consisting of the elderly and those too young to join the ranks of fighters. A small armed guard of ten men had also been selected to stay behind with the others, charged with the protection and defence of the settlement in the others' absence. Gabhran, who had become popular among the people of Neig, had been selected to take charge of the home guard, and the devout Christian man now looked down on the dawn assembly as he patrolled the ramparts above.

"Hear me now," Vandrad called out, addressing the men and women before him, his strong, clear voice ringing out in the frigid morning air. "In my life, I have seen much of war and blood. I have fought beside great warriors and commanded squadrons of skilled and fierce soldiers, men whose very lives were defined by war and struggle. Heroes and legends they were, all storied men of great deeds.

"But know this, my brethren - never have I stood before such a company as that which stands before me this morning. Never have I seen an army that fills my heart with such pride, for before today, most of you were not soldiers of great deeds, but simple folk. Farmers and thatchers. Potters and fishermen. Blacksmiths and weavers." Vandrad pointed his spear at individuals in the crowd before him as he named their trades, and saw them stand straighter, their spines stiffening under his recognition. He paused for a moment then went on. "But today, as we march to rid our land of the evil that has come among us, you are meek and humble no more. I have seen much of evil in this world, but in the games of the gods, for every monster there is a hero to slay it. For every devil, an avenging angel. No god, Norse or Christian, could match the wrath that you shall bring down upon your enemy."

A low muttering growl rippled through the crowd at his words. Several of those present nodded and unconsciously bared their teeth as their blood began to heat. Hands tightened reflexively on weapons and feet shifted restlessly in the dust.

"You are the flames that will burn these demons to *ashes* and the winds that will scatter them," Vandrad continued, his voice rising to a near shout. "You are the lightning that will strike, and the thunder that will roll down upon those that have killed and corrupted our friends and kin."

Again the assembled men and women responded, several more in the crowd adding their voices now as more cries of outraged anger rang out, increasingly vehement as their ire was raised with the promise of violent retribution for the horrors they had suffered.

"*I see before me a cleansing fire*," Vandrad yelled, thrusting his spear at the angrily simmering throng, "*one that only a great flood of wolf blood shall quench!*"

Several shouts of *aye!* and *burn them!* sounded out from the crowd. Vandrad nodded with grim satisfaction as he saw his fledgling warriors' confidence grow before his eyes, the desire for vengeance swelling and spreading through the clamouring ranks. The men and women of Acker and Neig stood taller, their jaws set and eyes bright.

Standing before them, the Norseman drew a deep breath, thrust his spear into the air and roared, "*You are HUNTERS! You are the SEALGAIREAN!*"

As one, the assembled crowd let loose a deafening war cry, stabbing their weapons to the sky and chanting the name with which Vandrad had just dubbed them.

"*SEALGAIREAN! SEALGAIREAN! SEALGAIREAN!*"

"Each and every one of you knows what must be done," Vandrad continued, his voice fierce and his pale eyes blazing as he paced back and forth before the eager fighters, gesturing with his spear. "You all know the enemies we face. The Sons of Fenrir and their bastard vargulfen hounds. You all know what is at stake. Should we falter, then the very existence of every man woman and child of this land is forfeit, for to the west there lurks evil such as has never been visited upon these shores. But we will march to meet this blight, and we will be as wildfire, and we will *burn it from the face of this Earth!*"

Again, the jostling band of fighters howled approval, the angry mob seemingly now on the verge of rushing madly out the gates in search of their foe. The newly christened Sealgairean roared as one again, banging their weapons together, the fearsome din rattling through the village, rising to the heavens and seeming to shake the very ground.

Satisfied, Vandrad turned away from them, and at his signal the tall gates of Neig swung slowly open. As the column of armed men and women filed out and set foot on the downward sloping path outside, those who stayed behind parted before them, touching the warriors' heads and shoulders as they passed and offering blessings and prayers for their protection and safe return. Small children wept as they clung to departing mothers and fathers. The parents embraced their sons and daughters tightly, whispering their love and farewells before turning their offspring over to the elders charged with their care. Then they forced themselves to turn their backs and walk away.

As the last of the company and their accompanying caravan of pack animals laden with supplies passed through the gates, the remaining villagers began to chant, their collected voices rising gradually until it was a defiant cry that echoed around the surrounding hills and rang out across the still morning waters of the misty loch below.

SEALGAIREAN!
SEALGAIREAN!
SEALGAIREAN!
SEALGAIREAN!

4

They'd been marching for about hour when Osvald, who'd volunteered for rear guard duty, turned round and looked back the way they'd come, letting the column draw ahead of him momentarily.

The settlement of Neig was now visible only as a slight bump in the horizon atop a distant hill behind them to the north. Osvald felt a pang of melancholy at leaving the village behind. He and his brother had made a good life there, and he knew there was a fair chance that he would now never see it again. He whispered a quiet prayer in his native tongue, an incantation of the northlands, asking Odin's protection over Neig and its people, then he turned south once more and broke into a trot to catch up to the rest of the Sealgairean who moved purposefully away down the valley.

The meandering path they followed wound south down through a series of steep rugged hills dotted with small patches of woodland, then rose again through a dark and narrow mountain pass that twisted between looming grey walls of granite that towered high above them on all sides.

During their journey that morning, there had been clear sign of the enemy's presence. In the hills outside Neig they had found tracks, the outsized paw prints of several very large wolves, and in many areas the air was rank with the pungent reek of canine piss where the beasts had marked their territory. As they travelled further south and the land rose toward the mountain pass, the Sealgairean had come across more than one isolated hill dwelling, their doors broken down and gouged with great claw marks, the huts themselves empty but for a gamey animal stench, the walls and floor splattered and smeared with dried blood and torn human remains. At each site, they offered prayers over the ransacked huts, then set them aflame before moving on, their hearts a little heavier.

They emerged from the bleak razor backed mountains in the late morning, passing from the narrow enclosed trail onto wide highland scrub, below which the entire south western corner of the island lay spread out.

Looking ahead to the southern half of the island, the land continued on the left into the far distance, pushing out of the sea in a series of dramatic mountains and scattered rocky islands, gradually narrowing to a long peninsula far off on the horizon. East and west of their position, the land sloped down on either side, flattening towards the coastline that was a haphazard series of cliffs, sea lochs, wide sandy beaches and rocky outcrops cutting into the sea. Beyond the western coast on the right the great ocean held sway, stretching away as far as the eye could see, vast and endless, to the very edge of the world.

Osvald's grandfather Agnar had always told him and his brother that the world *had* no edge beyond the sea, and the grizzled old warrior would often spin fantastic stories of a mysterious place far away across the great ocean - a vast land of unimaginable size, inhabited by strange animals and fierce red skinned warriors. A far off continent discovered by intrepid Norse heroes, who had named it Vinland.

From the Sealgairean's elevated position, Osvald could also make out in the far distance the forest that was the suspected lair of their enemy, a large area of dense woodland on the west coast that sprawled inland, smothering a sizeable portion of the land in a thick green blanket. He stood for a moment, letting the rest of the moving column flow around him as he stared at the far off trees.

Soon, my brother, Osvald thought as he looked toward the forest, and was startled from his grim reverie by a hand clapping him roughly on the shoulder. He turned to see Ulfar grinning at him.

"Come," the big man said in the Norse tongue as he passed. "The day grows short, and the hamrammr will not kill themselves."

Leaving the bare high ground behind, the Sealgairean descended down a steep valley where vegetation once more began to appear, precariously clinging to life on the high rocky slopes of the foothills. As they made their way down, they encountered more evidence of their quarry when they came upon a few smallholdings. Modest farms where crofters had scratched out a meagre living from the patches of fertile land amid the barren rock. The livestock here lay in humming, fly covered pieces. Torn open, their insides, limbs and heads scattered around, but the carcasses for the most part uneaten. The small dwellings where the herd owners had presumably lived were either cold and deserted, or familiar sickening scenes of mindless red slaughter. These too were put to the torch before the Sealgairean pressed on.

They moved quickly down from the foothills, bearing westward toward the coast and passing into sloping meadows of high grass, until cresting a rise in the folds of the land, they looked down upon a large settlement that sprawled out beneath them. Nestled beneath high cliffs at the mouth of an estuary, Halastra was more of a town than a village, with a busy harbour constructed along the waterfront which was ever lively with trade and merchants from the mainland and beyond. From their elevated vantage point, Osvald could see a flotilla of boats berthing just offshore. They hoped to reach the harbour town before nightfall.

Vandrad turned to Osvald as they marched. "We have made good time. I feared we might not reach Halastra before sunset."

Osvald nodded. "The Sealgairean move with purpose. Thoughts of vengeance can put extra miles in a man's stride. In a woman's too, it seems."

Although there had been no arguments against the recruitment of women into their force, many of the men of Neig had expected that their inclusion would inevitably slow and hinder their march. Despite these misgivings, there had not been a single complaint of tiredness or request for rest from any one of the Sisters, as the female members of the Sealgairean had come to be known, and they matched the men step for step in their passage down the pass through the mountains.

Those steps were coming harder now, though. It had been a long, hard day's march, weighed down not only with the equipment every member of the company carried, but by the terrible sights they had witnessed along the way.

"I for one will be glad of a bed this night," Osvald said, wincing and hitching his heavy shoulder slung equipment belt up on his back as he walked. Along with the short sword he carried on his hip and the bow and quiver of arrows secured across his back, he also carried a great double headed battle axe in a leather harness, and had felt the deadly weight of it in each step he had taken that day. "It has been a long time since I marched to battle."

"I heard that," a female voice said behind him. "You're not tiring are you, Osvald?"

Osvald turned back to see Kadlin, Ulfar's wife, grinning at him. By her side, Ulfar laughed and favoured her with a look of pride. The short, stocky Norsewoman, who carried as much equipment as anyone on her back, had become something of a mother figure to the Sisters of the Sealgairean.

"Never," Osvald replied stoically, facing forward again and making an effort to stand straighter. "I could march all day and through the night."

Kadlin snorted laughter.

"You carry a heavy weapon," Vandrad said as they walked on, nodding at the great axe on Osvald's back. "Along with your sword and bow, you bear that tree feller. Do you not think yourself over equipped?"

Osvald shook his head. "It belonged to my brother. Originally it was our grandfather's, then our father's. He passed it to Ospak as he was the elder of us, though only by a few minutes."

"I would have him with us in this fight," Vandrad said laying a hand on Osvald's shoulder. "Ospak was a fine warrior."

Osvald shrugged. "He died in battle. It was a good death."

To Osvald, the days his twin brother had spent lingering on the edges of the afterlife, raving and racked with fever did not matter. He had sustained the wound that killed him in battle, and as such, now resided with their fathers by Odin's side in the halls of Valhalla. He had not died a shameful 'straw death', expiring in his bed of old age. The great axe he carried, named **Rimmugýgr**, the Battle Hag, was a burdensome weight, however, and Osvald found himself partly wishing that their grandfather had passed down a simple dagger instead.

"Well, you can soon rest your poor weary feet, Osvald," said Kadlin behind him, continuing her good natured taunting. Osvald smiled to himself. It was just like Ulfar's wife to distract others' melancholy with humour. "Halastra draws near. You will soon be able to set down your heavy..." her words died away, and Osvald turned back to her.

Kadlin wore an expression of puzzlement, and was looking around as if searching for something. They were making their way along a path that cut through the wheat fields above Halastra, the tall ripe stalks on either side of the marching column swaying gently in the early evening breeze.

"What troubles you, my little shield maiden?" Ulfar asked his wife with a fond smile.

"It's so quiet," she said, frowning. "The field workers. Where are they?"

Osvald realised she was right. It was harvest season, and there was still at least an hour before sunset. Normally those who gathered in the crops upon which any settlement's prosperity depended worked as long as there was daylight to see by, and the air should have been filled with the lively conversation and reaping songs of the field workers as they collected and brought in the sheaves.

But the fields were empty, the only sounds the gentle soughing rustle of wind-stirred wheat and the cawing of crows, which Osvald then realised seemed to be overly loud and raucous. A sense of foreboding settled in his bones. Halastra was no isolated farmer's hut, nor even a small village. If a settlement of its size had shared the same fate as the other habitations they had passed that day...

Vandrad held a hand in the air, bringing the column to a halt. Osvald saw him frown in consternation, turning his head this way and that, looking and listening for some sign of human activity.

There was none.

"We must make haste," Vandrad said shortly. "Osvald, you and Ulfar fall back to the rear of the column and watch our back. Something is wrong here."

5

Drostan, walking at the head of the column with Vandrad and Uallas, felt a familiar sense of growing desolation as they continued through the fields above Halastra, and it was not long before their fears were confirmed.

They found the first body a short distance along the trail that ran between the crops. A young woman, lying in the dust in an undignified ragged bundle, her throat and belly torn open and an open mouthed expression of pained terror frozen on her face, as if she had died in mid scream. The crows feasting on her had already taken her eyes.

As the Sealgairean approached, the fat waddling birds cawed irritably at the interruption and took wing, reluctantly abandoning their grisly meal. The woman's overturned basket and hand sickle lay nearby, the curved reaping tool's blade streaked a rusty reddish brown, suggesting she had at least managed to wound her attacker before she died. All around the strewn red remains, great paw prints were clearly evident in the dusty surface of the trail, and here again, the air was rank with the pungent wild reek of wolf piss.

"No more than a day or two," Uallas muttered, squatting by the corpse to examine the sickening scene, swatting at the hordes of flies that buzzed and crawled over the body in a grotesque humming mass.

Drostan looked down on the ravaged, shattered mess of the girl's body and felt a great well of pity and loathing rise up within him. He had seen several corpses that day during the march south from Neig, but none so recently butchered.

As the Sealgairean continued warily down the field path, they found the broken and debased ruins of several more victims. At each kill, the remains were obscured by the obscene shifting black masses of squabbling overfed crows and clouds of flies enjoying their own harvest as they made fine fare of the slaughter. The befouled air about each bloody scene was eye stingingly ripe with a foul perfume was the very essence of death.

And everywhere, the huge paw prints.

Further along the trail, the hayfields came to an end and the terrain opened up to green pasture set aside for grazing. The only life in evidence in the paddocks, however, were the shifting, winged black mounds where flies and avian scavengers supped on the mutilated carcasses of Halastra's livestock. Hundreds more crows circled hungrily in the sky above, the shrill cawing of the murder a chilling auditory accompaniment to the macabre scene.

Beyond the pastures, the town of Halastra lay still.

Drostan knew the place well, having lived there for a time in his youth. Like Neig, the busy coastal settlement had in years past been often targeted by sea raiders from the Northlands who came for the rich pickings that were to be found in the small but prosperous trading port. To defend against attacks, around the settlement the inhabitants had erected a high wall of stone and timber that rose to four times the height of a man. Now, from behind the walls, a few trails of wispy grey smoke could be seen rising into the air. Not the thick black smoke of burning buildings, but such as was produced by a simple peat fire, a smokehouse or a smithy. Despite this sign that there *was* still life within the town, nothing moved outside or atop the walls. No one came and went to or from the settlement, and the wide wood and iron gated entrance to Halastra was barred shut. As the column drew closer, it became possible to discern that the ground in front of the gates was also littered with several more dark mounds, indicating further corpses, though from this distance it was impossible to tell if they were of animal or human origin.

As the Sealgairean cautiously approached the walled town, a voice rang out, coming from somewhere ahead. "Halt!"

Beside Drostan, Vandrad immediately raised a hand, and the column behind him came to an uneven stop as the order to remain still was passed back along the line.

"Do not think to move," the voice came again. Despite the implicit warning in the words, there was a discernible measure of fear in the speaker's tone. "There are a hundred arrows trained on you. State your business in Halastra."

Drostan stepped slowly forward. Before setting out from Neig, it had been agreed that as a chieftain known by many on the island, he would be the one to speak for the Sealgairean at any settlement they came to. "It is I, Drostan of Acker," he called to the unseen watchman. "I come with help, and would have words with Ronan, your chieftain. We mean you no harm."

There was no reply, and tense minutes passed while the column behind Drostan shifted nervously, glancing around the walls for the unseen archers with which they had been threatened. Drostan felt a touch on his shoulder and turned to see Vandrad regarding him.

"You are on good terms with the leader of this place?" the Norseman asked. "We can ill afford to spend a night in the open."

"Well enough," Drostan answered. In truth, it had been many years since he had last spoke with Ronan, but they had known one another during the time that Drostan had lived in Halastra. He only hoped that the chieftain remembered him, for to the west, the sun was not far from touching the horizon. Night, and all the terrors that it brought in recent times, was drawing near. The Sealgairean behind him had also noticed the encroaching dusk, and were beginning to grow restless as they stood there, the walled town before them and the fields of uncounted crow pecked corpses behind.

Drostan was about to hail the watch again when another voice, deeper and more authoritative that the first, rang out from the wall.

"Drostan? Is it truly you?"

Drostan at once recognised the voice. "Ronan," he called back. "It does my heart good to hear your voice, old friend. I come with the people of Neig, your neighbours to the north. We know of the evil that has beset you, and we seek an alliance, but we have been on the road since dawn and beg shelter for the night."

"Come closer," Ronan's voice responded from the wall. "Approach the gate so that I may see you clearly."

As he stepped forward, Drostan heard Vandrad whisper urgently at his back. "Be convincing, Drostan. Night is upon us."

He walked slowly forward, empty handed and arms raised in a gesture of peace as he approached the gates. As he drew closer, he was able to make out more details of the slumped dark shapes they had seen on the ground before the walls, and his heartbeat accelerated as he realised that they were the carcasses of neither livestock nor humans.

They were wolves.

Drostan counted seven of them. The huge bodies of the vargulfen were peppered with arrows and spears, and lay in bloody mounds in the churned earth before the gates, some with their jaws still agape, their massive fangs exposed. The crows and flies, notoriously uncaring about the type of carrion that provided their meals, had shunned the giant wolves' bodies, and the open eyes of the dead beasts, eerie and glassily opaque with death, regarded Drostan closely as he passed. The chieftain felt a cold tremor of dread as he stepped among the watchful corpses, and his step almost faltered as he wound his way between the enormous dead beasts. He could not help but imagine one of the slain vargulfen suddenly rearing up in snarling resurrection, all burning eyes and dripping fangs to pounce upon him.

He took a deep fortifying breath and struggled with the urge to vomit as he inhaled the unholy stink of two day old dead wolf, mingled with stale blood, shit and more canine piss. He forced himself forward, seeing as he drew closer to the main gate that its thick timbers had been deeply scored with claw marks, and appeared to have been gnawed upon in several places. The wolves had tried to chew their way into the settlement. Drostan shuddered at the insane ferocity and single minded hunger that drove the creatures.

A small hatch constructed between the logs and covered over with an iron grate creaked open to the side of the gate. Drostan stepped closer and beheld Ronan's grizzled face peering suspiciously out at him. The chieftain of Halastra had been a robust youth the last time Drostan had seen him, tall and broad of shoulder, with an open, handsome face that had charmed many of the young women of the settlement. The face that regarded him now was deeply lined and heavily bearded in wiry black curls shot through with streaks of silver. Ronan's eyes were still that peculiar and disarming shade of grey, but they no longer shone with the roguish carefree light of youth. The chieftain's eyes were as haunted as any Drostan had seen in recent times. Heavy purplish bags underscored them, and the haggard slackness of his face spoke of recent sleepless nights and the heavy burden of great worries.

"Drostan," Ronan said through the small opening, his tired eyes brightening slightly in recognition and a weary half smile forming on his lips. "It truly is you."

"Aye, Ronan. It is good to see you, but I beg you, can we greet each other within the safety of your walls? The sun sets and my people are in need of shelter."

"As are mine," Ronan replied sadly. "These are evil times."

Drostan noticed the other man made no move to open the gates. "We have seen what has happened here," he said, "and my heart is wounded for you, Ronan. The same befell Acker, my own village, not so long ago. It is a fate that has been shared by many other settlements."

Ronan nodded slightly, his expression morose. "I have heard the stories. A woman came to Halastra just three days past. Mad with terror she was, bloodied and half dead, babbling about demons slaughtering her family." Ronan paused a moment and dropped his eyes, a frown further creasing his already worried brow. When he spoke again, it was almost a whisper. "We took pity on the poor wretch and gave her shelter, tended to her wounds. She had been bitten, Drostan."

Drostan closed his eyes, dreading what he already knew the other man would say next.

"She *changed*," Ronan grated, his head still bowed. "She took on the form of a great wolf and ran wild through the settlement. Many were killed before we were able to bring the beast down. My own daughter..."

"I am sorry, Ronan," Drostan said gently. "Neig, where my people took shelter, was likewise breached. We lost many."

Ronan met his eyes again. They were full of regret. "Then you will understand why I cannot let you in," he said quietly.

"You mean to leave us out here?" Drostan asked in disbelief.

"I am sorry, Drostan, but I have my own people to protect, and you bring a large host to my door. How can I know that one, or many among you, are not such creatures?"

"Ronan, we march to rid the land of this evil, and would have your help in doing it. I swear to you, in the name of all that is holy, none of my people carry this blight in their blood. You must let us in."

"*I must do nothing*," the Chieftain hissed, his grief torn features twisting with bitterness. "You say that you have seen what has already been done to my people, Drostan, but *I watched it happen*. With my own eyes I saw my daughter's throat torn out and her body ripped to *pieces!*" Ronan's voice had risen to a shrill shout. He paused, his breath coming in ragged gasps, then continued, forcing a measure of calm into his voice. "I will not risk such a fate befalling those who still live under my protection. As a chieftain yourself, you would do the same."

Drostan stared through the iron grate at Ronan, his heart sinking. As he opened his mouth to reply, a deep mournful howl sounded out, floating across the land.

Drostan spun round in alarm, and saw that while he and Ronan had been speaking, the sun had begun to sink below the horizon.

"They fell upon the workers the next night, as they were returning from the hayfields," Ronan was saying behind him. "We could hear the screams from here. We sent men out to see what was happening, but they never returned. Then we saw them. Wolves, Drostan. A great pack of giant wolves. They came from the hayfields and fell upon the sheep and cattle. Then they attacked the walls." Ronan's eyes flicked momentarily to the huge lupine corpses lying on the ground behind Drostan. "We closed the gates, and slew those you see there from atop the walls. But there were many more, Drostan. Many more."

Another ululating cry slid across the dusk like a blade, high and hungry. It was joined immediately by a third. Then a fourth. They were getting closer.

Drostan turned back to Ronan, his eyes frantic. "Please, Ronan. You cannot abandon us. It is as good as murder."

Ronan held Drostan's desperate gaze for a moment, then looked away, averting his eyes. "I am truly sorry," he muttered. "May God be with you."

The chieftain of Halastra slid the wooden panel closed with a heavy thud, ending their conversation.

"Damn you, Ronan, you *cannot do this*," Drostan shouted at the closed panel in desperation. There was no answer.

Cursing furiously, he turned and began running back towards the Sealgairean, but stopped as he saw that the ranks of men and women were already coming to him.

6

The fields and hills behind the Sealgairean were being steadily consumed in shadow as the daylight failed, and night inexorably crept towards them in a black tide that slid slowly across the land.

Despite the horrors he'd already experienced and survived, when the far off baying of the wolves began, floating out of the gathering darkness in the west, it still had the power to turn the blood in Breck's veins to ice and to freeze his breath in his throat. The ghostly howling had barely died away before Vandrad began barking a series of curt orders.

"*To the gates!*" he bellowed. "Form up in two ranks, half moon formation, animals to the rear. Breck, Fionn. Take the torches and light the field. You know what to do. Let us see what we are killing. *Go!*"

The Sealgairean column surged down the sloping trail towards Halastra's gates. As they reached the walls and began organising themselves into two curving lines, Breck, with Odhran's son Fionn at his side, ran to one of the sturdy ponies laden with extra supplies and provisions. From the tethered mounds of equipment upon the animal's back, he took a long and thick leather wrapped bundle, and quickly cut the fastening rope tied around its middle with his belt knife. He unrolled the bundle on the ground and gathered up half of the ready prepared torches within, Fionn snatching up the others. Laden with armfuls of the torches, each one almost the height of a man, sharpened at one end and wrapped in oiled rags at the other, the two boys separated. Breck ran along the front of the curved ranks until he reached the extreme left of the front line where it met the wall of Halastra. From there, he walked left along the wall, counting out his paces as he went. When he reached a suitable distance, he dropped to his knees, set down the torches, and working as fast as he was able, drew his belt knife again and began stabbing at the earth, excavating a narrow hole in the ground. This done, he grabbed one of the torches on the ground and thrust the sharpened end into the thin fissure he had created, driving it firmly into the earth and repacking the loose soil, tamping it down firmly around the shaft with his foot. From his belt pouch he took a flint and steel, and holding it close, struck a spray of sparks onto the head of the torch. He was greatly relieved when the oiled cloth ignited almost immediately and a strong, bright flame bloomed from the dried rags, casting a wide circle of flickering orange light upon the swiftly darkening ground around him.

Breck was thankful for the hours spent rehearsing this task back in Neig before they had set out. For their youthful fleetness of foot,

Vandrad had said, he and Fionn had been given the roles of torch bearers, charged with lighting the field of battle as quickly as possible in the expected event of a night time skirmish with their nocturnal enemy. The task was a hazardous undertaking, as those placing the torches were vulnerable to attack, working in failing light and separated from their armed comrades.

The first torch placed, Breck gathered up the others, turned and ran ten paces back to the right, keeping parallel with the bowed front rank of the Sealgairean, and repeated the procedure, digging in the soil, planting a torch in the earth and setting it to flame. When he reached the wide path leading to Halastra's gate, he placed a third torch, then turned so his back was now to the walls, measured out ten paces and began again, now working right to left, staggering the second row of torches between those in front. Trying to ignore the chilling cries of the approaching wolf pack, he continued to move back and forth across the ground outside Halastra, methodically working side to side and outwards, precisely placing the torches ten paces apart in a wedge shaped pattern that threw back the darkness in front of the ranks to a distance of a hundred paces. The last torch planted and lit, he turned from the pooling darkness that now seemed to pour down off the hills to the west, and sprinted back towards the wall, running between the lit torches, glancing over to the other side of the path as he went and seeing Fionn had also finished the same task on his side of the path, and was rushing back to rejoin the Sealgairean, now fully formed up in front of the walls of Halastra. The double line of bow wielding fighters parted to let him through as Breck approached, and he joined the ranks, taking his place midway between the centre and left hand side of the standing rear line.

Those archers in the front rank had lowered themselves to one knee, allowing a clear field of fire for those standing behind. Bows were strung and arrows nocked in readiness. Those also armed with hand to hand weapons loosened swords and daggers in their scabbards, and spears, axes, pitchforks and the occasional shield were laid ready on the ground in front of the fighters where they could be snatched up quickly if needed. Behind the two rows of archers, the ponies whickered and tossed their heads nervously. The animals had been skittish all that day, unsettled by the scent of wolf urine at the site of each kill they had encountered, and now they grew more restless still, their eyes rolling in fear and hooves stamping at the earth as the ghostly baying continued to drift across the land, growing closer by the second.

To Breck's left stood Sileas, Vandrad's woman, and she nodded to him as he joined the line of archers and began stringing his bow. "It seems now we shall see if your mighty shot back in Neig was merely luck," she said, offering a nervous laugh.

Breck tried to smile back to show that he was unafraid, but it felt more like a grimace.

"It seems so," he replied, taking an arrow from the quiver on his back and notching it to the bowstring.

The pale half light of dusk had faded further, and full night now closed in around the Sealgairean, held back only by the large fan shaped area of illuminated ground before them, washed with the orange glow of the torches Breck and Fionn had planted.

"I am afraid, Breck," Sileas whispered at his side.

"As am I," he replied. "Your husband tells me fear is a good thing in small doses. It sharpens the mind. So he says. I'm not sure I agree with him."

Sileas gave him a half smile, but gasped and whipped her head to the left as another ragged howl tore through the blackness somewhere just beyond the light of the torches.

"*Stand ready my hunters!*" Vandrad's voice cried out from the centre of the front rank. "*Our quarry approaches!*"

"For Eanach," Breck said softly, pulling his bowstring to half draw. Sileas looked over at him at the mention of the village that had once been their home. There was fear in her eyes, Breck saw, but she stood with her back straight and head held high, a determined set to her jaw. She nodded once. "For Eanach," she repeated, and looked out into the blackness beyond the torchlight, waiting.

She did not have to wait long.

7

"They will die out there, Ronan."

Inside the walls of Halastra, the chieftain rounded angrily on the man at his side as they walked away from the closed gates. "And what would you have me do, Egil?" he spat. "Invite them inside, not knowing who among them may be another of those creatures? You saw with your own eyes what happened when we last offered shelter to a stranger."

Egil said nothing for a moment. The wiry shipwright's wind blown, pock marked face tightened at the memory of the horror he'd witnessed. "Yes. I saw," he replied in a near whisper. "I would not see such a thing again."

"Nor I," Ronan said, his shoulders slumping and his voice heavy with regret. "Drostan was once a trusted friend. Do not think I make this decision lightly, Egil. It wounds me greatly to turn him away from our door, but I cannot put the lives of our people at further risk."

"Our people are already at risk," Egil insisted, following in his chieftain's footsteps as Ronan turned and began walking away into the settlement. "What little supplies of meat and grain within these walls will not last long, Ronan. We cannot stay locked behind our walls forever, and this Drostan spoke of ridding the land of these monsters. A worthy cause, I think."

"Drostan was often given to unrealistic fancies," Ronan said, walking on without turning. "He came to Halastra as a young man seeking to make his fortune as a trader, but had no head for it. I think he has not changed in the years since last I saw him, and reaches still for things outwith his grasp."

"Ronan, we slew seven of the beasts ourselves. The wolves are flesh and blood. They bleed and die as well as any other animal. Perhaps there is merit in what he intends."

"Seven out of how many, Egil?" Ronan asked, turning suddenly to face the other man again. "How many fell upon our people? Those we were able to bring down were not even a quarter of those that attacked us. How many of those things do you think are out there now? *Listen to them.*"

The baying of the wolves in the hills outside Halastra was a cold and greedy many throated chorus that pierced the bones, seeming to come from every direction. Judging exact numbers of the approaching pack was impossible, but it seemed far more than a mere few. The discordant howling set Ronan's teeth on edge, ringing dread within his skull.

"I fear I will hear them until the day I die, Ronan," the shipwright said, the well defined muscles beneath the skin of his bare forearms bunching like thick ropes as he wrung his calloused hands on the shaft of the spear he carried. "I do not wish to live in fear, as I know you do not."

Ronan let out a long shuddering breath. Heart rending grief for his murdered daughter tore at him, but he had no time for sorrow with an entire settlement looking to him to somehow make the horrifying situation right. He was beset with regret and guilt at denying Drostan and his people sanctuary, but knew he had no choice. His people were frightened enough without a hundred more strangers suddenly appearing within their midst, any one of whom could potentially wreck as much bloody havoc as had the desperate woman they had foolishly taken in.

But Egil was right. Ronan could not live in fear. As chieftain of the settlement, it was his responsibility to shoulder the burdens of his people, to listen to their complaints, dispense justice when needed and above all, to protect them and to be strong for them.

"To the wall then," he said. "We cannot shelter Drostan and his party, on that I will not bend, but I will not sit behind our walls and do nothing while they are slaughtered. Gather the men."

8

The howling of the approaching wolves had faded and eventually ceased, and a tense, brittle hush settled over the torch lit ground outside the settlement.

The Sealgairean waited in taut anticipation, bows held ready, alert for the slightest sound or movement that would signal an attack. Beyond the perimeter of the torches, the night was a black wall of deep shadow, unlit by star or moonlight. The oppressive gloom pressed in from the front and sides, surrounding the fighters before the settlement walls.

Nothing moved. There was not the slightest sound.

Then the inky curtain of night beyond the torches seemed to suddenly billow inwards with shocking abruptness as the vargulfen burst from the shadows in a ravening, snarling rush, bounding towards the humans with frightening speed. A large pack of them, at least twenty in number, they came at full pelt, with no attempt at stealth or guile, streaking hungrily out of the darkness from all directions and charging into the illuminated section of ground in front of the waiting Sealgairean, their yellow eyeshine flaring brightly in the torchlight.

"*Front rank, loose!*" Vandrad roared.

With nowhere near enough time to turn each villager into an expert archer, a skill that took years to perfect, Vandrad had taught the men and women of Neig how to fight as a single unit, where numbers and discipline made up for a lack of individual accuracy. The men and women of the Sealgairean responded to the command instantly, the long hours, days, weeks and months spent in training for this moment making their reactions automatic, swift and sure, and with a loud *snap* of some fifty drawn bowstrings releasing as one, the kneeling front line of Sealgairean fired.

The volley of arrows whirred out from the half moon formation, flashing through the air to meet the rapidly closing pack, and high, yowling animal cries of pain rang out as several of the great wolves were struck. None were killed outright however, and they rampaged heedlessly forward, weaving and leaping between the torches as they came, arrows embedded in many of their bristling coats.

"*Second rank, loose!*"

The standing rear line of archers laid down a second volley. Already wounded, and with the range now shortened, a few of the onrushing predators fell this time to the barbed barrage that enveloped them, their great hairy bodies jerking and faltering as they were hit, then going skidding and tumbling ungainly along the ground, knocking torches to the earth as they thrashed and howled in their death throes.

"First rank, loose!"

Now only thirty paces from the front line and closing fast, the third concentrated volley ripped into the charging monsters with deadly effect, felling several more of the pack who pitched to the ground, kicking and snarling as they died. Several more still lived however, and they swiftly descended on the Sealgairean, pouring in from all sides, their great loping strides devouring the ground beneath as their claws flung divots of earth in their wake. Within moments, they were close enough that those in the front rank of fighters were practically staring into the wolves' red, gaping jaws.

The forward line of Sealgairean cast aside their bows, snatching up swords, spears and axes in readiness for the imminent melee.

"Second rank, loose!" Vandrad shouted, raising his spear and centring its long iron point on a massive black coated wolf rapidly bearing down on him.

As he gave the command, another voice, coming from somewhere behind and above bellowed, *"Now!"* and the air above the Sealgairean was suddenly filled with a storm of spears, arrows, rocks, axes and harpoons that rained down from the walls of Halastra behind them. The monstrous black wolf lunging at Vandrad was abruptly knocked out of the air as a barbed whaling harpoon punched into its back, the heavy projectile's falling weight driving it through fur, muscle and sinew, impaling the wolf and pinning it to the earth where it continued to thrash and scream.

The deadly hail fell among the wolves at the exact moment the fourth volley of arrows also ripped into them, the combined barrage tearing into the pack in a lethal torrent of sharpened steel, decimating the remaining beasts as they closed to within a few paces of the front rank. The vargulfen shrieked and howled as their bodies were skewered, pierced and riven by the devastating two pronged fusillade, and they fell in twitching heaps, their coarse wiry pelts matted and stained with gore, bristling with the shafts of arrows and spears. Incredibly, some yet attempted to drag their crippled, torn bodies forward, clawing at the earth as they snapped and snarled at the humans before them.

The Sealgairean needed no command from Vandrad to finish them off, and they fell upon the crippled vargulfen strewn around the blood soaked ground with sword, axe, hammer and spear, screaming in wordless rage as they laid waste to the enemy, mercilessly slashing, stabbing and pounding at the already dying animals in a wrathful frenzy.

It went on for some time.

When it was finally over, little was left of the wolf pack but formless pulped mounds of splintered bone, butchered meat and scraps of wet fur. The night air was thick and ripe with the hot coppery scent of blood, so prevalent it could be tasted upon the tongue.

As the madness of their battle fever finally dissipated and ebbed from their veins, a strange calm descended over the field, and the Sealgairean stood around, wide eyed and panting with exertion and the after effects of adrenaline, their clothing and weapons stained and dripping thick ribbons of gore that glistened blackly in the torchlight.

Not one of them had suffered so much as a single scratch.

For a long moment there was a perfect silence as the blood splattered men and women looked around at each other in confusion, regarding the horrific red butchery strewn about them as if unsure of what had just transpired.

It was Vandrad's powerful voice that sounded out over the battlefield, breaking the eerie lull. The Norseman stood tall over the carcass of one of the dead vargulfen, his great spear planted deep in the creature's chest. Dark splashes and streaks of blood patterned his face, arms and long golden hair, contrasting sharply with the pale skin and shining whites of his eyes and teeth as he grinned, baring his teeth in a fierce expression of triumph that was itself disturbingly wolfish. He spread his muscular arms wide and turned in a circle, indicating the surrounding carnage.

"*You see, my hunters?*" he cried. The others turned toward him. "*Stand proud and behold the terrible fruits of your wrath! Did I not tell you no god could unleash such ruin upon their enemy? SEALGAIREAN!*"

The brief numbing effect of battle shock broken, Vandrad's victory cry was taken up by the others, and the men and women of the Sealgairean screamed, chanting and raising their bloodied weapons to the night sky in triumph.

Absorbed in their savage celebrations, none noticed that the gates of Halastra had opened behind them, and a large party of the settlement's inhabitants now stood outside the walls regarding the blood caked, madly shrieking fighters with a combination of awe and fear.

The first of the Sealgairean to eventually become aware of the group of astonished onlookers was a young woman of Acker named Calike, who stood with one foot planted atop the smashed corpse of the giant wolf she had been intently pounding to hairy red paste. The farming flail in her hands - normally used in the separation of grain from sheave, but tonight used to part life from wolf - was caked in clinging lumps of wet viscera and coarse animal hair. Kadlin stood by her side, the stocky little Norsewoman clutching a short axe and similarly adorned in lupine remains. Calike shook her by the shoulder, pointing towards the silent throng of watchers, and Kadlin immediately called out to Drostan, who also stood nearby. The chieftain saw the watching townspeople, and indicating that Vandrad should join him, slowly made his way back across the slippery carcass littered field, the two men walking unhurriedly towards the wall where Ronan stood, a strange expression on his face that was somewhere between stark amazement and bald terror.

At Ronan's side was a thin but sharply muscled man with pale blonde hair and the salt weathered face of one who spent much of their life at sea. There was no sign of apprehension on his face. The man was actually grinning as he stood there, nodding in approval. Drostan recognised the features and tall stature of the smiling man as distinctly Norse, and his suspicions about the man's heritage were confirmed when Vandrad hailed him in their native tongue, to which the other man smiled and replied in the same strange language. The two men grasped each others' forearms in greeting.

Ronan opened his mouth to speak, but seemed to be struggling for words as he looked upon Drostan's gore splattered face and the tall, equally bloodstained warrior who accompanied him.

"Before you say anything," Drostan said, "know that I place no blame on you for your caution. We had the same doubts about taking in strangers in Neig, and you were right. In your place, with the tragedy of what befell you still fresh in the memory, I would have done the same thing."

"Dear God, Drostan…" Ronan muttered, staring over the other man's shoulder in disbelief at the corpse carpeted battlefield behind him.

"Those afflicted with the blood of the wolf turn quickly," Vandrad stated, "within a day of being infected, and the beast consumes the victim with the coming of the next night. You need not fear that any among us are so tainted, but if it will ease your mind, separate us from the rest of your people and have your men stand guard over us until morning. I ask only that you do so within your walls. Dawn is yet some time away, our people are weary from battle, and we may not have seen the last of the vargulfen this night."

"Your words do not convince me," Ronan replied after a moment's pause. He gestured at the bloody spectacle of the annihilated wolf pack lying in bludgeoned pieces about the ground before his walls. "*That* convinces me. Beyond any doubt, that convinces me."

From a scabbard on his hip, the chieftain of Halastra then drew a great broadsword and presented it in offering to Drostan. "Forgive me, old friend," he said. "You are welcome within our walls, and if you still wish an alliance, the swords of Halastra are yours to command."

9

The woods were dark.

Standing on the open moorland a ways back from the fringe of the forest, Drostan felt his belly tighten and twist as he gazed into the densely packed wall of trees that reared up before him. Ten paces to either side of him stood other fighters of the Sealgairean, each with bow in hand as they swept their gaze left and right across the treeline in front of them. Each one of them watching. Waiting.

Drostan could see only a few paces into the trees before the early afternoon daylight was consumed in the murk that pooled between the thick trunks and crowding tangle of underbrush. The high branches that made up the vast green canopy of treetops above intertwined and meshed tightly, creating a thick leafy roof that blocked the sunlight so that beyond the edges of the wood, day was as late twilight.

The Sealgairean had departed Halastra three days after they had first entered, bloodied and buzzing with adrenaline following their annihilation of the vargulfen pack. The time within the coastal town had been spent replenishing supplies, cleaning and sharpening weapons, recruiting more fighters from the population to their cause and discussing the plan to attack the lair of the Ulfhednar. Drostan and Vandrad had spent many hours poring over maps of the area and discussing strategy in the company of Ronan and Egil, the wiry Norse shipwright who acted as the chieftain's second in command. Making use of the daylight hours, runners had been sent out to other nearby settlements in search of others willing to join the fight. Most of the scouts returned to Halastra pale faced and trembling however, telling the now familiar tale of how they had found villages and homesteads abandoned or reduced to charred ruins about which lay the butchered remains of the inhabitants. Of the five villages and farms to which Ronan had dispatched scouts, only one returned in company, bringing with him the inhabitants of a sizeable crofter's farm that lay a morning's walk east of Halastra. Around thirty able bodied men and women along with their accompanying children, elderly and livestock.

Drostan and Vandrad's efforts to swell their ranks from within Halastra had gleaned better results. There was a ripe climate of fear and loathing among the large settlement's people after the infiltration of the vargulf and the slaughter of their fieldworkers and livestock. That first night, after seeing the Sealgairean sheltered and fed, Ronan had instructed Egil to spread the word among the people that Halastra was joining with the forces of Neig and Acker, and that anyone able and willing to take up arms against the wolves was urged to do so. The spectacle of the Sealgairean's crushing decimation of the marauding vargulfen had provided a sorely needed dose of hope and courage to the frightened Halastrians, and accounts from those who had witnessed first hand the defeat of the monstrous wolves quickly spread among the people. The stories were then excitedly repeated, passed on and embellished until the brief but brutal skirmish had become an epic battle of titanic proportions. Before the next dawn, the Sealgairean, the mighty hunters from the north, were revered by all throughout Halastra as conquering heroes.

When it became known that Ronan had called for volunteers to join with them, with the aim of hunting down and eradicating the demons that had brought death and terror to the settlement, the response from the Halastrians was immediate and widespread. The populace signed up in droves, eager to take their share of vengeance and to become part of the burgeoning legend of the Sealgairean.

As well as adding a great weight of numbers to the ranks, Halastra had a well stocked armoury, for although the frequent and brutal raids committed by the Vikings were a thing of the past, the busy trading port would from still time to time become the focus of unwelcome attention from other ocean travelling marauders. Ronan and the chieftains before him had for generations kept an arsenal of weaponry and maintained an active garrison of around eighty guardsmen to protect the settlement, mainly consisting of ex soldiers and mercenaries, many of them of Nordic stock. The experience, knowledge and skill in warfare of such men were a most valuable addition to the Sealgairean's relatively raw and untested ranks.

By the time three days had passed and all were counted, the small war party of barely a hundred souls that had set out from Neig less than a week before had swollen and now stood over five hundred strong.

They left Halastra at dawn of the fourth day, marching north west along the jagged coastline until they reached the southern fringes of the forest. From there, the Sealgairean turned north east, skirting the inland side of the woods. As they went, the marching column thinned as individuals dropped off the rear at regular intervals and immediately set to work clearing the ground before them of heather and grass, every man and woman excavating a section of earth until a wide shallow trench of raw soil formed and grew with each fighter that dropped off the back of the moving column to further lengthen it. So it continued all that morning, until by midday, the entire inland side of the forest was encircled by shallow trench and the long line of some four hundred armed men and women who stood guard behind it, each evenly spaced ten paces apart, their positions marked by the flickering flame of the waist high torches planted in the ground by their sides.

The remainder of the Sealgairean, over another hundred armed and ready fighters mainly made up of the Halastrian guardsmen, had taken up position along the western side of the forest, anchored offshore in a long flotilla of vessels from Halastra's harbour. The seaborne division completed the circle, hemming in the forest from the ocean side.

The plan that they had agreed upon was simple. Surround the forest, and reduce it to ashes by launching fire arrows into the treeline. It had been an unusually hot summer, with little rainfall, and the trees and underbrush of the forest would be dry and prone to burning, especially with the westerly winds blowing in from the ocean to fan and spread the flames. If all went as hoped, the cleansing blaze would immolate the entire forest, along with the unholy creatures that had made it their domain.

Any remaining doubt that the Ulfhednar and their vargulfen offspring *were* in fact located within the forest had been dispelled after scouts and trackers from Halastra had reported finding strong sign of them in that vicinity. They discovered paw prints, hundreds of them, leading in and out of the treeline as well as several tufts of coarse hair snagged on bramble and gorse along the forest fringes. If one drew close enough to the edge of the wood, the trackers said, the stench of wolf piss in the air was ripe enough to singe the hairs in man's nose. Along with the stories of nocturnal carnage previously related to Vandrad and Drostan by the refugees that had fled the villages close to the forest's edge, no more evidence was required. They were there. The western woods had become the realm of the wolf.

Glancing up into the cloudless blue void above, Drostan raised a hand to his brow, squinting against the glare to gauge the sun's position in the sky. His heart quickened a beat as he saw that it had reached its midday zenith, the agreed time at which the assault on the forest was to commence.

After the forest fire was lit, it was the role of Drostan and the other four hundred fighters who covered the north, east and south sides of forest to take down anything that escaped the flames and attempted to flee inland. And now, with a wince of discomfort, Drostan rolled his ageing shoulders in their sockets and stretched out the muscles and tendons in his back and arms. A full quiver of arrows hung across his back, and the longbow he held was strong and supple in his hands. His spear was planted in the ground by his side, beside a tall wooden shield on the grass at his feet. The sheathed sword belted across his waist was a business like weight that pulled on his left hip.

A distant shout floated across the moor, coming from the south. He turned towards the sound, and in the distance saw a figure several places further down the line waving a white flag high in the air.

The signal, relayed from the coast and passed north along the guard line.

The attack had begun.

As Drostan looked to his left, he saw scores of bright orange points of light flickering into existence, then rocketing skywards as the inland guard lit their arrows and sent them arcing towards the treeline before them. It was a hauntingly beautiful sight to behold, and he looked on in wonder as the flaming arrows dropped like falling stars amongst the trees and underbrush at the forest's edge. The woods began to burn.

Dropping his bow, Drostan took hold of the tall flag on the ground in front of him, raised it as high as he could, and with a grunt of effort began sweeping it back and forth in the air.

"Make ready your bows," he shouted to those around him as he relayed the order.

There were forty such signal bearers spread evenly along the enclosing ring of archers. Like him, each one in command of a division of ten men and women. Looking north, he saw another white flag rise into the air as the next signal bearer in line, which he knew to be Ulfar's wife Kadlin, received and relayed the order to fire.

Discarding the flag again, Drostan dropped to one knee and took up his bow and one of the three fire arrows laid out ready before him. Notching it to his bowstring, he turned to the small torch planted in the ground at his side and lit the oiled wrapping of cloth wound around the shaft behind the arrowhead. He leant back slightly to raise the trajectory of his shot and drew his right arm back till the fletchings brushed his cheek and his arms trembled with the strain. *"Loose!"* he roared, and fired. With a long stuttering series of snaps and whooshes that rolled across the plain, his section added their own falling stars to the incendiary assault on the woods. Their second and third shots quickly followed, aimed slightly to either side of their first to aid the spread of the flames. He saw small fires wink into life along the treeline where his arrows fell.

He looked to his right and felt a savage excitement in his breast as he beheld the breathtaking spectacle of hundreds more blazing arrows fired from the guard line streaking up into the sky and falling back to the earth, adding their spark to the rapidly growing blaze already spreading among the trees and undergrowth along the forest's fringes.

Turning his attention back to the smouldering trees before him, Drostan then reached over his shoulder, drew an arrow of simple wood and steel from the quiver on his back, and nocked it to the bowstring in readiness.

"Mark your targets," he barked to his section, *"and let nothing through."*

10

Standing at the rail of a large fishing boat anchored just offshore on the other side of the forest, Vandrad watched silently as the woods burned.

When the hail of flaming arrows fired by the ten man crew aboard the ship had fallen among the trees that grew right up to the land's edge, the dry sap heavy trunks and branches had ignited with frightening ease. Fanned by the brisk westerly sea breeze, the fire had spread rapidly, leaping from tree to tree in all directions along the thickly wooded coastline, hungrily consuming the forest like a ravenous living entity.

Looking north and south, Vandrad could see several other thick columns of smoke in the distance, rising high above the treetops and marking the areas where the other nine ships in the flotilla had also set the forest alight. It was not long before the separate plumes became one as the individual fires spread and combined to create a single massive wall of flame that chewed its way east through the woodland. A thick, suffocating cloud formed above the entire width of the burning forest in a vast dark pall of choking woodsmoke and ash, amid which a galaxy of glowing embers danced and swooped like fireflies. Even from his position aboard the ship anchored a safe distance offshore, Vandrad could feel the heat of the rampant flames on his face, and the hot crackle and roar of the blaze was like the sound of a dragon's breath.

Behind him, several of the guardsmen on the ship whooped and yelled in celebration as the wildfire razed the ancient forest, and it was not long before above their gleeful cries and the roar, pop and snap of the burning wood, that the terrible screaming howls began ringing out from within the fire. The hoarse shrieks of the wolves trapped inside the blazing wood, their tortured screams floating out across the water as they were burned alive.

Vandrad smiled at the sound of it.

Even as he watched, a large fiery shape suddenly came hurtling out of the burning treeline off to his left and leapt off the high craggy rocks at the land's edge, the huge lupine body a living, shrieking torch. The burning wolf dropped through the air and plunged smoking into the choppy dark water with a stinking hiss and crackle, then disappeared, only to resurface moments later, thrashing and snarling, most of its coat burned away to reveal raw half melted skin and scorched flesh beneath. The nightmarish animal snapped and yowled as it floundered in the stinging salty waves, its hate filled face a twisted mess of charred skin, blazing eyes and flashing fangs.

"Finish it," Vandrad said without taking his eyes off the screaming animal. A quick volley of arrows from the other men aboard the vessel silenced the vargulf and sent it under again. It did not resurface.

A few minutes later, Vandrad saw another of the great wolves attempting to flee the fire, leaping in a ball of flame from the cliffs north of his position. It too surfaced briefly before meeting the same end, the arrows and spears of the men in the closest boat dispatching it permanently and sending its half roasted carcass to the seabed.

11

The death cries of the burning vargulfen in the forest had been going on for some time. Breck had never heard anything like it, and his skin crawled at the hideous sound.

The entire forest and parts of the heathland surrounding it were well ablaze now, an immense bonfire that dominated the landscape, clawing at the heavens with great talons of flame and tentacles of writhing smoke. The sun cowered, hidden behind a roiling grey overcastting of soot and ember flecked ash, and though it was still only early afternoon, the day had the dimness of twilight.

The soaring temperature of the superheated air around the burning woodland had driven him and the rest of the Sealgairean back several paces from their positions on the moor behind the firebreak they'd dug, and Breck stood looking on in wonder at the mass destruction they had wrought upon the landscape. The sheer size of the blaze made him fearful that the firebreak would be unable to hold it at bay, but Vandrad had ordered the wide, shallow trench of overturned soil to be excavated far back from the trees, the distance of a long range bow shot. By the time the fire reached the ring of bare earth, he told them, the flames would be smaller, only as large as the heather and gorse bushels they consumed, and would be halted easily by the firebreak. Breck hoped he knew what he was talking about, as parts of the moorland at the forest edge had now started to go up in a several places as the fire reached flickering red fingers outward from the massive central inferno.

Then the wolves started to come.

As during the battle outside Halastra's gates, Breck was initially unnerved by the blistering speed at which the first vargulf came at him. It burst from the treeline and seemed to fly across the scrubland, trailing fire, leaving rank smoke and smouldering heather and grass in its wake.

He brought it down with his first shot. At a range of thirty odd paces, the charging animal's hoarse scream was abruptly cut off as Breck's arrow plunged deep into its chest between the forelegs, and it tumbled and somersaulted in a puff of smoke and sparks before disappearing beneath the scrub. On his right, he heard the snap of a bowstring and looked over to see Fionn quickly notching another arrow. A great black coated wolf was coming at Odhran's son fast, weaving through the undergrowth and bearing down on his position with terrifying speed. The arrow from Fionn's first shot bobbed in its thick furry shoulder as it ran, having had little or no effect. He drew and fired again, but rushed his shot and missed the oncoming beast. Another arrow, fired from the archer to Fionn's right, streaked by the wolf, flying harmlessly over it head. Fionn drew a third arrow from the quiver on his back, but it was already too late. The wolf leapt into the air, wide red jaws yawning, dagger teeth flashing. Fionn screamed and fell back just as Breck's arrow punched into the vargulf's body just below the shoulder.

The monster pitched off to the side with a pained yelp, crumpling to the earth. Fionn looked over at Breck, and nodded his thanks before rising shakily to his feet again. Casting the bow aside, Fionn took a spear planted nearby in the earth, walked cautiously over to the huge animal writhing and snapping in the grass, and thrust the spear through the base of its skull. The vargulf let out a short bark and then was still. Fionn withdrew the spear, stooped and pulled his first arrow from the wolf's shoulder, nocked it to his bow again and resumed his position.

And so it went the rest of the afternoon. Every once in a while, another wolf would break from the forest and come tearing towards the Sealgairean line before being brought down, but as the day wore on and the fire ate deeper into the wood's depths, there were fewer, and those that made it out of the fiery treeline were horribly burned, weakened and slow, easily finished off by the archers' arrows.

Eventually, the screams of the wolves yet trapped in the burning forest faded and died away, till the only sound was the deep crackle of the forest fire as it consumed the last of the trees. The scrubland between the woods and the firebreak had by now also been completely burned away, leaving a black smouldering plain dotted with red embers, smoking wolf carcasses and charred skeletal shrubbery.

Looking in both directions along the rank of archers within his field of vision, Breck could see that the guard line seemed to have held. Along this section at least, not one of the fleeing vargulfen had made it past the Sealgairean archers.

For the first time in months, he felt a small, cautious swell of hope rising in his chest.

12

The fire quickly consumed the rest of the forest, eventually burning itself out well before sunset. The woodland and surrounding moors were simply gone, replaced by a great smoking swathe of scorched terrain branded into the coastal landscape.

The Sealgairean remained in their positions on the land and ocean the rest of the day and through that night, still encircling the great smouldering scar on the Earth. As the sun set, those in the inland guard line gathered into groups of five, each group's members taking turns to keep watch throughout the night. Those manning the ships off the coast also bedded down for the night, sleeping out in the open on the decks while one among each vessel's crew kept vigil.

The night passed without incident, and in the morning, the embers of the fire had cooled enough to allow the Sealgairean to move into the charred wasteland where the forest had stood. The intention was that the crews of the flotilla would land, spread out and push eastwards through the burned forest, sweeping the area and ensuring that nothing had survived the fire. Although the plan to immolate the forest had gone perfectly, Vandrad had been aware even when planning the attack that it was far from foolproof, and that even if the plan worked and the woodland was razed, it did not necessarily mean an end to their struggle.

Simply burning the forest was no guarantee of total victory in their fight, which, they all agreed, could only be theirs with the complete and utter eradication of both the Ulfhednar and their vargulfen brood. They had made a good start, but now the hunters had to confirm exactly how decisive a victory they had won. Although the numbers passed along the ranks reported that eighty seven vargulfen wolves had fallen to the Sealgairean's arrows as they had tried to escape the flames, there was no way of knowing how many the fire had claimed in the interior of the forest, and there had been no word that any of the dread Ulfhednar warriors themselves were among those confirmed slain.

That made Vandrad nervous.

At a flagged signal from Vandrad's command ship in the centre of the seaboard line, passed north and south along the offshore guard, each vessel in the flotilla raised anchor, and rowed for shore, beaching at planned landing points along the rocky coast where the jagged cliffs occasionally gave way to small sandy coves and inlets. Once ashore, the crews of the ten ships dispersed and began to spread themselves out along the charred woodland's western edge, organising themselves into a long single ranked skirmish line consisting of a hundred men, the north and south ends of which met with the Sealgairean forces already on land at the north and south reaches of the dead forest.

When word was passed along the line from each end that the men were in position and ready, Vandrad drew a horn from his belt and blew a long single blast that resonated and carried clearly on the still grey morning air. As the mournful sound died away, the men unslung bows from their backs, strung them and notched arrows to the strings - arrows tipped with points of wolf blooded steel produced in the forge back at Neig.

Ailde and Camran had managed to form almost a thousand of the arrowheads, reforged from the various damaged weapons recovered after the Ulfhednar's attack on the hilltop settlement. Each man in the skirmish line, save those few who carried other hand to hand weapons of blooded steel, was equipped with two such arrows capable of wounding the shapeshifters, each barbed projectile's fletching marked with red dye to identify it. The rest of the special arrowheads had been distributed evenly among the archers on the inland side of the forest, again, two wolf-blooded arrows for every man and woman.

They began making their way slowly and carefully forward through the desolate smoking terrain, each footstep of their passage raising puffs of ash from the still warm ground underfoot. A deep silence descended as they moved cautiously forward among the field of tall charcoaled sticks that were all that remained of what had only hours before been tree trunks, centuries old.

Beyond the fringes of the devastation, deeper into the deadened grey depths of the burned forest, they began to find the remains of the vargulfen. The blackened canine skeletons lay in cauterized contortions upon the ashen ground, their singed bones stripped of flesh, skin and fur. The eyeless black sockets in the skulls of the wolves still seemed to glare balefully at the men who stepped nervously around them, even then irrationally wary of the fearful fangs and claws of the dead creatures.

No one among them stopped to claim a tooth or talon as a victory token.

No one among them dared.

13

As he made his way through the burned out woodland near the centre of the skirmish line, Ailde flexed his aching shoulders and rolled his neck, wincing at the hot jolt of pain that flared along the tendons beneath his jaw and the thick ropy muscles across the top of his back.

He had not slept well upon the wooden deck of the ship the night before, and had been plagued by sea sickness all the previous day. It had been the first time he'd set foot on a boat since he'd fled back to the island from the mainland all those years ago following his escape from the slaughter at Hastings, and he'd been dismayed to discover the debilitating nausea that had assailed him as a young man still had the power to leave him fearfully sickened and weak.

During the long hours the boat had been anchored offshore as part of the flotilla, rising and dipping ceaselessly on the undulating surface of the ocean, he'd spent much of the time leaning at the rail, trembling, weak kneed and green faced as his stomach revolted and his head swam sickeningly to the constant motion of the deck beneath his feet. He'd lost count of the amount of times he'd retched and heaved the diminishing contents of his stomach over the side of the accursed boat. Ailde's misery had been compounded further by Ulfar, who had cheerfully stood with him at the boat's rail, the giant Norseman, like the rest of the damned crew, infuriatingly impervious to the seasickness that crippled him.

Ulfar had stood there, chortling in amusement and heartily swatting Ailde on the back each time his lurching stomach had spasmed, ejecting rank burning strings of sour bile into the choppy water. Although the two men had become friendly over the course of the past few months, Ailde hated him with a passion that day, and would cheerfully have taken his smith's hammer to Ulfar's infuriating smiling face, if only he'd had the strength to lift it.

The spectacle of the burning forest had distracted Ailde from his illness though, and for a time, the rampant sea sickness that plagued him was almost forgotten as he watched the woods going up and heard the screams and howls of the dying wolves trapped within. Ailde had felt a savage satisfaction listening to the agonised baying and guttural shrieks of the creatures being roasted, and for a while he revelled in the terrible sounds emitting from the blaze.

Now, cresting a gentle rise in the soot blanketed terrain of the seared forest, his throbbing neck and shoulders competing for his attention with his still unsettled gut, Ailde paused at the top of the slope to catch his labouring breath, and saw it.

Just ahead. A cave. A shadowy opening in the rock at the base of a cliff face that thrust up from the earth some twenty paces further on. The sight of the darkened cavity immediately caused the big blacksmith's hands to tighten on the shaft of his hammer, and he stood staring at the lightless opening, a cold flower of foreboding blossoming in his chest.

Ulfar, who'd been walking beside him in the line, noticed Ailde had stopped moving and looked over. The blacksmith pointed, indicating the dark crack at the bottom of the cliff ahead. Seeing it now, Ulfar also stopped where he was, holding up a hand and calling out for the line to halt. As the instruction to hold was passed along the line, Ulfar crouched low, his longsword held in his right hand, and moved slowly toward the opening in the soot blackened rock, gesturing for Ailde to join him.

A cave, the blacksmith thought as he drew closer, the word repeating in his mind. The hairs on Ailde's forearms prickled and stirred, twisting as the same idiot word clamoured in his mind over and over in rising tones of alarm.

A cave.

A cave.

A cave.

Glancing over his shoulder, he saw the other men in the line behind him looking on in unease as he and Ulfar drew nearer the inky gap in the cliff face. Several of them exchanged nervous glances, and Ailde knew that the same frightening thought that had occurred to him was now catching hold in the other men's minds.

A cave. A hollow of dry bare stone, deep beneath the ground, safe from the ravages of fire.

A den.

He turned forward again in time to glimpse a quick shifting suggestion of movement in the shadowy cavity before him. He drew a breath to alert Ulfar, and had the briefest glimpse of something streaking out of the cave mouth.

The spear took him dead centre in the upper chest, punching into his body with incredible force, passing through his clothing, skin, flesh and bone. The iron head burst from his back between his great shoulders in a spray of blood, the force of the sudden skewering pitching him backward, and Ailde went crashing to the ash choked forest floor, run clean through.

Then he heard a bellowing battle cry rattling out from the cave. A great bestial roar rebounding and reflecting off the stone walls. As he lay there looking up at the sky, he was peripherally aware of several tall, half seen figures moving past him, emitting that terrible war cry, then he heard shouts of alarm and panic. Ulfar's deep voice roaring commands. The grinding clash of steel on steel. The whizz and hum of loosed arrows. Urgent blasts of a horn in the distance. Wet squealing blurts of pain. Terrified screams.

It was all getting further away, the clanging racket of battle growing mercifully fainter as Ailde's senses began to fail.

It was getting dark.

He'd expected death to be like this. A cool dark shade drawn over his eyes, ushering him into a long, deep sleep. But no, it was the dull half shaded light of the morning itself that was dimming, not just his perception of it.

Ailde looked up into the sky above him, ringed from his point of view by dead treetops, and through the shifting veil of woodsmoke that hung over the land, he beheld the sight of the sun disappearing behind a black disc that had almost completely obscured it, blocking its light and darkening the day.

His eyes widened in awe at the astonishing spectacle as the black circle moved into the centre of the sun's pale disk, and a brilliant flaring ring of cold fire blazed out around the edges in a flashing corona.

It was literally a breathtaking sight, and Ailde's last exhalation escaped his skewered chest in a thick wet rattle.

Then the perplexing sight of the sun being devoured dimmed too, as the big blacksmith's eyes fluttered and closed.

PART NINE

1

"The last thing he saw was the sun being eaten."

Mark took his eyes off the road and glanced over at the pretty brunette in the passenger seat next to him. They were the first words Sharon had uttered since they'd fled the Calanais visitor centre and the crazy shit that had happened there twenty minutes ago.

Since he'd half walked, half carried his semi-catatonic girlfriend back to the car and belted her limp body into the passenger seat after the bizarre incident at the standing stoens, she'd been completely silent, unresponsive to him repeatedly asking if she was okay, and had kept her face turned away from him, awake, but looking blankly out the passenger side window. Even the spectacle of the much talked about and anticipated solar eclipse that had occurred as they'd driven away from Calanais hadn't grabbed her attention, despite Mark shaking her shoulder and urging her to look, anything to get her to react.

He'd had to abandon his efforts to rouse Sharon and concentrate on the road as the sun's light was shaded by the passing moon. Weird how all that mental shit earlier had happened right before an eclipse, Mark had been thinking as he drove along the darkened road, then decided that such thoughts were just too spooky at that moment. It was just then that Sharon had spoken.

She was all of a sudden sitting bolt upright, her body rigid, staring intently out through the windshield as they made their way along the remote backcountry road in the direction of Stornoway where they were staying for the weekend. Despite the strange random words she'd spoken, it was good to hear her voice. At least she was saying something. He'd been starting to get a little freaked out, well, in all honesty, he'd been more than a little freaked out, and had been for the past half hour. Worried for Sharon following her collapse and apparent seizure at the standing stones, Mark had made up his mind to drive to the hospital instead of the hotel when she'd finally spoken.

"What'd you say, babes?" he asked her now, frowning. "Who saw the sun being eaten?"

"The big man with the black hair and the hammer," Sharon replied after a long moment, speaking in a strange, tight voice, her eyes bright and shining, but still not looking his way. She smiled a little.

"Okaaaaay..." Mark said, dragging his eyes back to the road. "Babe, what are you talking about?" Again with the freaky nonsensical shit. It wasn't so much the words themselves, but the way she said them that made his scalp feel like it was covered in scuttling insects. He glanced back at Sharon again, and saw she had turned in her seat and was now looking back at him, that strange little smile still in place and a new mischief dancing in her mad staring eyes. Her smile grew broader and she started to giggle.

"Get tae fuck, ya daft cow," Mark blurted in a mixture of relief and disgust, letting out a shaky nervous breath as Sharon's giggles became genuine belly laughs and she slapped her thighs in delight at having wound him up. She had a bizarre sense of humour. One of the reason why he loved her.

"Hahaha! Had you going there, doll!" she crowed triumphantly, ruffling her fingers affectionately in his hair. He huffily jerked his head away from her hand, shooting her a sulky look. It had been a good one, he had to admit. She'd freaked him right out there for a second.

"Jesus Christ, Sharon, don't do that. I was about to rush you the local A and E there. Silly bint."

"Awwww, your concern's touching, babe. You're my hero." She leant across and planted a big wet kiss on his cheek, still giggling in amusement. He didn't pull away this time. Mark smiled. Couldn't help it.

"Are you okay though," he asked. "What happened back there?"

"Dunno," Sharon replied, making a nonchalant shooing gesture with her fingers. "Probably just ate something dodgy. I'm fine."

"You weren't fine, babe. You went white as a sheet and screamed, then just keeled over in the grass and had some sort of fit. And what about all the others?" Mark insisted. "You should have seen it. It was fuckin' nuts. People just started running around shouting and bawling, rolling about on the deck. And that *noise*..."

He'd heard it as he'd dragged Sharon away from the stones towards the car park. Something like laughter, but so deep and gravelly it had been like boulders being ground together. And something else. Something that was like... wolves howling, as crazy as that sounded. It had seemed to come from nowhere and everywhere, and had turned Mark's knees to water.

Sharon just shrugged, as if the mass hysteria and inexplicable sounds had zero interest for her. "They probably served some bad food in the canteen. Maybe someone spiked it with acid or something."

"I still think we should go to the hospital," Mark said, thoroughly unconvinced by Sharon's half arsed explanation. Something seriously fucked up had just happened. "Seriously, babe, you had a seizure or something. I'm worried."

"That's sweet," Sharon said, "but really, I'm okay, Mark."

He felt her gaze linger on him and turned towards her again, taking her hand in his. "You're sure?"

"I'm sure. There's nothing wrong with me. Plus, if we go to the hospital, we'll just end up stuck waiting in the casualty department for hours. I don't want to miss the festival tonight."

Mark held her eyes for a few moments, then relented. She could be stubborn as a particularly uncooperative mule when she dug her heels in.

"Okay, fine," he said. "But promise me you'll go the doctor's and get checked out when we get back home."

"Honest engine," Sharon vowed with a bright smile, then leant over and kissed him on the cheek again, then nuzzling at his ear. Mark felt a delicious shiver rush over his skin as she nibbled gently, flicking and probing with her hot wet tongue.

"Woah, easy there, missy," he chuckled. "I'm driving here. Keep it in your pants till we get back to the hotel, eh?"

"Can't help it," Sharon murmured in his ear. "You're so *sweet*. I could just eat you alive right here…"

"Oh my!" Mark laughed as her hand dropped down into his lap and began stroking him through his jeans. "Somebody's feeling frisky."

"There's a lay by just ahead," Sharon breathed, her voice thick with desire. "Pull the car over."

Mark grinned and did as she said, easing the car to a stop in the lay by as she continued rubbing his crotch and nipping gently at his neck with her teeth. They were in the middle of nowhere, with nothing but miles of empty moorland stretching to the horizon in every direction. Looking quickly ahead and behind, he saw no other cars on the lonely stretch of road. A fine spot for a bit of al fresco sauciness.

Mark hurriedly unbuckled his seat belt and turned towards her, reaching. Sharon abruptly disengaged herself from him though, and holding him at arms length, leaned back against the passenger side door, her head tilted back slightly, looking down at him from under sensually lowered eyelids.

"I want you inside me, Mark," she said, her eyes seeming to flash with green fire. "I want you in my mouth, and then inside me."

It drove him crazy when she talked dirty like that. He'd been considering proposing at the festival tonight, and this little interlude was the definite clincher. He figured he could find a jewellery shop in town when they got back to Stornoway, maybe sneak out from the hotel and buy an engagement ring when Sharon was in the shower getting ready to go out. This was turning out to be a fucking *awesome* weekend.

Feeling a great rush of love for this beautiful, funny, smart and thoroughly bewitching girl whom he'd been with for three amazing years, Mark lifted one of her hands to his lips to plant a tender kiss upon it, which was when he noticed her fingernails.

Thick and dark yellowish in colour, each one four inches long, they tapered to wicked hooked points, like the claws of some predatory animal.

Mark made an inarticulate sound of horror and thrust Sharon's freakish clawed hand away from him. Raising his eyes to her face, he saw her smile.

Saw her teeth.

They crowded her grinning mouth in two rows of hideously oversized interlocking fangs.

It's just another practical joke, Mark's yammering mind desperate tried to reason. It's a fake rubber hand and pretend vampire fangs you can get them in any toy shop she put them on somehow when you were distracted with her tonguing your ear and rubbing your dick good one Sharon hahaha very funny...

It wasn't until she lashed out with her claws and disembowelled him that Mark was finally convinced that this was no laughing matter.

Thick ribbons of blood flicked against the inside of the windshield, the metallic stench of it immediately filling the car's interior. Glistening coils of intestine bulged from the four long incisions across Mark's stomach, spilling out from under his shredded t-shirt and into his lap with a wet *slurp*.

"I could just eat you alive right here," Sharon said again.

And that's just what she did.

2

Patricia Lock, twenty four years old, slightly plump with mousy brown hair cut in a sensible bob, was a young woman from Southampton, in no way particularly remarkable.

She led a quiet life, eking out a low key existence working in a low to middle paid office job, going home each night to her cramped one bedroom flat above a kebab shop, where she lived alone but for a parakeet named Dexter. She had a few friends, but not many. Sometimes she had boyfriends, most times not. She smoked a twenty pack of Regal every day and worried about her mother, who also lived alone and had been starting to show early signs of Alzheimer's, even though she wasn't even halfway through her fifties. Particia liked pizza. Mushroom and anchovy pizza, and Chardonnay wine. She'd never known any other holiday destination but the Costa del Sol until a week ago.

That was when she'd got a message on Facebook from a girl she'd gone to university in Glasgow with. Shona. A lively blonde Scottish girl from the Outer Hebrides. Both freshmen, they'd shared a student flat in the halls of residence, and had become BFFs for the four years it had taken them to get their respective degrees. Then they graduated and went their separate ways. Shona took off travelling round Europe, while Patricia, who'd been close to going with her, had instead jumped at a lecturing job offer she received from a college back home in Southampton. It didn't pan out, the teaching job, so there Patricia was, two years later - customer service rep for a mobile phone network, solidly on the bottom rung of the corporate ladder and her degree in philosophy bitterly redundant as her mind was numbed and her soul destroyed, twelve hour shift at a time.

She'd been on her half hour lunch break, gazing wistfully into the small beige plastic coffee cup in her hand and glumly pondering her existence and place in the universe when her mobile gave a cheery whistle, and there was a friend request from Shona on Facebook. A few LOLs, OMGs, WTFs and PMSLs later, and Patricia had been invited up to the Isle of Lewis in Scotland to visit her old uni mate. There was a music festival on, and she could stay at Shona's flat. It'd be like old times.

Patricia booked a few days holiday from work and a flight up to Stornoway.

Now she stood in the middle of a lonely country road, surrounded by empty darkened moorland, staring south down the unspooling ribbon of tarmac that rolled and twisted away across the remote landscape into the dim grey distance. Her eyes were fixed on the horizon, at the vanishing point where the road south disappeared behind a fold in the land. Normally she wore thick glasses and could see maybe a foot in front of her face before everything became a blur, but that was before.

Before the standing stones.

Before the wolf got in her.

Now she could see everything, even in the much reduced daylight of the eclipse. She could hear everything. Smell everything. Taste everything.

It was wonderful.

Shona had taken her to the Calanais Visitor Centre. She'd known Patricia liked that kind of stuff, and her friend had always been thoughtful that way. Shona was in the car now. What was left of her anyway?

As she stood there, facing south and watching the road, Patricia flexed her hands. They felt strong. Very big and very strong. She wiggled and flicked her long, claw tipped fingers, felt them brush stickily against each other, tacky from the half dried blood that covered them. Without taking her yellow eyes from the road, she lifted one long sinewy hand to her mouth. Her curiously elongated jaw opened slowly, revealing the cruel array of pointed teeth, still stained pinkish with Shona's blood. An obscene tongue slithered out from between her new teeth, freakishly long and dog-like. Patricia licked delicately at the drying gore on her right hand, as a bonus, finding a happy little morsel of juicy flesh hiding beneath the hooked talon of the eight inch long middle finger.

Behind her, Shona's car, its interior awash with drying blood and torn body parts, was parked lengthwise across the two lane road that led north to Stornoway, creating a roadblock. On Particia's right, another car was likewise parked, obstructing the road that ran west, back towards Calanais. A second woman stood by the other car. An older lady of about sixty. Patricia had never met her before today, but the elderly woman had also been there at the stones when it had happened.

She had a wolf in her too.

As the crowd of tourists had fled the site of the ancient standing stones earlier, Patricia and this stranger had turned to each other and shared a look. Before that moment, Patricia had only seen the silver permed lady peripherally, being jerked into the air, levitating there while her body spasmed and shook. Patricia had meanwhile been convulsing on the ground, her skull full of laughter and howling, the wolf brutally forcing its way inside her in a nightmarish spiritual rape, an ordeal far worse than anything she ever had or ever could have imagined.

The invasion of their bodies complete, they'd stood there before the standing stones, before the gateway, their eyes burning into each other while the crowd of human cattle fled around them, making for the exit. An unspoken communication had passed between the two women

Feed.

The others also came through. A further three of their kind, tearing through the thin veil that was the barrier between realities, slashing with tooth and nail into the human world, the talisman that had kept them at bay for a thousand years finally removed. They ripped their way beneath the skin and into the flesh of nearby human hosts - another young woman and two males - then took up the instinctive mental call that pulsed between them, flashing irresistibly in their ancient predatory minds, reborn under the diminished sun.

Feed. Spread.

The other three leaving the site in their new human guises, Patricia had rushed to the elderly woman's side, calling for Shona to help her aid the poor stricken pensioner. Shona, being a gentle, caring sort, had been only too willing to help Patricia get the frail looking woman to her car, where the three of them had then driven away from the visitor centre and its looming grey monoliths.

Now, the two women, one elderly, one young, but both with souls millennia old, were waiting. Something was approaching from the south. Something of consequence. They both felt it. An instinctual pull at their hot pumping blood, a whispered warning that had urged them to join together, that had told them some strange presence was heading their way, something of a similar nature to themselves, but different.

Whatever it was, they would destroy and feed upon it. They had been asleep for a long time, and were ravenous.

Killing and eating Shona had barely begun to touch the fierce hunger that tore at them.

As the daylight continued to fade under the eclipse, Patricia felt the bones of her shoulders shift and stretch, popping and creaking painfully as her body gradually gave itself over to the wolf inside her. She had grown in height by almost a full foot in the last half hour, and had a new powerful muscularity around her formerly thin shoulders. Little by little, Patricia's mind and will, her very *self* grew smaller and smaller inside her own slowly transforming body, which was being relentlessly devoured by the ancient entity that had invaded it, taking possession of her flesh. She didn't mind.

Such power. Such terrible, irresistible *power*.

Above, the arcing black silhouette of the moon continued to move in front of the sun. Broken beads of light flared around the foremost edge of the obscuring dark disc as the eclipse crept toward totality, the sun's light bleeding through the valleys and rough barren topography of the dead lunar rock passing before it.

And the more the moon held sway, the more the thing lurking beneath Patricia's stretching twisting skin and flesh came to the fore, impatiently scratching at her insides, clawing behind her eyes, shuddering behind her teeth and nails, eager to be let loose upon the Earth once more.

3

Aaron Latharn, forty two years old, standing a barrel chested six foot three and dressed in thick black biker's leathers, applied the brake on his Triumph Thruxton motorcycle and cruised to a halt in the empty car park of the Calanais Visitor Centre.

He turned the key in the ignition, silencing the low burbling purr of the vehicle's 865 cc engine, and hauled his imposing frame off the bike in a practiced, almost graceful dismount. He removed his helmet and stood for a moment looking down on the darkened and deserted grounds of the tourist attraction, the sea breeze blowing in from the Atlantic on his left, cool on his shaven head and stirring the wiry brown hairs of his goatee beard.

Straining his eyes in the reduced light of the ongoing eclipse, he saw that the area outside the single storey building was devoid of any living presence but for Jack Powning and Gordon McLeod, who stood together close to the main ring of standing stones, engaged in animated conversation. Jack was restlessly pacing back and forth, gesturing at the stones and shaking his head while Gordon stood holding his arms out to the sides in a helpless gesture that plainly conveyed the message How the fuck should I know?

Aaron quickly took the short flight of steps that led down the gentle hill from the car park and walked across the grounds to where the two men stood. Gordon looked up at his approach and met his eyes. Right then, Aaron, who had up until that point only held a strong suspicion, knew for certain that something very bad had happened here. Only on rare occasions had he seen another human being look so singularly afraid.

There was a similar look to Jack as well. The young weaponsmith couldn't stand still, continuing to pace back and forth on the grass, chewing nervously on a thumbnail, occasionally giving another quick shake of his head as if ruminating on some vexing problem, considering and rejecting possibilities.

Gordon continued to stare at his old friend for a few more seconds, and Aaron wondered how scared he looked himself. On the ride over from his house, he'd had time to think some very troubling thoughts.

"So what came through?" Gordon asked eventually. "On the phone you said 'something's coming through'."

Aaron thought about saying he didn't know, or couldn't be sure. He thought about trying to be evasive. After all, what did he really know? Some dead birds and a few accidents. Some greeting weans and interference on the phone. No biggy said the piggy. All everyday occurrences.

Except it hadn't just been some dead birds, kitchen mishaps, crying children and faulty phone lines, had it?

Three separate incidents of the inexplicable avian suicides, each time with exactly five birds. And then there was the eclipse. And the fact that all the day's tourists had apparently fled from the visitor centre. And Gordon's description of the little ones crying and being afraid when in the immediate vicinity of the standing stones - the same stones that those fifteen birds had apparently intentionally sacrificed themselves upon. Then on top of all that were the other things he knew. Things that caused his nutsack to tighten when considered in the context of everything else Gordon had told him had happened that afternoon.

No, Aaron decided. This was no time for evasive humming and hawing, so instead of answering Gordon, he turned to Jack who continued to stride back and forth close by.

"Jack, we need to go to your place," he said.

The younger man stopped his nervous pacing and looked up at the mention of his name. "My place?"

"Aye."

"What for?"

"I'll explain in the car."

"I'd rather know right now if it's all the same, Aaron. I'm really badly in need of some clue as to what the fuck just happened here."

Aaron could tell by the manic shine in Jack's eyes that he wasn't going to do anything or go anywhere until he had a least a little information. He thought about how to quickly explain the frightening, and frankly insane, theory which he'd arrived at while riding over to the centre. If he was correct, and he was pretty sure that he was, then time was very much of the essence.

Or it could already be too late.

Looking up, he saw behind the veil of clouds that the eclipse was now practically in a state of totality, the black disc of the moon aligned almost dead centre in front of the sun, blocking out most of the day's light and dimming the world around them to a murky grey shadowland. The sight caused a fresh shudder of unease to quiver through his bones. It would take too long to explain the whole deranged business, so in an effort to mentally slap Jack into action he said, "Fair enough. Do you still have that set of throwing knives you made? I think we're going to need them."

Aaron was spared the need for further explanation as a high wavering scream split the air. The three men looked towards the main building, where the shriek had come from. Then Gordon was moving, jogging as fast as his ageing legs would allow in the direction of the centre. Jack shot a quick glance at Aaron then took off after his boss.

"No, wait," Aaron called urgently after the two men, but they paid no heed. "Shit. *Shit!*" he cursed, and then followed them.

As they neared the glass walled main entrance to the building, another scream sounded from somewhere inside, followed by a heavy crash and the sound of breaking glass. More shouts of alarm, another high pitched wail of terror, quickly followed and overlapped by several more, and then another noise, one that caused Aaron's already chilled blood to seemingly freeze solid in his arteries. The deep, guttural snarling of what sounded like a large, angry animal, rumbling and barking out from somewhere in the east wing of the building where the cafeteria was situated.

Gordon was first to the entrance, pushing hurriedly through the glass set of double doors. He stood in the entrance foyer for a second, looking around frantically as Jack and Aaron joined him. The reception desk was unmanned, no sign of Claire, the cheery blonde who worked there dispensing tickets and information flyers.

Aaron was the first to spot the dripping splash mark that stood out against the white painted wall behind the reception desk, as if someone had thrown a cup of some dark liquid. With a sinking sensation, he suspected that if the light were better, that spray of liquid that ran in rivulets down the plaster would show up as bright arterial red.

"Gordon..." he said quietly, pointing.

Gordon saw the mark on the wall and immediately hurried round to the other side of the desk, where he abruptly stopped, looking down at the floor behind the counter and emitting a strangled sound of revulsion. Aaron and Jack ran to his side.

The screams, crashes and unearthly animal roaring that continued to blare from elsewhere in the complex seemed to fade momentarily as Aaron looked down at Claire's body.

The young receptionist lay facedown on the ceramic tiled floor, her golden blonde hair fanning out, soaking into the widening puddle of freshly spilled blood that pooled around her head. In the dim grey light, Aaron could see the blood collecting and running in straight black lines, turning at right angles as it flowed along the narrow grouting spaces between the square floor tiles.

The entire back of Claire's neck at the base of her skull had been ripped away, leaving a horrific gaping wound of raw shredded flesh, mangled tendons and exposed, splintered vertebrae.

That was when the door behind the three men suddenly slammed open and the rest of the centre's staff came bursting into the foyer from the corridor beyond in a yelling, stampeding rush, running, pushing, stumbling and crying in frantic goggle eyed panic.

Aaron saw that several of them were splashed with gore. No one stopped to explain the situation to the three men who stood in dumfounded shock behind the reception counter, watching as the terrified stream of jostling employees raced by, running for the exit.

Gordon reached out and grabbed hold of one employee's arm as they ran by, a young guy of about seventeen dressed in blood splattered chef's whites. The boy, who hadn't even seen the three men as he rushed past, yelped in alarm and tried to struggle loose as Gordon seized him.

"Barry, it's me, it's Gordon," the older man gasped, fighting to keep a hold of the lad's red stained sleeve. "What the hell's going on?"

The teenager, Barry, finally recognised his boss and looked at Gordon with an expression of total bewildered terror as he continued to try and pull away. "Holy fuck, Gordon we have to get out of here!" he said in a girlish, high pitched voice. "There's a fucking monster in the café! *Run!*" And he tore loose from Gordon's grasp, joining the press of other workers who were fighting and pushing to get through the exit doors.

Aaron saw a middle aged woman dressed in a waitresses uniform grab a fire extinguisher mounted nearby on the wall and hurl it at the large floor to ceiling window at the side of the doors, which shattered and exploded outwards, allowing the panicked throng to stream outside in a rush, heedless of the sharp falling shards of glass that cascaded down on their heads as they poured through and bolted, many of them still screaming.

Aaron, Jack and Gordon then made an unconscious group decision to follow the young kitchen porter Barry's advice, and ran out from behind the reception counter to join the escaping mob.

They were halfway across the glass littered foyer when there was a savage bellow and a tremendous rending crash from behind them. An instant later, something large slammed with immense force into Aaron's back, knocking him from his feet and sending him skidding on his belly across the polished tiled floor. He collided head first with a wire display rack that held a selection of colourful postcards before he came to a painful thumping stop against the far wall. Dazed but unhurt, he groggily rolled over and raised himself up on his elbows, looking back across the foyer.

It was the door leading to the cafe that had slammed into him and sent him sprawling across the floor. The heavy piece of reinforced wood, glass and plastic had seemingly been ripped off its hinges as if by a violent explosion, and now lay in the centre of the reception area where he'd been standing a mere second or two ago.

But Aaron's attention was directed to the towering creature that then strode through the splintered door frame, ducking under the lintel in order to pass through the gap in the wall where the door had been a moment previously. Although the actual physical appearance of the immense bipedal animal confirmed the wild theory Aaron had arrived at following his earlier phone conversation with Gordon, his mind could not at first process what he was seeing, and seemed to be stuck like a scratched record, repeating the same word over and over until it was a nonsensical sound of no meaning.

Werewolf.
Werewolf.
Werewolf.
Werewolf.

Then the thing roared, a deafening explosion of sound that was pure rage and bottomless hunger. The terrible noise seemed to shake the building's very foundations, punching the air from Aaron's lungs, who gasped before the tremendous sound as if slugged in the gut.

Boulder thick in the chest and powerfully muscled beneath its bloodstained coat of coarse, rippling fur, the huge creature stood an easy seven feet tall, the tufted tips of its pointed ears brushing the ceiling of the reception area. Its long sinewy arms tapered from the heavy shoulders down to monstrous quasi-human hands, each freakishly long finger ending in a viciously hooked four inch talon, the canine-jointed legs terminating in clawed appendages that were somewhere between paws and human feet. Although the creature's torso and limbs were a horrifying mixture of lupine and human anatomy, the head was unmistakably that of a wolf. The bloodstained muzzle protruding from the broad skull was crammed with a ridiculous amount of huge pointed teeth, and Aaron fancied that he could see shreds of fleshy tissue dangling amid the tightly clustered fangs.

Tearing his gaze away from the creature, Aaron saw that Jack was standing off to his left by the shattered glass wall, looking back at the monster with an expression of idiotic incomprehension. Gordon, who'd been running at Aaron's side when the door had come flying into the foyer, was lying facedown and unmoving on the floor a mere five metres or so from the beast, which let out another nerve shredding bellow and stalked towards the helpless man before it, flexing its claws. It covered the distance in three great strides, and before Aaron was even on his feet again, it had bent down and hungrily fastened its dripping fangs around the back of Gordon's neck. Aaron heard the quick wet crunch as the werewolf's jaws closed. Saw Gordon's body spasm once, and then go limp.

Someone was screaming. Jack. Aaron saw the younger man sprinting across the foyer at the huge beast as it worried at the nape of Gordon's shredded, broken neck. Aaron found himself also striding across the foyer towards them, reaching with his left hand into the inside right hand pocket of his leather biker's jacket. The wolf ripped its wet muzzle away from the dead man in its grasp and turned its blazing yellow eyes on Jack as he ran at it, screaming in grief driven fury. Just as the young weaponsmith leapt to the attack, heroically, stupidly, completely unarmed, the lycanthrope swung one massive hairy hand in a contemptuous backhand which caught Jack in mid air, sending him careening across the reception area to go smashing face first into the wall. There was a dull muddy crack, and he dropped like a stone to lie face up, his mashed nose pouring red.

With fluid animal quickness, the wolf then spun round again to face Aaron who had closed in from its blind side, and with a deep snarl, it sprang at the big man. Quick and nimble as a dancer, with his weight on his right foot, Aaron leant back and rotated his body counter clockwise in a smooth, perfectly executed balletic pirouette, spinning away from the lunging predator. Halfway through the dextrous twirl, his left hand flashed out from inside his jacket, holding a flattish glass bottle of amber liquid which he gripped by the neck. As he completed the turn, he swung his left arm backward with all the force he could muster and smashed the bottle with the half loosened cap over the back of the wolf's neck as it passed him. The high, rich smell of brandy instantly filled the air. Stepping smartly away, only vaguely aware that his left hand was cut and bleeding, Aaron then fished into his jacket pocket with his right had and withdrew a Zippo lighter emblazoned with the Triumph logo, knocking its lid open and sparking the wheel with two quick practiced flicks of his thumb. He turned back to the werewolf as it wheeled round and closed on him again, reaching with those long spindly fingers. He was almost casual as he tossed the metal lighter.

Fwuuuump.

The creature screamed and instantly reeled away, thrashing and howling as it tried in vain to beat out the sudden explosive ball of blue and yellow flames that wreathed its body as the highly combustible booze ignited. It staggered across the reception area, shrieking horribly and leaving a pall of thick stinking smoke in its wake, colliding with walls and glass display cases which toppled and smashed on the floor. Aaron carefully tracked the burning monstrosity as it blundered in panic around the foyer, his eyes watering from the thick smoke and putrid smell of flaming hair and dog meat.

The lycanthrope eventually went to its knees, then onto all fours, weakly crawling into a corner, still burning as the accelerated fire ate into it. Its screams became hoarse croaks and dry, brittle barks that sounded like human coughing. Eventually, these grotesque sounds ceased, as did all movement from the werewolf as it was burnt up, and Aaron stood dispassionately, watching as the flames did their work.

When the fire guttered and finally died, Aaron calmly walked over to the scorched, vaguely humanoid ruin, and unceremoniously kicked it over. It hit the floor with a crisp sizzling sound and a puff of rank smoke, leaving a greasy smear of melted skin and ash in the corner where the walls met. Then he knelt over the remains, reached into his jacket once more and withdrew a steel letter opener with a thin stiletto like blade. Crouched over the carbonized carcass, he located the top two vertebrae of the creature's warped spine amid the gnarled mess of flaky black and blistered red tissue, and thrust the slender blade deep, working it back and forth and few times and twisting it this way and that before pulling it free again.

It was then that he noticed Jack standing nearby, watching him with horror-glazed eyes, the bottom half of his face a red mask of dried blood from his broken nose. Aaron got up from the roasted werewolf and walked over to him.

"Now," he said, placing a hand on Jack's shoulder, "how about those throwing knives?"

4

The sun was setting. He was in a line of archers, a bow in his hands, kneeling on the ground in front of the high wooden walls of a fortress, his eyes fixed on a wide area of torch lit grass before him.

The hills echoed with the howling of wolves.

A woman with long dark hair knelt at his side, like him, looking out over the torchlit ground, an arrow in place, her bowstring at half draw. *For Eanach*, she said, and...

"Aww for fuck's sake, what is *this* pish?"

Ian jerked awake in the back seat of the northbound police cruiser. The healing always took it out of him, and that had been a bad one. His stomach still felt tender and sore, as he knew it would for probably another couple of days. He'd had similar injuries in the past. Self inflicted ones, sustained when he'd been in the very depths of the nightmarish passage of time after the accident.

Ian opened his eyes at the sound of the voice from the front seat and looked forward. The grey haired sergeant who he'd spoken with the previous night, and who'd witnessed his regeneration on the little island earlier, was in the passenger seat. Poor Sergeant Harrison, Ian thought, recalling the stricken, blank eyed look he'd seen on the man's face when he'd woken up. Ian remembered how he himself had felt the day all the madness and terrifying *realness* of the supernatural was made apparent to him. That cold, draining feeling of having your perception of what's real and what isn't permanently shifted. Ian knew first hand that when you figure out that the existence you think you know is just a single thin skin in an infinitely layered and hopelessly deranged onion, the realisation is traumatic to say the least.

The other copper, the one with the broken nose, Wallace, was driving, and the patrol car slowed as it approached the jam of vehicles blocking the road ahead.

Ian sat up, rubbing at his face and trying to wake himself. Trying not to think about Clyde and Matt. He felt like he'd lost a limb. Two.

Looking through the windshield between the driver and passenger seats, he saw the ambulance stopped twenty metres or so further along, just round a curve in the road. He saw the silver saloon car parked across the width of the road in front of the ambulance, and the second car parked at a right angle to the first, barring the adjoining road that wound away to the west. The uneven rock littered terrain of the moors on all sides made going round the blockade impossible, and there was no one standing at the vehicles waiting on assistance. No sign of the ambulance crew or the owners of the two cars.

"What in the name of Christ is this?" mumbled Harrison in the passenger seat, and snatched up the radio. "Dispatch, this is Sergeant Harrison. Be advised, we have two vehicles blocking both roads at the junction of A859 and A858. Can you patch me through to the ambulance, Jim?"

"Roger that, Murdo," replied the dispatcher. "Standby." They waited. A few seconds later, Jim was back on the radio. "No response from the ambulance, Sarge."

Ian saw Harrison and Wallace exchange a quick look.

"Roger that, dispatch," the sergeant said into the radio. "Proceeding on foot to investigate." He flicked a switch and then addressed the other patrol car and the police van behind them. "Papa Charlie seven, Papa Victor two, come in. John, Peter. Stay put and keep your eyes open. Going to see what the story is here. Standby." He put the radio down and turned to the younger constable in the driving seat. "Let's go," he said, and opened the passenger side door.

"Don't go out there," Ian heard himself blurt. The two coppers in the front turned to look at him. "Just... don't."

Now that he was fully awake, he was feeling it. That same indefinable sensation of being watched that he'd carried around with him all day yesterday. It was growing stronger by the second.

"We need to go and see what's happening, Mr Walker," Wallace said.

Ian saw the way Harrison was looking at him. That realisation thing again. The polis could see that something had Ian on his toes.

"What is it?" Harrison asked him quietly, a very sincere look in his eye. The younger guy, Wallace, frowned across at his superior, obviously not understanding Harrison's question or the need for it. Ian opened his mouth to reply, but found he had no voice as he saw from the corner of his eye the huge shadowy shape abruptly looming up outside the car.

The driver's side window suddenly imploded at that moment, and a massive hairy arm snaked into the police car's interior, the enormous clawed hand at the end of it closing around Wallace's face. The young constable let out a muffled scream as the claws sank into his flesh, and then he was dragged out through the shattered window, kicking and shrieking in a cascade of falling glass and blood.

*

"Woah, what the fuck is *that*?" Constable Peter McAuley said, sitting up in the driver's seat of the second patrol car as he spotted the large shadow rushing low to the ground from the gloomy moorland on the right.

In the near darkness of the total eclipse, the vague shape that slid with eerie fluid speed through the undergrowth toward Sergeant Harrison's car was just a formless darting phantom. In the passenger seat next to McAuley, Lorna McDaid gasped as she saw it too and began to say something, but whatever it was turned into a wordless, shuddering groan of horror as the indistinct shadow then reared up at the driver side of Harrison's car, and was momentarily revealed in the glow of McAuley's headlights.

Although there were no zoos on the Isle of Lewis, at first he thought it must be a bear. It was certainly about the right size, reaching well above seven feet tall as it stood on its hind legs, but it was too lean to be a bear, the pointed ears too big, the huge, almost apelike arms and thick angular hind legs too long. Caught for a second in the bright lights, the facial features of the animal were revealed in terrifying detail as it turned toward McAuley and looked straight at him.

He saw the elongated canine snout, the bottomless glowing yellow eyes. The thing peeled its lips back in a leering doggish grin, displaying its teeth. McAuley felt an alarming loosening sensation in his bowels at the sight.

Then it punched through the driver side window of the patrol car in front and dragged Niall Wallace, shrieking and kicking, out of the frame. The thing wrapped its other huge arm around the struggling policeman's chest, enfolding him in an inescapable embrace, then darted its head forward and closed its massive jaws around the back of Niall's neck. His screams were abruptly cut off as his body began to jerk and quiver in the monster's grasp. It held him there, its mouth fastened around his neck for a second before it gave a savage twist of its jaws. Even from inside the car, McAuley heard the wet, popping crunch as Niall's head was torn clean off. It fell to the ground and rolled a short distance, coming to rest in the middle of the road, facing McAuley and illuminated hideously in his headlights. Paralysed at the horrific spectacle, he numbly regarded the frozen expression of dead eyed terror etched on the torn, bleeding features of his colleague's face, which still wore the plaster cast across the broken nose.

In the passenger seat, Lorna screamed. McAuley was also half aware of Cal Dempster and Scarlett Mathie yelling in the back seat. He himself couldn't make a sound. His throat had locked up and he was frozen rigid in his seat, unable to breathe. It was only the sound of Lorna opening the passenger door that roused him from his petrified state.

"*Lorna, no!*" McAuley shouted after her, but she was already out of the car. He threw off his seatbelt and reached for the handle of his own door. As he made to exit the vehicle, he saw Lorna in the headlights as she ran in front of the car, incredibly, she was drawing her baton and sprinting toward the towering beast that still held Niall's limp headless body. Half in and half out of the car, McAuley saw a second huge shadow suddenly burst out from the darkened moorland to the left of the road. It snatched Lorna up in the blink of an eye, bowling into her like a freight train and bounding away across the road, vanishing again into the dark undergrowth. A thin spray of blood splashed softly across the windshield, like gentle drops of thick red rain. McAuley had an insane urge to flick the windscreen wipers on. He heard Lorna's diminishing screams as she was carried off into the murk.

Then the gunfire started.

*

In the police van at the rear of the three car convoy, Authorised Firearms Officer Paul McShane was doing his level best to keep his shit together as he fumbled with the key to the secure safe between the seats, his violently shaking hands almost dropping the small piece of metal before he managed to unlock and open the metal box and grab the two Glock 17 pistols inside. He slapped a full clip into the hand grip of one of the guns, disengaged the safety and thrust it at John MacAllan, the big red haired second sergeant at the station, who was riding in the van with him. MacAllan wasn't an AFO, and had no official clearance to be using the hardware, but in Paul's mind the rule book had swiftly taken a flying fuck to itself the moment he'd seen what could only be described as a big fucking *werewolf* drag Niall Wallace out of the lead car and bite his fucking head off right there at the side of the fucking road. He knew it was no fucking bear. He'd seen *The Howling*. He knew what a fucking werewolf looked like.

Fuck.

Taking and loading the second Glock for himself, Paul and MacAllan exchanged a quick Are we really doing this? Look. Paul drew a deep, shaky breath, trying to steady his fried nerves and ricocheting thoughts, and nodded once.

"Slide over and get out on my side after me," he said to the older man, gritting his teeth as he spoke so his jaw would stop shaking. "Stay low, keep moving. Wait for my word, aim for the chest, make your shots count." He was trying his best to stop his voice coming out in a terrified squeak. "Let's go."

Paul opened the passenger side door quietly and got out, followed a moment later by MacAllan. Crouching low, the two men began advancing up the road, moving along the grass verge on the left hand side of the road. They were in line with the back end of the patrol car in front of them when Lorna McDaid suddenly threw open the passenger side door and ran into the road, screaming incoherently and drawing her baton. Paul was just about to shout at her to clear the line of fire when another fucking werewolf came bursting out of the shadows on his left no more than three metres in front of him, seizing Lorna in its jaws before disappearing again in the thick undergrowth on the other side of the road. It was gone before Paul could even level his weapon.

His attention was then drawn back to the first creature, which discarded Niall Wallace's decapitated body, casually dropping his dripping corpse onto the road like a piece of litter, and with a grating snarl, advanced on the second car containing Peter McAuley and two of the civvies. Paul saw McAuley, who had half stepped out of the car, hurriedly retreat back inside and slam the door closed. In two massive strides the monster was there, drawing back a huge muscular arm, about to again punch through the driver's window.

"*Hit the cunt!*" Paul shouted, and opened up with the Glock, joined a second later by MacAllan.

The two men opened fire on the werewolf, blasting round after round into the huge creature over the roof of the car, pistols spitting flame. The flat *pop-pop-pop-pop-pop* of the Glocks echoed across the darkened moors, and Paul saw the monster jerk and twitch, driven back a few paces as a fusillade of hot Parabellum ammunition slammed into its body. Spent shell casings leapt from the ejection port of the bucking pistol in Paul's hands and fell around his feet, jingling and tinkling on the tarmac as he continued firing at the roaring creature. But it wouldn't go down.

Sighting carefully on the centre of the creature's huge lupine skull, Paul pulled the trigger again, and felt a hollow sinking sensation when there was only the dry click of an emptied magazine. His breath coming in rapid, wheezing gasps, he groped with numb fingers for another ammo clip on his belt. There was a sudden blur of movement in his peripheral vision, and he turned to his right in time to see the second wolf come streaking out of the undergrowth again, this time from the right hand side of the road, hurtling from cover and coming straight at them. "Watch out, John!" he yelled, but too late.

MacAllan saw it, raised his pistol, but didn't even get a shot off before the onrushing creature sprang across the roof of the car and slammed into him, jaws clamped around his throat. Locked together, man and wolf tumbled back off the grass verge and rolled away down the steep shadowy embankment, leaving Paul alone. He turned back to the first werewolf still standing in the centre of the road, its huge hairy body pocked with bleeding bullet holes. It snarled deep in its chest, stalked forward again, seemingly undeterred by its injuries, and then simply wrenched the entire driver side door away from the chassis of the patrol car between them, stooping low and forcing its massive upper torso into the gap as McAuley, mewling and gasping in terror, tried to scramble away on his back across the front seats and escape through the open passenger door. As the creature fell on him and he began to scream, Paul slammed the fresh magazine into the Glock and crouched down, firing one handed into the car's interior, aiming across McAuley's body and unloading at near point blank range into the werewolf's face, which was revealed in a rapid fire series of starkly detailed snap shots in the yellow strobe of the Glock's muzzle flashes. He was half aware of the man and woman in the back seat yelling and screaming, frantically kicking at the windows in their own bid to escape the car. Paul reached out with his left arm, grabbing hold of the thrashing McAuley's jacket, desperately trying to pull his screaming colleague from the car which had become a little piece of hell, the enclosed space of the vehicle's interior filled with bestial roaring, gunfire, screams, the smell of cordite, blood, wild animal and madness. A jet of warm thick liquid gushed across Paul's face, spraying in a hissing fountain and splashing across the inside of the windscreen. McAuley's panicked screeching reached a new ear splitting top note, louder even than the continuous roar of the Glock which Paul continued to fire, pulling the trigger again and again even as something gave way in the desperate tug of war and he fell backwards, landing on his arse on the tarmac and pulling Peter McAuley's shredded upper torso out onto the road beside him.

*

Murdo Harrison tore open the rear door of his cruiser and roughly hauled Ian Walker from the back seat. Grabbing the musician by the shoulders, he began running for the ambulance halted at the roadblock in front of the patrol car, pushing and shoving the struggling man ahead of him as they went, the crack of sustained gunfire coming from somewhere behind and echoing across the murky twilit countryside.

"*No! Wait! Scarlett and Cal...*" Walker shouted, fighting to be free of Harrison's grip as they arrived at the ambulance's rear doors. One handed, Harrison threw them open and hastily bundled Walker inside, practically tossing the skinny freak into the back of the ambulance.

"Stay here. Lock the doors. Don't fucking move," Harrison ordered, then slammed the doors closed. He drew the telescopic ASP baton from his belt, extending it to its full length with a hard flick of the wrist, and began sprinting back down the road towards Peter and Lorna's car, where he could see Paul McShane crouched by the open front passenger side door, laying down a furious barrage of gunfire into the vehicle's interior.

As he ran past his own car, there was a faint sound from his right and Harrison turned, instinctively raising the baton as the second of the huge wolfish creatures suddenly sprang up from the darkened embankment and leapt at him with a rasping grunt. He got the twenty-one inch steel truncheon up just in time, jamming it sideways into the monster's gaping jaws, but the immense weight of the lunging creature pitched him backward and drove him to the ground where he fell heavily onto his back, crunching to the unforgiving surface of the road between the two patrol cars. His mind whirling with the sheer madness of the moment as the creature bore down on him, his hands locked in a desperate death grip around the ends of the metal baton still jammed in the creature's mouth. Harrison struggled to hold the unholy array of impossibly large bloodstained fangs at bay, only his own strength keeping the dripping canines a few precarious inches from his face. The thing's hot breath, all blood and carrion, washed over him in a stinking miasma. Thick bloody drool dripped from the cavernous red maw onto his upturned face as he lay there, futilely trying to resist the overwhelming force of the enormous snarling animal bearing down on him, the hungry abyss of its fiery yellow eyes yawning, seeming to suck him in. Harrison felt claws ripping at his chest and shoulders and he screamed, bellowing with effort and pushing the steel baton back against the hinge of the beast's encroaching jaws with every last ounce of his strength, its claws raking through his heavy jacket and shirt, finding and puncturing the skin and yielding flesh beneath. The wolf's huge open mouth inched closer. The diseased amber eyes flashed in triumph. Harrison closed his eyes and prepared to die.

Then there was a metallic sounding *whoosh* of parting air followed by a thick meaty thud. The grating snarl of the werewolf was abruptly silenced, the pressure on his arms gone. He rolled away and sat up, wiping rancid drool and blood from his face.

The body of the enormous bipedal wolf lay there on the road next to him between the two patrol cars, a spreading pool of dark blood pumping in regular spurts onto the tarmac from the red stump of its neck. Its severed head lay four metres away on the other side of the road.

A strange, dislocated sensation began to drift through Harrison's body, like a slow soothing tide. He had trouble ordering his thoughts. Somewhere, someone was screaming. Something else, something that sounded like an enraged bear or an angry tiger, was roaring and snarling. There was gunfire. The crackle and hiss of a radio and urgent, static distorted voices saying things that he couldn't make sense of, but that seemed desperately important. It was all very confusing. Murdo Harrison shivered, and began pushing himself to his feet, but froze as he felt something sharp pressing into the flesh on the right side of his neck just beneath his jawbone. He turned his head very slowly.

Standing over him was the giant psychopath. The same nameless killer Harrison had personally witnessed die only an hour or so earlier, a large portion of his head reduced to a grisly mulch of pulped brain and shattered skull by Paul McShane's well placed rifle round. But all the same, here he was.

He towered above Harrison, glaring down at him, eyes glowing a glacial blue in the dimmed daylight, and looking for all the world like some angry giant from a children's fairy tale as he held the massive broadsword tight against Harrison's neck.

*

Sealgair woke in darkness.

He lurched up with a convulsive spasm, gasping in a great mouthful of close, hot air. His eyes snapped open, but remained sightless. Had he gone blind? Disorientated, his mind whirling with a thousand thoughts that cascaded through his head in a great confusing rush, he tried to think. What had happened? The last thing he could recall clearly was standing over the Harbinger on the island. His spear poised above the back of the intruder's neck, about to deliver the killing blow. Then something had struck him sharply on the back of his head.

Then... nothing.

The grave. The grave had been disturbed. The seal was broken.

Shuddering black horror shot through his bones as the realisation hit him.

He had failed.

They were loose.

He tried to move, but found his body was tightly cocooned somehow, encased in some sort of smooth material. With a roar of fury, he flexed his huge arms. The restrictive shell that imprisoned him split and burst apart, and he sat up, his senses flowing back to him, his strength buzzing through his now fully restored flesh.

There was no light, but with his heightened vision he saw that he was in a large metal box. There was the smell of motor oil and petrol, of machinery and blood and death. From somewhere outside, there came a confused bedlam of noise. Screams, men shouting, gunfire, and the sound he dreaded. That deep and terrible snarling. A wholly unnatural and loathsome sound, aeons old.

He had failed to protect the grave, and the Ulfhednar were once more loose upon the Earth. There was no more he could do to prevent it from coming to pass.

He could only hunt.

Kicking away the rags of the vinyl body bag, he stood up in the metal box, stooping slightly to accommodate his height and resisting the urge to immediately burst outside. He closed his eyes and cast out with his mind, searching for a particular energy signature. He found what he sought instantly, turned round and stepped to another shelf at the rear of the metal box, which he now knew to be the rear cargo area of some motor vehicle.

His weapons were encased in labelled plastic evidence sacks, and he quickly tore three of them open, slinging the longbow over one shoulder, the half full quiver of arrows over the other, and hefting the great longsword in his right hand.

He stepped to the doors of the metal box and kicked them. With a huge booming clang, the doors burst open and Sealgair jumped down onto the road outside the van, sweeping his gaze left and right across the dim shadowy landscape.

There.

Stepping round the back of the van, Sealgair strode silently up the left hand side of the road in a half crouch, hefting the sword. Ahead of him, a youngish policeman with close cropped hair was kneeling on the grass verge, shouting and firing a pistol through the open front passenger door of a patrol car. On the road next to the armed man lay the upper body of a second policeman, the uniformed corpse ending just below the ribs in a bloody mess of torn skin, shredded clothing and trailing viscera. The lower half of the dead man was clutched in the claws of the beast backing away from the car on the other side.

Seeing it, a jolt of hate filled recognition surged in Sealgair's blood.

Hamrammr. Ulfhednar.

A short distance further along the road, half obscured by the patrol car, Sealgair saw another policeman locked in a desperate struggle with another of the shapeshifters, which was crouched over him, tearing at him with its claws as he somehow managed to hold its teeth away with a short metal baton jammed deep into its jaws.

The gunfire abruptly ceased with a dry click as the young policeman's ammunition ran dry, and the creature in the middle of the road lifted its distorted lupine face, misshapen and cratered with bullet wounds. Ignoring the armed man, it locked its one good eye on Sealgair for a moment, then it turned and fled, vanishing in the blink of an eye into the gloomy bracken on the far side of the road.

Disregarding it for the moment, Sealgair turned back to the ongoing struggle in front of him. As he strode forward, the one with the pistol, who already was busily groping for a replacement ammunition clip, turned and saw him, his mouth dropping open in stupid disbelief as he saw Sealgair bearing down on him. Sealgair had no wish to harm any humans, but with the Ulfhednar loose, he could afford to waste no more time. There was a dully metallic *whaaang* sound as the flat of his sword met the side of the young man's head. He went down immediately, the pistol falling from his limp fingers and clattering away across the tarmac. Sealgair stepped over the unconscious man and the mangled torso beside him, bringing the sword back over his right shoulder in a firm two handed grip as he approached the figures struggling together on the road between the two patrol cars.

With a low grunt, Sealgair swung the sword left to right in a rising arc. The wolf's head came away in a gout of blood, bounced across the second police car's bonnet and rolled into the road. Its body collapsed onto the man beneath it, who managed to thrash and struggle out from under the dead weight, coughing and spitting.

It was with some regret that Sealgair then laid the bloodied blade of his sword against the big policeman's throat as he pushed himself halfway to his feet, but his flesh had been marked by the wolf's claws. Left alive, he would change. Become *vargulf*. He could not allow that to happen.

With the Ulfhednar once more walking the Earth, Sealgair's mission of prevention was over. He was now in the business of containment. Of eradication.

He began his backswing.

*

Move.

Scarlett sat rigidly in the back seat of the patrol car. Cal was next to her, also frozen in place, staring blankly ahead, drowning in the same deep sea of shock. She was cold all over, her skin seemingly sheathed in a layer of paralyzing black ice that rendered her completely, helplessly immobile.

Move, some small part of her mind urged again.

She was only half aware that she was hyperventilating. Small, frightened whimpers squeaked from her constricted throat with each rapid whistling breath.

Move.

It was quiet now, except for the high feedback howl of tinnitus that rang in a sustained note in her head.

Fucking move it, the voice in her head said.

No chance. No danger, ranger. No way, Jose. That thing...

Werewolf. Have some balls and call a spade a spade.

...that thing that had torn the copper in two, right there on the front seat less than a metre away, was out there somewhere. Not to mention the huge bearded psychopath that had killed Clyde and Matt, now back from the dead and standing in front of the car holding a huge sword to Sergeant Harrison's neck.

Scarlett wasn't leaving the car. Not ever.

Aye, because you're totally safe in the car, eh? The other half of her mind said, dripping with sarcasm. *Staying in the motor worked out really well for that first poor bugger that got dragged out the window and got his head bitten off, didn't it? Nevermind the copper that you just watched get ripped in half after the WEREWOLF tore the car door off like it was made of paper. And that big bastard out there's not going to be put off with you staying in here bubbling like a wean if he wants to kill you. Besides, you saw him take that other WEREWOLF'S head off. Maybe you don't even have to be worried about him. Maybe he's on your side.*

Logically, theoretically, Scarlett supposed that made sense, but the past few minutes had been anything but logical. The application of logic could go and shite. Even if the guy had killed one of the... wolf... things... he had still killed Clyde and Matt. He'd tried to kill all of them. Scarlett squeezed her eyes closed. She was faintly aware of tears tracking down her frozen cheeks.

Scared, are you? Afraid? You? Staunch as fuck Scarlett Faye Mathie?

Fuck yes. First the horror of what had happened to them on the island earlier, now this. There were *monsters* out there. Real life honest to God *monsters*. She'd never been so afraid.

Don't talk shite, the other, far braver voice in her head chided. *This is fuck all. Remember when Reece was born? How he came out all blue, with the umbilical cord wrapped round his neck? How he almost died? How he spent three weeks in an incubator almost dying? They told you to be prepared for the worst. Remember when Stu had his cancer scare? Remember the days of wondering, waiting for the test results? You know fine well what real fear is. So move your fucking arse.*

Then she *was* moving. The layer of petrifying ice covering her skin shattered, and Scarlett found herself clambering in a desperate scramble between the two front seats of the patrol car, crawling into the front, forcing herself not to think about the still warm pools of blood and ropes of intestine she slid through as she struggled past the steering wheel, out the gap where the driver side door had been, and fell onto the road outside. On her hands and knees, her heart hammering in her throat, she seized the outside handle on the rear driver side door and pulled it open.

"Cal, move!" she said, her words coming out in a hoarse, breathless gasp somewhere between a scream and a whisper as she reached out to her friend, still sitting frozen in the back seat. Cal flinched at the sound of her voice, as if he hadn't even realised that she'd left the vehicle, then scrambled across the back seat and joined her on the road. Holding each other up, they began running south, back down the road in the direction they'd come, not thinking about where they were going. Just trying to get away. They'd just passed the back of the police van at the rear of the convoy when Cal suddenly pulled up, dragging Scarlett to a halt beside him.

"Where's Ian?" he asked breathlessly.

"Oh, shit." Scarlett felt a pang of shame. In the madness of the past few minutes, she'd totally forgotten about Ian who'd been riding in the other police car. "He was in the car in front of us. We have to go back..." She turned from Cal, but instead of immediately running up the road again, she climbed through the open rear doors of the police van they stood beside. Back at the loch, sitting in the patrol car, shivering, sore and grief stricken, she'd watched the police load the huge body of Clyde and Matt's murderer into the meatwagon. Then, from the tiny earth and wood hut where the killer had apparently lived, the cops had brought out a number of large see through evidence sacks.

Scarlett stepped to the wire storage shelf at the back of the cargo area and quickly found what she was looking for.

*

Cal stood with his back to the open rear doors of the police van, nervously scanning the darkened moors. He grit his teeth together as he whipped his head left and right, trying to control his breath as he watched the bleak terrain for any signs of movement. The tall grass and clumps of gorse that whipped and rippled in the brisk wind blowing across the landscape provided ample cover, and there were plenty of rocky outcrops and dark folds and dips in the land where anything could be lurking, watching him. Glancing up, through the strange opaque veil of fast moving clouds, he saw that the eclipsing moon had now passed the point of totality and was slowly edging away from the centre of the sun, slinking past with horrible sluggish slowness as if reluctant to give up being the centre of attention.

He could hear Scarlett moving about inside the van behind him, and turned to see her emerge carrying a pair of spears. She jumped down from the back of the van and held one out to him. He took it, surprised by the hefty weight of the weapon. The long wooden shaft was almost as thick as his wrist, some two and a half metres long, and was topped with a leaf shaped metal head, itself a further half metre in length.

"Ready?" Scarlett said.

Cal looked at her. "No. You?"

"Nope."

Then they were running back up the road in search of Ian.

They didn't have to look long, because as they came to the front end of the police van, Ian emerged from the rear doors of the ambulance, two car lengths away. Relieved to see him alive, Cal called out to his friend. Ian raised his head at the sound of his voice and stepped down from the ambulance, but then froze. At the same moment, Cal became aware of voices to his left, and skidded to stop, lowering the spear. Between the two patrol cars, he saw the huge bearded madman with the sword, still standing over the kneeling form of Sergeant Harrison. The policeman was talking to the long haired giant, speaking in Gaelic as he knelt there looking earnestly up over his right shoulder at the killer, the edge of the sword blade still pressed against his neck. Cal heard the big lunatic reply in the same language. His voice was surprising soft. Almost tender. There was a short pause in their brief conversation, then Cal saw Harrison sigh and lower his head, offering the nape of his neck to the man standing over him.

*

With his sword's edge tight against the big vein under his jaw, the stocky grey haired policeman slowly turned his head, looked up at Sealgair, and calmly spoke to him in the old tongue. "What happened here today?"

Sealgair saw no harm in telling him. He would be dead soon. "There are demons loose on the island. I tried to stop it from happening. I failed."

"And now?"

"You have been marked. You will turn soon. I am sorry."

The big man dropped his gaze briefly, nodding in grim acceptance. "I feel it. Something in my blood. In my bones." He paused, then met Sealgair's eyes again. "What happens after?"

"I will kill them. Are you ready?"

The policeman let out a long, shuddering sigh. "Make it quick." He bowed his head forward, presenting the back of his neck. Then he made the sign of the cross and began to pray in a soft whisper. Sealgair, impressed with the man's courage, stepped behind him and carefully placed the point of the sword between atlas and axis. It was ill fortune that the policeman had to die. There was iron in him. He would have made a fine hunter.

"Journey well, *Sealgair*," he said, and drove the sword down.

*

Ian watched in numbed horror as Sergeant Harrison's body spasmed once, then seemed to deflate like a punctured balloon as the life rushed out of him. The hulking killer, his eyes glowing a vivid gas flame blue, gave a twist of the wrists, then withdrew the great sword from the back of the copper's neck with a moist *sniiiiick,* and Harrison's body collapsed out of Ian's sight behind the rear end of the patrol car that separated them.

For a long moment no one spoke or moved, and a heavy silence settled over the little stretch of road. Then the brief lull was torn as Scarlett let loose a wordless scream. Ian looked across the road, saw her draw back her arm like a javelin thrower and hurl her spear at the killer. She was only about five metres away from her target and could hardly miss, but as if he'd been sent a letter in the post a week beforehand warning him of the attack, moving with an inhuman quickness, the grizzled giant leant back slightly and neatly snatched the spear out of the air with his left hand as it passed him.

Cal rushed him, that black, sunken look in his eyes that Ian had only ever seen once or twice before, the spear held low in his hands as he charged at the big fucker. He was promptly knocked to the ground though, his feet flying up into the air as the towering freak performed some ridiculously fast ducking spinning manoeuvre, slashing out with the spear in his left hand and sweeping Cal's legs out from under him.

Cal lost his grip on his own weapon as he was flipped arse over tit, and then it too was in the giant's grasp, who now stood holding the massive sword in his right hand and the two spears in his left.

Ian then found *himself* running forward, but stopped in a hurry a few metres away as the big nutter shot him a look that could have frozen a lava flow, and placed the point of the longsword against Cal's throat. Scarlett had also started forward, but like Ian, thought better of it as she saw that Cal's life could be abruptly ended with a flick of the giant's wrist.

And so they remained there, frozen in a bizarre sort of uneven Mexican standoff where one person had all the weaponry, the big man silently holding the business end of the sword against the soft flesh of Cal's throat, switching his cold blue eyes between Ian and Scarlett, who stood on either side of him, powerless to intervene but unable to walk away while Cal lay on the road, looking up at the huge man standing over him.

Ian's mind was frantically playing catch up as he stood there, trying to process everything that had occurred in the last few insane minutes, and at a complete loss as to what might happen next. He had no doubt that the big psycho – who was apparently a fellow immortal - could swiftly end the lives of himself, Scarlett and Cal with a few deft slashes of that sword, probably before they could even so much as flinch. But for some reason, the huge glowing eyed madman who'd wreaked so much carnage that day remained still, just flicking those disturbing gas flame eyes left and right.

And of course, there was the deranged icing on the huge triple tiered cake of crazy; the enormous decapitated body of what could only be described as a werewolf lying in the road.

Ian had an urge to simply burst into laughter. The reality of supernatural forces on Earth was nothing new to him of course, but still. Fucking *werewolves?*

And so he stood there, waiting for whatever insane and probably fatal turn events would take next. Above, the sun was slowly reappearing from behind the moon, and the shadows painting the wind blown landscape began fading to grey and inching back, reluctantly slinking away like vampires before the lazily gathering daylight.

There were still a lot of deeply shaded areas where the returning sunlight had not yet reached though, and it was from one of these - the steep, bracken tangled embankment to Ian's right - that the second werewolf sprang.

*

With the broad shouldered man powerless at Sealgair's feet, the sword point nestling in the hollow of his throat, the woman and the Harbinger stood helpless. Frozen in place and watching him, no doubt expecting Sealgair to kill their friend, who even then looked up at him from the road, meeting his eyes defiantly.

The sudden prickling jolt that shot up Sealgair's spine in warning came a fraction of a second too late, and he only managed to half turn before the other shapeshifter slammed into him.

He was thrown across the road by the wolf's savage impact. He lost his grip on the two spears which went clattering across the tarmac as he stumbled and reeled, the shapeshifter bearing down on him. He tried to set to his feet and bring the sword in his right hand to bear, but the wolf was too close. Sealgair barely managed to get his balance before the beast lashed out with a forepaw and ripped the sword from his hand, immediately following up with another slash of its claws which he only half evaded. Off balance, he was sent blundering further across the road as the great talons ripped across his shoulder. The wolf pressed its attack before he could regain his bearings, and the head darted forward, angled to seize his throat in its long flashing teeth. Sealgair got his hands up in time, locking them in an iron grip around the roaring creature's thick hairy neck. With a tremendous roar of his own, Sealgair focussed all his strength into his forearms, forced the wolf's snapping jaws to one side, and smashed a crushing headbutt into the side of its face. The beast's momentum momentarily broken, he pushed it away to the side, trying to give himself room, but the wolf would not be denied, and caught him a devastating backhanded blow across the face with its left forearm. White light exploded in his head as Sealgair's jaw and cheekbone broke apart. He fell heavily to the road, and just had time to look up and see the wolf's clawed foot come down and plough into his face. He heard the crack of his skull giving way between the awesome force of the grinning beast's stomp and the unyielding road surface beneath his head. All strength left him, and Sealgair was powerless to resist as he was hauled to his feet and lifted off the ground.

The wolf drew his face up close to its own and stared deep into his eyes, and Sealgair felt the foul essence of its mind smother him in a diseased embrace. Felt its gloating, malevolent joy.

The monster opened its massive jaws to receive him, and its entire head abruptly burst apart in a flash of steel and a great fountaining explosion of blood, bone and brain matter. The clawed hands gripping his shoulders loosened, and Sealgair fell to the ground again in a great boneless heap. The world was going grey, a dark mist edging in at the sides of his vision.

Just before he faded out, he saw the Harbinger standing over the huge twitching corpse of the shapeshifter, Sealgair's sword gripped in both his hands, dark blood and hair dripping from the edge of its blade.

5

Forming. Treating. Finishing.

Jack recited the stages of weapon making in his mind, mentally underscoring each word for emphasis.

Annealing. Heating. Sharpening.

Drowning in the unknown, in the unreal, bloody and inexplicable, he clung to the certainty of metallurgy, the sure, familiar and unchanging processes and laws that didn't change, that were free of impossibilities. The solid, unshakeable physics and incontrovertible principles of the forge.

Malleability. Stock removal. Filing. Grinding.

The outcome of weapon making only depended on the skill, knowledge and experience of the smith. There were no uncertainties in the applied science of metallurgy.

No monsters.

Cutting. Folding. Welding.

He absently fingered the thick nylon knife holder under his jacket, strapped diagonally across his chest like a bandolier. Ran his fingertips gently over the protruding handles of the six throwing knives tucked snugly into the sheaths. He had no memory of leaving the visitor centre after... what had happened. He only half remembered being in his house with Aaron sometime later. Had a vague recollection of being in his workshop, taking the knives from the display case on the wall with numb fingers. Then he'd been in his car, in the passenger seat while Aaron drove.

Normalisation. Quenching. Tempering. Work hardening.

Jack was about to begin mentally going through the periodic table and listing the composite elements of various metal alloys when Aaron spoke. The big man hadn't said much up until that point. Jack couldn't recall him speaking at all in fact.

"Did Gordon ever tell you about the wolves of Langabhat?" he said now.

A wintry judder rippled through Jack. *Gordon.* Gordon was dead. Killed. By that... thing.

He looked across at Aaron. He was frowning ahead, keeping his eyes firmly on the road, an intense scowl of concentration on his face as he piloted Jack's car along the twisting country road east. Outside the Jeep's windows, under the diminished light of the eclipse, the moors, fields and tundra rolled by, the long grass and coarse scrub washed in a dismal grey version of weak daylight.

Gordon had told him the story of the Langabhat wolf men when Jack had been a teenager, not long after he'd started working at the visitor centre. He remembered Gordon and him sitting in the centre's café on a stormy autumn day, with the elements screeching and clawing at the large floor to ceiling windows of the restaurant, thick grey sheets of wind driven rain gusting, rattling and spitting against the glass. Jack remembered sitting there in one of the booths, the taste of Isa Shaw's patented cream scones still fresh in his mouth. Gordon sitting across the table with his huge mug of coffee, both hands wrapped around the enormous bowl like vessel, a present from his niece, Jack remembered. Funny how you recall the little things after someone dies. The tiny, inconsequential details of a person's life. All the more heart breaking for their unimportance.

It was just one of those old folk tales. The kind that Gordon had loved and had an encyclopaedic knowledge of. The kind that usually start with the words 'long, long ago'.

Long, long ago, this particular story had gone, there once lived a colony of wolf men on the Island of Lewis. For many years they terrorised the villagers all across the land, but eventually the men of the island hunted them down, surrounded their lair, a tiny village deep in the forest. The villagers set fire to the woods during the day, when they knew the creatures were weak and could not take the shape of wolves, but it was said that one of them escaped the fire and fled. The lone survivor was hunted all across the island, and was eventually trapped on a small island on Loch Langabhat. Knowing that he would be killed by the villagers, in a final act of revenge and defiance, the last wolf man cursed the islanders, and vowed that his pack would one day return. Then, rather than give the villagers the satisfaction of capturing him, he took his own life, throwing himself upon his sword.

"Aye, I know the story," Jack quietly said to Aaron. He sniffed and coughed. "Fucking werewolves? Seriously?" he asked, trying to inject a tone of outraged disbelief into his voice, as if berating someone who'd played some ill advised practical joke that he found in no way amusing. Despite his bluster, he knew he just sounded badly scared.

Aaron, without taking his eyes off the road, only shrugged. "You saw it. What would you call it?"

Jack had no answer to that one. That seven foot nightmare back at the visitor centre, all hair, fangs, muscles and claws, had been decidedly werewolfish, and decidedly real. Very real. Real enough to...

He closed his eyes and fought against the sinking grief that threatened to pull him down and bury him under a landslide of horror. Although his memory of the last half hour or so was patchy at best, his traitorous brain had no problem gleefully replaying in visceral detail the insane sight of that thing clamping its huge bloodied jaws on the back of Gordon's neck, and only too glad to happily recall the sound of Gordon's screams and the noise his spine had made as it crunched and popped between the monster's teeth...

Jack squeezed his eyes tightly shut and bit down on his tongue, hard enough to taste blood. Something else. Think about something, *anything* else.

"You seemed to know what was going on," he said to Aaron. "And the way you killed it..." He had a half coherent, dreamlike memory of looking up from the floor and seeing Aaron gracefully dodging away, avoiding the wolf's claws, smashing something on its back and setting it on fire somehow. Then he'd passed out. Then there was a foggy semi-conscious recollection of Aaron kneeling over a huge burnt carcass on the floor, sliding a knife or something into the back of its neck.

"Jack, to be honest, I don't know much more than you about what's going on," Aaron said. "When I was on the phone with Gordon earlier and he told me everything that had been happening today out at the centre... then there was that noise on the line. Like something howling. I remembered the old story about the Langabhat wolf men... It was really just a best guess scenario."

"But you knew something was going on," Jack pressed. "You told Gordon something was coming through."

Aaron shrugged. "The birds at the standing stones. The lass in the kitchen cutting herself. The kids crying. The eclipse. You know what a portent is, right?"

Jack nodded. "A sign something's going to happen."

"Right. An omen. I don't need to tell you that no one really knows what standing stones were for. Time keeping, burial sites, astronomical significance and all the rest of it, yeah? You know the theories." Jack nodded again. "There's a few people though," Aaron went on, "that think standing stones are gateways. Portals."

Jack thought about that for a very scary second. "To where?"

Aaron looked across at him with a vague hand gesture. "Who knows? The only thing I know for sure, Jack, is that in my experience, there's a lot to be said for the theory that every myth, superstition and legend has a grain of truth at its origin. Like the wolf-men of Langabhat, or burning and beheading. Think of all the stories you've read and heard about vampires, dragons, witches and... you know, werewolves. How many say you have to remove the head and burn the body to kill them for good?"

Jack nodded silently as his mind tried to keep up with Aaron's insane rationale.

"You boil water to make it drinkable. You can clean a wound by burning out infection. Fire kills just about any organism you can think of, natural or not, but it's also thought to be spiritually cleansing, which is why the Inquisition used it during the witch hunts in the sixteenth century. Purification by fire and all that. The act of beheading, it's all about parting the body from the spirit." He reached across and tapped Jack lightly on the nape of his neck. "Right here. Between the top two vertebrae of the spine, the atlas and axis as they're known, is where the brain stem fuses with the spinal column; where you could say the body and mind come together. Separate that, and it's game over. Physically, it's the quickest, cleanest way to kill any living vertebrate. That's why the Romans, the Samurai and other ancient cultures used it as a means of delivering a 'warrior's death'".

As much as things could right then, Jack had to admit it made sense. The act of decapitation popped up all over the place in myths and folklore where immortal beings were concerned. Bizarrely, the one example that stuck in his head right then was of Sean Connery's Ramirez in *Highlander*, schooling Christopher Lambert's Connor MacLeod on the rules and regulations of their deathless kind. Only decapitation could kill an immortal, Sean had taught him, speaking with a Scottish accent far more convincing than Lambert's. That had always struck him as weird in that film. Christopher Lambert - a French American actor with a horrendously bad Scottish accent playing a hairy arsed highland clansman, and Sean Connery - a dyed in the wool Scotsman with a broad home grown brogue, playing an Egyptian swordsman from Japan, but with a Spanish name. The finger clicking opening bars of Queen's *A Kind of Magic* began playing in Jack's head when he realised Aaron had started speaking again.

"All you need to know and believe right now, Jack, is that some of the freaky shit that people call supernatural and paranormal, is *real*. Very real and very dangerous." He looked across to gauge Jack's reaction, as if waiting for the young blacksmith to laugh in his face and call him a nutter. Jack probably would have laughed, if he hadn't seen what he had seen, and if he weren't so dangerously close to soiling himself at the memory.

"What happened to you?" he asked the older man. The matter-of-fact tone and total unquestioning conviction in Aaron's words were the type you only hear in someone who is speaking from hard learned personal experience. "How'd you know all this?"

Aaron didn't reply right away. A strange look passed over his face, and Jack saw the other man's knuckles whiten momentarily on the steering wheel, saw the tightening of the muscles around Aaron's jaw. Then, speaking in a hollow, toneless voice, he just said, "My daughter," before clamming up again. Jack knew better than to press for details. The bleak expression that had flickered across Aaron's features for a second was that of a man who'd suffered a terrible, unknowable loss.

Aaron was silent for a few more seconds, then he sniffed, cleared his throat. "After Libby... died..." he went on, "I read a lot of books, Jack. I travelled. All over the world. For years, I followed stories and news reports. Chased up urban legends, rumours, folk tales, ghost stories. Most of them turned out to be nothing, but sometimes.... I've seen a lot, Jack. Enough to know that there's a whole other world, maybe an infinite amount of them, just a scratch in the surface away. You're a smart lad. You know the theories about parallel universes?" Jack did. Aaron paused a moment, as if considering his own words. "Now and then, not often, but sometimes, something from somewhere else... slips through. The good news is that there's always a way to fight back."

Jack had a million questions, but elected not to voice them right then. He thought it would be best for now if he just tried to absorb what Aaron was saying. He drew in a deep breath, let it out slowly and tried to balance and calm his mind. It wasn't easy. It was actually really fucking hard. He tried to imagine what Gordon would have said. Gordon, a man whose opinion and advice he had trusted and valued above all others', would probably have smiled, favoured him with one of those wry grins of his and simply told him to roll with the punches. He turned to Aaron. "So what do we do?"

Aaron considered for a moment. "When it happened earlier, at the standing stones, when there was the panic. You told me people collapsed? How many?"

"Everyone really. Everybody ended up rolling about on the ground with their hands over their ears."

"But that first girl, she collapsed before that happened?"

"Aye."

"Did you see anyone else like the girl? Anyone actually unconscious? Anything... weirder than people with their hands over their ears?"

Jack thought back to those few strange minutes that had preceded the tourists' mass exodus from the Calanais Visitor Centre. "There was one kid, he looked like he saw something, and was backing away from it. And another older woman, she looked like she was… levitating. That was pretty weird."

"Anyone else?" asked Aaron, a note of worry in his voice.

"I don't know. Everyone just seemed to hit the deck. I had my eyes closed most of the time. I don't know."

"Five birds? Three times?"

"What? Oh, right. Aye, five birds, each time."

"Fuck."

"What?"

"Best guess?"

"Aye?"

"Numbers are powerful, Jack. That's something else I've learned over the years, mate. They're *relevant*. Especially the number three. Look it up. From what you've told me, there's a good chance that there's another four of those things running about somewhere."

"Ah. Fuck."

"Aye. How good are you hitting moving targets with those knives?"

Jack was too upset about the prospect of another four werewolves loose somewhere on the island to say that he was, as a matter of fact, pretty damn good indeed with moving targets. He was thinking about what kind of carnage a free roaming quartet of seven foot tall, man-eating, bipedal wolves could inflict when let loose in any kind of population centre, Stornoway for example.

Oh, Christ.

The festival.

His mind reeling from the day's bloody madness, Jack only just then remembered there were a few extra thousand people in town that weekend. He was about to mention this to Aaron when the car rounded a bend and they saw the roadblock just ahead. Two cars parked at right angles, one barring their way east and the other parked lengthwise across the intersecting road which ran north and south. Behind the roadblock, an ambulance and three police vehicles sat stationary. There were people there. Two men and a woman. One of the men, a slim long haired guy, appeared to be holding a sword, and there were what looked like several bodies littering the tarmac.

6

ARO Paul McShane woke up lying on the gurney in the back of the police van.

A woman, a very attractive woman he noticed, was leaning over him, applying something cool and sterile smelling to his temple, which hurt like a bastard. He could feel a lump there that had to be the size of an unusually big ostrich egg, and it pulsed and throbbed through his skull in aching, nauseously regular swells. The dentist drill whine of tinnitus in his ears was horrendous. There'd been gunfire. Lots of gunfire.

"Uuuuurrrghhhh..." he moaned, with much feeling. He was pretty sure he was about to throw up.

"Don't move," the woman said. Scarlett. That was her name. One of the civilians.

"Aaaaaaahhhh. Ooooooooft. My fuckin' heid..." It hurt to speak, to breathe. The blood pounding in his head was a constant and repetitive hammer blow synchronised to the beating of his heart. To simply have a pulse was to know the deepest bowels of hell.

"It's okay," Scarlett said. "You're safe. Cal says you've got a concussion... I thought he killed you."

"Carol? Who's Carol?" He'd had a girlfriend called Carol once. Big lass. Serious eyebrows on her. Bit of a munter in all honesty. He couldn't think why she'd want to kill him though. That made no sense. This was all really confusing.

"*Cal.* My friend. The one who broke your pal's nose last night?" Scarlett prompted him.

"Oh. Right. Dempster," Paul grunted. "Right. Why'd he want to kill me?"

"No, for fuck's sake," Scarlett sighed impatiently. For a nurse, she didn't have much of a bedside manner. Her tender healing touch with the medical swab or whatever it was on his doubtlessly grotesquely mangled head could have been a touch more gentle as well. "The big hairy bastard," she said. "The one you shot earlier. I thought *he'd* killed you. He smacked you on the head with a sword."

"Ah." Paul remembered now. Sort of. It was hazy. Confused and fractured, like a half recalled nightmare, but the full horrible jist of what had happened was coming together in his head quickly. He really wished it wouldn't. People, his fellow officers, were dead. "Aw, for..." he groaned as it all fell insanely into place. "Werewolves? Tell me that didn't really happen. That had to some mental concussion dream, right? Are there fucking *werewolves* out here?!"

"It's okay. They're dead," Scarlett said. She looked down at him, pausing for a moment in her clumsy swabbing of his temple. Her eyes, deep blue flecked with light green, really were something else. Slightly slanted. Like a cat. A really hot cat. "You know... your friends?" she said gently "The other cops..."

"I know."

"I'm sorry."

Lorna. Peter. Niall. John MacAllan. All gone. Just like that. "What about Murdo? Sergeant Harrison?" He remembered seeing Harrison running towards him from the ambulance, drawing his baton, then the second werewolf had come flying up out of the embankment, and then the big beardy psycho - who's melon Paul clearly remembered blowing a large hole in with his rifle - had been there, swinging a huge sword at his head. Then nothing. The woman, Scarlett, met his eyes and gave another sad little shake of her head. Harrison too, then. He'd liked and respected the big sergeant. Never had a bad word to say about anyone, but no soft touch either. Just a good big guy. Paul closed his eyes. Later, he told himself. Keep that shit for later.

He pushed himself up into a sitting position, manfully managing to stop himself from whimpering like a six year old girl as the horrific pounding in his head swelled like a rolling timpani building to a crescendo. "Painkillers," he almost sobbed. "I need painkillers."

"Here," Scarlett said, handing him a brown pill bottle, which he eagerly unscrewed before gratefully dry swallowing four of the fat white tablets inside without so much as a passing glance at the label. Paracetamol, Codrymadol, morphine or elephant tranquilizers, he wasn't fussed about what he was necking as long as it made his head stop feeling like it was about half a psi from bursting like an over inflated beach ball. "Cal took them from one of the medical kits," Scarlett said, nodding at the pills.

"What happened to the ambulance crew?" Paul asked.

She looked away. "We found their bodies... what was left. Down in the embankment."

"Jesus Christ." Paul murmured. More dead. His mind was clearing, beginning to function again. "Where's my radio?" he asked urgently "I need to call this in."

Scarlett handed it to him. "It's okay," she said. "We used it already, spoke to someone called Jim at the station. Help's coming. We found your gun as well." She gave Paul the Glock. It had a fresh magazine. He had one more spare in his belt.

"Good," Paul said, checking and holstering the weapon then thumbing the radio switch. "I need to tell them what's going on." This should be a laugh, he thought, raising the radio. "Come in control. This is ARO Paul McShane. Jim, you there? Over."

"This is control. How you doing, Paul?" Jim's voice came back. "We've got cars en route. What in the name of Christ's going on out there? The civvie that radioed in told us some kind of animal attack? Can you confirm there's officers down? "

"Affirmative," Paul stated. "Sergeants Harrison and MacAllan, Officers Wallace, McDaid, McAuley, and the ambulance crew. All ten-double-oh. Jim..." *How do I put this? Suggest immediately arm all officers with firearms and silver ammunition?* Paul broke contact with the dispatcher for a moment and turned again to Scarlett. "Where's the big fucker with the sword?"

*

The big fucker with the sword had lay there on the road, unconscious or dead. Ian couldn't tell which, though he strongly suspected the former. He stood over the massive body, the broadsword still gripped in his hands, watching him closely, which was difficult considering the distraction presented by the corpses of the two headless werewolves also lying nearby, one of which he'd created himself.

After the thing's head had burst apart on the edge of the sword, the giant, on his hands and knees, his face all slanted in peculiar angles and grotesquely dented at the back, had looked up Ian. He'd stared intently at him for a few seconds with those sapphire eyes, then slumped unmoving to the road, lying in a battered bloody pile. The three of them, Ian, Scarlett and Cal, had just stood there silently for what seemed like ages, looking down at the huge lifeless figure and the two decapitated werewolves sprawled out on the road nearby. Impossible, yet there, clear as day and a million times as ugly on the tarmac right in front of them.

It was Cal who'd eventually got them moving. He didn't try to come up with some futile explanation for what had happened, just quietly started giving calm, practical instructions to him and Scarlett to keep their reeling minds occupied.

Dazed and brittle with delayed shock but still functioning, they found the only surviving policeman by the roadside next to the second patrol car, lying beside the half-a-body of his colleague. Cal checked him over, then had Ian and Scarlett help move the unconscious man into the back of the police van and onto the gurney formerly occupied by the reanimated bearded behemoth. Then he got through to the police dispatcher on the radio and told them what had happened. As best as he could anyway, giving only the salient points. Cal didn't mention anything about rampaging werewolves or reanimated corpses.

They found the mostly eaten remains of the two man ambulance crew in the tall grass close to the roadside. There was little left of them. The hollowed out, limbless and headless ruins were barely recognisable as human cadavers. It was only the blood stained scraps of familiar green uniform that identified the scattered red heaps as the remains of the missing paramedics. They also found the two cops who'd been snatched off the road, again stumbling on the partially devoured bodies half hidden in the tangled undergrowth by the side of the road.

The sun fully re-emerged by then, they'd trudged silently back to the road, Scarlett going inside the police van to check on the unconscious cop in the back, Ian and Cal again standing over the still form of the resurrected killer, Ian once again armed with the sword and Cal holding one of the spears at the ready. They'd both previously seen the dead man zipped up in a body bag, half his head missing, unquestionably deceased, but he'd come back.

Ian, freaked out as he was, was less perturbed by this particular facet of the situation than Cal probably was. He was, after all, a fellow immortal to the big psychopath with the penchant for mediaeval weaponry. He supposed given their unnatural natures, it wasn't all that strange that he felt at least a little sense of kinship with the man who'd been trying so hard to kill him for the past two days. Disgusted at the undeniable feeling of relief he felt in finally knowing that there were others in the world like him, knowing that he wasn't alone, Ian also felt like an absolute prick. The bastard had murdered two of his best friends. He was thinking how completely fucked up that really was when they heard the car approaching.

Ian and Cal looked over and saw it; a dark blue four by four, approaching them along the adjoining country road that led to the western side of the island.

"Dude, what do we do?" Ian asked, glancing at Cal.

"I don't know," Cal replied, frowning over at the jeep as it came to a stop before the car blocking the road west. "We should probably keep them away from all… this," he said, gesturing at the bodies, human and not so much, the drying splashes and pools of blood, weapons, spent shell casings, car parts and smashed glass littering the little stretch of road.

Two figures emerged from the four by four. A big shaven headed guy with a goatee and dressed in motorcycle leathers, accompanied by a younger, slim built guy who had a badly scared look about him, and who kept glancing uneasily at the wind blown moors surrounding them on all sides. He had something on under his jacket that looked like a bandolier.

"Ah, shit," Cal muttered. "You okay to watch this big cunt while I go and speak to them?"

"Aye, on you go. Doesn't look like he's getting up anytime soon. I'm cool."

"Just be a second." Cal turned and jogged towards the two newcomers.

Ian sighed and hefted the sword in his hands. It felt far lighter than he would have imagined, given the size of the thing. He'd been amazed that he'd even been able to swing it with any degree of accuracy. In truth, he'd made no conscious decision to do what he had. Getting involved in the vicious brawl between man and beast had been the last thing on Ian's mind as the enormous hillbilly and the even bigger werewolf had gone toe to toe. Then, for some strange reason, he'd found himself picking the sword up off the blood slicked road surface, a helpless spectator as his impetuous body overruled his horrified mind, and rushed gallantly in to join the fight. The sword had felt alive and responsive in his hands. Hungry. He'd barely had to strain himself to swing the weapon in a high, handsome arc and send it bursting through the monster's skull in such explosively spectacular fashion.

He looked at the sword now, studying it closely for the first time. Just by having it in his hands, he could tell it was very old. Simple in its design, with practically nothing in the way or ornamentation, the sword had a feel of hard use and long antiquity about it. The only decoration evident were the Runic characters etched into the dull grey steel along the flat of the blade, scrawling in a straight line up the first foot of its fearsome length. This time, when Ian saw his self designed monogram inscribed among the other unknowable hieroglyphs and ciphers, he wasn't quite as freaked out as he'd been on the island when he'd seen the same symbol on that cairn. There was that sense of alignment again.

Ian thought about that for a second. *Alignment.* The eclipse. That creeping mental sensation that all this horrendous madness had a warped feel of predetermination about it. That strange feeling of homecoming as he'd paddled along the loch, his head alive with music for the first time in months.

Although he of course had the natural male urge to do so, Ian refrained from running his thumb along the edge of the sword to gage its sharpness. He felt it was safe to assume that the ancient weapon was well honed, possessed of razor like keenness fit to trim a midge's moustache. Ian knew nothing about sword fighting save what he'd learned from watching movies. Before today, he'd never even held a real sword. He gave it a few tentative practice swipes through the air, again surprised by the lightness of the weapon. It felt good. Right. As if he'd owned and used the sword for years.

It was while he was practicing his mastery of the blade that the giant hillbilly suddenly got back to his feet and was abruptly towering over Ian, glaring down out of that terrible craggy face, which was, of course, now completely healed.

Stupidly, Ian tried to swing the sword, but he didn't even manage to move it more than an inch before it was simply wrenched out of his hand and he felt the point pressed into the soft flesh under his chin.

"Go ahead, fucker," he heard himself say in a weary groan of defeated acceptance. "Give it another shot. I sure as shit can't figure out how to do it."

The huge killer just kept staring down at him. Ian felt something prodding and poking at his thoughts. He stared right back into the giant's face. Sick of it all. Tired. Angry. Grieving. Terrified. He just wanted it to be over.

Your coming is as a plague, Harbinger.

The words that shimmered in his thoughts weren't spoken in any language he knew, but Ian still understood them. His eyes still held on those of the deathless man looming over him, there was the feeling of something momentous happening, some moment of great significance which he couldn't even begin to comprehend.

My weapons are washed with the blood of the Ulfhednar, the voice in his mind said. *Take them, and try to undo some of the damage you have done. There are more of them.*

Then he was gone. The murderer turned, leapt off the embankment and sprinted away through the scrub and long grass of the surrounding countryside, swift and agile as a deer. Ian lost sight of him after a few seconds, and was standing there on the road looking out into the cold empty wasteland when Cal, the two newcomers, Scarlett and the armed policeman walked over and joined him.

"Where the fuck's Grizzly Adams got to?" Scarlett asked, looking around in confusion.

Ian pointed off into the moors in the direction the man had vanished, just as the mournful whining wail of approaching sirens rose in the distance.

"He said there are more of them," he muttered to no one in particular, still gazing away into the bleak windblown tundra.

"Ian, this is Aaron," Cal said. Ian turned and saw he was indicating a goateed, built-like-a-brick-shithouse bald dude in bike leathers. "He's a local. He thinks he knows what's going on." The newcomer nodded to Ian, who nodded back.

"Does the word Ulfhednar mean anything to you?" Ian asked him.

From the look on Aaron's face, Ian could tell that it did, and that it didn't mean anything good.

7

Bryan Goodman shut off the hot water and stepped from the walk in shower cubicle. His skin pink and tingling from the high pressure shower jet's pounding, he took a towelled bathrobe from a hook on the bathroom door, shrugging into it and fastening the belt across his expansive waist. Taking a towel from the heated rail on the ceramic tiled wall, he left the spacious en suite bathroom and stood in the farmhouse's master bedroom, briskly rubbing at his face and balding pate with the luxuriantly soft cotton towel.

He felt pleasantly bloated and sleepy, the way one did after a large and satisfying meal. A nap would be great, and the large oak four poster bed on his right looked extremely inviting, but he resisted the urge to lie down and catch forty winks. He had plans to make. Things to do.

He shrugged out of the bathrobe and thoroughly dried himself, considerately depositing the damp robe and towel into the wicker laundry basket in the corner when he was finished. Naked, he left the bedroom and descended the stairs to the farmhouse's ground floor, admiring the glowing sheen of the highly polished walnut steps and banister as he went down.

In the spacious lounge, he found his clothes neatly folded in the corner where he had left them some time ago, and unhurriedly dressed himself. Clothed again, he stepped to the large bay window. Outside, beyond the low red brick wall bordering the neatly landscaped front yard, empty moorland stretched away to the horizon on all sides in a rolling patchwork of dull brown and sullen green, gloomy and wan under the tumultuous blanketing of racing grey clouds above. But for the heather which trembled in the wind, nothing moved. All was silent but for the faint murmur of the hard gusting gale outside, pushing against the windows.

Turning back to the living room, he looked down thoughtfully at the mostly skeletonised human corpse lying spread-eagled on the large Persian rug on the floor before the fireplace. The rug was completely ruined, of course. A shame really. It truly had been a singularly beautiful piece of artwork, and must have cost at least a couple of grand. Maybe a dedicated and well equipped carpet restorer, armed with a variety of industrial strength stain removers and a liberal amount of elbow grease could have some success restoring the rug, but it would likely never again fully regain its former complex glory, with its dazzling array of intricate patterns and skilfully weaved design. There was only so much blood, shit, piss and other various other bodily fluids stain removers, industrial strength or not, can be effective against.

Bryan had been surprised by how easily he'd gained access to the farmhouse. In times such as these, when horrific stories of murder, assault, child abuse and an endless variety of other human cruelties were humdrum everyday news, he'd expected at least some wary suspicion from whoever opened the door. Surely no one just welcomed complete strangers who turned up uninvited on their doorsteps into their homes anymore? Then again, Bryan was from Los Angeles. He figured the crime rate on this quaint little Scottish island was very different to that back home.

As it turned out, the man who answered the door, an ageing hippy type of about fifty with a lush head of silvering pony-tailed hair and an open, friendly face, had readily bought Bryan's story about his car breaking down nearby and the unfortunate lack of mobile coverage out here in the countryside, miles from anywhere. The farmhouse's owner, who introduced himself as Liam Kilsyth, had warmly invited Bryan inside to use his phone and call for a mechanic, ushering him through a bright, many canvas adorned hallway and into a small but clean and well equipped kitchen that was filled with the delicious spicy aroma of simmering chilli.

While Bryan had been making his fake call, just punching in random numbers and then having a fictitious conversation with the dead tone on the line, his gracious host had put the kettle on. When Bryan hung up, Liam insisted he have a cup of tea to warm him from the bitter cold winds outside. They'd chatted a little.

Liam was a landscape artist. Watercolours mainly, though he dabbled in oils from time to time. He did not bad. Had a steady enough stream of business with a few of the gift shops in town, his work popular with the tourists and locals alike. He'd even sold to a gallery or two on the mainland. Yes, he lived there alone. Wife had passed on a few years before, and the kids had moved away, as most of the kids on the island did.

It was when the painter turned away momentarily to stir the bubbling pot of chilli on the hob, that Bryan picked up the heavy wooden chopping board from the counter. A quick, glancing blow to the back of the skull had sent the artist folding neatly and silently to the kitchen floor.

Bryan had found some duct tape in the cabinet beneath the sink, and Liam had eventually regained consciousness in the lounge some time later, finding himself naked, his ankles, wrists, chest and forehead securely bound with the duct tape, immovably anchored to one of his stout oaken kitchen chairs. Bryan had also taped his eyelids open. But he didn't tape Liam's mouth. He wanted to hear the artist.

Bryan hadn't said a word as the pony-tailed painter had wept and begged and cursed and screamed. He just stood there, a few feet away from his bound, naked and defenceless prey, similarly disrobed, the heat of the merrily crackling fireplace warming his bare skin.

He just stood there, and let the shift slowly take place.

In the fading light of the ongoing eclipse outside, Liam Kilsyth's screams had reached new and impressive levels of ear piercing shrillness, his taped open eyes helpless to avoid witnessing Bryan's transformation from man into wolf in close up, visceral detail. He'd been close enough to hear the small squeaks, snaps and pops Bryan's body made as it stretched, twisted, shifted and reformed itself.

To Bryan, the mind buckling fear pouring from the bound, shrieking man had been like a long cool drink of water on a hot day. By the time the change was complete, the watercolourist's throat had finally given out from all the screaming, and he was making strange, hoarse barking sounds, like an injured dog with laryngitis. He'd also lost control of his bodily functions. The ripe, fecund stink of his shit and piss had been strong and delicious in Bryan's newly sensitive nose.

He'd taken his time eating Peter Kilsyth, keeping the naked, bound artist alive as long as possible as he leisurely stripped the meat from his bones with tooth and claw, beginning with the calf muscles and working his way up, wringing every last possible drop of sweet terror that he could from the human. It really was fascinating how much of a person's body you could remove before they eventually expired. As long as one was careful not to damage any of the major arteries or vital organs, it could go on for quite some time.

And it did. *Quite* some time.

When Bryan, who wasn't just Bryan anymore, felt the skinned, partially eaten and for the most part deboned human was drawing its final tortured breaths, he neatly separated the axis and atlas with a quick, accurate snap of his jaws, drinking in the human's essence. Its *manna*. The wolf in him had been asleep for over a thousand years, and like the others of its kind who had been reborn that day, it needed to feed. On the fear and flesh and souls of humans, it needed to feed to come completely alive and regain its full strength.

Some time later, when the eclipse had passed and the hated sun once more held sway in the sky, Bryan, once again in human form, had pushed himself painfully up from the carpeted floor of the lounge, his bones aching and awkward beneath his skin. His face, chest and arms had been coated with drying blood; the tacky, semi-congealed dark red paste irritating on his naked body, every inch of which crawled and prickled with the insectile scuttling sensation of pins and needles. He went upstairs in search of a shower.

So it was that he now stood, freshly scrubbed and dressed again, looking thoughtfully down on his kill. He turned away from the carcass and walked back down the hall to the kitchen, stepping to the laptop lying open and powered up on the counter. Liam had been checking his email. A piece of his had been accepted by a gallery in Manchester. Shame.

Bryan clicked on the search box at the top right hand corner of the browser screen and googled Stornoway harbour. Within seconds he was directed to the Stornoway Port Authority website and presented with a full schedule of all the vessels coming, going and presently docked at the large marina, complete with each ship's type, country of origin and destination. Finding a notepad and pen in a kitchen drawer, he quickly jotted down some of these details, considerately shut down Liam Kilsyth's laptop, and exited the farmhouse, a little reluctantly leaving behind its warm intermingling aromas of fresh home cooked chilli and spilled blood.

PART TEN

The giantess old in Ironwood sat,
In the east, and bore the brood of Fenrir.
Among these one in monster's guise,
Was soon to steal the sun from the sky.
There feeds he full on the flesh of the dead,
And the home of the gods he reddens with gore.
Dark grows the sun, and in summer soon,
Come mighty storms.
Would you know yet more?

The Poetic Edda

1

His eyes flicking left and right, scanning the burned out wood for any survivors of the fire, Ulfar isn't paying any attention to the sky above, and so doesn't notice the day's stealthily growing dimness until it is too late.

It is only as he slowly approaches the cave mouth with Ailde, straining to peer into the murky opening in the cliff face ahead, that he realises that the early morning light is unnaturally weak, and rapidly growing fainter still. A sudden dread tickles the hairs on his bare arms, and he glances up, gasping in superstitious awe at the sight of the mist veiled sun already more than half obscured as the dark circle of the moon passes in front of it.

In that instant, Ulfar is transported back through the years, suddenly a small child again, sitting at his mother's feet in the tiny earthen floored hut in which they'd lived. He is gazing up at her, rapt in the gentle sound of her soft voice as she tells him the stories of their people, all the wondrous myths, legends and fables of mighty gods, brave heroes, and terrible monsters. Monsters such as the trickster Loki's demonic offspring Fenrir, and *his* sons Hati and Skoll, great wolves who eternally chase the sun and moon across the sky.

Beware the day that turns to night, little Ulfar, his mother had warned him, *for when the daytime sun grows dark, it warns us that the wolf Hati has seized it in his jaws and brought it to bay. That is the time to fear, my son, for Ragnarok threatens.*

Momentarily frozen, his mother's words still whispering in his mind, Ulfar glimpses the spear whipping out of the dark opening in the cliff face just ahead. Sees it pierce Ailde's chest, running him through and throwing him backward. The impaled blacksmith lands several strides away in a big cloud of smoke and disturbed ash.

Then the wolves come, roaring out of the black.

A score or more of the Ulfhednar, accompanied by as many again of their vargulfen offspring. In the absence of daylight brought on by the eclipse, the berserkers are fully transformed, and every one armed for battle. They wield great swords, axes, spears and maces. Several carry wide iron rimmed shields, and all wear armoured vests of either chain mail or lamellar plates. The vargulfen come with them, pouring out of the cave mouth and streaming around their masters' legs, liquid fast, running low to the ground, baying hungrily like an eager pack of monstrous hunting hounds unleashed.

They spill out into the darkened forest in a shrieking horde, immediately dispersing, leaping and bounding down the slope toward the Sealgairean line. The demons roar as they fling themselves at the men, frenziedly cleaving into the humans in a savage, unstoppable wave of iron, claw and fang. The skirmish line shatters, breaking apart under the sudden onslaught, the orderly single rank of men bending, fracturing and dissolving until a desperate sprawling melee spreads across the charred forest floor.

Ulfar, roaring at the men behind him to form up and stay together, backs down the hill, and sees one of the berserkers single him out and lope forward. The huge armoured creature roars as it swings an enormous double headed axe in a vicious arc at his head. Ulfar gets his shield up, angling it to deflect rather than block, but he's still sent reeling under the impact, staggering away to the side, his left arm numb to the shoulder. The shapeshifter follows him as he stumbles across the sloping ground, fighting to find his balance, the monster closing in and lashing out with the claws on its left hand. Ulfar manages to duck beneath the blow and scrambles back, raising his sword and shield again. All around them, the air is filled with the savage sound of battle, the dead black forest ringing and clashing with the scraping clang of steel on steel, the booming roars of the marauding lupine pack and the screams of dying men.

The shapeshifter lunges again, leaping across the ground and brining the axe down in a huge downward swipe. Ulfar raises his shield above his head to meet the assault, grunting in pain as his left arm buckles under the blow. The wolf once again follows up with a left handed slash of its claws, but Ulfar, anticipating the tactic, twists his body away, draws back his sword arm then springs forward, pushing from his toes to gain momentum, ramming the half shattered remains of his shield into the shapeshifter's body with his left arm and thrusting at the its unprotected groin with his right. The blade cuts deep, sliding hungrily into the huge creature's flesh beneath its plate vest, severing the large artery in the thigh. It screams and backs away, dark blood pumping freely from the gaping wound and soaking the matted hair of its muscular canine legs. Ulfar follows it, pressing his advantage, easily evading the wolf's next blow with the axe, which comes at him clumsily, almost slowly. He ducks beneath the sideways attack and slashes at his opponent's legs, chopping his sword backhanded into the outside of the creature's right knee. Even as it shrieks in pain, he is reversing the blow, twisting his wrist and swinging the sword upward. The heavy blade cleaves deep into the underside of the shapeshifter's upper arm, almost completely severing the limb. The demon roars, falling away to the side, its maimed arm flapping uselessly, dropping the great axe, blood bucketing from its wounds. Ulfar brings his sword back over his shoulder, meaning to take his enemy's head, then the vargulf hits him. The dim lit forest spins crazily as he is bowled over and sent rolling down the slope, the huge wolf snapping and clawing at him as they turn over and over, locked together, kicking and thrashing in the warm blood splattered ash carpeting the forest floor.

*

The enemy has chosen their ground well, Vandrad thinks grimly as he draws back his arm, feeling the straining tension of the bow and the brush of the feather fletches on his cheek. The cliff face from which the snarling horde had suddenly poured was situated at the top of a slope in the forest floor, hiding them from sight and giving them the advantage of high ground from which to launch their crippling assault, launched under the ecliptical cover of near darkness, giving them further advantage.

It was a perfect ambush.

Vandrad releases the bow string. One of the rampaging vargulfen bounding past screams and rolls, skidding and tumbling across the ground, an arrow embedded in its throat. He reaches over his shoulder and draws another from the quiver on his back. He fires again and brings a second wolf down, his arrow plunging into its chest and stopping it dead as it charges toward him.

Of the hundred men in the line, only ten of them, himself included, are armed with a sword, axe or other close combat weapon of blooded steel capable of wounding the Ulfhednar fighters. The other men wear their own weapons, but before leaving Halastra, each had also been equipped with a compact bow and a brace of the blooded arrows Ailde and Camran had fashioned in the forge at Neig. With no time to arrange themselves into properly organised formation however, with the uphill lay of the land against them, greatly reduced visibility and the close range nature of the fighting, the arrows are all but useless.

Now, everywhere he looks, the Sealgairean are being overwhelmed. The towering berserkers tear into the men, deep in their infamous battle frenzy, howling as they madly hack and slash and bite and claw. Protected behind their armour and shields, they rip into those few who have managed to form small groups, battering and bludgeoning apart the desperate knots of men while the vargulfen dogs dart here and there, lightning fast, bounding from the shadowy areas between the skeletal trees, coming at the men from all directions. They pick off those who stand alone, snatching the isolated fighters up in their jaws, tearing out throats, ripping into hamstrings, dragging their shrieking prey away into the enshrouding murk. All around, the cindered forest floor is already littered with maimed and bleeding bodies.

More men are arriving, emerging from the murk between the singed tree trunks, rushing into the vicious conflict from the north and south flanks of the line and trying to bolster the fast dwindling ranks of the men in the centre. They throw themselves bravely into the battle, but to little effect.

"TO ME!" Vandrad thunders. *"FORM UP ON ME!"* A few of those nearby look up and run towards him, rallying to the commanding battlefield roar of his voice and quickly forming a defensive four man formation, but it is no sooner formed than a huge black coated vargulf comes out of nowhere and steams into them, dashing the small group apart again. Vandrad is sent sprawling, thrown face first into the warm ash of the forest floor. He rolls and pushes free of the thrashing, kicking tangle of bodies, snatches his spear from the ground and turns to see one of the men pinned beneath the massive wolf. It is worrying at his neck as he kicks and shrieks beneath.. The huge bristling animal tears its long bloody muzzle free of the fighter's flesh and turns in a quick circle, glowering balefully at the surrounding humans. It leaps forward, powering into the man on Vandrad's left with shocking speed, clamping its jaws down on his sword arm, which flings ribbons of blood and breaks with an audible *snap*. Man and beast topple to the ground, and the wolf then has the man's entire head gripped in its maw even before Vandrad and the remaining fighter fall upon it, stabbing and thrusting with their spears until the wolf is still. Vandrad instinctively looks up to see another vargulf charging toward them through the dead trees, eyes afire in the murky half light. His spear takes it directly in the chest at ten strides. He sprints forward, wrenches

his weapon from the animal's corpse and turns back to see yet another vargulf pounce upon the last man in their short lived formation, knocking him to the ground and tearing into his belly with its teeth. Vandrad runs back over and thrusts his spear through the animal's neck, severing the spine. The beast yelps once and then drops, slumping on top of the already dead and gutted man beneath it.

"TO THE RIDGELINE!" Vandrad screams, desperately trying to marshal his rapidly diminishing forces and instil some sort of order to the vicious bedlam. He begins forcing his way up the slope, eyes on the rock face at the top. If they can form up there and gain the high ground with the cliff at their back...

Another giant wolf leaps at him, lunging from the shadows on his left. Vandrad throws himself flat, feels the big creature's looming bulk sail over him, catches the fetid wild musk of it in his throat. He punches out a hard one handed thrust with the spear before the wolf can turn on him again. It howls as the razor sharp edge of the spearhead slides between its hind legs and opens up its groin and belly, spilling its guts. Vandrad is already up and moving again, making for the hilltop, shouting for the men to join him as he goes, scrambling up, up, up the slope, tripping and stumbling over hidden roots and singed tree trunks. He glances back, half seeing that amid the shadowy chaos below, several others have heard his command and are now also making for the cliff face, climbing desperately for the high ground, harried and assailed from all sides by the wolves as they come. *"TO ME!"* he bellows, waving his spear in the air. *"THE CLIFF FACE! MAKE FOR THE CLIFF FACE!"*

There is a booming roar close by, coming from the darkened area between the scorched trunks to his right. Vandrad turns just as the colossal blonde coated berserker appears from the shadows and launches its spear at his face.

*

Osvald, his snarling face splattered with wolves' blood, emits a hoarse battle cry as he presses forward, his late brother's axe, **Rimmugýgr, the Battle Hag,** alive in his hands, slashing and hacking ceaselessly at the huge bestial warrior facing him, forcing the monster to give ground. The berserker handles its massive two handed broadsword with the practiced skill of a warrior of many years experience however, deflecting and turning each of Osvald's attacks with ease. The axe and sword meet time and time again, clashing, clanging, sparking and grinding. Osvald cannot find a way through the berserker's defence as it continues to parry and block his attacks. His arms are tiring, his legs leaden, his breath coming hard, and he knows he must end it soon before his foe moves to the offensive. He feints to the left, chopping the axe down over his left shoulder, swinging it toward the berserker's right knee but watching its guard, waiting for the crucial moment... there. The wolf spins its sword blade round and down to the right to block Osvald's low slashing cut, and he wrenches his wrists round, painfully twisting, straining the muscles and tendons in his shoulders and arms under the weapon's weight and momentum as he fights to alter the direction of the feint. Osvald hollers with effort, pours all his strength into it, and **Rimmugýgr** responds, arcing suddenly upward again, the axe head rising over the wolf's countering parry. At the peak of its skyward arc, he reverses the swing once more and screams like a demon as he brings the sharpened double crescent of steel down once more with all the killing force he can muster. The Battle Hag bites deep into the Ulfhednar warrior's broad, hairy forehead, splitting it apart all the way down to the jaw. A hot broth of thick bone splintered gore sprays all over him.

For you, brother.

It is as he is wrenching **Rimmugýgr** from the ruined lupine head that the two vargulfen come bounding from behind a charred tree trunk, streaking over the ground towards him. He takes the first one full in the face with the Battle Hag, but he cannot evade the second beast, which barrels into him, its crushing jaws savagely clamping down around his left shoulder. They tumble and roll across the ground, locked together, the huge animal's teeth sunk deep into Osvald's flesh, gnawing at the bone beneath. The axe gone, Osvald manages to draw his short sword with his right hand, and he spits curses as he punches the foot long blade again and again into the snarling horror's side. The vargulf screams, loosening its killing hold. He rolls away, his left arm hanging uselessly from the open, grisly crater of his chewed shoulder, then pushes himself to his feet, with the last of his fading strength thrusting down at the bucking, blood soaked monster on the ground, plunging the short sword deep into its chest and twisting the blade.

Something hits him in the neck, and the world around him turns upside down. There is a strange, disembodied sensation of flying before he feels the thumping impact of the forest floor as his head hits the ground, his teeth clashing painfully together.

He then sees the bizarre sight of his own decapitated body, still grasping his short sword, slumping to the earth several strides away, pushed aside contemptuously by the snarling shapeshifter that strides past, the blade of its sword glistening with his blood.

A good death, Osvald thinks, and smiles.

2

Breck and the other Sealgairean on the inland side of the burned out forest were standing looking up at the sky, watching in an almost reverential hush as the moon inched across the face of the sun, throwing the land below into deep grey shadow. The unexpected disappearance of sunlight came as a creeping portent of disaster, as the enemy were creatures of the night, such was the reasoning for the Sealgairean offensive taking place during the daylight hours. Now, looking around in growing fear as the land was swallowed in darkness, Breck tried to convince himself that the strange event taking place was simply a case of extreme bad luck, an unfortunate fluke of cosmic timing.

Except it didn't feel that way.

He knew it in his very bones that this fatal turn of ill fortune had somehow always been planned, and that he, Vandrad, Drostan, Ulfar and everyone else were dumb pieces unwittingly playing out some elaborate and cruel game.

It was as they were staring in fascinated terror at the spectacle in the sky that the faint sound of battle began drifting over the smoky air towards them, and all along the enclosing line, the men and women shifted and glanced at each other nervously as the indistinct clamour of far off combat gradually intensified. They'd been waiting on those in the forest to emerge from the charred treeline, marching victorious from the ruin of the woods and bringing news of the wolves' eradication.

From points along the rank of archers came the voices of the signal bearers, harshly instructing those around them to stand fast and hold the line. Before setting out from Halastra the day before, Vandrad had ordered the inland division to remain in place at all costs and to let nothing through. They were only to break rank and move into the forest if…

Three strident blasts of a signal horn rang out from the wasteland before them, sounding out above the distant clash and clamour of battle. The spit in Breck's mouth instantly dried up and his heart missed several beats. The guard line was only to move into the forest in the direst of circumstances, which would be relayed to them by three blasts of a horn. The signal for reinforcements.

As the sounding of the horn died away, the signal bearers called the order to advance, and the four hundred odd archers obeyed, all across the moor, the long line immediately sweeping forward as every man and women advanced at speed into the singed heathland.

What weak light remained was barely enough to see by, and running forward, Breck staggered through the skeletal remains of the scrubland in front of the dead forest, tripping over roots and rocks already blackened by the fire. As he stumbled through the wasteland and then on into the scorched treeline, the sound of battle ahead grew louder, detailed enough so that he could now make out individual voices shouting and screaming, the distinctive metallic ring of clashing blades, and the bowel loosening roars of the Ulfhednar.

The terrain ahead of him cleared somewhat as he ran on, breathing hard, his skin frosty with fear and excitement. The charcoaled tree stumps all around began to thin out and the lifeless forest opened up before him till Breck found himself standing atop a near vertical cliff, perhaps four times the height of a man.

He gaped in horror at the slaughter unfolding below.

The burned out wood beneath him, dim and indistinct in the sunlight's absence, was an appalling greyed out tableau of death. The broken and savaged remains of men lay all about. The huge hulking shapes of the Ulfhednar, in full wolf form, armed and armoured, stalked among the chaotic butchery, roaring and cutting men down at will as they went. The vargulfen wolves ran amok, bounding sleek and deadly quick amid the brutal skirmish, swift as predatory shadows, running down and mauling any who crossed their path. It was impossible to tell accurately in the indistinct melee, but Breck doubted there were many more than a score of the seaborne division yet alive, and his heart quailed as he witnessed the annihilation.

Most of the few humans still breathing were making for the top of the slope below Breck, struggling up the uneven terrain, trying to reach the relative cover of the bottom of the cliff face, desperately trying to fend off the relentless assault of the wolves as they went. A handful of fighters had already gained the ridgeline, and stood with their weapons drawn, backs to the rock face, some of them throwing spears and firing arrows down into the wolves below, attempting to cover their comrades' ascent.

Breck was only half aware of the arrival of the rest of the inland guard, who joined him along the cliff top, drawn to the screams and roars of combat. He looked away from the battle below as the signal bearers began barking orders to take position and form two ranks along the cliff top, and draw the blooded arrows from their quivers.

Breck closed his eyes and tried to block out the terrible jarring sounds floating up from the madness below. He forced himself to breathe deeply and evenly, as Vandrad had taught him.

Vandrad. Was he down there lying among the maimed and the dead?

A cold focus settling in his mind, Breck opened his eyes again, knelt and readied his bow.

*

Drostan, his arthritic knees and hips grinding painfully with each step, forced himself on between the bare black trees of the wood. The exertions of the past few days were finally catching up to him, and he struggled forward, guided on by the sound of battle somewhere ahead. When he'd given the order for his section to advance after hearing the three blasts of the horn, he'd found himself quickly left behind the younger, faster men and women under his command as they raced forward. He did his best to keep up, but the weight of his years had meant that that he'd been some distance behind the others as they'd entered the scorched woods. He now found himself alone, breathing hard and his heart pounding painfully in his chest as he pushed himself onward. He yelped in alarm as his foot was seized by a hidden tree root, and he stumbled and fell to the soot blanketed ground. It was as he pushed himself wearily to his feet again, cursing and spitting ash, that he heard a cry of alarm ring out from somewhere ahead and to his right, separate from the distant noise of the battle. A woman's voice.

Kadlin.

A fresh jolt of fear spurring him on, Drostan lurched forward, angling toward where the cry had come from, weaving between the thinned blackened tree trunks and squinting into the gloom ahead, trying to get a fix on the source of the commotion. More voices, shrill with fright rang out. Someone screamed. Something else roared. There was the snap of a loosed bowstring. Close by. Just ahead.

"There! On the right! Bring it down!" someone yelled. It sounded like Sileas.

More guttural roars rumbled out from somewhere in the shadowy murk ahead. There was another piercing female scream of terror and pain. *"To me, Sisters!"* Kadlin's urgent command bawled out. *"On the left! There! Loose!"*

There was the low *snap, snap, snap* of bowstrings in quick succession, followed by an inhuman shriek of rage.

"Another one! On the right!"

"No!" another woman cried out, a rising note of panic cracking her voice. *"Behind us! Don't let them through!"*

Drostan frantically stumbled on, the sword grip slippery in his sweaty hands, bouncing off half seen tree trunks, near blind in the sunless depths of the wood and fear squeezing his throat as he followed the terrified cries.

3

Midway up the rise beneath the cliff face, Ronan, chieftain of Halastra, stood side by side with Egil, his second in command. Both men were battered and bloody as they backed their way up the corpse littered slope, their shields overlapping, weapons trained on the snarling, blood painted berserker that stalked up the hill after them, its own glaring yellow eyes boring right back into them with sinister, hungry intent.

The slope all around them was carpeted with bodies, the vast majority of them clawed and bitten humans. Although heavily outnumbered, the speed and sheer bloodthirsty ferocity of the enemy's ambush had been overwhelming, and the wolves had torn the hundred men of the seaborne Sealgairean division apart, falling on them in a frenzy of unholy violence.

The slaughter was not entirely one sided though, and strewn among the mangled fallen were the carcasses of several of the vargulfen wolves. Through sheer weight of numbers, the men had even managed to bring down and behead a few of the armoured berserkers, and one or two of the Ulfhednar had fallen to well placed blooded arrows, though these small victories counted for little, as the Sealgairean had lost a far greater portion of their forces, and several more of the towering wolves still roamed across the slope, hacking, clawing and snapping at the rapidly thinning ranks of the islanders trying to gain the top of the hill and join the small group of men at the cliff face.

The monster stalking up the hill after Egil and Ronan wore an ancient dented breastplate patinaed with age, splashed with gore, its bristling pale fur streaked and matted with blood. Weaponless, the berserker shadowed them, moving hunched over in a half crouch, its long sinewy arms held out to the sides, red claws twitching as it feinted left and right, looking for an opening while keeping out of range of Ronan's sword and Egil's spear.

A sudden low snarl and the rush of heavy padded feet snapped Ronan's attention to the right, and he half turned as one of the vargulfen streaked along the slope towards him, the great wolf bounding over the ground and springing at his face. He met its attack with his shield, turning aside from Egil, putting his shoulder behind the wide heavy circle of wood, leather and iron and pushing forward with his knees bent to absorb the impact. The huge animal yelped and twisted away to the side, but the weight of its bulk as it crashed against his shield was still enough to send Ronan reeling back, stumbling away from Egil's side.

Their two man shield wall broken, the shapeshifter in front roared and immediately sprang forward, slashing out at Egil with its claws. He ducked aside and thrust out with his spear, burying the point in the monster's shoulder. It howled, and took an arrow directly in the face, courtesy of one of the growing number of Sealgairean gathering at the bottom of the cliff face above. Undeterred by its wounds and the arrow still hanging out of the side of its drooling, bloody snout, the thing screeched and came at him again, striding forward and lashing out with its long muscular arms, tearing deep gouges in Egil's shield as it tried to get at him. He staggered back, no room or time to draw his arm back and thrust again with the spear.

To his left, Ronan hacked down with his broadsword, cleaving the vargulf's head as it wheeled round to leap at him again. Dragging the blade free from the wolf's split skull, he leapt back to Egil's side, throwing his own shield up to bolster that of the other man. Their shield wall was of little defence in the face of the enormous creature's fury, and it lunged forward, darting its head to the left and seizing the rim of Ronan's shield in its jaws, the thick, pointed fangs biting deep. With a deep snarl, it savagely jerked its huge head back to the right, its irresistible strength brutally twisting Ronan's shield aside. A flaring jolt of agony shot through his left arm as it was wrenched from the shoulder socket, and even as he drew breath to scream in pain, the Ulfhednar's left hand smashed into the side of his head. Ronan careened into Egil, his face and scalp shredded by the berserker's claws.

Egil was thrown off balance by the impact, stumbling off to the side, his left foot coming down in the slippery open stomach cavity of a disembowelled corpse lying on the slope at his feet. His ankle twisted and he went down, falling onto his side with his left foot still ensnared in clinging warm entrails. The monster roared in triumph and pounced, its wide open jaws descending on him, the mottled, ridged tissue of the inside of its mouth filling his vision with deep glistening red and curved yellow teeth.

Then there was a sudden hoarse bellow followed by a deep grunt and the sound of impacting bodies. Egil opened his eyes again and saw the shapeshifter staggering backwards down the slope, fighting for balance as Ulfar, coated head to toe in blood, shieldless and roaring like a demon himself, hacked and slashed at the monster with his longsword, tearing into it in a furious flurry of blows, the great two handed weapon a razor edged blur of wolf blooded steel in his hands. A mighty backhanded cut opened up a gaping red gash across the shrieking beast's throat. Screaming, the badly wounded monster staggered away before the overpowering, raising an arm to ward off the ceaseless cuts. That arm went leaping into the air in a spray of blood as Ulfar hacked it off at the elbow before skilfully reversing the sword's momentum and thrusting forward with blinding speed, burying the wide blade deep in the centre of the thing's neck, the point sliding clear from the back of its skull. The berserker went rigid and made a brief, wet gurgling noise before the light faded from its eyes and it toppled lifelessly to the ground.

Ulfar wrenched his sword free, turned and grasped Egil's arm, heaving the rangy shipwright to his feet. "Go!" he snarled, pointing up the hill to where the few remaining members of the Sealgairean line were clustered at the foot of the cliff face, their backs to the rock, reigning down the last of their spears and arrows at the creatures that continued to advance up the slope towards them. Egil stooped down to help Ronan to his feet, but then saw the glaze of death in his open, staring eyes and the grotesque, impossibly canted angle of his chieftain's head atop his broken neck. Much of the tissue had been flayed from the right side of Ronan's face, scraped down to the bone, which gleamed white amid the open red. Egil bit down on the bitter lump of revulsion and grief that rose in his throat.

Looking back downslope, he saw there were still several Ulfhednar fighters making their way up the hill towards them, their scarred shields absorbing the occasional arrows and spears whipping down at them. Egil looked for Vandrad among the men there, but couldn't see him.

The vargulfen stalked at leisure around the hillside, pouncing upon and tearing out the throats of wounded and savaged men still feebly trying to crawl up the blood slicked incline. Glancing back up towards the ridgeline, Egil saw the last group of Halastrian guardsmen scramble over the top of the slope and join those standing at the bottom of the cliff, leaving him and Ulfar alone on the cadaver choked slope, the oncoming berserkers, he counted nine of them, spread out on the hill beneath them. They ascended unhurriedly, knowing that the few Sealgairean still standing had nowhere to go.

It was just then that Egil heard the sound of several nearby voices barking orders, and he turned to see the cliff top above rapidly filling with men and women. All along the ledge of the tall precipice, the arriving inland division of the Sealgairean formed up, arranging themselves into two tight rows that stretched across the width of the cliff, the front rank kneeling, those behind on their feet. The wooden rattle and clack of four hundred arrows being fixed to four hundred bows clattered blessedly around the cliff tops as the archers readied their weapons and prepared to fire.

Egil felt a momentary flicker of hope, then realised he and Ulfar were standing in the field of fire. "Let's go," he grated, urgently grasping the big man's shoulder. Ulfar shrugged his hand away, never taking his eyes off the wolves below.

"I can't," he replied simply, raising his right hand and pushing his long blood matted hair back. Egil's saw the four parallel furrows scored into the side of Ulfar's neck and face, the deep slashes already inflamed and swollen.

He heard a series of harsh guttural barks, the grating sound inflected with the unmistakable intonation of some twisted form of language. Egil saw that the Ulfhednar had spotted the archers on the cliff top. They quickly reformed into two tight rows, their wide shields raised and overlapping in front, above and on the flanks, creating a four sided overlapping shield wall from which swords and spears bristled. They began moving again, the formation advancing relentlessly up the hill toward the Sealgairean.

A new dread swelled in Egil at the creatures' display of tactical awareness and intelligence. He had seen the Roman testudo deployed more than once in his life. He'd been in one himself, and had fought against others using the tactic, and knew all too well how effective the defensive mobile formation could be.

Beside him, Ulfar grunted in grudging admiration as they watched the tightly grouped berserkers come on, then he laid a big gore streaked hand on Egil's shoulder. Incredibly, he grinned, his large square teeth starkly white in the crimson mask of his lacerated face. He offered his sword to Egil, hilt first. "This is wolf blooded steel," he said, his pale blue eyes holding the other man's. "Use it well."

Egil wordlessly accepted the longsword, and then watched in astonishment as Ulfar stooped, slid his arms beneath a thick fire scorched tree trunk the length of two men, and with a roar of effort, heaved the heavy section of blackened timber up from the ground onto his chest, holding it across his body in his huge arms. Trembling with effort, Ulfar fixed his furious eyes on the approaching wolves advancing up the hill toward them, now only some twenty paces away, their snarling faces glimpsed between the gaps in their tightly meshed shield wall. He turned one last time to Egil and grinned again. Egil had never seen a man look so content, so at home.

"If you should see my Kadlin," Ulfar said, "tell her I died well. I was never a fucking farmer." With that, he turned back to the berserkers.

"*Come to me then, dogs!*" he roared at the oncoming phalanx, his voice ringing out strong and clear, echoing from the cliff face behind him. "*I am Ulfar! Named for the wolf, and the wolf and the dog do not play together!*"

Egil watched in awe as the big warrior let loose a deafening battle cry and took off down the slope, the tree trunk still held across his body. He hurtled downhill at full pelt toward the Ulfhednar, gathering speed, using the slope's decline to build speed and momentum. At a distance of only a few strides, he dove headlong into the air, releasing the tree trunk from his arms and immediately drawing a pair of short handled axes from his belt.

The result was spectacular. The long heavy trunk of scorched pine bounced once then rolled beneath the front of the shield wall, ploughing into the foremost berserkers' lower legs and toppling them forward while the weight of Ulfar's bulk simultaneously smashed into and broke through the roof of their protective formation. The wolves' testudo shattered and broke apart under the tremendous double impact, sending several of the Ulfhednar sprawling and rolling downhill. Egil heard Ulfar screaming for the archers to loose, and caught a final glimpse of him, flaying frenziedly at his enemies, a bloodied short axe in each hand, his heavily muscled arms a red blur as he hacked and chopped, slashed and cleaved at the berserkers trying to regain their balance.

The order to loose was repeated by the signal bearers above, and a great rolling *snap* rattled across the cliff top, reverberating around its curved stone façade as four hundred bowstrings were released almost simultaneously. Egil ducked under the splintered remains of his shield, turned and sprinted up the slope to cover as the heavens spat barbed iron.

Made from damaged weapons salvaged from the fire outside its walls, the arrows that Ailde and Camran had spent weeks producing back in Neig fell on the broken enemy formation in a devastating and inescapable fusillade of wolf blooded steel. Amid a withering storm of Sealgairean shafts, the exposed Ulfhednar fell shrieking to the ground, their huge hairy bodies several times ventilated by the massed hail of arrows. A second volley swiftly followed as the archers used the last of their blooded shafts, and when they were spent, they turned their remaining arrows on the last of the vargulfen. Unable to escape from the sheer scale of the barrage, the wolves were engulfed, their hides pierced and skewered by the lethal torrent of slashing metal that rained down from the cliff top.

4

The carcasses of the Ulfhednar and vargulfen were heaped into a great pile, soaked in oil, and set to flame.

Some time later, when the pyre had died down, a lone vessel set out from where the scorched land met the ocean, and sailed west into the blue, dropping sail and anchor only when the island was a thin blurry line on the eastern horizon. Stone weighted sacks containing the blackened bones that remained after the blaze were unceremoniously dumped overboard, the hard faced men watching as the last physical remnants of the demons disappeared beneath the waves. The weapons and armour of the Ulfhednar followed their bones, consigned to the crushing deep.

Back on land, Breck was sat upon a boulder, his back, arms and legs aching from the past few bleak hours spent hauling corpses and preparing them for burial. He was filthy with a rank greasy coating of sweat dampened ash and dried blood, more tired than he could ever remember being in his life, and numb with the after effects of the battle. Now, his mind felt curiously detached, his flesh and bones icily tremulous with delayed shock.

Over the course of the last months, with the loss of so many of those whom he had known and loved, Breck had become somewhat inured to death and dismemberment. Nevertheless, he was not immune to fresh stabs of grief and horror as he and the other survivors had begun the grim undertaking of picking their way through the bloody aftermath of the battle. Amid the butchery they discovered a few crippled and arrow rent vargulfen and Ulfhednar fighters, incapacitated by their wounds, but even yet twitching and snarling, that baleful yellow light weak, yet still stubbornly smouldering in their eyes as they writhed and snapped weakly at the grim faced men standing over them. Each was dispatched with a decapitating blade through the neck.

Harder to undertake were the mercy killings.

In Halastra, during the feverish few days spent in preparation for this expedition, before they committed, all who signed up to the ranks of the Sealgairean were first made fully aware of the hard facts regarding the nature of the enemy. Every man and women who joined the hunters was told plainly of the risks entailed, and about exactly what it meant to be infected by the Ulfhednar. The pestilent nature of the enemy meant that the Sealgairean operated under one simple decree. Any man, woman or even child found to be marked was put to the sword and burned. No exceptions.

In the aftermath of the forest battle, they'd found several men bitten and clawed, but damnably alive. To their credit, none of them had begged for their lives, and each welcomed the merciful steel, sparing them their awful fate and sending them on their way.

It had been hard to witness, Breck thought dismally, staring down at his filth encrusted hands as he sat there hunched over on the boulder. He couldn't stop clenching and unclenching his fists.

Practically every one of those infected had kin and kith among the survivors, and where possible, it was respectfully left to friends and loved ones to dispatch them. Breck had watched as one such tragic tableau had played out, his heart breaking in his chest as he witnessed the poignant sight of a tearful woman gently holding her man's head in her lap, tenderly stroking his blood matted hair, looking into his eyes and murmuring final words of love and farewell, before compassionately slipping a dagger into the nape of his neck. The howl of pain and grief she had let out after had barely been human.

There had been many more cries of loss and bitter weeping as bereaved brothers, sisters, children, mothers and fathers found family members amid the dead and infected. By the time it was over, Breck knew he would never again hear a sound so chilling as the screams of those forced to take the life of someone they cherished.

Trying to shake off the maudlin depression that hung on him like a wet grey cloak, he told himself that they had won. The wolves had been eradicated, the nightmare finally over, and yet Breck couldn't force himself to feel any jubilation or sense of triumph in the vanquishing of their enemy. After the all consuming hail of arrows had petered out and finally ceased, there had been no massed cry of victory from the Sealgairean on the cliff top as they looked grimly down on the field of battle, the full horror of which was slowly revealed with the drawing back of the curtain of false night as the eclipse passed and the sun re-emerged.

Too many of the Sealgairean's own had been lost in the battle for anyone to take joy in victory.

Osvald. They found the Norseman's decapitated body at the bottom of the slope. Lying about him were the corpses of several vargulfen, as well as that of one of the huge berserkers, its wolfish head practically split in two down the middle. Osvald's axe, Battle Hag, lay close by, the crescent edges coated in drying blood and wolf hair. On the ground, his own severed head smiled with glassy eyed satisfaction. Breck had often sparred with Osvald during the weeks and months of training back in Neig, and though the stocky Viking had been a quiet sort, especially after the very bad death of his beloved brother, they had often talked with one another during breaks in practice. A patient teacher and a skilled, fearless fighter, Breck hoped that Osvald was now at peace, reunited with his twin in the halls of Valhalla, a mystical place he had often spoken of with longing, where he and his brother could drink and feast and fight for eternity, happy and content in the raucous afterlife of the Norse.

Ailde they found close to the cave entrance. Speared through the chest, his eyes stared sightlessly at the sky above, a look of mild surprise on his waxy features. Breck had knelt by his body and whispered a short prayer of thanks to his departed spirit. Without the big blacksmith's efforts and skill in producing the blooded arrowheads, the day would in all likelihood have turned out very differently.

And Ulfar. Breck knew that he would never again in his life see a sight so awesome as that of the giant Norseman, armed with a *tree trunk*, fearlessly charging the Ulfhednar testudo like a one man battering ram. In single handedly breaking the impregnable shield wall of the enemy, Ulfar's incredible display of strength and courage had been the deciding action of the battle. They'd found him in the middle of the dead berserkers, his twin short axes still tightly clutched in his great ham sized fists. Caught in the devastating volley of arrows, his body was just as riddled and pierced with shafts as those of the wolfish hellions lying sprawled about him. He too was smiling.

They found Vandrad close to the top of the slope beneath the cliff face, his body pinned beneath the massive bulk of a dead berserker. The handle of a large dagger protruded from the thick ruff covering the beast's neck, and it had taken three men to roll the dead weight of the enormous plate armoured corpse off his body. The Norseman was unconscious, and the back of his head was gashed and bloody from where it had struck the rocky ground, but he was alive, and mercifully free of any bite or claw marks. He'd regained consciousness a short time later and had been informed by Egil of the outcome of the fight. The last Breck had seen of him, Vandrad had been midway down the slope, kneeling over Ulfar's body, his head bowed in mourning.

Breck was sat there lost in his own weary thoughts, sleepily wondering where he and the rest of the island's inhabitants went from here, when a hand roughly shook his shoulder. His head jerked up and he saw Uallas looking down at him, a grim look on his face. Like Breck, the tracker was sheathed in grime and rusty dried blood, his long brown hair hanging in sweat dampened ropes around his stubbly haggard face. He looked every bit as exhausted and heart sick as Breck felt.

"It's Drostan," Uallas said.

Breck frowned up at him, his exhausted mind trying to catch up. He'd last spoken to Drostan in Halastra in the early morning of the previous day, just before the inland Sealgairean division had set out and marched north to take their position along the outskirts of the forest. Like Breck, he'd been part of the line of archers standing guard beyond the eastern edge of the woods. He hadn't seen Drostan in the aftermath of the battle, but there were over four hundred people milling about amid the carnage, and his thoughts otherwise occupied with the grisly work of sorting through the dead, he hadn't been looking for, or even thinking about his adopted chieftain.

Seeing the deep disquiet in Uallas' eyes, Breck wearily pushed himself to his feet and followed the tracker as he strode hurriedly away into the dead wood. He thought he'd reached his limit for the day, but a new sense of gathering unease was slowly mounting as he went.

They didn't have far to go. Just a few minutes later, Breck followed Uallas over a small ridge to the north east of where the battle had unfolded, and stopped dead.

There'd been a slaughter here. Separate from the engagement back beneath the cliff face. There were so many glistening red shreds that it was impossible to tell how many individual corpses there were scattered and strewn about the area. Ten? Twenty? No way of knowing. There was hardly anything left.

Egil, the shipwright from Halastra was there, knelt over the only body still in one piece. Drostan lay prone on the forest floor, his eyes open, as he whispered something to Egil, who nodded, gripped one of the older man's bloody hands briefly and then rose to his feet. He turned from Drostan and walked slowly over to Breck. "He is asking for you," he said quietly, then turned away, his head hanging, leaning on his spear like it was the only thing holding him upright.

Breck stumbled over, seeing as he drew nearer that Drostan had been badly wounded. The chieftain was bare chested, revealing four long straight gashes that had been slashed across his torso, running from his left shoulder down across his chest and belly to his right hip in red parallel furrows.

Fresh despair wrenching him, Breck sank to his knees beside the chieftain of Acker and took hold of his hand. "Drostan," he said. "I'm here."

"Breck..." Drostan croaked, opening his eyes and fixing the younger man with an intent look. Breck had to resist the urge to lurch back in fright as he saw that Drostan's irises had already taken on a sickly ochre tinge. "I'm sorry," he whispered. "We couldn't stop them..."

"What happened here?" Breck asked gently, though he wanted to scream the question.

"Attacked..." Drostan groaned, wincing as a quivering spasm jolted through his body. "The Sisters... tried to hold them back, but... overrun..."

The Sisters.

Breck glanced back over his shoulder at the mess of bloody remains strewn around the wasteland. He realised that he hadn't seen Kadlin, Sileas or any of the other warrior women of Acker and Neig in the aftermath of the earlier battle, and the terrible realisation of what had transpired in this lonely section of charred wood dawned on him.

"The wolves? They got through the line?" he asked, unable to help the tremor in his voice.

"I tried... tried to help..." Drostan went on, his halting, pain wracked words slurring and hoarse, "but they were... everywhere... they made me watch... *made me watch what they did to the Sisters...*" Another wracking spasm took hold of the chieftain, and he gripped Breck's hand painfully, crying out in agony. Beads of sweat emerged along Drostan's blood smeared brow, and Breck could feel the sour heat radiating from the wounded man's skin. There was an abrupt series of low popping noises, and Drostan screamed, his body arching up off the ground as the infection of the Ulfhednar worked its way through his flesh and bones. Breck could only gape in horror as he saw that the weeping claw marks etched across the width of Drostan's body had almost closed over, and that around the wound there now sprouted several strands of coarse hair that hadn't been there a few seconds before.

Looking skyward, Breck reckoned from the sun's position, there was a little over an hour till sunset.

Drostan opened his eyes again. "Please..." he growled, his roughened voice thick with gravel and grit, "Neig... they *told* me... got inside my head...they're going back to Neig... six of them."

Breck grit his teeth. Neig. Left practically defenceless with a mere ten men standing guard.

"They'll be there... before nightfall..." Drostan gripped Breck's hand tighter. "Please... Breck..." he said, in a guttural near snarl, "...end it."

Breck let go of his chieftain's hand and drew a large dagger from the sheath on his hip. He remembered the day, so long ago it seemed, that Vandrad had given the formidable weapon to Egor. He had later presented it to Breck after the fire at Neig, telling him that Egor had died with it in his hand. A warrior's death.

Turn terror to wrath.

Breck rolled Drostan onto his side and knelt behind the now violently shuddering man. He carefully positioned the point of the dagger at the nape of his neck, finding the soft hollow between the top two vertebrae of his spine, just as Vandrad had shown him.

Gritting his teeth, Breck closed his eyes, felt hot tears spilling down his cheeks, and pushed.

There was a brief moment of tension as the dagger slid between the bones, then Drostan seemed to shrink. After a time, Breck wiped his eyes and got to his feet.

"Egil..."

"I will have the ships ready and crewed," the shipwright said. "With fair sailing we can land on the shores of Loch Shiphoirt before sunset."

5

Each of the ten shallow drafted vessels beached on the edge of the burned forest were quickly packed with as many of the Sealgairean as was possible, while those that remained on shore were charged by Vandrad to head east on foot under the command of Uallas and to make for the village of Neig with all possible speed. Egil hoped that the short sea journey round the south of the island would have them at the hilltop settlement before nightfall, but for the second time that day, nature turned on the Sealgairean.

The skies darkened with billowing back clouds. An ugly storm blew up mere minutes after they set sail, rolling in off the ocean in great gusts of wind and white capped waves, and Egil's hopes for fair passage were dashed like the turbulent swells of dark water smashing onto the rocky outcrops they left behind as the small fleet set out.

Braving the storm, the ten ships sailed south down the western coast, passing by Halastra before turning east and cautiously navigating the narrow tidal corridor that separated the island's upper and lower halves. From there, their course took them a short distance north up the eastern coastline to where Loch Shiphoirt cut diagonally inland to the north west, leading to Neig. Even in fair conditions the voyage was dangerous, the coastline riddled as it was with jagged peninsulas, unpredictable currents and treacherous shallows that appeared and vanished with the coming and going of the tide. The buffeting winds and rough seas made the journey all the more perilous, and the Sealgairean fleet had to fight the waves and wind all the way, every last ounce of the crews' seafaring skill and experience necessary to keep the ships from being blown onto the fangs of rock that jutted from the water and lay beneath the surface, ready to tear out their hulls. It was something of a minor miracle that every ship made it around the coast unscathed, but severely delayed by the tempest, the sun was already setting even before they rounded the southern side of the island and turned north onto the eastern coastline, and except for an ominous orange glow on the horizon ahead, it was full dark when the Sealgairean ships entered the calmer inland waters of Loch Shiphoirt.

By the time they reached the head of the loch, and the men and women of the Sealgairean leapt over the sides of their vessels, wading with pointless haste through the surf onto the beach, Neig, perched on the plateau above them, was well aflame.

After a while, as the Sealgairean stood on the beach looking up the slope and watching helplessly as the village on the mound was devoured, floating eerily out of the darkness to the north west came the howling. Mocking. Challenging. At the unearthly sound of it, the weeping of the several men and women on the beach who'd left loved ones in Neig gradually began to change tone. Their plaintive, tearful wails of loss twisting into angry curses and shouts of rage which spread quickly through the crowd gathered on the shore. A palpable sense of impending violence and outrage rapidly swelled through the mob, kindling wrath and the desire for reprisal. Then the clamour abruptly lessened and quieted, diminishing to a reverent hush as Vandrad walked slowly up the beach through the crowd to stand beside Breck at the foot of the hill.

The Norseman stood looking up at the burning settlement as the distant howling of the Ulfhednar bled across the night, his knuckles white around the shaft of his spear, eyes glinting in the firelight. Other than to give the order for Uallas to take charge of those who wouldn't fit on the boats and to head for Neig on foot, Vandrad hadn't spoken a single word since learning of the terrible end that had befallen the Sisters, his wife Sileas among them.

During the journey round the island, their ship had been tossed around like a toy on the waves, seemingly on the verge of capsizing several times. Vandrad had remained stony faced and implacable the whole time, barely flinching, seemingly oblivious to their imminent peril.

Now, standing on the shore and looking up the hill toward the burning ruin of Neig, he remained silent. He gave no rousing speech, let loose no thundering battle cry. He didn't even speak. Vandrad simply turned from the burning settlement above and began climbing the darkened slope at an angle, heading instead in the direction the wolves howling was coming from.

The Sealgairean followed.

6

They skirted the fire topped plateau, cutting round its base on the western side and leaving the destroyed settlement of Neig behind, guided ahead through the night's darkness by torchlight and the ceaseless baying of the Ulfhednar, floating out of the north west. The storm that had delayed their arrival at Neig had blown itself out, and the clouds above thinned and parted to reveal a vast canopy of stars, their heavenly glow and the glare of the full moon washing the land below in a spectral gray light. As the Sealgairean marched onwards across the moonlit landscape, the defiant shrieks of their enemy continued, growing ever nearer.

It wasn't long before their route led them up a steep rise in the terrain, and cresting the hill, they found themselves looking down on the northern end of Loch Langabhat, the great body of black water glittering under the starlight.

The Ulfhednar were on one of the many small islands lying offshore. Five of them standing in a circle, stripped of their armour, weapons planted in the ground, heads thrown back and arms raised to the night sky as they howled and shrieked. They were close enough now to discern that amid the baying, the largest of them was emitting a series of strange garbled barks and short grunting calls separate to the rest of the pack. A twisted, nauseating sound. A mangled form of speech, never spoken in any tongue of men.

A low murmur of fury rippled through the Sealgairean gathered on the hilltop as they looked down on the last of the Sons of Fenrir. The humans standing above the loch numbered close to two hundred, and held the advantage of the high ground, while there was only a mere five of the berserkers, stranded on the barren little island with nowhere to go.

As he stood beside Vandrad looking down, Breck frowned. This made no sense. The Ulfhednar had shown time and time again that they possessed a well developed sense of strategy. Now they'd cornered themselves and announced their position, calling the Sealgairean down on them when they were heavily outnumbered and exposed in an indefensible position with no means of escape.

As he fretted on this turn of events, in his peripheral vision Breck caught sight of something flashing orange in the gloomy terrain just across the loch to the north, and looked over to see a long line of flaming torches emerge from behind the nearby hills. The rest of the Sealgairean, almost another two hundred men and women who'd made the overland journey from the burnt out forest on foot, also drawn here by the howling of the Ulfhednar. The men and women standing around Breck also saw the others' arrival, and began shouting and waving their torches back and forth in the air. An answering cry carried back across the night from those on the other side of the narrow bay, the dots of torchlight there waving back in response.

Rather than feeling a surge of joy to find their numbers bolstered, Breck again experienced that peculiar sense that he and the rest of the Sealgairean were victims of some sick jest. Something was pulling urgently at his memory, and Breck looked down again at the five Ulfhednar trapped on the little island.

"Vandrad," he said. "Something's not right with this."

Vandrad turned to him, and Breck almost recoiled the hatred twisting the man's features. "*Right?*" he hissed, "There has never been anything right about *any* of this."

Breck wanted to voice his concerns about the Ulfhednar's apparent recklessness and poor choice of ground. He wanted to say that this must be some sort of trap, that they had obviously been lured here on purpose, but looking at Vandrad's face, seeing that black, all consuming rage, Breck knew any protests he offered would be useless, and perhaps dangerous. The deaths of Ulfar and Sileas, and now the burning of Neig and those within, had finally broken him. He was blinded by hate. Deaf to reason. And now, the enemy lay a mere bowshot away, taunting him.

"This ends *now*," the Norseman spat. "Ready your weapon, boy."

Vandrad turned away from him and addressed the Sealgairean, his ear splitting command loud enough to be heard by the second division on the hill across the water to their right.

"*TAKE POSITION! READY YOUR BOWS!*"

Before setting out for Neig, the Sealgairean had salvaged close to four hundred blooded arrows from the battlefield in the forest, recognisable by the red dye marking the fletchings. Now, they arranged themselves into the familiar long line two rows deep along the crest of the hill, planted their torches in the earth behind them, nocked the scavenged shafts and prepared to loose.

Breck, still sensing that something was badly amiss, felt the now familiar pull on his back, arm and shoulder muscles as he reluctantly drew the bowstring and took aim, seeing as he did so that the Ulfhednar on the island below were still making no attempt to shield themselves from the imminent storm of arrows. They just stood there in their circle, bathed in moonlight, heads still thrown back, gaping muzzles pointed skywards and howling and roaring into the night. Breck had to struggle to keep his arms from shaking in irrational terror.

Their ultimate victory was mere seconds away, yet all the time, something in the corner of his mind kept yammering in horror and insisting that this was *wrong, wrong, wrong.*

"LOOSE!"

The great stuttering snap of bowstrings slapped around the surrounding hills and the loch below as the Sealgairean fired. Then an almost perfect silence fell as the arrows shot out into the darkness, and the men and women on the hill held their collective breath.

Below, the wolves at last ceased their demented baying, and now spread their arms wide as if welcoming the arrowheads. In the momentary hush, the fear in Breck's heart swelled till he felt it would burst.

Wrong, wrong, wrong...

Several arrows missed the mark, sending up thin splashes from the loch's surface and clattering off the rocky ground of the little island, but many many more fell true. The berserkers were riven with shafts, and began jerking and twitching as they were hit again and again and again, falling to the ground, their huge hairy bodies bristling with shafts.

"LOOSE!" Vandrad screamed again.

There was little need for the second volley, as each of the five berserkers had already been struck several times in the first wave and now lay prone and still on the island's barren surface, but the Sealgairean grimly obeyed Vandrad's command, pouring all their hate and fear and pain and loss into another torrent.

After the second round of arrows had been loosed, Breck saw Vandrad immediately cast down his bow, snatch up his spear and begin running down the steep hillside toward the loch's shoreline. Caught up in the killing fever, the others followed, drawing weapons and voicing battle cries as they went belting down the hill after the roaring Norseman in a mad rush. Breck was swept along with them, and as he blundered half blindly down the steep heather shrouded slope, across the bay he could just make out the rest of the Sealgairean following their lead, swarming down the adjacent hillside. Looking ahead again and fighting to keep his balance, he saw Vandrad had now reached the bottom of the slope and was racing toward the shoreline, tearing off his helm and chainmail vest as he went. Without so much as breaking stride, the now bare chested Norseman dove headlong into the dark water and vanished beneath the surface, appearing a moment later still clutching his spear and swimming one handed for the island just offshore. The black water was then churned to foam as the rest of the Sealgairean ran heedlessly into the loch after him, following in

Vandrad's wake. With no option but to go along, Breck's half panicked breath was punched from his lungs as the shockingly cold water enveloped him, and he broke the loch's surface gasping for air. Treading water and whipping his sodden hair from his eyes, he saw that Vandrad had already reached the island ahead, and was now standing motionless near the centre of the small patch of land. As he struck out after the rest of the Sealgairean, that small voice in his head continued to whimper and protest like a frightened child.

Wrong, wrong, wrong...

He clamped down on it, pushing the insistent thought away. Whatever was wrong, it was too late now, and so he grit his teeth, ducked beneath the dark surface and swam, limbs burning and heart pounding with effort as he dragged himself through the frigid water.

A few minutes later, as he stumbled, cold and dripping from the loch onto a small cove on the island, Breck heard Vandrad's voice somewhere ahead, sternly ordering the others back. He pushed his way through the tightly packed crowd of wet, shivering bodies and found the half naked Norseman crouched on his haunches in the centre of the ring of dead berserkers that lay sprawled and bloody on the ground. Vandrad was looking down with a strange expression Breck had never seen on the Viking's face. It took a moment for him to realise that it was fear.

Then he saw it, and all at once Breck couldn't breathe as everything fell horribly into place. With a slap of realisation, he suddenly understood the reason for the fearful doubt that had been pulling frantically at his thoughts since arriving on the crest of the hill above loch Langabhat.

Six of them, Drostan had said.

Six.

Not five.

The massive skull of the sixth berserker lay in a large pool of drying blood on the stony ground at Vandrad's feet. Freshly skinned, its hard pale surface was still moist and gleaming, hanging with tattered stringy threads of raw flesh. Strange runic cuneiforms had been etched into the bone, carved in jagged lines across the wide sloping brow, and the curving upper fangs were pushed into the ground beneath the skull, as if biting into the very Earth beneath. Of its body, or the rest of its bones, there was no sign.

Transfixed by the malevolent tableau, Breck was only aware Vandrad had moved when he felt his hand on his chest, pushing him back from the circle of dead Ulfhednar and the rune marked skull they surrounded.

"We have to go," the big Norseman was muttering, a strange haunted quality to his words. "All of you. Back to shore. *Now!*"

"What is it Vandrad?" Breck whispered as the Viking led him away. "What have they done?"

7

The sun was coming up in the east, the red morning light dashing crimson across the dawn sky and the surrounding hills.

Vandrad stood before the shivering bedraggled Sealgairean gathered around on the beach. Their bewildered faces looked to him expectantly, and he wondered how to tell them that it had all been for nothing, that the victory they thought was finally theirs was just another ruse. Another deception.

With no easy way to break the news to them, he simply told them the bald truth. "The wolves have cursed this place, sacrificed themselves and used the blood of their own to bedevil the earth." He paused for a moment, and a murmur of confusion muttered through the crowd as they looked at each other. At him. At the little half darkened island just offshore where the silhouetted corpses of the berserkers lay, unquestionably slain. Before the crowd could assail him with the inevitable barrage of questions, Vandrad continued. "They have sacrificed themselves, and marked the skull of one of their pack with a dark spell. A hex." He paused again, ensuring that he had their complete attention. "They will return."

His words hung in the air like a hanged man, then the shocked silence broke and the crowd's confused muttering turned to raised voices strained with anger, despair, and the beginnings of fear. Vandrad let them go a while, knowing it was pointless to try and quell the agitated crowd right then. They eventually quieted down when they realised he wasn't going to speak over them.

"The only thing we can do is cleanse and protect the land as well as we are able," he went on when the crowd settled again. "We must prepare. And we must keep watch."

"For how long?" someone in the crowd called out. "When will the beasts return?"

Vandrad only shook his head. "Days. Years. Centuries," he said. "There is no way of knowing. All that is certain is that they will come back."

*

They did what they could.

Led by Vandrad, a number of the Sealgairean swam back out to the island that afternoon to deal with the carcasses of the Ulfhednar. Under the Norseman's strict instruction, they took great care not to touch the rune marked skull that lay on the ground near the centre of the island. The corpses of the shapeshifters were burned, then, as before, their haunted weapons, armour, and the charred remains of their bones were gathered up, taken far out to sea and thrown to the deep. For what it was worth.

Back on Langabhat's shore, Breck stood watching, as using his knife, Vandrad etched a single rune onto a large, flat piece of slate. The strange figure he painstakingly carved into the piece of stone had the look of a skeletal tree.

"What is it?" Breck asked, looking over Vandrad's shoulder. The peculiar figure stirred an eerie feeling in him. It frightened him, yet at the same time was strangely comforting to look upon. Somehow it seemed familiar, but he had never seen it before.

"It is the mark of Algiz, the Elk." The Norseman replied without looking up.

"What does it mean?"

"Like all runes, many things. Protection. A ward against evil. Connection with the gods. Instinct. It is also a warning of danger. A repellent."

They turned at the sound of footsteps on the beach behind them, and saw Egil as he came toward them, carrying a small sack in one hand. "I have them," the shipwright said.

At Vandrad's bidding, Egil had left that morning and sailed back to Halastra to collect what was in the little bag of woven cloth. He handed it now to Vandrad, who silently nodded his thanks. "Will these charms work?" Egil asked, raising an eyebrow. "My grandmother back home placed great stock in the power of runes and plants. She was mad."

"I pray to all the gods that they do," Vandrad replied, getting to his feet. "And that your grandmother was simply misunderstood. Wait here." He walked once more to the shore line, the etched piece of slate in one hand, the small sack in his other.

"I'll come with you," Breck heard himself say. He hadn't meant to speak.

Vandrad stopped and turned back to him, a sad look in his eyes. "Very well," he said quietly.

They swam out to the island, and Breck watched as Vandrad slowly approached the skull on the ground, water dripping from his bare torso and long hair.

"What do the symbols mean, Vandrad?" he asked, staring with trepidation at the huge rune scrawled wolf's skull. Vandrad looked over at him and hesitated before speaking.

"They are a summons," he muttered, "a beacon that calls to the harbinger of their return." The shiver that rippled through Breck's flesh at that moment had little to do with the cold water of the loch.

Then Vandrad was whispering something under his breath, some reverent sounding incantation spoken in his native tongue. He knelt, and excavated a small hollow in the rocky ground with his knife before using the blade to quickly knock the monstrous cranium into the hole and filled it in again. With the greatest of care, he then placed the flat piece of slate over the buried skull, the marking facing outward, and made a strange, slashing inflection in the air with his hand, warily backing away, never taking his eyes off the little grave. He reached into the small bag of sackcloth Egil had retrieved from Halastra, and scattered the contents on the rocky ground around the burial skull. The hawthorne plant, used in many cultures as a protective charm against evil forces and harmful spells, was not native to the island, but as a trading port, Halastra was a place where such things could be found. Vandrad continued to chant and pray softly under his breath as he spread the seeds.

Watching him, Breck again felt something pulling insistently at his senses, warning him that still, something was not right. But no, that wasn't it. This time it was instead a feeling of something that was *too* right. A queer sensation of something colossal rushing inexorably toward him. Something inescapable as death.

"It won't work, will it Vandrad?" he said, unable to take his eyes off the rune marked slate. "If it takes centuries for them to come back I mean." That rushing feeling of impending *forever* grew stronger, stronger. Unstoppable as fate. Immortal as God.

His hand, as if by its own volition, slid slowly behind his back, down towards the belt fastened across his wet tunic.

Vandrad lowered his head morosely then turned to face Breck. There was an awful truth in his eyes. "No," he said. "Like all myths, over time, this will just be another legend. Even if we keep generations of Sealgairean watching over this island, and pass the duty of guarding this grave down through the years, eventually..." He left the rest unsaid, shaking his head. "We were never meant to win this," he said, looking back over at the etched piece of slate on the ground.

When Vandrad looked back toward him, Breck held the big hunting knife that Vandrad had originally given to Egor.

"Have you never wondered," he asked the Viking now in a quiet far away voice, "why I was so good with the bow?" Was he saying those words? They seemed to be coming from someone else. He lifted the knife before his face, intently studying the blade as he turned it back and forth, letting the afternoon sun's rays dance and glint along the steel. Strange that aside from the accursed steel of the berserkers, the huge hunting knife had been the only blade recovered from the ashes of the fire outside Neig that had kept its balance and edge. Vandrad didn't reply. There was a grim acceptance on the Norseman's face, as if he'd always known, but refused to acknowledge the thing that was growing and swelling in Breck's mind. "I'd never even held a bow before. I was a quick study with the sword as well, wasn't I, Vandrad?"

"You were, Breck," the Norseman replied in a near whisper. He took a tentative step forward. "A very quick study. I've never seen the like."

"The games of the gods," Breck said thoughtfully, gazing dreamily at the oversized knife in his hand. "In the games of the gods, for every monster there is a hero to slay it. For every devil an avenging angel. That's what you told us." He lifted his eyes from the knife and stared at Vandrad. Breck let out a long breath as a terrible, fateful truth unveiled itself in his mind. Then he smiled.

He only half heard Vandrad scream his name, as gripping it with both hands, he turned the huge blade inward and rammed it into his own stomach.

PART ELEVEN

1

"So," Paul said to Aaron. "Viking werewolves, eh?"

"Aye, looks that way," Aaron replied from the four by four's driver seat, not taking his eyes from the road. "Viking werewolves."

They'd had quite the info dump from Aaron, who seemed to be some sort of ghost busting Hell's Angel with an encyclopaedic knowledge of mythology and folklore. Prompted by Ian earlier, he'd told them what he knew about the Ulfhednar, the wolfskin wearing berserker warrior elite of King Harald Fairhair, first King of Norway in the ninth century. Aaron had then lectured at length about how the Isle of Lewis had strong historical connections to the age of the Vikings, and filled them in on the local legend of the wolfmen of Loch Langabhat, illustrating how extremely fucking relevant it all was to their situation. Paul had never liked history that much in school, but given their predicament, he found himself a suddenly attentive student.

They were well tooled up, their little hunting party, Paul thought. After a recklessly quick crash course in their basic use, he'd entrusted Cal Dempster with a Heckler & Koch MP5 submachine gun which Paul retrieved from the police van, and had given the two Glock 17 pistols to Scarlett and Ian, each of whom also carried one of the undead hillbilly's spears, the almost three metre length of the weapons requiring the Jeep to travel with its boot open. Jack, the boy from the Calanais Centre, who said he wasn't comfortable with firearms, had his bandolier of throwing knives, and Aaron had also declined a gun, instead augmenting his meagre arsenal of the letter opener in his jacket by claiming the big fuck-off double headed axe they'd found at the resurrected hillbilly's bothy. He was the only one of them big enough to lift the damn thing.

Paul equipped himself with the last item of firepower at their disposal which he'd also taken from the police van; a PSG-1 sniper rifle.

He'd been told via radio by Inspector Scally himself to remain at the crime scene with the civilians and wait for backup to arrive, and to then brief the incoming officers of the situation. To avoid wasting time trying to tell his CO what had happened and what he intended to do next, Paul had simply rogered that and said over and out, then he and the civilians had been piling into the Jeep, armed to the teeth and ready to go on the most fucked up safari imaginable. Equipping untrained civilians with firearms and disobeying a direct order from a ranking officer would normally land him in serious bother, but Paul figured that by the time the day was over, Martin Scally would have bigger fish to batter, and far crazier shit to deal with than a little insubordination. The rulebook had been shat upon, set on fire and merrily thrown out the proverbial window long ago. The incoming officers would be briefed just fine when they arrived and saw for themselves the aftermath of the bloody lunacy that had occurred. Out of professional courtesy, Paul had also scribbled a hasty report in his notebook recounting in broad strokes what had gone down. Werewolves, reanimated sword wielding hillbillies and all, and left it open on the bonnet of one of the patrol cars for the arriving officers to find. He'd ended the note by advising that he and the civilians were en route back to town via the back road, and that all available officers should also immediately return to Stornoway, as he'd been led to believe that there were a further two werewolves somewhere on the island, in all probability heading for the largest population centre. The seven foot zombie who'd kicked fuck out of the entire station that morning was also still at large. Now there was a line Paul had thought he'd never put in a police report.

"So, you're something of an expert on freaky shit like this then?" he now asked Aaron.

"Wouldn't say that," the big guy replied. "Don't think it's possible to be an expert on this kind of stuff, but I've seen a fair amount of it, so I'd say I probably know a fair bit more about it than your average Joe."

"So what else is real?"
"Like?"
"Aliens?"
"Oh aye. Shady bastards."
"Aye? For real?"
"Kid you not, man."
"Shit. Vampires?"
"Never met one."
"Zombies?"
"Immortals, aye, zombies, no."
"Ach. Ghosts?"
"Aye. All over the place."

"Fuckin' knew it. My mum had a sister who point blank refused to stay more than a couple of minutes in our house when I was growing up, and was always trying to get us to move out. Never saw or heard anything myself, but my auntie Ida always said there was something bad there. Up in the loft."

"There might well've been. I worked as an investigator in the states for a few years when I was younger. Some of the cases I got involved in were horrendous. What happened to your auntie?"

"She died a few years ago."

"Young?"

"I guess. She never made it much past fifty."

"Sorry to hear that. Happens sometimes. With people who're a bit more... tuned in."

"You mean like psychics?"

"Fuck psychics. Most of them anyway. If I ever meet that Derek Acora prick he's getting a burst lip. The people who experience and really know about this kind of thing tend to keep very quiet about it."

"No doubt. Straight jacket material."

"Well, yeah. But not just that. It's as if *they* know you know. You know?"

"I think so. *They?*"

"The freaky shit. The bad ones. From other places. They."

"So you think they'll be going for the festival?"

Aaron shrugged. "Possible. From what I've seen and heard before, most things like this, daemons, whatever, whenever they get a way in, they want to spread. Like a sickness. It's like they feed and thrive on bad vibes, and need to pass them on as much as possible. A crowd of a few thousand people would be a good place to start. But you can never really tell how their minds work or what they're going to do. It's like trying to imagine a colour that doesn't exist."

"Can you actually *use* that axe?"

"Aye. I've done a fair bit of weapons training. Spent one summer down in England working for one of those outfits that re-enact mediaeval battles for exhibitions and stuff. That was some laugh. Some of them boys are mental."

"You're an interesting cat, Aaron. We'll need to go for a beer later."

2

Sharon Blackwood was tired. She'd had a very busy day.

Bloated and sleepy after she'd finished eating Mark, regrettably she'd had no time for rest, and now, with a long lingering, open mouthed kiss, she thanked the kindly middle aged gentleman who'd picked her up by the roadside out in the moors, then smiled at him mysteriously and stepped from his car onto the busy High Street in Stornoway town centre.

The place teemed with prey.

Hundreds, *thousands* of humans went to and fro on the crowded streets, and Sharon's newly heightened perceptions were assailed by a great flood of sensory information. All the sounds, sights and most of all the smells of the throng thrilled and enthralled her. Buskers. Stalls. Bars. Music. The scent of fried food and alcohol. Cigarette smoke. Laughter. A child crying. Excited squeals and rowdy beer fuelled cheers. All of it washed over and around her in a dizzying riot of colour, sound and smell.

So many. A great flock of dumb sheep with absolutely no idea of what was about to happen to them.

Sharon Blackwood, and the ancient thing that now owned and rode her mind, flesh and soul, joined the merrily bustling throng and had a very pleasant afternoon just like any other happy go lucky girl enjoying the festival. She walked the streets, did a bit of bar hopping, had a few drinks, saw a few bands. All the while, the thing inside her assimilated her thoughts, knowledge and experiences. It had last walked the Earth a millennia ago, and the world of men had changed much during its slumber.

Many young men that day, and one or two giddily experimental girls as well, were left bewildered and charmed by the alluringly pretty blonde girl with the captivating green eyes who smiled flirtatiously and chatted with them, leaning in close and bestowing a deep, slow and thoroughly bewitching kiss before slipping away into the crowd again and vanishing. She hadn't really been keeping count, but Sharon figured she must have snogged at least forty individuals that afternoon.

Now, as the day waned and the sun started to go down, the entity inside her pulled impatiently at her blood, eager to run, yearning to be free, and her bones and muscles twitched and tingled in anticipation. Her gums and fingernails beginning to throb, Sharon left the town centre and joined the crowd of festival goers heading to the main stage in the castle grounds across the harbour. Once across the bridge and into the large open area of parks and woodland, she casually slipped out of the travelling throng, stepping off the footpath and heading off through a thick grove of trees. She walked for a few minutes until she found a quiet, private spot a suitable distance away from the crowds.

She had to change for a big night out.

3

In his bedroom on the upper floor of a terraced house on Scotland Street back in the town centre, nineteen year old college student Ross Michelson shivered and shook under his sheets.

He'd come home from a day at the festival feeling unwell, and had retreated to his bed, hoping to get a few hours kip and recover before heading back out to the main stage tonight with his mates. Through his sweat soaked tremors, he couldn't shake the image in his fevered head of the strange girl who'd kissed him in the bar that afternoon. She smiled at him through his delirium, just as she had earlier, those incredible eyes flashing with irresistible, almost predatory sexual promise.

*

Three streets away on James Street, Albert Knox, a thirty-one year old industrial washing machine technician, was also feeling a tad shady. He couldn't stop pacing his living room floor. He felt very hot and itchy. Felt like he needed to run. Naomi, his two year old daughter hadn't stopped screaming since he came in the door, and his wife Laura kept fussing over him, trying to press cold compresses to his forehead and insisting that he should be in his bed. He shrugged off her attentions irritably, thinking to himself that the fine wee bird who'd winched the face off him in the pub earlier wasn't such a pain in the arse. No. She'd been sexy. Mysterious. Not at all like the frumpy, nagging bitch whom he'd shared his bed with the past twelve years.

Naomi's ear splitting screeching went on and on, and the whining voice of his wife grated on his nerves like a rusty knife on a dinner plate. The two of them were really doing his head in.

Seriously.

*

In a flat on the south side of the town, not far from the car rental place where Ian and the others had been that very morning, twenty-four year old bar manager Scotty Sanders was acting very strangely indeed. He was sitting naked in a bathtub of iced water, working his way diligently through the half kilogram of raw fillet steak he'd bought from the local butchers on the way home from town. His eyes, normally a shade of cornflower blue that girls loved, were a sick jaundiced yellow, and he had a scraggly three day growth of beard on his oddly distended jaw, despite only having shaved that morning.

*

On Cromwell Street down by the harbourside, apprentice cabinet maker Joe Conner was crouched naked at the bottom of his twilit back garden, his aching fingertips weeping blood as his fingernails thickened, lengthened and became claws. The skin all over his body stabbed with hot needles as coarse strands of hair sprouted from his pores. He looked down in horror at the cooling body of his girlfriend, Lisa, who's throat he'd just torn out with his teeth.

Then, a thick guttural chuckling escaped his twisted mouth as the hideous transformation continued, buckling and contorting his limbs, his ears stretching and flowing like liquid wax into tufted points, his skull and spine reshaping in a series of wet cracks, crunches and thin squeals of shifting bone.

4

The Accident and Emergency department of Western Isles Hospital had been unusually busy that day, first dispatching an ambulance crew out to Loch Langabhat where there had been an incident concerning the fugitive who'd escaped from Stornoway police station that morning. Multiple casualties, the police officer who'd called it in had said.

Less than an hour after dispatching the ambulance crew, who'd later gone missing and couldn't be raised on the radio, another call had come in. Some kind of animal attack out at the Calanais Visitor Centre. When they brought the casualties in, the medical staff on shift, all well trained and competent professionals, had been badly shaken by the condition of the victims.

Six dead, all badly mutilated, and several more walking wounded who'd come in bleeding and panicked, marked with bites and scratches that could only have come from some large predatory animal.

The breathless, wide eyed accounts of exactly what had transpired at the tourist attraction varied wildly. Something about an enormous animal, a bear, wolf or gorilla depending on who you spoke to, running amok. One of the injured survivors, a seventeen year old kitchen porter who'd only come in to cover a shift at the last minute, had been babbling nonsensically about monsters. Werewolves.

Each of the injured patients had been running exceptionally high fevers, their various wounds already bearing the angry inflamed look of infection. Such had been their agitated state that more than one of them had had to be physically restrained, their limbs strapped securely onto the rails of their beds and gurneys.

Then more bodies had come in, some of them in several chewed pieces.

There'd been yet another incident, this time out on the A859 road to Stornoway, which had resulted in unspeakable carnage that had claimed the lives of five police officers and the two missing paramedics. Most of the bodies looked to have been extensively eaten, and there were whispers among the overwhelmed staff in the casualty department that a further two corpses, large unidentified animals, had been bundled quickly into a police forensics van and rushed away.

And as if all that hadn't been enough, as the strange and bloody day wore on, more people, young males mostly, came through the doors of A&E suffering with the same rampant fever that continued to burn through the wounded survivors from that afternoon's incident out at

Calanais. None of these new walk-in patients bore any sign of having been bitten or clawed however.

It was when the sun began to go down that things got really weird.

Quarantined by then in the ICU by the increasingly nervous and thoroughly baffled medical staff, the fever infected patients, around twenty of them, almost as one began to scream and snarl in their beds, biting at their restraints as their thrashing fever ridden bodies began contorting and shifting into new inhuman forms. The horrified doctors and nurses who witnessed the mass transformation gave scant thought to their Hippocratic oaths as they ran from the intensive care wing in terror.

As the sun sank below the western horizon, the vargulfen broke out of the ICU department and spread through the hospital like an unchecked virus, rampaging through the building, attacking any living thing that crossed their path.

5

Jack Powning's four by four was doing close to sixty miles per hour entering the tiny village of Marybank, just a single street of houses a mile to the north west of Stornoway, when full darkness came down.

Cal's attention was on Paul McShane, who was half turned around in the front passenger seat addressing him, Ian, Scarlett and Jack in the back, running over his plan for when they reached the festival main stage.

"The folk at the gig are too exposed out in the open," he said. "We need to try and get them inside somewhere secure. The college is just behind Castle Lews so I'm thinking that's our best bet as it's big enough. There's about three thousand people at the gig. We'll get you all kitted out with security crew jackets and you can help to start herding them in that direction while you keep an eye out for... you know what. Without the jackets, you're just going to look like nutters with souvenir spears and axes and shit, and no one's going to listen to you. At least with the jackets on you'll look official and people'll be more likely to do what you tell..."

"*Jesus Christ!*" Aaron suddenly yelled, and the car swerved violently with a sick lurch and the squeal of tortured brakes and skidding tyres. There was a hard thump, then Cal saw the world beyond the windshield spin madly as the vehicle lost its grip on the tarmac and went over with a rolling series of metallic bangs and scrapes, shattering glass, screams and shouts as the large vehicle rolled and spun clumsily along the road, through a fence and into an adjacent field.

Cal had never been in a car crash before, his only experience of them coming second hand from what he'd seen in films and read in books. In the dazed seconds after the four by four came to rest, he expected groans and cries of pain from the wrecked car's occupants, the constant blare of the car horn so often heard on screen, the smell of fuel and the accompanying panic at the thought of being burned alive as the petrol tank went up.

Apart from a few groans however, there was none of that. No car horn sounding an ugly unison. No smell of gas. No dread of being trapped and immolated in the wreckage. There was just a cool, almost soothing night breeze blowing softly in through the empty window frames and the burnt powdery smell of deployed air bags.

Then Cal looked over and saw the fence post protruding from Ian's torso, slightly left of centre just beneath the point where his ribs met.

He stared at it for a moment, at first not understanding what he was seeing. Then it all fell horribly into place. The long days and weeks spent engulfed in medical textbooks in the library of the University of Glasgow almost twenty years previously bore detailed and bloody fruit. Forgotten anatomical terms, iatric terminology and diagnostic jargon resurfaced from the depths of his memory, and he knew Ian likely only had moments to live.

Traumatic aortic rupture. Possible secondary rupturing of the celiac trunk with damage to common hepatic, splenic and left and right gastric arteries. Massive internal blood loss. Onset of shock. Death from exsanguination in minutes, if not seconds.

Someone was speaking to him. He didn't know who. There was a radio crackling somewhere, a tinny urgent voice saying things. Bad things. Then everyone seemed to be talking and shouting and screaming all at once. It was all just a blurred rush of nonsense sounds and words that he couldn't make sense of. Cal thought he heard wolves howling somewhere out there in the dark.

"...Ian oh Jesus God no no no no..."

"...something ran in front of the car..."

"...all units be advised...animal attack..."

"...stay with me Ian..."

"...oh fuck there's so much blood..."

"...multiple fatalities...Western Isles Hospital...holy Christ..."

"...phone a fucking ambulance..."

"...I saw it...a huge dog or something..."

"...I don't believe it there's another one...animal attack...Scotland Street..."

"...don't you die don't you dare die you bastard..."

326

"...Cromwell Street...I've got four dead here...mother of fuck they've been half eaten..."

"...backup we need backup now...holy Christ what's that...*what the fuck*..."

"...Ian please..."

"...a wolf..."

"...*holy shit...other there*..."

Howling.

A scream.

Gunfire.

6

Standing in the field by the wrecked four by four, Paul opened up with the MP5.

He let go a controlled three round burst that took the enormous animal running at him full in the face at a range of just five metres. Its head blew apart in a small but grisly explosion that sprayed black in the orange sodium glare of the streetlights behind it.

The passenger side door of the Jeep had buckled in the frame during the crash and wouldn't open, and Paul had to painfully haul himself out of the empty window frame. Amazingly, most of the totalled car's occupants had escaped serious injury. He'd been about to radio for an ambulance for the one passenger who hadn't been so fortunate – the gruesomely impaled Ian Walker – when he'd seen the massive wolf charging across the field at him.

Now he had time to get a good look at it, Paul could see that although it was undoubtedly a monster in anyone's book, this wasn't the same type of creature that had attacked the police convoy earlier. It ran on four legs, was smaller than the enormous bipeds, lacked their humanoid appearance and resistance to bullets, and was to all intents and purposes, just a wolf, albeit a fucking big one. Looking down at the huge animal's body, a single word from a TV show he enjoyed watching formed in his head.

Direwolf.

The big ass wolves from *Game of Thrones*. That's what this thing was like. An easy two metres long, not even counting the tail, its head would come up to almost the level of a man's chest.

He came back to the present as the frantic voices coming out of his radio got his attention again. Jim Maxwell, the dispatcher back at the station, was having the worst shift of his life. It sounded like the entire island had descended into utter bedlam in the few minutes since it had gotten dark.

Paul thumbed the transmitter switch on his own handheld. "Control, this is ARO Paul McShane. Jim, I know you've a lot to deal with right now but if possible I need an ambulance..." his words tailed off as he turned round and looked in at Ian Walker in the rear of the wrecked four by four.

The broken fence post that had come arrowing through the windshield, scraping along the side of Paul's head as it flew into the car's interior, had taken the poor cunt directly through the torso, impaling him, effectively *nailing* him to the back seat. He'd stopped breathing, was staring ahead sightlessly, and his skin had taken on that horrible slackness and waxy sheen unique to the dead. His heart already sinking, knowing it was pointless, Paul stepped closer and felt under the man's jaw for a pulse.

Nothing.

He turned to Scarlett who was standing close by, her intense eyes already shimmering in the orangey half light, and gave a single shake of his head.

"Nevermind, Jim," he said morosely into the radio, stepping respectfully away from the wreck as Scarlett Mathie went to her dead friend and began to weep quietly. "If you can," he continued, pitching his voice low, "get as many men as possible out to the festival grounds. They need to be armed. Tell them to look for wolves, and to shoot on sight. Out."

He turned back to the group of people by the wreck. Scarlett was half in, half out of the car, her body shaking with grief as she embraced Ian Walker's skewered body. Jack and Aaron stood nearby, facing out into the night, weapons drawn, keeping watch. Cal stood behind and to the right of Scarlett, his hand on her shoulder, an expression on his face that was somewhere between sorrow and rage as he stared into the car's interior. Paul noticed that *he* wasn't weeping. He didn't know *what* you'd call the weird look on the guy's face, but it was unnerving.

He walked back over to the vehicle after a moment, laying a gentle hand on Scarlett's shuddering shoulder. "There's nothing we can do here," he said quietly. "I'm sorry, but we need to go." Scarlett remained where she was for a second, then nodded, laid a gentle parting kiss on Walker's cheek, and stepped away. She turned to Cal, face wet with tears, holding out her arms to give and receive comfort.

"Oh shit oh fuck oh Jesus..."

Paul looked over his shoulder and saw Jack had approached, and was staring into the battered four by four, wheezing and pointing, the colour visibly draining from his face.

Then, despite all the impossible horrors the day had already thrown at him, Paul McShane came very close to shitting his pants as Ian Walker began to scream.

"You know about this kind of thing?" Jack asked, the words coming out in a cracked whisper.

Aaron just shrugged and went back to scanning the night around them, keeping watch for any sign of more prowling wolves, the huge double headed axe held ready across his body. The only sounds to be heard were the distant music of the festival, several far off police sirens, and the muffled grunts and low cries of pain coming from the recently reanimated Ian behind them, still pinned like a bug to the back seat of the four by four.

"But you said there were immortals. You're supposed to *know* this stuff, Aaron!" Jack insisted, hating and embarrassed by the pleading whine that he heard in his voice.

The big man looked at him. "I said I didn't think it was possible to be an expert in this kind of thing. I know that immortals exist, aye, but do I know everything there is to know about how or why it happens? Fuck no. I know this is more mind bending shit you have to deal with, Jack, but all I can say to you is accept it, keep your voice down and your eyes open. Cool?"

Jack was far from cool. He'd reached his daily crazy tolerance level quite some time ago.

"Jack? Aaron? Come here a minute, would you?"

Jack looked over his shoulder and saw Paul beckoning them over to the Jeep.

They went over to where Paul, Scarlett and Cal stood by the open rear door of the wrecked Jeep. Ian, still impaled by the fence post in the back seat, had stopped screaming, and in fact looked remarkably calm considering his predicament. Cal was clutching Ian's hand with both his own.

"What the fuck's happening, man? What in the name of Christ *is* this?" he was saying.

"It's cool, mate," Ian replied, "I know you're freaking out right now, but just try and chill and listen to me." The musician, who since Jack had met him had been broody and mainly silent in a nervous, twitchy sort of way, now possessed a remarkable measure of composure in his voice. He sounded in fact, like a patient father coaxing a frightened child through the finer points of stabiliser-free bike riding. "Paul, can you shine your torch here please, mate?"

Looking as astonished as Jack was by the skewered man's relaxed manner, Paul nevertheless obliged, and directed his compact Maglite toward Ian, who began undoing his shirt buttons. It was a surreal sight, with the fence post still stuck in him and all, seeing Ian carefully unfasten the shirt above, then below the thick fencepost, before suddenly yanking the garment open with a low growling scream to reveal the full bloody spectacle of his impaled torso.

He was as thin as you would expect, with not an ounce of fat to be seen. Ian Walker had to be at the most a thirty inch waist, but he was more wiry than puny, and there was visible ropy muscle there. Jack wasn't checking out the dude's six pack though. It was the way the terrible wound beneath Ian's sternum was... *moving*. Flaps of bloody torn skin undulated and slid fluidly around the thick wooden stake pinning him to the seat. Jack thought of the way a snail's antennae move as they sense out their environment.

"It took them two hours to find me after the stage collapsed at Reading," he said. "After the lightning rig went, the whole fucking thing just came down. They found me underneath the stage, buried under half the flooring, the big screens, the speakers, lighting rig, my kit and Ryan's cabinet stack. Unconscious, but alive. Un-fucking-scathed."

Jack remembered reading about the incident in the paper, how the bright future of the wildly successful band Ragged Mojo had been tragically extinguished in the freak on-stage accident which had killed two thirds of their group, the sole survivor of the band having miraculously escaped death with only a concussion, despite being entombed under several tons of AV equipment.

Cal and Scarlett looked at Ian in confusion, but when no one spoke, he went on. "These scars here and here," he pointed to the marks at his abdomen and throat, "I got these this afternoon. That big cunt that killed Clyde and Matt got me in the throat with an arrow, then speared me in the guts when he came out onto the island. Oh yeah, and last night? He didn't just scratch me. That knife went right into my neck. And on the ferry on the way here when that glass broke in my fist? My hand was slashed to fuck, but the cut closed over, two minutes after it happened." He leaned closer and put a hand on Cal's shoulder, meeting his eyes earnestly. "I've survived over twenty suicide attempts, mate. I've drank a bottle of bleach, hanged myself, slashed my wrists, tried to play electric guitar in the bath, shot myself, OD'd on every pill and powder you could name and driven my motor off a cliff. But I... just... keep... on... rolling.

"Ready?" Walker then asked quietly, his eyes flicking to the fencepost in his chest. Cal, who was staring at his blood streaked mate in open mouthed wonder, nodded, and took a firm two handed grip. "Do it, dude."

The scream he let out when Cal yanked the splinted wooden post out went through Jack like a clumsy dentist's drill. Then they all watched the hole in Ian's torso knit itself together, the blood caked fissure beneath his ribs quickly shrinking and folding in on itself like a puckering mouth, until there was just another patch of the same dark pink scar tissue that Ian wore. For a long moment, nobody said a word. Nobody could, it seemed.

"The wounds close fast," he said, almost as an afterthought, looking down contemplatively at his bloody, but whole torso. "The scars fade after a couple of hours."

Jack remembered to breathe. He hadn't been aware he was holding his breath.

Than Paul's radio crackled to life again and informed them that there had been a further three animal attacks reported in the vicinity of the festival grounds.

"We have to go," Paul said, breaking the awed hush. "Right now."

8

The beast's fangs bear down slowly, slowly, wringing every last possible shred of sweet agony and terror from the mewling prey in its claws before it dies. With a final ecstatic grunt, it snaps its incisors together and experiences a heady rush of exhilaration as its prey's life force erupts in its jaws. Everything the dying human has ever thought, seen, tasted, loved, hated and feared is contained in the burst of spiritual energy. It is the sum of the human's life, its very essence, and it is devoured.

After the last whispering traces have seeped from the human's mangled brain stem, the being that had recently wore the flesh of a human named Sharon Blackwood, releases the corpse, letting it fall to the forest floor. After a millennia of starved sleep, its hunger is fierce, and elsewhere in the woods lie a further four ruined human carcasses from which it has already fed.

Now, with the ambrosial, revitalising taste of blood and souls fresh between its fangs, the Son of Fenrir raises its muzzle to the stars and howls long and deep, a screaming primordial sound that rattles between the tree trunks and out into the night.

There is a tantalising fog of growing fear in the air, spreading gradually throughout the woodlands, seeping up into the atmosphere from the great herd of humans gathered in the area as they hear the roar of some unseen predator in their midst. The beast's sensitive ears pick up their cries of horror and the astringent scent of their burgeoning panic as the remains of its other victims are discovered, and every once in a while, it lets out another roar, its ancient voice spreading more delicious dread among those humans within earshot.

It senses its offspring, the vargulfen dogs also stalking the shadows, like itself, falling on those humans who stray from the crowd and leave the busy paths and greens to enter the darkened regions between the trees, seeking privacy to shit and mount each other. There are more of its brood approaching, running through the streets of the nearby town and the surrounding fields, homing in on the herd, mindlessly killing and maiming as they go. It feels the pack's eagerness to go tearing frenziedly into the large concentration of humans gathered nearby at the enormous tent in front of the castle, but it holds them in check, for it is aware of the presence of certain others in the vicinity.

Humans that bear the spectral shine signifying they have been touched by the void. Other immortals.

Although it feels no fear, which is an alien concept to its kind, the beast knows that these other deathless ones represent a threat, and it sends out a mental command, diverting its hungry offspring scattered throughout the woods toward the approaching immortals.

Growling deep in its chest, the beast drops to all fours and moves on, an immense fanged shadow flitting silently through the trees.

9

Nor for the first time that day, ARO Paul McShane supposed there was a hefty case of post traumatic stress disorder, and maybe even a full blown nervous breakdown in store for him when all this was over, assuming he managed to live through it of course. But for now, he continued to surprise himself with the amount of insanity he could take on board while still being able to function. Moments after Ian had undergone his inexplicable recovery, Paul had been on the radio, urging Jim Maxwell at dispatch to get in touch with whoever was running the show at the festival and order them to stop the concert immediately and begin moving the crowd to the nearby college. A big ask, but it was all he could do for now.

Fuck of a day, he thought to himself now as he looked over the civilians, standing there packing guns, spears, knives and axes, and looking for all the world like some bizarre troupe of time travelling mercenaries. Paul had to suppress a bark of laughter at the thought.

"Alright, troops," he now said to the group. "Keep together. Move fast. Keep your eyes open and be ready for anything. If you see a threat, yell 'contact' and give a clock position so we all know where it is. Remember, if you fire your weapon the recoil makes the barrel jump up, so aim low, go for centre mass, not head shots, and squeeze the trigger, don't snatch at it. We good?"

Paul would have liked to have heard a confident and resounding Marine Corps style *OO-RAH!* from the group, but was forced to content himself with a few reluctant nods and mumbles to the affirmative.

They left the trashed Jeep in the field and hurriedly made their way through the one street village of Marybank on foot, turning right at its eastern end onto Bennadrove Road, then right again onto the A859, the same road leading south that Ian and the others had taken that morning to get to Ardvourlie. After a short distance, they came to an opening in the stone wall flanking the road on their left hand side and passed through it, stepping onto the single lane track that led into the large woodland area encompassing the Raon Goilf golf course, Lews Castle College and the grounds of Lews Castle itself, where the main festival stage was located. The narrow road leading away through the tall pines that pressed in on both sides was illuminated by bollard lamps every twenty metres or so, which cast ghostly circles of luminescence on the darkened track. Paul taking point, the group moved quickly along the middle of the road in single file, making as little sound as possible, their heads on swivels, ears and eyes straining for any signs of movement in the shadows between the trees crowding the path. The tract of land was sizeable, some six hundred acres in total, threaded with over ten miles of paths, and Paul estimated it would take them around ten minutes to reach the festival grounds.

As they went, the sound of distant music coming from the main stage ahead gradually grew louder. Evidently, any efforts made by the festival organisers to evacuate the main stage area and move the thousands of punters to the college were still in the planning stage.

Paul could now make out the amplified double pulse of a bass drum followed by a single crack of thousands of hands clapping in unison. He recognised the familiar beat, and as they moved on, Paul was able to make out the melody of *We Will Rock You* played on bagpipes, and remembered the Red Hot Chili Pipers were on the bill for the evening's entertainment. He'd have really liked to see that show...

"Contact! Eight o'clock!"

A pistol fired. Paul spun left, raised the rifle, saw the huge wolf bursting from the gloom between the trees by the roadside and streaking out onto the path, frighteningly quick. He fired, but the attack happened so fast that his snap shot was off target and only spun the enormous animal, catching it above the left hind leg, before a quick burst from Cal's MP5 blew its head apart. Paul was about to congratulate him on a job well done when there was a sudden scrabbling sound from behind him and someone yelled another warning. He half turned and caught only a peripheral glimpse of the second wolf leaping into the air, coming at his face, fangs bared. He'd no time to get a shot off, and was knocked off his feet and thrown across the path, dropping the rifle as the huge animal ploughed into him and bore him to the ground. He landed hard on his back in the undergrowth to the left of the track, the crushing weight of the huge wolf on top of him slamming the breath from his lungs. He had time to look up and see its jaws open above him, had time to wonder what it would feel like when it bit into him, when there was a piercing yelp of animal pain and hot blood splashed across Paul's face. The creature's bulk pressing down on him suddenly gone, Paul scrambled to his feet in time to see Aaron bring the great axe down again, cleaving deep into the wolf's back. It collapsed to the ground, screaming horribly and tried to drag its shattered body away. Aaron had to use the axe a few more times before it finally stopped moving.

"Nicely done, big man," Paul said shakily when Aaron had finished and the giant wolf lay in several furry chunks on the road. He wiped its blood from his face with a trembling hand and bent down to retrieve his rifle from where he'd dropped it. "Guess you really do know how to use that thing."

"Erm... guys?" Scarlett said in a strained voice. Paul looked over at her and saw she was pointing her Glock into the treeline on the left, then swinging it right and back again. "Oh fuck," she whispered. "Oh shit, shit, shit..."

Paul saw them. Quick moving shapes darting around in the shadows in the treeline on both sides of the path, undefined patches of deeper darkness slinking within the gloom. He heard the snap of twigs, the rustle of undergrowth, and caught the occasional glimmering flash of yellow eyeshine, flitting between the half lit tree trunks like fireflies.

Taking aim on a monstrous black coated wolf that came rushing out from the trees on his left, this time Paul didn't miss, his round finding the beast's heart and stopping it dead.

Then the pack poured out from the shadows and came at them.

"Go! Go! Go!" he yelled, and the group ran, opening up on the wolves behind and to the sides of them as they went.

The night erupted in a strobe-lit bedlam of screams, snarls and gunfire.

10

Head ringing, arms numb from the Glock's recoil and her eyes stinging with gunsmoke, Scarlett ran with the others through the brightly lit car park in front of the main entrance of Castle Lews College.

The prolonged burst of adrenaline that had kept her going up until now was starting to wear off, and as they finally emerged from the forested path and entered the bright lit concentration of buildings and car parks of the college, she began to feel a heavy weariness weighing her down. Her legs were leaden, her heart a triphammer in her chest, her ragged gasping breath burning her fear parched throat.

The journey along the single track road through the woods was a confused, timeless blur in her mind, a chaotic series of mental snapshots that ran together like a jerky stop motion animation from the mind of a madman. Running, yelling, huge darting shadows, half lit trees, monstrous wolves, edged weapons of steel, blood and bursts of light and bullets.

All the way along the wooded single lane road, the predators hunting them had switched between stalking the group's flanks, loping through the trees on either side of the path, keeping pace with them while remaining half hidden in the gloomy treeline, and then launching sudden attacks, breaking cover and leaping out onto the narrow road in groups of threes and fours, coming at them from all directions and forcing the group to stop and try to hold them off. As their supply of ammunition had steadily dwindled, and the group began to tire from the constant running and fighting, each skirmish came a little closer to disaster than the last, with Scarlett and the others only just managing to hold the huge animals at bay with hot lead and blades.

But the wolves had just kept coming.

Scarlett didn't know how many of them they'd killed. Fifteen? Twenty? Impossible to tell in the chaos. She knew she'd got at least three of the cunts.

Since the group had exited the woods and begun winding their way through the various buildings of the college campus though, the wolves' onslaught had, at least temporarily, ceased. Looking about her now as she staggered through the car park outside the three storey main building of the college on her left, Scarlett did a quick head count, just to confirm to herself that by some miracle, each member of their group really *was* still alive.

Cal was limping along on her right. The machine gun Paul had given him had gone dry and been discarded some indeterminate time ago, and he now had one of the spears in his hands. Every few seconds he turned and jogged backwards as he checked their rear for signs of pursuit. His right leg was bleeding, the jeans above his knee hanging in tatters and stained dark from where a wolf had made it through their wall of gunfire, snaking out from the gloom by the roadside and going for his thigh. Aaron had intervened before it bit his leg off, smashing the enormous animal aside with his axe.

Aaron himself was running along behind them, grim faced, the enormous axe gripped in his hands and looking every inch the biker from Hell. His hands, face, shaven head and leather jacket and trousers were liberally splattered with blood, and the double crescent head of the axe he carried gleamed gorily in the orange glow of the car park's lights. In the mad confusion of their frantic dash along the tree lined road, Aaron had been their last line of defence, cutting down any lunging wolf that evaded the hail of bullets and came within reach of his weapon.

Jack was just ahead of Scarlett, one of his throwing knives held ready in his hand. She'd seen him take down at least three of the pack that had harried them as they ran along the forested road, sending his sleek symmetrical blades into their throats with unerring lethal accuracy in a display of skill that was uncanny, and which she would have regarded as extremely cool if witnessed in some other, less life threatening circumstances.

Ian was out on her left, armed with the other spear. His pistol had also run out of rounds some time ago, and Paul was at the front, at that moment standing on the roof of one of the parked cars, waving them on, covering the group with his rifle as he scanned the car park behind them and the grove of trees bordering its southern side on their right. She thanked God that the marksman was still with them. Without Paul, they'd never had made it this far. All the way along the woodland path, ceaselessly harried by the wolf pack, he'd kept them together, kept them moving, never wasting a shot as he efficiently dropped anything with more than two legs that came into his sights.

Even as she watched, Paul gave a sudden warning shout and raised his rifle, seeming to aim directly at her face. Scarlett ducked, then half a second later heard the heavy *crack* of his rifle and felt the air part directly above her scalp in the bullet's wake. There was a pained animal scream followed by a deep metallic thump close behind her. She looked quickly back over her shoulder as she stumbled on, and saw the body of the great grey wolf slide limply off the front end of a parked car on her right, leaving a wide trail of smeared blood across the bonnet.

"*Keep going!*" Paul yelled. He raised the rifle again, taking aim at something over Scarlett's shoulder, but this time, he didn't fire. Behind her there was a deep grunting growl, a scuffle, a harsh *clang*, someone roaring in pain, something tearing. Ahead of her, Paul cursed, leapt down from the car roof and ran forward. Scarlett turned and saw Aaron was sprawled on the road between the rows of parked cars, his dropped axe out of reach and his left arm seized in the jaws of a wolf as it gnawed and clawed and shook him like a terrier with a rabbit. Aaron hollered in desperation, frantically punching at the beast's head with his free hand while trying to get his feet under him, but the thing's brute strength and ferocity were too much even for him, and he was dragged helplessly back and forth across the tarmac.

Scarlett ran back, raising the Glock, praying it wasn't empty.

Close enough to smell the wild musky stench of the wolf, she leapt onto its back. It immediately twisted and bucked, trying to throw her off. It released Aaron's arm and craned its head round, snapping at her. Scarlett leant back, tightened her left arm around its thick neck, then jammed the Glock's barrel deep into the wide fleshy canal of its right ear, and pulled the trigger. Brains and skull fragments leapt in a lumpy explosion from the left side of the animal's head. The wolf jerked once, then slumped lifelessly to the ground.

Then Cal was at her side, telling her she was a crazy cow as he helped her to push herself free of the dead animal's heavy corpse. They rushed over to join Ian and Paul who were helping Aaron to his feet. The thick sleeve of his leather biker's jacket was torn and slicked in wolf spit, and he hissed in pain when he tried to raise his left arm. Grimacing, Aaron still had the fortitude to stoop and pick the axe up again in his right hand.

"Thanks, Scarlett," he said with a pained wince as he straightened up. "I owe you…"

"*Watch out!*" someone yelled.

There was a gun shot.

Something grabbed Scarlett's neck in a hot, jagged grasp and there was an instant of ripping agony.

Then the world turned upside down and everything dissolved in a red and black haze.

11

"Ladies and gentlemen, we have an emergency situation. Please remain calm and immediately begin making your way to the college car park."

Massed jeers and boos.

"We're sorry, but for your own safety, please follow the instructions of the event security stewards and make your way in an orderly fashion to the college grounds behind the castle. Again, this is an emergency situation."

The PA announcement and the subsequent angry reaction from the crowd at the nearby main stage area washed over Ian, barely heard. Sirens were rising in the distance. The cavalry finally arriving. Ian found he didn't give a fuck.

The wolf had come out of nowhere, sailing silently over the roof of a parked car on his left as they'd attended to the wounded Aaron, and Ian had only caught the sudden blur of movement in the corner of his eye before blurting out a warning. Paul's instinctive snap shot hadn't been enough to bring the animal down, and it had ploughed into the group, knocking them all flying. Ian had gone skidding across the tarmac, just scrambling back to his feet in time to see Paul, lying on his back, blow the entire right side of wolf's head away with his second shot, firing point blank into its face as it lunged at him. But by then, it'd already been too late.

Now, Ian and Cal knelt beside Scarlett, who lay on the ground in a rapidly spreading pool of blood.

Her neck had been laid wide open by the wolf's teeth.

Cal was pressing his wadded up t-shirt onto the wound, frantically trying to staunch the bleeding, urging the unconscious Scarlett awake in a cracked voice. "Please, Scarlett, hold on. Just hold on, babe. You can't... you can't go..." His features were so twisted with sorrow it was difficult to look at, and Ian realised he'd never seen his friend look so thoroughly distraught. Not at his family's funeral all those years ago. Not when Matt and Clyde had died earlier that day. He knew Cal and Scarlett had gone out for a while when they were in their teens, but that was years ago. Scarlett was married to Stuart now, and Cal was engaged...

"Open your eyes, babe" Cal was saying, his voice thick and hitching. "C'mon, Scarlett... please... open your eyes."

Scarlett's eyelids fluttered and opened slowly, as if she was waking from a deep and restful sleep. She looked up at Cal. "Hey, you," she murmured softly, her words distorted and sluggish, thick with blood. "Wha happened...?"

"It's nothing," Cal said, smiling down at her through his tears, gently stroking her hair with one hand while using the other to keep his t-shirt, now just a sodden red rag, pressed to her neck. "Just a wee scratch. You're fine. You're going to be alright."

"Don bullshit... bullshitter, Cal."

"No, really," he insisted, shaking his head. "It just grazed you."

Scarlett gave him a weak smile and reached up to stroke his cheek. Then she turned her eyes to Ian. "Tell im... t shut... the fuggup... will you, Ian?"

Ian's vision blurred and he felt tears tracking down his cheeks and rolling onto his upper lip. He could taste the salt. "Sure thing, missy," he croaked. "Shut the fuck up, Cal." Cal's eyes screwed up and he bowed his head. His shoulders started to shudder.

Scarlett fixed Ian with her eyes, her voice dropping to a near whisper. "Tell Stu... love him... an t... take care... Reece." A tear slid from the corner of her left eye at her infant son's name. "... sorry, baby... mummy gonna... miss you..."

Ian took her hand. It was very cold. Her eyes fluttered again and began to close. He felt her warm pooling blood seep into the knees of his jeans. "I'll see you around," he whispered, laying a gentle kiss on the back of her fingers. "Love you, Scarlett."

"Will you... sing me... t sleep?" she asked, her failing voice now hardly more than a soft breath. "You... such... lovely...voice..."

Choked up as he was, Ian didn't think he'd be able. But then, without thinking about it, he began to hum a slow, soft melody, and found it came note perfect from his throat, the pitch steady and unwavering. It was a strange, bittersweet tune, the rising and falling notes heartbreaking yet joyful in their curious mix of gospel and Celtic melodic patterns, and he recognised it as the haunting refrain that had come to him as they'd paddled along the eerie glass like surface of Loch Langabhat that afternoon.

Scarlett's eyes flickered opened again, and the corners of her lips rose slightly in a final, sad smile. "Beautiful," she breathed. Then her eyes closed for the last time, and Ian, still holding her hand, felt the last traces of life leaving her.

He continued to softly hum the strange, lilting melody while Cal, looking every inch an utterly broken man, leant down and whispered something in Scarlett's ear.

Ian thought he made out the words *it was always you.*

12

There's iron in you, son, *the old lifer said, sitting down on the bench next to him in the canteen of HMP Barlinnie.*

He was sore all over. He'd just got out of the prison infirmary. The dead eyed cunt that'd come at him with the sharpened toothbrush was still there, and would be for the foreseeable future. The old boy next to him didn't look at him. Just sat there shovelling gravy smothered mash potatoes into his mouth. His arms were covered in hand drawn tattoos and he had a large scar down one side of his wizened face, and...

... *it was a cold and grey Glasgow day in December. Sleet spitting from the grey sky above and an icy wind nipping his cheeks. He was walking through the gates of the prison, his time served. Free. Ian, Clyde, Scarlett and Matt were there waiting for him, smiling and laughing as they ran towards him, and...*

...*he was lying in bed. The weak early morning sunlight filtering through the thin curtains cast a subdued light across Scarlett's face on the pillow next to his. She smiled at him. Her dad had died last night, and she'd come to his flat, crying and in need of comfort. In need of a friend. It had just happened. But they both knew it would never happen again, and...*

...*he was in the library at uni, a thick textbook on virology and epidemiology open on the desk in front of him, medical terminology ricocheting around his head as he grappled with the dense text. Provirus. Retro virus. Symbiosis. Reservoir host. Host of predilection...*

"Cal? You okay?"

He blinked and looked up. Ian was standing over him, a hand on his shoulder. He heard sirens. Radios. Authoritative voices barking orders. The sound of a large crowd of people approaching. He looked down again. Scarlett lay on the ground in front of him. Eyes closed. A little smile on her lips.

Dead.

He bent forward and kissed her lightly on the forehead, then Cal wiped his face and stood up, turning to Ian, but found there was nothing to say.

"You cool, man?" Ian asked, studying his face. "You going to flip out?"

"Probably," Cal murmured, "but not right now."

A large column of people were emerging out of the trees that flanked the east side of the car park where Cal and Ian stood. The approaching crowd, the evacuated festival goers, mostly younger people in their teens and twenties, being guided along the path toward the college by yellow jacketed security staff and police. Cal saw that the cops in view were armed, visibly nervous, and were keeping a very close eye on the shadowy woodland.

"How you doing, lads?" Cal turned and Aaron was there, still in his blood splashed leathers. Still with the ridiculously large axe gripped in his right hand and the two spears over his left shoulder. "Sorry about Scarlett," he said simply. "That girl had some balls on her."

Ian burst out laughing.

A look of dawning horror spread on Aaron's face as he realised what he'd just said. "Oh, fuck, Jesus, I'm sorry, lads...I just meant..."

"It's cool, Aaron," Cal told him, grinning and shaking his head at Aaron's heartfelt, yet wildly inappropriate offer of condolence. "We used to say it to Scarlett all the time to wind her up. She had bigger baws that any of us." Then he let out a big snort of laughter and both he and Ian were gutting themselves. It really was a if-you-didn't-laugh-you'd-cry moment Cal thought. And it was alright. He knew Scarlett would've been pishing herself laughing as well. The day's madness and tragedy had to come out some way, and as he and Ian wiped their eyes, still chuckling and giggling, he felt a good ten pounds lighter. He knew the real hurt would come, and would never stop until he died too. But that was for later.

"Where's Paul and Jack?" Aaron asked.

"Paul got called away," Ian said. "They said he was needed over at the castle. Jack's still talking to the cops. How's the arm?"

Aaron shrugged and immediately winced at the movement. "Just dislocated. One of the cops popped it back in for me. Here." He held out his left arm, offering the spears to Cal and Ian. "One of the cops tried to confiscate these and the axe, but I told him to go and shite. He wasn't up for arguing with me."

Cal took one of the spears and frowned at the leaf shaped head of the weapon with an abrupt understanding. "It's like a... virus, this whole thing," he said distractedly.

"Eh?" Ian asked, frowning at him.

"What did the big beardy bastard say to you? His weapons were washed with the blood of the Ulfhednar?"

Ian nodded.

"I think it's kind of like the way we develop vaccines against viruses," Cal said, nodding now as he spoke and indicating the spear in his hand. "You use the virus to synthesise the cure. The big ones, the... Ulfhednar... they're the source, what a virologist might call the primary or definitive host. They spread the virus. They infect us. The ones that came at us in the woods... they were infected people."

He paused for a moment while that sunk in. *Fuck.*

They'd killed a whole lot of wolves in the woods, which meant they'd actually killed a whole lot of people who'd simply been unlucky enough to have been infected with a certain type of sickness. He filed that lovely little realisation away with the recent deaths of Clyde and Scarlett and Matt, and all the other horrifying lunacy he'd witnessed that day in a rapidly thickening mental folder marked *Crazy Shit to Deal with Later*.

"The ones infected. They die just like anything else, like with bullets and knives. If I'm right, they can't spread the virus. They're not carriers. They're what're known as dead end hosts."

Applying medical knowledge and logic to the situation, he found he was definitely more comfortable using epidemiological principles to make at least some sense of the deranged events. But he then became acutely uncomfortable as he realised what could happen if a virus such as this got off the island. Even if his theory was correct and the infected humans couldn't spread the virus further, he couldn't stop his medical mind morbidly considering the fact that viruses have the ability to spontaneously mutate and adapt according to their environment. If the dead end hosts were to become carriers as well, capable of infecting others...

The four of them stood in silence for a moment, digesting everything Cal had told them, then one of the event security staff approached and asked them to start making their way toward the reception area of the college. They were just walking across the car park, joining the confused and increasingly nervous crowd that had begun to file through the doors into the college's large glass walled reception area, when the sound of fresh gunfire cracked across the night, coming from the direction of the castle.

13

Paul let his breath out slowly. In the green washed circle of the Hensoldt scope's night vision, the illuminated crosshair reticle dropped slowly, inching downwards until it settled on his target. Holding his breath, he squeezed the trigger.

Half a mile away, just adjacent to the playing fields on Smith Avenue in the town centre, the enormous wolf with its muzzle buried deep in the open stomach cavity of a dead woman spasmed, a dark spray of blood splattering on the pavement behind it as the monster's legs folded, and it collapsed atop the eviscerated corpse it was chewing on.

Paul saw the glowing pinpoints of its eyeshine fade out of existence.

"Target down. Smith Avenue," he said into the microphone of his radio headset.

"Roger that," replied Inspector Martin Scally's tinny voice in his ear.

Paul had to give the gaffer his dues. He could have remained back at the station, safe behind his desk, but he'd come out into the field to direct the other officers in clearing and securing the festival site. As Paul had expected, Scally had had bigger concerns to deal with when the inspector had caught up with him in the college car park, and hadn't mentioned Paul's failure to follow his orders and remain at the roadblock earlier. After Paul had given his CO a full account of what had transpired with the civilians since then, tactfully neglecting to mention Ian Walker's death and resurrection right enough, Scally had simply nodded, then given him the broad strokes of what had been going on in and around town.

The streets of Stornoway had still been crowded when night fell and the wolves had suddenly appeared in the populace's midst. With so little manpower available to the local constabulary due to the day's other events, there had been precious little police presence on the streets to maintain order, protect the public or organise any sort of evacuation, and the carefree, bustling carnival atmosphere of the evening had suddenly deteriorated into mass panic and bloodshed as the wolves had appeared in the busy streets, running amok, attacking and mauling anything that moved.

Reports were sketchy at best, the details unclear, but the word was that the Western Isles Hospital on the outskirts of town had been particularly badly hit. A slaughterhouse, one of his officers had described it on the radio. The guy had sounded like he was about ready to burst into tears.

In the evening's confusion and chaos, there was no way of knowing the exact figures of dead and wounded, but through the sight of his rifle, Paul could now see that the streets of Stornoway town centre were littered with bodies. He'd counted eighteen so far.

There was no help coming from the mainland. Scally had confirmed that ever since late that afternoon, shortly after the passing of the eclipse, practically all forms of communication on the island had failed. Phone lines, mobiles, the internet, all gone. Some sort of freak atmospheric phenomenon caused by the eclipse the baffled techies at the station were guessing. The only line of comms still functioning was the police band radio, and even that was erratic, and reception was seemingly restricted to the confines of the island itself. They'd been unable to hail any vessels offshore. All attempts to raise the alarm and call for aid from emergency services on the mainland had been met with empty uncaring static.

Then there was the weather.

From what scattered information Scally had been able to gather, it seemed that a bizarre squall had blown up in the waters off the coast. Rough conditions were nothing new to the inhabitants of the Isle of Lewis, who lived on the very doorstep of the North Atlantic, but this particular storm, there was something wrong with it. It seemed to be blowing in from all points of the compass, surrounding the entire island in an impassable barrier of smothering thick fog banks, near hurricane level winds and twenty foot ocean swells. From Paul's vantage point high on the east tower of Lews Castle, across the bay he could see the huge waves crashing into the harbour walls and the wreckage of boats that'd been crushed against the quay. The end result of it all was that denied passage from the island by sea and air, and with no form of communication with the mainland, the entire Isle of Lewis was completely cut off from the outside world. They might as well have been on another planet.

When he'd finished briefing Paul on the grim situation as it stood, Scally ordered him up to the east tower of Lews Castle from where he could provide covering fire while the rest of the police and event staff evacuated the festival crowd to the college. The tower rose above the canopy of the surrounding woods, reaching a height of almost seventy feet, and now, standing at the open roof's crenulated parapet, Paul had a clear view in all directions.

Below him to the south east, the last of the festival crowd were quickly filtering out of the large lawn in front of the castle and joining the long column of people hurriedly making their way along the short woodland path that skirted the east facing side of Castle Lews and led to the college. The moving crowd was flanked by the yellow jacketed event staff and armed police officers, the festival workers keeping them moving and pointing the way ahead while the cops, now armed with more MP5, Glocks and Remmington shotguns from the station's small armoury, kept a wary eye on the trees that lined the right hand side of the path. To start with, the crowd had been moving sluggishly and with obvious reluctance, still pissed about the cancellation of the show, but they'd begun to move a damn sight faster after Paul's first shot from atop the castle tower had rung out, the sound of gunfire a far more effective means of motivation than the apologetic stage announcer had been.

To the east, Paul could see out across the bay into the town centre. In the grainy jade glow of his scope, Stornoway was a ghost town. The streets empty but for the dead, the survivors sheltering behind locked doors, seeking sanctuary from the wolves. His eye pressed to the lens, Paul adjusted the rifle's powerful telescopic sight, his elevated view of the streets expanding as he zoomed out.

His marksman's eye caught a dark flash of movement, and he panned the rifle slightly to the right, adjusting the scope's focus and zooming in again, locking onto the large darting shadow running west along the road by the waterfront, close to the ferry terminal.

"Target acquired. Westbound on Shell Street," he said into the headset. Despite the technicians back at the station still desperately tying to get lines of communication back up and running, the police band was still patchy and unreliable, and the unintelligible reply in Paul's ear was just a broken, static distorted noise.

He took a breath, tracking the loping figure of the massive wolf running along the quayside, keeping the crosshairs just ahead of the animal, leading it slightly, adjusting his aim for the downward angle of the shot and the animal's forward motion. His finger began to squeeze the trigger as he let his air out in a controlled, even exhalation. Again, when his lungs were empty, he held his breath and applied the last ounce of force to the three pound pull of the trigger.

Carried by its own charging momentum, the wolf by the ferry terminal performed a clumsy somersault as the bullet found it. It flipped, bounced, skidded along the pavement, rolled a few times, and was still.

"Shell Street target down."

Another replying burst of static in his ear. Inspector Scally's voice just a ghost in the hiss and crackle.

Paul zoomed out again, slowly panning his sights left and right, searching the town for another target, but nothing else moved on the streets of Stornoway. He went round the four walls of the tower, scanning the surrounding terrain in his scope, but there were no further wolves to be seen. None crossing open ground anyway. The immediate close vicinity around the castle was pretty much covered in thick woodland where his rifle, which ironically had an effective range of up to half a mile, was rendered useless. Anything could be down there beneath the treetops a stone's throw away, but there was nothing Paul could do about that. He'd just have to let the armed boys at ground level deal with that and hope for the best.

He leaned out over the parapet again, glancing down to check the progress of the evacuating festival goers. The tail end of the hurriedly moving column was just passing directly beneath his position, seventy feet below.

The earpiece of his headset suddenly came alive once again, and Paul made out snatches of raised voices amid the buzz of interference. "...Willow...multiple... coming... *fuck!*"

A series of sharp cracks. A fuzzed out scream.

Paul immediately swung the rifle to the north east. They'd placed armed officers at all entrances to the parklands in an effort to secure the area, and one of the entrances was on Willowglen Road. It was here that Paul now focussed, but a screen of tall pines bordering the far side of the golf course blocked his view of the junction where the officers were positioned.

More jagged pops of distorted gunfire in his ear. A scathing, rising wail of agony that made Paul wince, then nothing. The radio went dead. Dry mouthed, heart hammering, he kept his focus on the trees obscuring the Willowglen Road entrance to the grounds.

For a moment there was nothing, then several large shapes bounded out of the treeline and came flying across the second fairway of the golf course. An entire pack, at least fifteen wolves strong. They streaked across the wide open space, arrowing in his direction. Towards the castle grounds. Towards the evacuating crowd below him.

Paul liked golf, had enjoyed a few rounds on the Raon Goilf course during his posting on the island, and knew the second hole, named Manor, was a four-hundred-and-eighty-four yard par five. He did some swift sniper's maths, and estimated that at the speed the wolves was coming, he had maybe thirty seconds before he lost sight of the rapidly approaching pack in the thick grove of trees that separated the crowd below him and the golf course. Thirty seconds at most. Fifteen targets, give or take? A kill every two seconds if he hoped to get them all.

"Right, cuntos," he murmured, steadying himself. His mind sharpened, blotting out all distractions. The noise of the passing crowd below and the tinny, megaphone amplified voices directing the human traffic faded away as he applied all his senses and concentration to his rifle and his targets, seeking to make the weapon an extension of himself. Outside of what Paul could see in the night vision circle of the scope, the world ceased to exist. There was nothing else. Only the rifle and the target. The rifle and the target.

Paul drew a bead on the lead wolf, as before, letting the crosshairs of the reticle settle just in front of it. He fired, and some five hundred yards away, he saw the huge animal pitch forward, tumbling and rolling limply across the grass. He immediately trained the scope on another, again leading it a little. He fired. The wolf missed a step, then went down. Four hundred yards.

On the right. Another one separating from the main group and running off at an angle. He fired. The wolf faltered, then careened into a bunker, throwing a huge spray of sand into the air as it fell.

They were already more than halfway across the fairway, and coming on at terrifying speed.

Paul let muscle memory and instinct take over, adjusting his angle, scope focus and lead without thinking about it.

Two hundred yards.

He fired. He kept firing. The advancing pack left a trail of dead wolves in their wake, but still they kept coming. They began to fan out as they drew to within a hundred yards of the tree cover. He kept firing. Another two went down. There were still seven left.

Fifty yards.

He kept firing.

He never saw it because his back was turned and his eye was intently focussed on the oncoming pack below him. He never heard it because of the heavy continuous crack of his rifle. He never smelled it because of the pungent cordite miasma of gunfire surrounding him.

Paul only became aware that he wasn't alone on top of the stone tower when what felt like a huge leathery hand closed firmly over his head, and sharp claws dug into his brow and the back of his skull.

14

The beast roars as it pulls its arm back, pitching the human backwards across the stone tower while wrenching the rifle from its grasp. The human goes skidding across the flagstones on his back and collides with the low wall opposite, his scalp shredded and bleeding. This one, though not an immortal, has slain several of the beast's offspring this night, and now he will pay dearly.

The beast smashes the rifle against the stone flagstones of the tower, and the weapon breaks apart like kindling. As it starts toward the human, the bleeding man stands again, a pistol now in his hands, spitting fire. The bullets are mere bee stings, and in two great strides, the beast crosses the tower and tears the pistol from the human's grasp with a swipe of its claws before seizing him, pinning the man's arms to his sides. Snarling, it lifts him into the air and brings his bloody face level with its own. It glares into the human's eyes, wanting to draw forth every last drop of terror before it makes its kill. Its quivering black lips pull back to display the curving, pointed fangs inches from the human's face. It wants the man to know and understand that this *is how his life will end. Screaming, torn and bloody, ripped asunder between the beast's jaws and then devoured, body and soul.*

But the human just glares back at it, and it is not horror, but defiant anger that radiates from him as he curses, twisting and kicking, trying in vain to break the beast's iron grip on him. The human spits blood in the beast's face, and it is with some regret that it concedes that this is unfortunately one of those rare mortals that provide little in the way of fear spiced nourishment. Humans have several quaint names for their idiotic kind. Heroes. Champions. Slayers. They are flesh and blood, they bleed and die just like any of the rest of their species, but absent the flavoursome dread that sweetens the meat of other prey, eating them is a deeply unsatisfying experience. The only way to wring any terror from such a specimen is to use their deaths to inspire horror in others.

Still holding the kicking hero in its claws, the beast crosses the tower again, takes the human by the neck in one hand and holds him out over the edge of the parapet, still struggling and cursing, his legs seeking non existent purchase in the empty air as he dangles in the beast's grasp. The wolf lets out a bellowing roar to attract the attention of the humans passing along the path below the tower, then it reaches out its free hand, closes its long powerful fingers around the slayer's right arm, and slowly tears it off at the shoulder.

The hero screams, long and loud, and his blood sprays into the night air, falling like red rain on the faces of the horrified crowd watching from below. The beast pitches the severed limb down among them, already feeling and relishing the waves of purest fright that radiate up from them like a rising current of sweet fresh air. Shock is a fine immobiliser, and before the herd can regain their numbed wits and scatter, the berserker slashes its talons sideways across the torso of the writhing human in its grasp, slicing through clothing, skin and flesh. Then it launches the twitching, dripping body out into the night, watching with malevolent joy as the man drops and twists through the air toward the now screaming throng beneath, his entrails unspooling like wet ribbon from his opened belly as he falls.

Then the beast crouches on the low wall of the tower's parapet, and launches itself out into the night. As it plummets through the air, dropping toward the blood splattered herd below, it calls to its remaining offspring, inviting them to at last fall upon the crowd.

Come.

Feed.

15

Ian, Jack and Aaron were standing at the east facing gates of the college car park, keeping an eye on the trees, pointing the way inside for the bustling mob moving past them, all the while trying to reassure them and not look like psychotic nightclub bouncers armed with edged weapons.

The concert goers kept coming in a wide jostling river of frightened, running people, emerging in a steady stream up the short path leading out of the woods and heading for the college. Every now and again, from the direction of the castle behind the pine grove, a single gunshot cracked across the night and the crowd let out a short scream of fright and moved a little faster.

Ian had heard one of the security guys saying there'd been close to four thousand people attending the main stage. Already the event staff and police were struggling to keep things organised, and a panicky press of humanity was now bunched up around the double door entrance to the glass fronted college foyer. The car park continued to fill up rapidly as yet more people arrived from the evacuated main stage area and joined the skittish bottlenecked crowd, bewildered and afraid, calling out for friends and family separated from them in the confusion, eager to be inside, safely away from the sound of gunfire and the spreading rumours of wild animals roaming the woods around the festival, killing and eating people.

Another gunshot rang out from the castle, this time quickly followed by another, then another. An icy worm squirmed through Ian's heart as the now recognisable crack of Paul's rifle continued and intensified, sounding out every couple of seconds. Also aware of it, the crowd redoubled their efforts to reach the indoor safety of the college, yelling and squealing in fear as they fled, some of them with their hands over their heads.

Ian was jostled and bumped as they ran past him, then with Aaron and Jack following him, he pushed his way through the press of bodies and ran over to where Cal stood with Scally, the police inspector. The husky head copper was speaking urgently into his radio, a look of barely contained panic on his face. Ian could hear that there was no one answering the inspector's attempts to raise his officers, the radio stubbornly refusing to give him any kind of response but an unbroken crackle of static.

"*Fuck!*" Scally shouted, giving up his attempts with the uncooperative radio and looking around wildly, fists bunched in his thinning hair. "I can't reach anyone. What the hell is happening out there?"

The sound of gunfire coming from the castle stopped then, and in the brief lull, Ian found himself looking in that direction, holding his breath, his jangling nerves like frozen glass, unable to tell if the ceasefire was a good or bad development.

Then they heard it. A terrible roar like an violent gust of wind blowing across the night. A bladder weakening, inhuman scream of rage that echoed and reverberated around the car park and stone buildings of the college.

"Jesus Christ, what *is* that?" Scally muttered, looking in the direction of the castle and unconsciously taking a step back, his face now completely drained of colour.

Ian had last heard that dreadful shrieking howl when the creatures had attacked them that afternoon on the eclipse darkened moors, and any hopes he had of a positive development in their situation wilted as the already near panicked crowd were pushed over the edge by the ravenous cry of the werewolf.

The pushing, shoving mob trying to get through the doors to the college swelled, compressing tighter and tighter as more people joined the now frantic crowd seeking entry to the building. Scally saw what was happening and ran forward, roaring at them to make room and form a line, trying to get his officers and the event staff to control the rabble, but it was futile. They were too scared, and the situation deteriorated rapidly into a chaotic and violent free for all. People were getting trampled and crushed. Several onlookers on the fringes of the chaos abandoned the press of terrified bodies trying to force their way inside the college, and took off through the car park, bolting away into the gloom in blind, unthinking panic. Others who'd left their cars parked outside the college tried to escape the madness in their vehicles, but in the pandemonium, with the parking area choked with cars and several hundred people on foot all trying to flee at the same time in a disorganised rabble, the single track road exiting the college was blocked in seconds.

Then, audible even above the pandemonium, another sound drifted up from the direction of the castle. The massed screams of a large crowd of people further back in the woods, simultaneously raising their voices in absolute horror.

A moment after that, there came the metallic, coughing chatter of automatic gunfire.

Ian turned to the others. Cal, Aaron and Jack looked back at him, and an unspoken agreement flashed between the four men. Ian snapped his fingers in front of Martin Scally's face. The officer in charge looked like he was about to faint. He turned to Ian and looked at him blankly.

"You need to do what you can to get the people here inside," he said with a calmness he in no way felt. Scally just continued to gape at him, as if Ian were speaking in heavily accented Mandarin. Then Aaron stepped forward, grabbed a fistful of the police inspector's jacket and dealt him a reviving backhanded slap across the chops.

"Get your finger out your arse, Marty!" he yelled in the cop's face. "Do whatever you have to, but get these people inside the fuckin' college and get some lads with guns down to the woods!"

With that, Ian, Cal, Jack and Aaron turned and ran back across the car park, fighting against the oncoming tide of the stampeding, screaming crowd that continued to pour out from the darkened woods below. They ran, weapons in hand, heading in the direction of the castle as the shrieks of terrorized hundreds somewhere ahead continued unabated.

16

Before today, Jack Powning had been the kind of guy who felt bad if he accidentally stepped on an insect, and so he marvelled at the ease at which ruthless and efficient killing had come to him in the past hour or so.

If Cal was right, these things, these enormous man-eating wolves, had been *people* not so long ago, people with lives and families, jobs, favourite TV shows, friends and Facebook profiles, and despite his almost obsessive fascination with edged weapons, the Jack Powning who'd got out of bed that morning would have been appalled and sickened at the thought of actually using one of his creations for the purposeful taking of life.

That was this morning though. A lot had happened since then, and as he, Cal, Ian and Aaron ran toward the woods around the castle, a small part of him wondered with some disquiet at the sense of high blooded excitement and anticipation thrumming in his veins. As they approached the treeline, he recalled Aaron's words to him earlier, about there being no such thing as coincidence, and how life was a room full of mirrors that reflected time, people, actions and worlds. An unsettling thought, but Jack couldn't deny that the idea had the feeling of truth to it. Hadn't he always felt most himself, at his most natural, when working and practicing with his blades? Earlier, on the tree lined path, with the wolf pack stalking and rushing them as they made their way to the college, it wasn't disgust and remorse that he'd experienced as he'd sent his knives spinning into the throats of the attacking wolves, but a deep sense of satisfaction and resonant rightness, a feeling of being completely in his element, as if his whole life had been leading up to that moment.

Deep philosophical musings about the nature of fate, destiny and free will would have to wait though, as they were in the woods now, and ordered, rational thought had no place in what Jack witnessed there.

In their panicked rush to escape, the fleeing crowd of festival goers had abandoned the pathway leading through the woodland, and people ran through the trees and undergrowth on all sides, many of them splashed and smeared with fresh blood. All around, echoing between the tree trunks, the darkened woodland was filled with the frantic voices of people shouting, crying and gibbering incoherently. Nerve shredding shrieks of pain and the rapid fire cough of automatic gunfire rang out from the shadows, and then, from the shifting blackness beyond their field of vision, Jack began to make out deep hungry snarls and bestial growling. A few more bloody, terror stricken individuals continued to push past them on the path, paying no heed to the four armed men, but looking fearfully back over their shoulders as if pursued. As they ran by, Jack saw that some of them were wounded, their clothing ripped and stained dark red.

The stream of people sprinting and staggering past them gradually thinned and petered out, and Jack and the others were alone on the path.

That was when they began to find the bodies.

Cleared now of the fleeing festival crowd, they could see that strewn along the path and lying along the verges lay an increasing number of torn corpses, like a combine harvester had driven along the path, mangling and shredding pedestrians as it went.

"Oh. Fuck," someone behind Jack stated grimly.

He turned and saw Cal levelling his spear as one of the enormous wolves stepped slowly out onto the body littered pathway, fangs bared, hungry yellow eyes fixed on the four of them and snarling deep in its chest in a continuous, unnerving rumble. The lantern eyed monster began circling them, keeping out of reach, evidently wary of the men and their steel weapons. The sounds of screaming, snarling and gunfire in the trees around them had lessened now, and the night was almost still as they stood there, turning in concert with the circling wolf, trying not to slip on the blood slicked surface of the path. Jack drew one of his three remaining knives and cocked his right hand over his shoulder, the blade held between his thumb and first two fingers, ready to let fly, but then there was a rustle of disturbed undergrowth behind him. He spun around and saw another wolf detach itself from the brush at the side of the path, its shaggy pale coat matted with blood, its open jaws red and dripping. Another one joined it, a jet black monster. Then a fourth emerged from the trees on the right, its claws clicking on the tarmac as it stalked out from the underbrush to stand on the path, barring their way ahead.

Jack drew a second blade from the bandolier across his chest with his left hand and held it ready. He flicked his eyes back and forth, closely watching the shifting quartet of wolves for the slightest twitch which would signal an attack.

They didn't attack though. The four huge creatures just crouched there with their powerful legs braced, bloody muzzles furrowed in hateful snarls, strings of torn flesh and ropes of saliva hanging from their jaws.

Then the bushes on both sides of the path writhed with stealthy movement, and several more wolves slunk from the shadows and closed in, now completely surrounding the four men on the path. Jack counted twelve of them. His stomach flip flopped and seemed about to drop out of his arse. His throat constricted, and a cold layer of nervous sweat sheathed the skin beneath his clothes.

Still the ring of wolves didn't lunge to the kill. They remained in their shifting circle, enclosing and watching them, yellow eyes glowing, those terrible curved fangs on full display.

Jack could feel a strange tension surrounding the predators. They quivered and yowled impatiently, snapping at each other and occasionally taking a tentative step closer to the four men before whining and yelping as if struck, wheeling round and retreating again. Their pained frustration and eagerness was palpable though, and their sawing snarls and barks began to increase in intensity. Jack shifted his feet, sure the inevitable attack was only heartbeats away, and that in the next few seconds the creatures would finally rush forward and tear them limb from limb. Still though, the wolves held back. It was as if they were being intentionally restrained, held in check by some unseen master.

Even as he had the thought, there came a heavy crunching of footsteps from somewhere behind the trees on their left, followed by a low grating purr of pure malice. Something huge moved in the darkness of the forest beside the path, and Jack saw the bushes sway as if disturbed by the passage of some looming giant.

Then the alpha dog stepped out onto the road.

On all fours, the immense lycanthrope was almost twice as massive as the overgrown wolves. Then it reared up onto its hind legs, an eight foot spectacle of hair, fangs, claws, and muscle, and let loose an earth shaking bellow as it glared down at them. The force of the monster's terrible scream seemed to knock Jack's air clean out of his lungs, and he had to fight to stay on his feet before the terrifying sound. The werewolf then made a sweeping gesture with one massive clawed hand, and the surrounding pack retreated, slinking submissively into the trees again and vanishing.

"What the fuck?" Ian asked in a strained whisper, looking around in disbelief as the encircling wolves disappeared into the underbrush.

"Ermm, I think this big cunt wants a square go," Cal said. "Shit."

It seemed Cal had called it spot on, Jack thought, as the towering creature then stalked toward them, flexing its long, hook tipped fingers.

Jack immediately whipped his arm forward, sending the knife in his right hand flashing through the air. The one in his left followed a half second later. Both were fine throws, the first blade embedding itself dead centre in the chest of the advancing werewolf, the second directly in its throat.

The monster jerked, gave a low grunt and took a step back. Then it reached up and simply plucked the knives from its body, dropping one on the ground. Jack watched in astonishment as it brought the second knife up to its face and seemed to study the streamlined blade with interest, turning it back and forth in its huge hand, even bouncing it in its wide leathery palm as if testing its weight and balance.

Then it looked at Jack, and in a blur of movement, launched the knife right back at him.

17

Aaron flinched as the blade flashed by his face. At his side, he heard Jack let out a squawk and felt warm liquid copper splash the side of his face. The werewolf roared again, and came at them.

Aaron stepped in to meet it, ignoring the sudden shooting flare of pain in his left shoulder as he brought the axe sweeping through the air, left to right. The lycanthrope was eerily quick for such a massive creature though, and it twisted neatly aside from the blow. The force of the axe's iron head cleaving nothing but air pulled Aaron off balance, and weakened by his injury, he was half spun, helpless to resist the centrifugal force generated by the heavy weapon. His back turned, something hard and fast smacked him on the back of the head, and he went sprawling face down in the bushes at the side of the path. Waves of nausea radiating from the blow to his head, he struggled onto his back and in his blurred, star spangled vision, saw Ian and Cal backing away from the approaching nightmare, jabbing their spears at it. It feinted left, then right, then suddenly lunged straight forward with blinding speed, seizing Ian's spear halfway along the shaft in its left hand, simultaneously swaying aside from Cal's thrust and dealing him a crunching backhanded blow across the face which sent him skidding and rolling along the path. The werewolf, still holding Ian's spear in its enormous hand, twisted at the waist and sent the wiry musician catapulting high through the air. He flew a good twenty feet before landing badly on his side further along the pathway with an audible *crunch*. The beast nonchalantly tossed Ian's spear after him, returning the weapon it had so easily taken from him, and letting out a hideous stuttering bark that could only be mocking laughter.

And as he lay there by the path, his head ringing, listening to the grotesque laughter of the werewolf, Aaron realised that it was toying with them, taking malicious pleasure in the consummate ease with which it outfought them.

Well fuck that for a game of soldiers he thought angrily as he grabbed a fist sized rock from the ground and pushed himself to his feet. He drew back, then launched the heavy stone at the monster now advancing on Ian, putting all his weight behind the throw. He felt a grim satisfaction as the rock nailed it an absolute cracker, square on the side of its head. The wolf's hateful barking laughter cut off abruptly and it turned to him, eyes flaring. Aaron raised the axe again. "Haw!" he yelled, stepping back onto the path. "C'mere you, ya big manky hairy bastard!"

The werewolf roared and strode towards him. It slashed out with its right hand, aiming to rip Aaron's face off, and he only just managed to avoid the blow by leaning back slightly. He quickly brought the axe round in a counterstrike, chopping low at the creature's right knee, but it nimbly stepped over the axe's arc and twisted clockwise, spinning on its left foot and slamming its long muscular left arm into Aaron's right shoulder. The power of the blow sent him reeling, and Aaron fought desperately to keep his feet under him. The wolf followed as he staggered along the pathway, snarling and snapping its jaws. Hoping to catch the monster by surprise, Aaron turned suddenly and slashed out with the axe again, bringing it up from left to right, aiming for the thing's head and trying not to scream as the force of his movement painfully wrenched his weakened left shoulder. Again though, the creature dodged the blow, smoothly swaying away out of reach, and Aaron groaned in agony as something finally ruptured inside his shoulder with a white hot twist and pull. His entire left arm instantly went numb, and he staggered back, red flashes of agony blinding him, the axe falling from his nerveless fingers with a dull *clang* onto the road.

The lycanthrope came on mercilessly, and gave a triumphant wolfish grin as it raised its long right arm high up over its shoulder, poised to take his head off.

Then it gave an unearthly screech and suddenly wheeled away, clawing behind its shoulder at the spear embedded mid way up its broad back. Cal stood there on the path, his eyes cold and dark with loathing, his right cheek oddly misshapen and blood pouring from his nose, sheeting the lower half of his face. The creature lurched across the road to the treeline as if seeking escape, but then spun round quickly. The shaft of the spear in its back swung up with its momentum, clacking violently against a pine trunk, and the head of the weapon was ripped free from the flesh of its back, leaving an ugly gaping tear that bled copiously. The werewolf howled in rage, then bent down and snatched the bloodied spear from the ground before striding back across the path in Cal's direction, glaring straight at him, the spear poised with lethal intent.

Aaron, wincing through the tearing agony in his ruined and useless shoulder, looked over at Ian. The musician was only now struggling to his feet and was obviously in a great deal of pain, hunched over and holding the ribs on his left side. Jack was lying motionless on the ground, a spreading circle of dark blood pooling around his head, and Aaron felt a heavy grey blanket of inevitable defeat drop over him. Together, armed and able bodied, they might just have stood a slim chance.

Now, they were fucked.

The werewolf reared back like a javelin thrower to launch the spear at Cal. Aaron looked on helplessly, knowing it would skewer the man like he was a piece of meat on a shish kebab.

Then there was a high, yowling animal shriek of pain from the treeline to Aaron's left, and a moment later, dressed in a torn and blood soaked shirt and tattered trousers, an enormous bearded guy with long iron grey hair came exploding out from the thicket at the side of the road. He was brandishing the biggest sword Aaron had ever seen.

18

Bitten, clawed and bloody, Sealgair is cloaked in the cruor of uncounted slain vargulfen as he breaks from the treeline and rushes the shapeshifter.

His arrows are long spent, embedded in the corpses of the many wolves he has killed on the way here, but the great sword, a wolf blooded blade that long ago belonged to a brave man named Ulfar, is alive and hungry in his hands, eager to cleave, its razor edge keen for killing.

He pays no mind to the four men on the path, nor to the several armed police now combing the surrounding woodland. He barely hears the iron stammer of their guns as they come upon the last few vargulfen stalking the trees. There is only the ancient enemy and himself. Nothing else matters. Nothing else ever had. He is the hunter, last of the Sealgairean, and the extermination of the aeons old entity before him is his only reason for existence. And so he raises the sword high, and charges.

The wolf whips its head round at his approach. It roars a challenge, then turns from the bloody faced man standing before it and faces him, one of his own spears clutched in its clawed hands. Sealgair pivots to the left as the wolf thrusts the spear at his chest. Feels the keen edge of its head slide across the fabric of his shirt, parting the coarse material and slicing a shallow cut into the flesh below. He takes a step back and brings the sword down, seeking to cleave the spear's shaft in two, but the beast moves with evil fluidity, and sweeps the spear out of his sword's downward arc, spinning to its left and ramming the butt of the weapon into Sealgair's ribs. He staggers forward, propelled helplessly across the path by the brutal impact to his side, the snarling berserker now behind him. He anticipates the oncoming thrust to the unprotected back of his skull and ducks, twisting round again and bringing the sword up. It meets the darting spearhead and sparks fly as steel meets steel with a grinding clash. He reverses his cut and brings the sword back, left to right, aiming for the demon's head, but it crouches beneath the blow and sweeps the spear along the ground, trying to take his legs out from under him. He jumps over the low attack, and using his still swinging sword's momentum, allows it's weight to twist his body clockwise in mid air. He spins a full revolution, stamping down with both feet as he lands, snapping the spear's shaft and simultaneously slashing the great sword across the still crouching wolf's back. The creature screams and backs away, blood gushing from the deep cut across its shoulders. Sealgair bares his teeth and strides forward, already bringing the sword back over his left shoulder, ready to swing again, But the retreating berserker suddenly lurches forward again in a rushing storm of slashing claws and fangs, surprising him. It's too close to strike with the sword, and Sealgair is forced to twist out of its way, but is not quite fast enough to evade the pouncing monstrosity, and though he avoids the killing claws, it's thick muscled shoulder smashes into his head as it lunges past. Something crunches in his face under the heavy blow, and then he is reeling backwards off the path into the undergrowth, skull ringing, blood and shattered enamel filling his mouth. He manages to stop himself from falling amid the weeds, and trying to blink away the pinpoints of light filling his vision, he staggers back onto the path.

He raises his aching head, and as his vision gradually clears, he sees the berserker standing before him again a short distance along the road. It is now brandishing his axe, **Rimmugýgr**, the Battle Hag, which long ago belonged to another brave man named Osvald.

The demon snarls, a low, hoarse rumble of black gravel and hate, and with one clawed hand, beckons him forward like a taunting prizefighter.

Sealgair spits blood and broken teeth from his mouth and raises the sword again.

19

The distant, rapid fire cough of machine guns echoing through tree trunks. Men's voices raised in the darkness, some of them barking orders, others shouting warnings, some screaming in terror. The rasping snarls and howling of wolves.

It's all just background noise coming from points unseen in the woods around him as Ian stands there on the path, leaning on the spear and hunched over, spitting aerated blood and cradling his side with his left arm as if trying to hold himself together.

He's had broken ribs before. A few times. It's among the most painful injuries he's sustained, and he's sustained more than a few. He is acutely aware of the splintered jagged ends of the bones in his left side grinding and grating against each other, sending fiery shocks of agony through his torso all the way out to his extremities as the fractured ribs realign and begin to fuse together again. He's aware of the laboured wheeze and gasp of his faltering respiration caused by a punctured lung. Can taste the air bubbled blood in his throat and mouth, seeping up from the burst football in his chest which even now he senses slowly reinflating.

Even this though, is just interference.

The chattering-screaming-snarling bedlam in the woods, and the oxygen starved pain of his injuries and their healing, are pushed to the back of his consciousness as he stands there, his attention hopelessly fixed on the insane spectacle unfolding on the road in front of him. He watches with car crash fascination as the two huge figures, man and wolf, come together again, now violently having at each other with sword and axe in a furious blur of slashing steel. The unceasing swipes, parries, cuts, thrusts and blocks are almost too fast for the eye to follow, and the huge sword and equally massive axe spark as they collide again and again and again, the grating, grinding squeal of the weapons a metallically violent, razor edged tattoo. The eerie grace and quickness with which the two huge combatants move is incredible, should be physically impossible given their freakish size, and as the giant hillbilly and werewolf duck, spin, weave and lunge, attacking and blocking, feinting and thrusting, the brutal fight has the lethally choreographed look of some murderous ballet.

Ian sees that further back along the road, Aaron and Cal have dragged Jack's motionless body off the path and are standing on the verge, separated from him by the battle on the road between them. He sees the others watching on, like him, rooted to the spot, helpless spectators unable to look away from the two enormous figures hacking and cutting at each other with brutal abandon.

Ian can see that both man and wolf are striped and gashed with deep lacerations to their limbs and torsos, their blood dripping onto the butcher's shop floor of the road surface beneath them. They're starting to slow, exhaustion and blood loss finally beginning to rob each fighter's movements of speed and accuracy. Their lunges become less precise, clumsier, their evasions slower and more desperate. Both are breathing heavily as they disengage once more with a sparking scrape of grating iron and begin to circle one another warily.

It's the werewolf who breaks the standoff, striding forward with a throaty grunt and bringing the axe round in a low arc, left to right. The man steps forward, already bringing the sword down, angling it low to block the attack... and the wolf subtly alters the direction of its swipe, raising it slightly with a twist of its sinewy wrists, and then letting go of the axe. It flies over the giant's guard, and too close to evade, slices into him, opening a terrible gaping wound that lays his left shoulder and the top of his chest wide open.. He is knocked from his feet by the devastating force of the blow, landing hard on his back on the road, the raw wedge chopped into his shoulder gushing blood.

In an instant, the beast is upon him, dropping to all fours and pouncing on his inert body, locking its jaws around his hewn shoulder and neck and slashing with its claws, tearing into him, savaging him. Killing him.

Ian is unaware he's moved until there's a particularly nasty crunch from deep in his side, and he finds he's taken a few steps to the side, rearing back with the spear.

His right arm whips forward as if by its own volition, and he screams as something just *bursts* inside him. Blood blurts from his open mouth as the spear flies from his hand and arcs up into the air. Red lights flash behind his eyes and he collapses to the ground on his hands and knees in breathless, choking agony. He looks up through the hair covering his eyes, and at the end of a long black tunnel, Ian sees the spear plant itself directly in the nape of the werewolf's neck.

The immense creature stiffens, its entire body suddenly tensing as if hit by a strong electrical current, then it falls to the side, slumping off the torn giant beneath it.

Ian blacks out.

Then finds himself stumbling along the path, trying not to trip on the scattered red detritus of human remains that litter the single lane road. Someone up ahead is calling his name. Clyde? No. Clyde's dead, he remembers. Matt maybe? Nope. He'd dead too. Someone's laughing. Ian realises it's him, and makes himself stop. Laughing hurts. He wipes blood from his chin and stumbles on up the path, his feet dragging, weaving drunkenly as he approaches the two huge corpses lying side by side on the road.

He closes his eyes, and a swirling cascade of images, names and words rush through the canals of his mind in a sudden torrent of insane understanding. A burning longship with the graven image of a snarling wolf at the prow. Ulfhednar. Vandrad. Drostan. The remains of an obliterated village above the blood soaked sands of a small cove. Fenrir. Neig. A high walled settlement perched atop a lonely hill. A great forest fire. Ulfar Halastra. Sealgairean. Sealgairean. *Sealgairean...*

...and when he opens them again, Ian is standing over the big bearded man. He doesn't look good. His face, neck, arms and torso have been torn up to fuck. He's all wet and red, a badly flayed mess of exposed flesh, tendons and glinting bone. There's a massive chunk of him that's just plain *gone* where his left shoulder, upper chest and the side of his neck should be. His guts are all over the road, scraped out of him and strewn around by the werewolf's burrowing claws.

But he's alive.

From the ruined confusion of his shredded half-a-face, the big swordsman's one remaining blue eye blazes up at Ian, pinning him in a cycloptic glare. Ian turns away, looking down at the dead werewolf on the ground next to him. He plants a foot on its back and wrenches the spear free, his vision swimming as a fresh wave of blinding pain washes through him. When he can see and breathe again, Cal and Aaron are standing beside him, the three of them looking down at the mangled living corpse with the one glowing blue eye.

An image of Clyde's face appears in Ian's mind. He remembers him coming up to check on him after the incident on the ferry, standing there with him, rambling on in that uniquely Clyde way. He remembers him misquoting *Jaws* in the Norseman bar. He remembers him yelling *Eskimo roll!* on the waters of Loch Langabhat. Not long before the man now lying helpless on the ground in front of Ian put an arrow through his neck. He thinks of Matt and his maps and timetables, of him sitting there on the island, an arrow in his chest and babbling about javelins for midgets. He thinks of Scarlett, drunkenly singing along to *Chiquitita* in that God awful voice of hers at her wedding, and lying in a pool of her own blood, asking him to sing her to sleep.

Ian calmly slides the spearhead into a large gristly tear under the man's chin and applies a little force, pushing the tapered blade further into the already yawning wound. The giant makes a funny gurgling sound. His heels drum on the path. Ian feels the point of the spear nestle between bones, and simply knows he's found the narrow gap between the two vertebrae at the top of the man's spine. The keen iron point slots neatly into place, as if guided. Ian only needs to lean slightly on the shaft.

Then the raw open meat and shredded skin around the blade begin to writhe and flow like melting wax. Tissue unfolds from nowhere and knits together, severed tendons stretch and reconnect.

I am Sealgair. *I am the* Hunter, the giant roars defiantly in Ian's mind. *There is another. It is* not *over.*

No, Ian thinks back at the hunter. *It's not.*

He pushes down on the spear.

EPILOGUE

He wakes in a fever.

Pain in the belly like gnawing teeth. White light behind his eyes. There are unseen others holding him down. Urgent voices, filled with fear and wonder. Someone is screaming. He realises it is himself. He forces his eyes open. The big man is there. The Norseman. Cold blue eyes looking down at him, his long blonde hair framing his stern face.

Be still, Breck, *the Norseman says.*

Breck? The name is familiar, but it is not his. Not any more. He wonders if it ever truly was.

Time passes.

Days, weeks and months are spent in constant hard training with the Norseman, practicing with the sword and bow, the spear and axe. On the steep hills above the northern end of Loch Langabhat, they build the watch post where a vigil can be kept over the cursed little island.

Time passes.

When stories begin to circulate that not all of the vargulfen perished in the great forest fire, and that some yet roam the land, taking humans and cattle alike, he and the Norseman turn their minds to the hunt. To the east and west, the north and south, across windblown moors, along lonely coastlines and through high mountain passes, they scour the island, tracking down and exterminating the last remnants of the rogue wolves.

Time passes.

During their travels, it is in an isolated village in the far north of the island where they first hear of one previously unknown horror of the Ulfhednar's occupation.

The rapes.

Rumours of women in the area that had vanished, snatched from their homes in the night and carried off, violated and debased by the Ulfhednar, then left alive, broken and raving, hopelessly insane. Fearing what ungodly horror might be birthed from the ruined women's bellies, the few victims who had not taken their own lives had been dealt with by their neighbours and families. Mercy given by a knife in the back of the neck and a funeral pyre. A kindness.

Time passes.

In the seasons and years that follow, he is wounded many times during the hunt, clawed and bitten by the wolves. But the injuries always heal, and with impossible speed. He grows. And keeps on growing. By the time he has seen seventeen summers, he already towers over the Norseman. He grows, but he does not grow old. Not like everyone else. It seems that for every ten years that come and go for those around him, only one passes for him.

But time passes.

The years turn into decades. The islanders who lived through the black time of the Ulfhednar grow old, entrusting their stories and knowledge to their children and grandchildren, before succumbing to the inescapable creeping doom of illness, infirmity and age, then slipping beyond the veil. Even the Norseman, even with all his great strength and skill. He dies the only way he possibly could, while on a hunt, well past his sixtieth summer and facing down a vargulf they have tracked to the snow capped peaks of the mountains in the south of the island.

He dies with his dagger in the beast's heart and its fangs in his throat. It is a good death.

Time passes.

When all who lived in the time when wolves walked as men have gone to their graves, he finds himself alone in the world. People begin to fear him, and make the sign of the evil eye whenever he is near. Ogre. Ageless One. Devil. Monster. He is shunned, and goes into exile, separating himself from others. He and the Norseman built the watch post above the northern end of Loch Langabhat for exactly this purpose, knowing the day would come when he would be forced to exist in solitude, and keep watch. He makes the cramped bothy his home and lives in isolation. No one goes near Loch Langabhat any more. It is a cursed place, they say. Tainted by evil. Haunted.

Time passes.

All too soon there are three, then four, then ten generations removed from the time of the Sons of Fenrir, and the people forget. Just like the Norseman predicted, the dire warnings and stories of that evil period become legend; myths retold and embellished down through the centuries until the horrific reality of what actually took place is distorted, forgotten and lost to the passing of Father Time. The Ulfhednars' final and finest trick. Only he knows the truth.

And so, time passes.

Through the passing of a millennia, the Hunter, Sealgair in the old tongue, watches from his hide. He watches for the foretold Harbinger that will wake the wolves from their slumber.

And he waits.

CODA

The storm that had cut the island off from all sides blew itself out and died around sunrise, vanishing with the same eerie suddenness with which it arrived.

By Sunday morning, Stornoway harbour was packed with overdue vessels that had been forced to spend the previous night anchored off the coast, prevented from docking anywhere on Lewis by the bizarre wall of dense fog and rough seas surrounding the island. On land, the weekend's carefree festival vibe was well and truly gone, and the entire waterfront area of Stornoway was teeming with a large crowd of frightened people, tourists and locals alike, eager to get the fuck off the island.

By late Sunday afternoon, the beleaguered and shell shocked remains of the local police force were mercifully reinforced by newly arrived emergency services personnel from the mainland. The military arrived soon after, and hastily set up armed checkpoints at the small airport and every harbour, pier and dock on the island. Every last person seeking to leave the Isle of Lewis was extensively questioned and thoroughly checked over by army medical staff, who wanted to know what each individual had done and seen that weekend, and who were looking for anyone bearing specific kinds of injuries. Animal bites. Scratches. That kind of thing. Anyone who acted strangely, answered their questions evasively or who was found bearing suspicious wounds were immediately detained and quarantined. They found quite a few, and it had got a bit ugly that morning at Stornoway Harbour. More than a couple of fights and frantic struggles had broken out as friends and families were separated, and the attending authorities had only just managed to keep the situation from deteriorating into a full scale riot, though it had taken a few shots fired into the air above the crowd's heads to maintain order.

Earlier that morning, one of the first vessels arriving in the harbour was a large cruise ship making a stopover on the island before embarking for the United States. It took on fifty-seven passengers in Stornoway, both pre booked holiday makers and a few wealthy walk-ons who had the money and necessary travel documents.

Five days later, that same Cunard liner turned into the Hudson River, passing beneath the Verrazano Narrows Bridge with Staten Island on its port side, Brooklyn to starboard. The immense luxury vessel's foredeck rail was crowded with passengers excitedly pointing, waving to other passing ships and taking snapshots on their phones and digital cameras of the famous skyline ahead.

Ian could make out the Statue of Liberty in the distance. He liked New York. Had been here a few times with the band, and knew a few people in the city.

His mobile vibrated in his jeans pocket. Ian took it out, saw Cal's name on the screen and answered. "Alright, mate."

"Alright," Cal replied. "How's it going?"

"Almost there. Should be docking in about ten minutes."

Cal didn't say anything more, but Ian answered his unspoken question. "I don't know yet, dude. Not for sure. It's a big ship and it's fuckin' mobbed. There's over two thousand people on board, not including the crew, but they're definitely here. Somewhere."

"You've got the blades on you?"

"Aye. In my pocket."

That morning at the harbour, as the cruise ship had been docking, Ian had made a phone call to Ragged Mojo's old manager, who in turn made a few more phone calls and threw a lot of money around. Ian was met shortly afterwards on the harbourside by the vessel's head of security, who personally escorted him on board the Cunard liner bound for New York, carrying his bag for him, a bag that contained two throwing knives.

Ian felt a pang of sadness as he thought of Jack. The guy had still been alive after the werewolf and the hunter were dead, but only just. The throwing knife had been half embedded in his skull above his right temple, one edge glinting in the night air, the other buried in the side of his cranium. Jack's last few minutes were blurry in Ian's mind. In deep shock, he had a dreamlike recollection of himself, Cal and Aaron crouched round him as Jack lay on the ground. Aaron had been holding his hand and talking softly to him. About what, Ian couldn't remember. What he remembered very clearly however, was Jack opening his eyes at the end and looking straight at him, before grasping hold of the sleek leaf shaped blade and wrenching it free from his skull.

Use them, he'd said to Ian, offering the bloody weapon. Then he died.

"Aaron's taking the stones down tomorrow by the way," Cal added. "He says he knows a guy who works at the local quarry, and he can get him some explosives and a loan of a JCB." They'd discussed this while waiting with Ian at the harbourside. The Calanais Stones had been the doorway the Ulfhednar had come through, and Aaron was fixing to make sure nothing else followed them. Issues of cultural heritage and historical importance be damned.

"Cool," Ian said, then hesitated. "And...?"

Five time zones and three and a half thousand miles to the east, Cal sighed. "There was another attack last night. A farmhouse down in Harris. Three dead. A family. Only one left was a nine year old boy who hid in the loft. He said it was a wolf. A giant wolf."

"Jesus," Ian whispered. Despite the warm July New York sun beating down on the ship's deck, the hairs on his forearms writhed as if stirred by a cold draft.

"That's the third attack reported since you left," Cal said.

"You still staying on?"

"Aye. I need to…"

"I know, mate. I know." Just before Ian had left, Cal had told him that he wasn't leaving the island. Not until the rest of the wolves were dead. Maybe not even then. He said he felt like he *couldn't* leave. Like this was where he was always going to end up, no matter what.

"You speak to Lynne?" Ian asked.

Cal gave a harsh bark of humourless laughter. "Yeah. Want to know something fucked up? She didn't even seem that surprised I called the wedding off. She was pissed for sure. Screaming at me and crying down the phone, but it was like she'd seen this, well not *this*, but something coming." He paused. "It probably wouldn't have worked anyway."

Ian thought of Cal huddled over Scarlett's body, weeping and broken. He thought his friend might be right. His marriage to Lynne probably wouldn't have worked. "I'm sorry, man," he said. "I know you loved her." Whether he was referring to Lynne, Scarlett, or both, he didn't know.

"Yeah, well. Shit happens, right?"

"Frequently."

Cal was silent for a moment, then he began speaking again. "I've been thinking about it, man. Far as I know they only had checkpoints set up in Stornoway harbour and the airport, and even that took some time. The army didn't get here till the afternoon. How many people living on an island own a boat of some kind, and how many do you think got off the island without being checked? Before the quarantine. We saw a fuck load of people with bites and scratches in the woods."

"We did."

"And the standing stones. How many stone circles are there in the world, man? Hundreds? Thousands? How many of them are… like Calanais?"

"Probably at least a couple. More."

Scary thoughts, these. Cal didn't say anything more for a moment, then, "Ian? It's never really going to be over, is it?"

"I don't know, man. Probably not."

"Hmmm. Good hunting, dude."

"And you, mate. Catch ye, Apache." Ian ended the call, and looked around again at the crowd of passengers gathered at the ship's rail, chattering and pointing and *click-click-clicking* with their camera phones as the Manhattan skyline drew ever closer.

He'd had the dream again last night. The same dream he'd had the first night on board the ship. A vivid nocturnal vision of a heavily pregnant women in a tattered homespun shift of rough cloth, screaming and sweating in her labour agonies, which she endured alone in a ramshackle earth and wood hut secreted in a forgotten valley. In that dreamlike way, Ian had *been* the woman, and yet had been himself. He knew she'd been driven from her village and lived alone, hiding in the hills. And he'd known that she was at least half mad, driven insane by an act of unspeakable bestial violence. He felt the terrible ripping pain low in her belly, heard her birthing shriek, and saw the child enter the world in a red rush. He felt the woman's mounting terror as she peered down between her trembling bloodied legs, sure she would see some half human monstrosity...

But the child was normal. Just a tiny pink babe like any other newborn, helpless and squalling lustily. The nameless madwoman gathered her new son into her arms, holding him to her breast and cooing soothingly, her horror instantly forgotten, erased by the sudden flood of protective maternal love for her child, which her broken mind accepted unquestioningly, her previous dread cast off as if it had never been.

She named the child Valkyr, for the Valkyries of her homeland, and dipping her fingers in her own blood which pooled on the bare earthen floor between her thighs, she daubed the child's forehead with the rune of Algiz. The protector.

Ian had awoken that first morning in his luxury cabin on board the ship with the name Valkyr on his lips, feeling that onrushing sense of inescapable fate again. A quick Google informed him that Valkyr was an old Norse name, and that it was the origin of Walker, his own surname.

It surprised him less than he would have thought, though to be fair, his capacity for shock had diminished considerably over the weekend. It certainly explained a few things.

Now, standing watching the snap-happy passengers at the ship's rail, he was getting that squirrely feeling again. A feeling that he'd had ever since he drove that spearhead through the flayed giant's brain stem. He'd followed that feeling to Stornoway harbour, compelled, then after showering, changing and hastily packing a bag back at the hotel, he'd followed the feeling onto the cruise liner. But the awareness of some menacing presence that pinged in his brain every once in a while like some psychic sonar was new, strange and vague. Even after almost a week on the cruiser walking around, closely observing the other passengers, the *other* that Sealgair had thought of before Ian killed him, had remained elusive.

There was something about the balding, middle aged fat dude standing by himself at the rail a few metres to Ian's left though. Standing a little apart from the others, he was looking out over the Hudson at the city that never slept, just like the other passengers crowding the foredeck, but there was something in his eyes. Something like hunger.

As soon as he had the thought, a red warning light seemed to come on in the back of Ian's head, flashing and urgent. And he knew. Blood calls to blood after all.

That was when the man at the railing turned to him, and smiled.

Ian drew Jack's throwing knife from his jacket, and smiled back.

BIOGRAPHY

D.A. Watson spent several years working in bars, restaurants and call centres before going back to university with the half-arsed plan of becoming a music teacher. Halfway through his degree at the University of Glasgow however, he discovered he was actually better at writing. He unleashed his debut novel In the Devil's Name on an unsuspecting public in the summer of 2012, and has since published several more short stories, articles and poetry. He gained his masters degree in creative writing from the University of Stirling in 2015, and is currently working on a third novel. He lives with his family in Western Scotland.